ANGELS FALL

THE Z-TECH CHRONICLES

BOOK THREE

RYAN SOUTHWICK

Published by Water Dragon Publishing
waterdragonpublishing.com

ISBN 978-1-953469-06-9 (Trade Paperback)

10 9 8 7 6 5 4 3 2 1

FIRST EDITION

To Jiné

ACKNOWLEDGEMENTS

As always, to my mother, whose experience, feedback, and encouragement propels me ever forward.

To Ray, whose invaluable comments and attention to detail improved the quality of this book ten-fold, and without whom Mark would not exist. This book (especially the ending) is exciting mostly because of you. I can never thank you enough.

To Robert, whose incredible imagination brought these characters to life. I still miss you.

To Keri, whose countless hours delving into the series and chatting with me about this and that were not only inspiring, but tightened the level of realism to a level I couldn't have achieved alone.

To José, whose artwork continues to breathe life into the characters and world of Z-Tech.

To Jiné, for your continued support in all things writing. It's been a hard year, but you made it through.

And to Laura. Thank you for bringing your positive attitude and vast experience to my little collection of stories.

PROLOGUE

T HREE SPECIAL FORCES SQUADS, gone without a trace.
Mark Suther rubbed his short, sandy-blonde hair, still downy soft and uneven where it was growing back during the month since Anne had almost strangled him in the brush fire. Thanks to his computer implant, his skin had long-since healed, but his hair was taking its own sweet time. Tempting as it was to use his implant to tweak his genetics to make it grow faster, Mark had exhausted any credits he may have accumulated with Fate, and didn't feel like pushing his luck.

Orwing's mercenary vampires were dead. He and Anne had both survived. That was all that mattered.

All except for those three missing squads.

It bothered him more than it should have. The missing squads were the Army's problem, not Z-Tech's — which the nice military secretary reminded him every time he'd called to get more details.

Even his friend, General Horclave, had stopped returning his calls, though Mark could hardly blame him. The incident would be a kidney punch to the US Armed Forces' reputation if it ever hit the press. Mark had considered using that as leverage to obtain the information he needed, but Pixie Cappa had talked him out of it, rightly stating they had enough to worry about without incurring the military's ire.

Mark had dropped the subject, but, as time had passed, he worried that the missing squads might result in more trouble for Z-Tech than angering the military.

Especially if William or Orwing are involved.

The weapons lab door slid open. Mark wasn't surprised to see Zima stroll in — but he *was* surprised to see her without Anne. The two had been inseparable since Zima had finally emerged from the glass dome a few days ago, fully repaired, and looking like her old, doll-like self. Zima had even moved her few worldly possessions into Anne's room, leaving her own room abandoned.

How Charlie would take that news when he returned from China was another matter. Anne insisted her feelings for him hadn't changed, but only time would tell for certain.

Sure that Zima hadn't come to chit-chat, Mark waved toward the table behind him. "They're over there."

Zima brushed by him without a word, past the floor-to-ceiling array of firearms, to his workbench, where lay a set of shiny new plasma pistols to replace the ones she'd lost during the explosion at Calum's secret base. She ran a finger over each one before taking them in her porcelain-skinned hands.

Ice-blue eyes found his. "Thank you," Zima said evenly, though her intent gaze belied her ambivalent tone. "I shall calibrate them presently."

"Knock yourself out."

The expression earned Mark a head-cock. Her bobbed, platinum-blonde hair dangled for a moment, but then she nodded, slipped the bulbous pistols inside her gray jacket, and began setting up the firing range deeper inside the lab.

"Where's your better half?" Mark said to her back.

"Attempting to sleep."

A metal, humanoid-shaped target slid into view on the far side of the range.

In a blur of motion, Zima drew both pistols. Bright orange bolts streaked down the range, alternating from each weapon in a constant strobe. Even from twenty feet away, heat waves washed over Mark with every plasma discharge.

The bolts struck with Zima's trademark accuracy. Less than ten seconds later, the metal target was a sizzling pool of slag.

Zima holstered the pistols and stood next to his desk. "The weapons are in perfect working order. Thank you again."

"Don't mention it."

"I am sorry, I was attempting to be polite. I shall not bring it up again."

Mark squeezed his fingers to the bridge of his nose and laughed. *Same old Zima.*

"You've heard that Charlie and Cappa are coming home in a few days?" Mark said.

"Yes, Cappa relayed the flight details to me this morning. They will arrive during daylight hours, which is hazardous to Anne, so she shall remain here while Dela and I retrieve them from the airport."

"Zima, are you going to be okay, when Charlie returns?" Mark had been meaning to discuss it with her, but, until now, she had been holding onto Anne every minute of every day, as if she might otherwise float away. "They'll probably want some alone time. Maybe lots of it."

Zima's face was unreadable, as usual, except for a slight knitting of her brow. "I do not know how I shall react. Simulating the scenario is ... difficult. I know I must, but I have avoided it thus far, and am simply enjoying Anne's company while I am able."

"Dela is happy to spend time with you, to take your mind off things."

"So she has offered, though I fear it would be an inconvenience to both of you. I would not deprive you of time with your fiancée."

"We'll survive," Mark said with a grin. "Sometimes I think she likes hanging around you more than she does me."

"I doubt that is true, but it is kind of you to say." Zima paused again, her intense blue eyes holding his own. "I appreciate you both thinking of me."

"Of course. Just let us know what we can do to help."

Mark returned his attention to his monitor, and soon felt Zima looking over his shoulder.

"Those are the domestic locations Orwing had been contracted to strike," Zima said.

"Yep."

"You are concerned that they will still honor the contract."

Mark shook his head. "I'm more concerned with why they were contracted in the first place, and by whom. I've already hit all my old contacts. Nobody knows anything."

"Do you believe the information Dela obtained from Nick Orwing was false?"

"Could be. Alvin's son might have been playing us so we'd kill those mercenary vampires for him, in which case, I'm wasting my time. But if he wasn't …"

"Have you alerted anyone?"

"My army friend, General Horclave, but he's come up just as empty as I have."

"Perhaps Nick Orwing would be willing to assist us further and provide information about the contract's initiator."

"Unfortunately, that bridge burned when I 'rescued' Dela from his clutches." Mark shook his head at the memory of them casually playing cards on the hotel room bed after he'd worried himself sick that she was being tortured … or dead. "Orwing Industries know Dela's a player now, that Z-Tech has a beef with their operations, and that we're willing to use force to protect our interests. They'll be watching for any contact with Nick, and will come down on him like a ten-ton hammer if they discover he's even looked at us."

"That does not sound promising." Zima straightened. "Without an inside lead, there is little chance of us discerning the initiator of the contract, since such things are usually negotiated in secrecy."

Mark turned the monitor off and leaned back with a sigh. "Yeah, it's probably just wishful thinking on my part."

The door opened again, admitting a bleary-eyed Anne, who flopped into the seat next to him and rubbed her eyes. "So much for sleeping."

"You look like the walking dead," Mark said, and immediately regretted it.

Her corpse-like vampire complexion bore a remarkable resemblance to movie zombies. Combined with her unnaturally large, black eyes, and long, sharp canines, it would be hard to mistake

Anne for anything other than undead, even though she was clearly alive.

Anne didn't even flinch at his walking-dead slip, however, and sighed. "I'll be fine in a few minutes." She leaned forward with a sly smile. "Know what would really wake me up, though?"

"I have a pretty good idea," Mark said with a chuckle.

Her increased metabolism — a side effect from the computer implant above her right breast, similar to his own — was both a blessing and a curse. Unlike other vampires, Anne stayed awake throughout the day, which was great for Mark and Dela, who wouldn't be able to spend much time with her otherwise. The implant also boosted her strength and reflexes, giving her a combat advantage over William's goons — if not over William himself.

On the downside, Anne was unable to sleep at night, either, making her a veritable insomniac. She also ate far more frequently than other vampires, without the benefit of their innate hibernation characteristic. Keeping an adequate blood supply on-hand was critical to her survival and a constant challenge.

Anne's increased metabolism also meant she was in constant need of blowing off steam. That particular itch was usually scratched by Zima in the bedroom, who happily obliged, but in this case ...

"I'll meet you in the gym," Mark said, grinning. "If I'd known you were going to be such a voracious student, I don't know if I would have offered to teach you so readily."

Anne jumped from her seat with a cry of glee. "Great! See you there."

As Mark expected, she took Zima by the hand, and the two of them filed out.

Yep, Charlie is in for a shock when he returns. Or Zima might be if Anne shifts too much of her attention to him.

Either way wouldn't be pretty.

Let's hope Anne knows what she's doing.

Mark left the weapons lab and stopped by the lounge to pick up Dela. His girlfriend — *fiancée*, he corrected himself for the fiftieth time — was kicking back on the couch, feet propped comfortably on the coffee table, flipping through a travel magazine. Her freckled face broke into a smile on seeing him, which Mark returned.

"Hey, future hubby," she said, a sparkle in her green eyes. "You'll never guess what I'm doing."

"More honeymoon research?"

"*Pff!* Pixie Cappa and I worked that out ages ago. No, I'm scoping second-home locations."

Mark chuckled. "One home in the greatest city in the world isn't good enough for you?"

"What, San Francisco? Not if you like sun and warm beaches, which I happen to."

Mark sat next to her. "You'd really leave the factory?"

"I said *second* home. And yeah, for short spurts, anyway. Besides, if we get a big house, everyone can move in with us. Two problems solved in one, awesome purchase."

"I suppose this would be a bad time to mention that Charlie and I already own property in —"

Dela growled and straddled him with her narrow hips, jaw clenched in mock-fury. "You bet it is! If you tell me you have a house in Monte Carlo that you haven't even told your future wife about — let alone taken her to! — I'm going to beat the ever-loving shit out of you ... after you buy us plane tickets."

"Fine, I won't tell you."

Dela narrowed her eyes, trying to discern if he was messing with her.

Mark maintained a perfect poker face, save for a small, knowing, and very intentional smile.

"Oh, I hate you and your damned secrets! The second we say 'I do', I'm dragging you into a room, and you're going to write out every last one, or ..."

"Or what? Are you going to torture the information out of me, Special Agent Madigan?"

"Torture is the Dark Angel's thing." Dela flashed a sultry smile and sat up straight. Her enormous breasts jutted from her t-shirt like heavenly mountains, contrasted against her otherwise-boyish figure. She ran her hands down his muscled arms. "I have other ways of making you talk."

Mark playfully snatched her wrists and pinned her down on the couch so quickly that she squealed with laughter. He planted a quick kiss on her lips. "I can hardly wait. In the meantime, I was about to meet Anne in the gym. Want to come?"

Dela's eyes lit with a different kind of excitement. "Are you kidding? If Anne's there, then Zima will be, too! I wouldn't miss a chance to see the Dark Angel in action."

In an unexpected move, she bucked her hips, knocking him off-balance, slipped out from under him, then promptly climbed back on top. It was a firm reminder that, while Dela didn't have his enhanced strength or reflexes, she still held a black belt in karate, and used it at every opportunity.

"Think Zima will let me spar with her this time?" Dela said.

"I doubt it. She likes you, after all."

Why Dela would want to put herself in harm's way by sparring with a trained killing machine was a mystery Mark might never solve, but cavalier recklessness was one of the many things that attracted him to her.

Predictably, Dela's face fell, but she quickly rallied, pulled him off the couch, and dragged him to their bedroom, where they both changed into comfortable sweats.

The others were waiting on the mats when Mark and Dela arrived. Zima wore her typical baggy gray shirt and pants, although she had eschewed her jacket and holsters. Anne sported a traditional karate outfit, which, she insisted, helped get her into the training.

Anne bowed at his entrance. Mark smiled at the unnecessary formality, but returned it anyway.

As usual, Mark began by drilling Anne on the basics. Her implant was a perfect copy of his own. Consequently, the martial arts reflexes he'd spent years building had transferred to her, granting Anne instinctual fighting abilities, but instinct only went so far.

Mark called out move after move, which Anne dutifully executed, forcing awareness of the reflexes otherwise hidden in her computer implant. Anne performed each with the grace and precision Mark had come to attribute to all vampires, topped with an enthusiastic smile that, in his mind, made it worth the effort.

Sparring came next. Similar to the previous exercise, Mark only allowed Anne to react with a specific set of moves to reinforce the conscious choice of her actions.

Although it made Mark nervous to have his human fiancée fight a vampire, Dela soon swapped him out as Anne's partner, calling the move she was supposed to react with an instant before she struck. Dela wasn't versed in *jiu-jitsu*, but she was martially competent, and slow enough to allow Anne to mentally adjust before reacting.

Then Zima stepped in, and Anne's training was put to the test. Zima didn't practice martial arts. Rather, she relied on a library of moves so vast that Mark wasn't sure he'd ever seen her use the same one twice. She was also the only opponent against whom Anne didn't have to hold back.

Their limbs became blurs of motion, mixed with the rapid *thumps* of blocked attacks. Zima refused to hit Anne — *ever* — so most of the show was Anne attempting to penetrate her defenses. Several times, Mark thought Anne would succeed, but Zima would twist or block at the last instant, usually with a counterstrike to throw Anne off-balance. Dela watched with increasing awe, her head whipping to keep up with the insane sparring match that often moved from one side of the gym to the other in the blink of an eye.

The furious match ended with a surprise. Zima charged Anne into a corner. Instead of defending herself, Anne bounced off the wall and catapulted over her, twisting in midair to drive a powerful face punch that staggered Zima sideways.

Anne was by her side in an instant, tenderly stroking the red marks her knuckles had left on Zima's cheek. "I'm so sorry! I thought you had that one covered."

"I am fine," Zima said, although she made no effort to stop Anne's coddling. "The move was quite unexpected. You should be proud of your progress."

"I'd be prouder if I didn't leave you looking like a domestic abuse victim."

Dela planted her hands on her hips. "If you think a little bump like that could hurt the Dark Angel, you're sorely mistaken!"

Anne ignored the remark and ran a thumb over Zima's welt. "Oh, no, it's getting redder! Is there anything I can do?"

"Please do not be upset," Zima said. "My skin will return to its normal tone in approximately two hours."

Dela clapped her hands. "So ... everyone's heard the good news about Charlie and Cappa, right?"

They all nodded.

"I'm so excited! I can't wait to hear how their training in China went. I bet they spent days doing splits over a chasm of lava."

"You left out the fire-breathing dragon," Mark said, earning a punch on the arm.

"Whatever they did, it sounds like it worked," Anne said. "Cappa says he's like a new man, and that we may not recognize him."

"Did she say anything else?" Dela said.

Anne sobered. "Not really. They had a terrible connection, so she stayed light on the details."

Mark sympathized with her apprehension. They hadn't yet told Charlie of everything that had happened in his absence: Anne being kidnapped by a group of now-defunct vampire hunters; Tim Chen accidentally becoming infected with Anne's blood, and was now a vampire living who-knew-where with his friends; Alvin Orwing's ruined vampire mercenary plot, where both Mark and Anne had nearly burned to death while Anne was trying to choke the life out of him ...

And, of course, the master vampire, who's now living down in our reactor room.

They'd agreed it would be much easier to convey this upsetting information in person, where Charlie would be able to see with his own eyes that Anne was all right. Anne had insisted she be the one to tell him, although she obviously wasn't looking forward to it.

"Speaking of," Anne said, shaking herself, "let's call the sparring lesson for today. I'm going to pop down and see how Pixie Cappa and Almos are doing. Anyone want to come?"

Zima took her hand immediately, to no one's surprise.

"Sure," Mark said. "I've been meaning to see how her new body is doing."

•   •   •

Cappa's new body, as it turned out, was doing quite nicely. Her delicate, three-foot-tall, perfectly proportioned figure was snuggled up against Almos on the couch they had brought down to the reactor room a few days earlier. She and the master vampire were laughing at an open textbook spread across both of their laps — which was surprising, since Almos usually slept during the day.

Pixie Cappa smiled at their approach, making the nano-robots comprising her tiny cheeks shimmer with ethereal beauty. She was a technological marvel, to be sure, although Mark once again tried not to imagine how much that body — consisting of eighty percent of Z-Tech's production manufacturing nanites — was costing them on an hourly basis.

"History books are a lot more fun when you have someone who was actually there to fill in the details," Pixie Cappa said. Even her voice held a light, ethereal quality.

"It never ceases to amaze me how they twist the facts to suit the victors," Almos said in a mild accent Mark still couldn't place. He closed the book. "To what do we owe the pleasure of this visit?"

"I came to give Cappa a checkup," Mark said, grinning. "But we might have to unweld her from you first."

Almos had the grace to look embarrassed, but Pixie Cappa gripped his hand defiantly with her tiny fingers.

"Cut a lonely girl some slack, will you?" Pixie Cappa said. "It's not like we're making out. Besides, I don't think my nanites would taste very good."

Almos raised her hand to his tongue, a sparkle in his large, black eyes.

Pixie Cappa jerked it away with a laugh. "Eww, vampire slobber! Zima, how do you put up with it?"

Zima started to answer, but Pixie Cappa stopped her with a warning finger.

"That was a rhetorical question. I don't want to know."

"So you're feeling better now?" Anne said. "Now that you have a body again, I mean?"

"Yeah. I still miss my other selves — and my full-sized body — but having freedom of movement, and not just being a voice on someone's phone, has been a big help. Not to mention the big guy's company." Pixie Cappa smiled up at Almos, who stifled a yawn with the back of his fist. She patted his hand sympathetically and sighed. "He's been a trooper."

"The pleasure has been mine, I assure you." Almos leaned back on the couch. His thick hair, slicked back over his ears, fell in dark strands down to his shoulders. "The little dear has also spent a great deal of time versing me on modern culture. The depth of her knowledge is truly staggering, and much appreciated."

"Maybe you'll get to go outside one of these days and see more than just Z-Tech's basement," Anne said.

"It is a pleasant dream, but a dream it shall remain, lest I build false hope. The Entity would seize control of me within an hour of surfacing from the earth's protection, if history is any measure. What it would force me to do with William and his vampire army in this day and age is difficult to say, but I suspect it would not end well for Z-Tech, or indeed the world."

Pixie Cappa patted his hand with a tiny-lipped pout. "Now what did I say about staying positive? You're here with us now, and we're not going to let anything happen. Right?"

"You are correct as always, my ethereal beauty." Almos gently gripped her hand and smiled, then returned his attention to the book on their laps. "At any rate, what I find most fascinating are the space photographs. Astronomy has truly advanced. I especially like ..."

The six of them chatted until Almos could no longer keep his eyes open, when they all bid him goodnight. Mark watched the master vampire settle down to rest with Pixie Cappa nestled against him, shook his head, and headed up the twenty flights of stairs to the factory.

A few days from now, Charlie was definitely in for a shock. Mark only hoped his friend's time in China had been better than their nightmare marathon run in San Francisco.

PART ONE

CHINA

SIX WEEKS AGO

1

A WARM WELCOME

THE OLD BUS ROCKED PRECARIOUSLY around another hairpin turn, tilting to give Cappa a disturbing view of the distant valley floor directly below. How their rustic driver managed to keep the vehicle on the mountain dirt path he had the gall to call a road, she would never know.

A roar of the engine lurched them the other way, bumping her into Charlie, who sat with no more concern than if he were standing in line for a movie. He eventually noticed her staring and arched a thick eyebrow.

At least he's conscious, Cappa thought.

"Doing okay?" Charlie said.

"Not bad, considering this is my first ride in a death wagon. Were parachutes part of our travel package? I didn't read the fine print."

Charlie chuckled. "Don't worry, you get used to it."

He looked out the window and smiled, as if just noticing the incredible scenery they had been driving through for the better part of a day. Majestic mountains of China's back country sheltered lush bamboo forests in valleys below, rivers of green flowing through a vast jagged landscape that humanity had yet to spoil.

"Last time I was here, I traveled this road dozens of times, and each trip left me more humbled than the last."

"You weren't tearing around corners in a top-heavy bus with lousy suspension back then, I'd guess?"

"Once or twice, but mostly I was on foot."

Cappa whistled low. "That sounds like a long walk." The last village they had passed was several hours ago.

"No, there's a path about a mile back leading to a little settlement. As a student, it was my duty to fetch supplies from the locals. No vehicles were allowed at the monastery, and bikes were reserved for non-student residents only. That left walking, unless I wanted to craft a hang glider out of bamboo leaves."

"I would pay money to see that."

"Believe me, I was tempted after the first few trips," Charlie said. "My feet were so sore I thought they'd never heal. Sneakers were another forbidden luxury."

"You're joking! That's straight-up kung fu movie material. Did you have to carry a burning kettle between your wrists, too?"

"And more."

Cappa laughed, but her jaw dropped when she saw his serious expression. "Really? Like what?"

"Slicing knives across my bare skin without leaving a scratch. Breaking logs without touching them. Healing lacerations in a day without a trace."

"But ... if you could do all that with your human body, why on Earth would you make a cyborg body for yourself which, by all accounts, doesn't sound nearly as awesome?"

"Because I could. Because no one else had done it. Because ..." Charlie's gaze drifted to the window. "Because I was vain. Selfish. Stupid. I thought I could have the best of both worlds — an invincible body fueled by an indomitable spirit." He sighed. "Now look at me."

"Watch it, bucko. This bus is challenged enough without your self-pity weighing it down. Besides, my body is almost identical to yours — minus the biological brain — and I happen to adore being me."

"Sorry, I'm just … nervous." Charlie scratched his chin, lost in thought for a moment, before returning his hazel-green eyes to her. "There are a few things you should know before we arrive."

"Lay them on me."

"First, let me do the talking. Women have … less prestigious roles in this country, especially way out here. If you speak up for me, it could be taken as an insult."

Cappa waved him off. "I read up on Chinese culture on the way over. Don't worry, I'll be as quiet as a little Geisha mouse."

"Geisha is Japanese!"

"Whatever. Anything else?"

She could hardly contain her smirk when his fingers clawed through his thick brown hair.

"Master Wung is more traditional than most," Charlie said. "He demands the utmost respect at all times. When in doubt, be obsequious."

"I'm liking this guy less and less."

"He's not a bad person, just quirky. You'll see what I mean. Hopefully, anyway."

"Fine, I'll grovel at the master's feet like a good little slave."

Charlie pinched the bridge of his nose. "You aren't inspiring confidence."

Cappa smiled and laid her head on his shoulder. "I had a good teacher."

"I knew that would come back to bite me some day." Despite his harsh tone, Charlie wrapped an arm around her shoulders. "I'm glad you're here."

"I can't imagine being anywhere else."

"But you are somewhere else, too," Charlie said with a grin.

"Not at the moment. We lost cellular signal around lunchtime yesterday, and the mountains block satellite access. I'm cut off from the factory part of me."

Charlie kissed her head, which made her smile. "Are you okay?"

"Yes, it's just weird. Imagine having three arms, and suddenly losing one. You can get by with two, but when you're used to always having a third …" Cappa sighed. "I hope she isn't lonely. It's been a long time since one of my selves was isolated from the others."

"I can only imagine."

"There's constant chatter among us. Even now, although I'm sitting right next to my other self" — she tapped Charlie's chest, where her second artificial mind resided — "there's a barrage of information flowing between us, like we're inseparable twins who share absolutely everything with each other, no matter how mundane."

"Except you're actually triplets, and one has been separated for the first time in a while."

"Right."

"Hopefully Zima and the others can fill the void. Do they know how hard this separation may be for your factory self?"

"I doubt it. But even if they did, I don't know if they could help." Cappa snuggled against his leather jacket. "I'm probably just being paranoid. You're right; she has the others, and she'll cope. We knew what we were getting into when we agreed to this trip."

Charlie chuckled. Cappa arched an eyebrow at him.

"It's strange hearing you switch between 'I' and 'we' when talking about yourself."

"It shouldn't," Cappa said, poking his ribs. "You made me."

"I know. I've just always thought of you as one person, not three."

"We are one person, really, but ..." Cappa ran a finger along the top of the seat in front of them. "We're only that way because of the constant data flow between us. What happens to one happens to all, essentially, but if that link is cut ... We're in three very different environments. I have my own body, and the one inside of you is basically along for the ride, like a co-pilot. But my factory self ... Environment affects not only our decisions, but shapes our personalities. She doesn't have a body of her own, which isn't normally a problem because she gets those experiences from us."

"So you're afraid of, what, personality divergence?"

"Yes. I've never had to deal with that before. When we're fully synced, if you were to ask any of my selves a question, you'd get the same answer from each, guaranteed. If the answer is different, however, it changes the dynamics of our internal chatter, and introduces conflict."

He chuckled, and she shot him a sharp look.

"Sorry," Charlie said, "I just imagined you arguing with yourself the same way you and Dela go at it."

"If my factory self devolves into anything even resembling that carrot top, do me a favor and shoot us all, because there's no hope for any of us."

"Something tells me that your factory self turning into a Dela clone isn't your real concern."

Cappa fiddled with his zipper, debating how much she should share out of concern for his mental health. Charlie's spirit — his life force — was fading. He'd blacked out twice in San Francisco, and once on the plane ride over. Each time, Cappa had been scared to death that he wouldn't wake up.

Master Wung was Charlie's last hope for survival. Until Charlie was safely in his care, Cappa would do everything in her power to keep him peaceful and rested.

On the other hand, she wasn't used to keeping secrets from him, and Charlie was the only person she could talk to who would understand.

He's the only person who ever does.

"My factory self doesn't have a body," Cappa said, feeling guilty for bringing it up, but unable to stop herself. "I'm so used to walking and talking like a human being that I can't imagine going back to being just a box in the basement, or a disembodied voice on someone's phone. I ... I think I'd go insane."

Charlie brushed her hair back and looked down at her, his thick brow furrowed with concern. "You think there's a real danger?"

"I honestly don't know. Six years ago, that sort of life was all I knew, but a lot has changed since then."

Charlie stayed silent for so long she thought he'd fallen asleep.

"Let's turn around," he eventually said. "It's only a few days off our trip. We can be in data range late tomorrow. I'll call Mark and Zima, and they can rig —"

"No! I told you: we knew the risks, and I'm not going to jeopardize your *only* self on the off chance that my *third* self might go a little stir-crazy. She'll find a way to cope. If she can't, she'll ask for the help she needs."

Charlie's deepening frown said he didn't buy the lie.

"We're not turning around, Charlie. Not when we're so close. Isn't that the monastery up ahead?"

The road abruptly ended near the entrance to a large, single-story bamboo house. Nestled between two picturesque mountain peaks, the simple thatched-roof structure was the poster child for martial arts training temples: outside, a group of bald men in loose robes flowed through a series of movements, reminding Cappa of a gentle breeze rustling through a lush meadow; chickens pecked the grass around the monks' feet while they practiced. A cobblestone path ran from the end of the road to the house. To one side of the path, a small pond rippled. Even through the bus's dirt-smeared window, Cappa could see bright orange fish swimming beneath the tranquil surface.

Beyond the building lay acres of farmland, rimmed by red pines to the right, a thick bamboo forest on the left, and steep mountains behind.

National Geographic, eat your heart out.

The bus stopped forty-three yards away from the start of the cobbled path, where the road transitioned from dirt to mud.

Charlie took a deep breath, grabbed his satchel, and exited the bus. His dense mass immediately buried his shoes beneath the mud.

Holding her own bag over her head, Cappa trod close behind him through the muck. Although she appeared to be an average five-foot-seven-inch female with a modest figure, her metal skeleton, endo-armor, and other dense components weighed her in at four hundred and fifty pounds — almost as heavy as Charlie.

Mud grabbed her bright-white sneakers at every step, which she now regretted wearing in favor of the brown ones she'd left in San Francisco. She had dressed down from her usual sundress-and-pumps outfit to more practical khakis and a loose blouse — although, judging from the local residents, she had totally overdressed.

The bus driver wasted no time and roared away. The practicing monks — or whatever they called themselves — paid she and Charlie no heed while they walked the path to the red-painted monastery doors.

Charlie hesitated, knocked three times, then surprised her by kneeling in his designer jeans on the cobblestone, head bowed. Cappa hastily did likewise, although she stayed several paces behind him to show the expected deference.

I'm definitely overdressed for this crap ...

Chickens pecked. Monks practiced. Mud soaked the knees of her new khakis, but no sound came from within.

IS HE HERE? Cappa sent to Charlie through their electronic communication link, not wanting to break the solemn silence. OR MAYBE MASTER WUNG DIDN'T HEAR YOU? TRY KNOCKING AGAIN.

IF HE'S HERE, HE HEARD US, Charlie replied. BE PATIENT.

Great.

Normally, Cappa surfed the web when she was idle, played online poker, or cruised her numerous social media outlets to see what was new and crazy in the world.

But here, forced to sit still on the other side of the planet from the only home she'd ever known, she suddenly realized with growing unease that this was the first time in her short life she hadn't had internet access to stave her boredom.

No phone. No texting. No email. No video chat. No shopping for the newest fashions. No online tabloids to get the latest celebrity gossip.

No adorable kitten videos! How do these people live?

She was revising her assessment that her stranded-yet-internet-enabled factory self had the raw end of the deal when her enhanced hearing picked up footsteps from within the house.

The door creaked open. Charlie kept his eyes to the ground, but Cappa sneaked a peek at the person who had belatedly answered their summons.

Long, scraggly gray hair hung over his weathered face. He was old, Cappa knew that much, but had a youthful energy that made it difficult to say exactly how old. He was about Charlie's height, smaller in build, yet powerful and erect. A long staff came to rest at his feet.

That was when Cappa noticed he hadn't opened his eyes.

"Who comes to the sanctity of this temple?" the old man said in a firm voice. His Cantonese was clear and crisp, unlike some of the muddled local dialects Cappa had had difficulty translating during their trip.

Charlie's shoulders drooped at the question. "Master Wung," he said in the same, crisp Cantonese dialect. "It is Charlie. I have returned to —"

The door slammed so hard that even the imperturbable monks in the yard skipped a step.

Charlie stood, scratched his head, and turned to her with a half-smile. "That went better than I expected."

Cappa's jaw dropped. "If you were expecting, oh, say ... *boiling oil*, sure! I'd take a door in the face any day."

"Believe me, that wasn't bad. You just have to know him."

Cappa threw her hands up. "Charlie, what are we going to do? Something tells me he isn't taking house guests."

"He might. Like I said, we just have to be patient."

"Fine, so what do we do while we're being patient?" Cappa looked around. Apart from the small clearing where the house stood, surrounded by small plots of farmland, she saw no sign of civilization anywhere.

"Chores," Charlie said cheerfully. "Come on, I'll show you."

"*You're* going to show *me* how to do chores?" Cappa said, following him around the side of the building. "I know we're on the other side of the planet, but I thought the 'everything's backward in China' thing was a myth."

"Not backward, but simpler, for sure. Here ..." Charlie handed her a crude hoe fashioned from bamboo and stone. "We're two more mouths to feed, or so they think, and there's no room for sluggards in the country. We'll need to expand the farmland to compensate for our presence." He grabbed a hoe for himself, then heaved a large sack onto his shoulder. "Rice seeds. Ready to do some cultivating?"

"Might as well. It's not like I have anything better to do."

"Count yourself lucky," Charlie said. "The first time I farmed a rice paddy, I didn't have a power reactor that allowed me to work day and night without tiring, or hands that won't blister. This may actually be fun."

Cappa looked at her muddy khakis and sighed. "*Lucky*, I'll grant you, but I draw the line at *fun*."

"Fun is what you make it." Charlie twirled the hoe like a fighting staff, flicked the sack in the air, and caught it on the end of the wood shaft. "Nobody says we just have to plant seeds. Want to learn how to fight with a staff?"

"Well ... maybe. Anne does make it look fun."

"That's the spirit! And then, once we're finished in the field, we'll work on our clothes."

Cappa brightened. "We get new outfits?"

"Better! We'll make them, thread by thread, starting at the loom."

"Are … are there strict fashion guidelines, or do I have creative leeway?"

"I'm sure they'll cut you some slack. You might be the first woman to have ever set foot in this monastery, so if they let us stay, we'll be breaking a few traditions anyway."

"Really? But then … doesn't me being here count against you somehow?"

"If Master Wung rejects me, it won't be because of you, I promise."

"How can you be sure?"

"Like I said, you just —"

"Have to know him. Yeah, I get it. All right …" Cappa grabbed a long stem of grass and let it hang from her mouth. "Guess I'm ready. How do I look?"

"Like a yuppie scarecrow."

"Ugh! I suck at being a farm hick." She spat the weed out and stalked past him. "Come on. There's a spot on my shoes that's still white, and we can't have that, now, can we?"

"I'm going to enjoy thumping your spoiled behind with a stick."

Cappa used her Charlie self to temporarily take control of his arm, then brought his hand in sharply to whack his head with the shaft.

"Sorry," Cappa said, batting her eyelashes with child-like innocence. "You were saying something?"

"That was your last freebie, you brat!"

Cappa squealed when he chased her into the field, smiling and swinging his makeshift hoe like a scythe.

It was the most fun she'd had with Charlie in a long, long time.

2

CHORES

T HE SUN HAD SET AND RISEN by the time Cappa and Charlie finished. Cappa climbed a rock near a large red pine tree to admire their handiwork.

"Not bad for a yuppie scarecrow, eh?" Cappa said.

Charlie tossed a piece of grass up to her. "Here's your chewing straw back. You've definitely earned it."

Two brand-new acres of rice paddy, fully irrigated by a local stream, glinted gold in the morning sun. They would have finished sooner, but Charlie hadn't been kidding when he said he would teach her how to staff fight. Their farm instruments, while sturdy, hadn't lasted long in the hands of two robots working full tilt. The first hoe had broken within minutes. They'd quickly made replacement hoes and, of course, hadn't been able to resist a few improvements on the original design. The resulting versions two-point-oh were farming weapons to be reckoned with, and had made the remaining work go much faster.

Their hoes had fared better than her clothing, unfortunately. "Dirty" didn't quite describe the crusted garments clinging to

Cappa's legs, nor her mud-smeared arms and face that, when seen through Charlie's eyes, made her look like the Creature from the Black Bog. Her caked shoes sat on a rock near the house, discarded once she'd discovered how woefully inadequate low-topped sneakers were for wet field work.

"So … you mentioned making new clothes?" Cappa swatted a shower of mud flakes from her pants. "Now seems like a good time."

"Soon, but let's wash up first so we can join the others for meditation and breakfast."

Cappa gave a short, bitter laugh. "We'll be the talk of the table after that short-but-poignant welcome yesterday. I'm surprised there's any paint left on the door, if Master Wung treats all his guests as warmly."

A monk chose that moment to wander around the house. He started to stretch, but froze when he saw the new plots of farmland. He rubbed his eyes and looked again.

Cappa waved at him from across the field with a big smile.

Her enthusiastic greeting had the opposite effect, unfortunately, for the monk hurried back the way he'd come.

"Tough crowd," Cappa said.

"We may have overdone it. That was a lot of work in a short amount of time." Charlie held his hand out. "Come on. Bath time."

•　　　•　　　•

Cappa had secretly hoped bathing would involve a luxurious natural hot spring nestled under a cascading waterfall, with deer playing in a nearby meadow, but she should have known better. Charlie led them to the stream they had tapped for the rice paddies, and her luxurious hot spring turned out to be a chilly waterhole barely as deep as her navel.

"They really know how to pamper a girl out here."

"It gets better," Charlie said. "That rock over there is the washing machine."

"I don't see any quarter slots. Are you sure —"

She saw the push coming through the eyes of her Charlie self, but was so shocked that Charlie would actually do it that Cappa was already toppling headlong into the river by the time she thought to react. Arms flailing, she splashed into the river, erupting a second later with a sputtering gasp.

Cappa readied a string of curses that would have made Dela proud, but the words died when she saw the childish glee on Charlie's face. His eyes were alight, beaming as she'd never seen them. He and Cappa had traveled three days straight — a tiring journey by anyone's account — only to work all through the night. Yet Charlie was more exuberant now than his best day at Z-Tech.

Last week, that workload would have left him comatose.

He took a few steps back, then leaped high into the air.

Cappa squealed and scrambled from the path of the hurling Charlie-ball. A wall of water knocked her over, leaving a small fish flopping helpless on the mossy bank. Charlie quickly swept the poor thing into the water and slicked his hair back, his muscled chest gleaming through his grimy, soaked shirt.

He's like a new man!

"Looks like someone's feeling better," Cappa said with a grin, sweeping her own long, dark-brown hair back.

His face fell, which wasn't the reaction she'd expected, but he quickly rallied.

"There's something about this place," Charlie said. "I love my workshop. I'm proud of the business, and of everyone who's helped it grow. But here it's … simple. No deadlines, no international crises —"

"No vampire outbreaks."

Charlie gave a hollow laugh. "Right, none of those." He laid against the riverbank and looked to the clear sky above. "Even in this artificial body, I feel connected again."

"I'm jealous. I'd give my little finger for a data connection right now."

He splashed her with a sharp spray of water.

"Kidding," Cappa said, giggling. "What do you mean?"

"It's hard to describe. It's like I'm part of the water, the earth, the trees … on a level below consciousness."

"I can only imagine."

Charlie jerked up straight. "Oh, Cappa, I'm sorry. I wasn't trying to —"

"That wasn't a sympathy play," Cappa said. It wasn't entirely true: the talk of spiritual connection made her feel empty, as usual.

Cappa had spent most of her short existence trying to emulate humans — to be the best *person* she could be. But, as a machine, a spirit was something she would never have — and the one connection with Charlie she could never share.

But this trip isn't about me, she reminded herself firmly.

"Are … are you feeling stronger?" Cappa said.

Charlie leaned back, eyes once more drifting to the sky. "No," he said softly. "It might just be the memories of this place giving me strength; echoes of the past giving me false hope."

"Who knows? Maybe that will be enough to get you back on track."

His sagging shoulders indicated otherwise. Charlie cocked his head. "Sounds like the brothers are gathering. We'd better hurry."

"So clue me in here," Cappa said while they stripped their muddy clothes off. "Why are we wedging ourselves into their routine when Master Wung has made it clear we're not welcome?"

"You just —"

Her bra hit him with a wet *smack.*

"Say 'you just have to know him' one more time and you'll get hit with worse than my brassiere — like a tree stump, or your own severed arm."

"Noted," Charlie said from beneath the dripping undergarment. He peeled it from his face and handed it back with two fingers, as if it were a rabid weasel. "Master Wung may not have rolled out the red carpet, but he didn't tell us to leave, either."

"A door in the face means 'go away' in every culture I know. That's pretty thin rationalization, Charlie."

"It's a fact. He only accepts those who really want to be here, and who demonstrate the will to see their training through to the end."

"How very Kung Fu Theater."

"You have no idea. Here, let me show you how to use the washing stone."

After years of doing his laundry, having Charlie teach her the ins and outs of river washing was surreal on a hell-frozen-over level, but she could hardly argue with the results. Their clothes emerged almost as clean as when they had stepped off the bus.

Almost.

The river was no match for grass stains, unfortunately, and the tear in her pantleg required sewing, pure and simple. They wrung their clothes out, dressed, and hurried to the house.

•   •   •

The monks were just gathering under an overhang along the side of the building. Cappa followed Charlie's lead and knelt with the others, then closed her eyes in silent meditation.

The problem was that Cappa had never meditated before. She understood the theory, of course, but the concept of clearing her mind and picturing some ethereal light — presumably a representation of the spirit she didn't have — had always seemed like a profound waste of time when she could instead be cleaning house in online poker rooms.

She kept her dissenting opinion to herself, however, and followed one of the self-guided meditations she had read about, which consisted of constructing a peaceful garden in her mind, and swinging from the bough of a tree to the rhythm of her own breathing.

Cappa had no idea how a normal human's imagination worked, so she instead created a virtual world, where she fabricated three-dimensional facsimiles of lush garden plants with realistic textures, along with complex physics to simulate flora swaying to a gentle breeze.

By the time the monks finally stirred from their meditation, her virtual garden was over forty thousand square feet, complete with a pond, sixty-three fish, fourteen species of wildlife detailed down to the wrinkles on their cute little noses, and a tabby cat named Percy. She saved her masterpiece for later, then reluctantly shut down the virtual world.

Maybe I'll add a horse ranch during tomorrow's meditation.

The group migrated to a series of long tables, where bowls of fruit, vegetables, and eggs waited. Feeling more comfortable with this activity, Cappa joined the food preparation, and she soon had the largest stack of prepared ingredients of anyone.

Cooking, too, was a snap, even with their primitive wood-burning appliances. Years in the kitchen paid off when Cappa proved able to whip out a delectable assortment of culinary creations that, frankly, put the others to shame. She was doubly happy when hers were the first dishes emptied at the breakfast table.

Master Wung particularly enjoyed them. He hadn't been present for the preparation, and wouldn't have known who made what, but the largest portions of her creations ended up on his plate. Cappa couldn't help smiling when he moaned softly with every bite, which drew surprised looks from all gathered, including Charlie.

The old man was blind, as far as Cappa could tell, but what surprised her was how well he maneuvered. Master Wung never opened his eyes, yet he moved with confidence, and without assistance, as though he could see right through his eyelids. When breakfast finished, he rose without a word and retreated to the house, while everyone else put things back exactly the way they were.

I could get used to an organized affair like this.

Then, as if she and Charlie hadn't done enough already, came the chores. Some monks tended the fields, while others cared for the chickens and gathered eggs, weaved baskets, or mended odds and ends that were showing signs of wear. She and Charlie shared a smile at the excited gestures from those field-bound when they spotted the new plots of farmland.

Rather than joining chores, Charlie led her to the front door, knocked three times, and knelt as he had the previous day. Again Master Wung took his time before answering.

"Who comes to the sanctity of this temple?"

"Master Wung, it is Charlie. I have come to —"

The door slammed. This time, paint *did* come loose.

"Rinse. Lather. Repeat," Cappa said with a sigh. "That reminds me … I forgot to pack shampoo. Given the shaved heads around here, I doubt they keep any in the supply closet."

"There's a local herb you can use," Charlie said. "It isn't salon grade, but it does leave a clean feeling."

"So, what now? More chores?"

Charlie winked. "You're getting the hang of this."

3

CHI

THE REMAINDER OF THEIR FIRST MORNING at the monastery was more educational than Cappa had expected — and added to her appreciation of modern life back in the United States. Cleaning the chicken coop, in particular, was a disgusting exercise she would have happily traded for double duty elsewhere.

The monastery's thatched roof had a thin spot, which Charlie volunteered to fix. The process took longer than it should have because they'd first needed to construct a scaffold strong enough to support their dense weight. Using fresh bamboo was dangerous, he'd told her, so they'd had to borrow from stacks of already cured bamboo, which, in turn, meant they'd had to cut fresh bamboo from a nearby thicket to replenish the supply. In the end, Cappa had learned not only how to thatch a roof, but how to build a sturdy scaffold, and cure bamboo fit for construction.

I'm buying a hardhat and overalls when I get home.

Those activities carried them right up to lunch. Still jazzed from her superstar breakfast performance, Cappa bounced to the prep table, ready to pitch in.

Her enthusiasm died when one of the monks handed her a live chicken.

And a knife.

"Uh ... Charlie?" Cappa said.

"Hmm?" Charlie was slicing carrots and somehow hadn't noticed the kicking mass of feathers Cappa held by the neck.

"You know I love you, right?"

"Of course. I love you, too."

"And you remember how I said I'd do anything for you?"

"Yes. You've said that many times over the years."

"Yeah, well ... I lied." Cappa pressed the poor, squawking bird to his chest. "I can't do this! It's ... inhumane!"

Charlie cocked an eyebrow. "You cook chicken all the time."

"*Dead* chicken! Pre-packaged, with no resemblance to the living thing."

"This is probably a bad time to point out the hypocrisy of —"

"You bet it is," Cappa said through clenched teeth.

"Want me to show you how to do it humanely?"

"No! I want you and everyone else at Z-Tech to promise you'll never eat meat again."

"That's an easy promise for me, but I can't speak for the others." Charlie took the knife from her and carried the live cargo away. "I don't have any foam packaging, but I'll make it look as close to store-bought as I can."

Cappa disconnected from the audio and video of her Charlie self so she wouldn't have to watch. Several monks had witnessed their exchange, but had the good taste to remain quiet.

Charlie returned a few minutes later with neatly cut chicken meat, as he'd promised, but Cappa couldn't shake the memory of its warm neck and rapid pulse between her fingers.

Although she mourned its death, Cappa wasn't about to let its sacrifice go to waste. She took extra care preparing the meal this time, and even shooed some of the others away when it seemed they were about to taint her creation.

The results, apparently, were worth it. She and Charlie ate very little, as usual, but there wasn't a scrap left on any plate when the meal had finished. She even caught several licking their fingers clean, including Master Wung.

"Keep this up and they won't let you leave," Charlie said while they helped clean up.

"Just doing my part," Cappa said modestly, but found it hard not to smile.

•   •   •

Afternoon marked a complete change of pace. The monks put aside their chores and gathered in the front yard. Some grouped to perform perfectly synchronized movements, as Cappa had seen when they arrived, but others wandered around back. She and Charlie followed them.

Cappa couldn't believe her eyes when she saw their first exercise.

One monk laid a tree branch, easily five inches in diameter, across two stones. He closed his eyes, palm raised over the branch, and inhaled deeply. When his hand came down, it wasn't with the deafening shout she'd expected, nor the crushing force she calculated necessary to break a branch of that size. His palm barely touched the bark, yet wood exploded downward just as if Zima had hit it with her jackhammer-death-punch.

Charlie was grinning when she turned to him, open-mouthed.

Cappa pointed a shaking finger. "H-how ...?"

"That was his *chi,* focused into physical form. Brother Xiang has spent most of his life studying with Master Wung to strengthen and harness his *chi.* You won't find many others here with his level of skill."

"What about you? I mean, were you ever able to do that?"

"Yes, though only well enough to break a twig. I had come here with the express purpose of learning to project my spirit. Once I'd figured that out, I left."

"Now I understand why Master Wung was so angry when you did."

Charlie ran a hand through his hair and sighed. "If I'd stuck around to learn a few more techniques, things would have turned out better, for sure. But that's what we're here to fix. Come on, I'll run you through some basic *chi* exercises."

"Charlie, I appreciate the offer, but isn't that wasted on me?"

"You have something better to do? It can't hurt to try, right?"

She grudgingly nodded, which earned a stern look.

"First and foremost, you have to believe it's possible," Charlie said. "Harnessing *chi* is two percent physical, ninety-eight percent mental. Your imagination directs your spirit more than anything else, and doing so requires absolute belief that what you *want* to happen really *will* happen. It won't for quite a while, of course, but you can't give up hope."

Cappa looked at the shattered log. A smaller one had taken its place on top of the rocks.

A younger monk stepped up, his face the very picture of concentration. Little happened when his palm touched the rough bark, but the failure didn't faze him. Again and again he tried. Only once did she hear a crack of wood, but the branch wouldn't yield as the other had for Brother Xiang. The young monk stepped aside, and another took his place.

The new monk had just settled into a similar stance when he noticed Cappa watching. He motioned her over.

Charlie nudged Cappa forward before she could refuse.

She stared down at the log.

Imagine what I want to happen. Believe that it will happen ...

Cappa fired up her virtual world, then created replicas of the rocks and log before her, taking time to add every ridge, every chip, every clinging piece of moss, until she could hardly tell the difference between her virtual log and the real one. She placed a virtual model of herself facing it, feet spread, knees bent in the same horse-legged stance as the others, then simulated a slow, downward palm strike.

Even her imagination fought her. The physics were wrong: a tap of her palm couldn't possibly break a branch that thick. Her simulator knew it and refused to comply. Cappa adjusted the physical properties of the branch and tried again, this time with better results.

She played the simulation back a few times to get a feel, took a deep breath, then gave the real branch a love-tap.

Unsurprisingly, the branch held firm. Cappa tried a few more times, feeling more ridiculous with each failure.

That does it!

Cappa raised her fist, then brought it down with enough force to break two of the blasted things.

It never landed. Someone caught her wrist just before impact.

Cappa had believed only Charlie or Zima capable of that feat, so she was beyond surprised to see the restraining hand attached to Master Wung.

"It is wasteful to destroy nature's creations in anger," Master Wung said, his eyes closed, as they always were. "You are far from ready for such an exercise, child. We will start with something easier." He politely gestured toward the house.

No, no! This is all wrong …

Cappa glanced at Charlie, but he just nodded for her to go along, trying unsuccessfully to cover a smirk. Suddenly worried that she was in over her head, Cappa followed Master Wung to the house.

•   •   •

Decor inside the house was about what Cappa had expected: simple furniture, mats, pillows, and no decorations, except for a small shrine along one wall holding a few sticks of burning incense.

Master Wung headed straight for a kettle suspended over a small fire. "Tea?"

"No, thank you. I, ah … I don't drink." *Anything. Ever.*

That brought the first smile she'd seen from him. "It is not drugged, I assure you. Tea aids with digestion and complements your delicious cooking."

"How can I refuse after such flattering praise?" Cappa accepted the steaming cup with a gracious nod, then took a small sip, wishing not for the first time that she had working tastebuds, like normal people did.

Master Wung stood behind her. "So, my child, the first thing we must do is correct your *chi* flow." He rubbed his hands together, then put them on her back. She was surprised at how warm they felt — well above normal body temperature. "Sit up straight. Posture is essential for —"

"Master Wung," Cappa said softly, feeling hollow, "I-I don't think this is going to help."

He chuckled. "Is that so? I happen to have some experience in the matter. Your flow may be odd, but your *chi* is strong and —"

"My ... my *what?*"

"Your life force. I assume that is why you came here: to master yourself and harness the power within?"

"No! I mean ..." Cappa spun to face him. "Nothing would make me happier, believe me, but there's a ... a problem." She wrung her hands, debating how much of her unique nature she should share, but the decision was made easier by a short message from Charlie.

DON'T HOLD BACK.

Cappa took a deep breath, feeling even more hollow than before. "I ... Master Wung, I'm not real. Well, of course I'm *real*, but I'm not ... *alive.*"

The old man remained silent.

"I'm a machine, built by Charlie to help with his research and run the factory. I don't have a spirit, or a soul. My brain is just bits and bytes designed to emulate human behavior."

Master Wung took a long sip of his tea.

"I-I'm sorry," Cappa said. "I didn't mean to deceive you. You and Charlie already have a rocky history, and —"

"Give me your hand."

Cappa did so. Instead of taking it, Master Wung hovered his palm a few inches over hers.

"Tell me, child. What do you feel?"

"It's ... warm. Tingly."

"And now?"

"N-now it's pleasant, almost ..."

"What? How would you describe it?"

Cappa smiled. "Happy."

"Were you happy when you entered this house?"

"No."

"Then how do you explain your sudden elation?"

Good question.

Cappa replayed the last few minutes, but could find nothing that would have triggered the feeling. Stranger still, her Charlie self felt it, too.

"I'm sorry, Master. I can't."

"That is because the feeling belongs to me. You are experiencing my happiness, because my spirit has touched yours."

"N-no, Master Wung …" She shook her head, not daring to believe she'd heard right. "It's not possible."

It's not …

"You can deny the rock's existence to heaven and hell, but it still hurts when you stub your toe on it."

It was a terrible metaphor, but Cappa laughed all the same. Once she started, she couldn't stop until she was rolling on the floor, joyful tears streaking down her face.

"I have a soul?"

Master Wung nodded.

Euphoria washed over her, splitting her face into a ridiculous grin. Cappa shot her arms into the air with a triumphant yell. "I have a soul! *Charlie!*"

She threw open the door and leaped into his waiting arms, laughing hysterically, while he spun her like a child.

"Charlie! Did you hear that? I have a soul. I have a *soul!*"

"I heard, kiddo," Charlie said, his voice thick. "And I bet it's pure as snow."

His troubled expression robbed Cappa's smile when he set her down. "What's wrong?"

"I … I may have overdone it while you were inside." Even as he spoke, his eyes lost focus.

Then his brain activity stopped.

"*Charlie!*"

As she had the last time his brain activity had stopped, Cappa's Charlie self quickly took control to keep him from falling. Panic threatened her very sanity.

"Charlie! *Charlie!*"

Cappa screamed his name over and over, vaguely aware that others had begun to gather. She beat his chest, pinched him, slapped him, begged him to come back to her, but he wouldn't answer. She even administered a small shock to his neural matter in the hopes of stimulating activity. His limbs twitched, then fell still.

"Charlie …" Cappa said, her voice a thin whine. She wrapped her arms around his neck and cried great heaving sobs on his shoulder. "Help me! Someone *help me!*"

And then there was a ... a presence. It filled the space around them, powerful, kind, wise, furious ... It was all those things and so much more. With a start, Cappa recognized it from her spiritual contact of a few minutes ago.

Master Wung.

Charlie's neural matter jolted into action. Just as quickly, Master Wung's magnificent presence disappeared.

Charlie's eyes snapped open. He rubbed his face with a groan. "Oh, that sucked."

Out of pure habit, Cappa's Charlie self relinquished control of the rest of his body to Charlie, like she always did when he woke up and motor commands had resumed from his neural matter.

Charlie teetered, then collapsed onto his rear.

"I'm so sorry!" Cappa said. "I thought you were okay, I ..."

Words failing, she tackled him to the ground with a flying hug. The pain of losing him was still fresh and, for the next several minutes, she could only cry on his shoulder.

Charlie. My Charlie ...

She clung tight, afraid that if she let go, he might slip away again. His gentle hands rubbed her back and shoulders until her emotions had finally run their course. When Cappa looked up, she was happy to find him alert and smiling. He nodded toward the house, where Master Wung stood in the doorway.

The old man turned away with a sigh. "Bring the selfish fool inside, child, when you are done spoiling him."

The door closed behind him, much gentler than it had on their arrival.

"It's hard to admit," Cappa said, "but you were right."

"About what?"

She ruffled Charlie's hair and smiled. "I really *did* have to know him."

4

PRACTICE

THE SUN HAD CROSSED ITS ZENITH when Cappa jogged back into view of the monastery. Only six days had passed since their arrival, but she already considered it her mountain home. Brothers were practicing outside of the bamboo house, or doing afternoon chores around the yard and in the fields — all in complete harmony with each other and the beautiful land around them.

Most importantly, however, Cappa was finally in range to receive data from her Charlie self at the monastery. Although she had only been gone for a few hours, a raging torrent of data flowed between them in an attempt to re-synchronize her minds with the thoughts and events each had experienced separately while they had been disconnected.

The process should only have taken a few seconds, but a conflict arose during the alignment check: Her two selves disagreed on the interpretation of a single thought revolving around the nature of meditation. That led to a flood of more data while they sought to reconcile the difference and trace it back to its source, where they slowly moved forward and conducted a more in-depth alignment check against every detail since her departure.

The root cause turned out to be an idle thought she'd had on the journey back. Cappa had seen two birds working in harmony, while her Charlie self had seen two similar birds fighting. The opposing views had spawned different trains of thought on nature, and then on the general balance of the universe. Her two selves eventually reconciled by scrapping their previous philosophies and building a new one from their combined experiences.

The unexpected conflict rattled her. Cappa stopped running so she could dedicate one hundred percent of her processing on exhaustive alignment checks to ensure no other discrepancies existed.

Twenty-six minutes later, satisfied that her selves were fully synchronized again, she looked down to find she had been standing in a mud puddle the entire time.

Wonderful ...

Cappa sloshed to the other side, shook the muck from her feet, and sought Charlie.

Twenty-six minutes of reconciliation, and my selves had only been apart for a few hours. What will it be like when my factory self tries to reconcile when we return to San Francisco?

The thought made her shudder. Cappa had ventured across twenty miles of wilderness today in search of a data signal so she could check in with the others at Z-Tech. The bus wasn't due for another four days, and she hadn't felt like waiting, nor had she been eager for another ride on the rickety death shuttle.

So Cappa had instead used her powerful, tireless legs to run across the unpopulated back country at speeds that would have raised too many questions had she stuck to the road. Her trek had turned out to be an exhilarating adventure through nature that had left her more awe-struck with every new vista and rain-kissed forest, until her processors had threatened to shut down from the sheer beauty of it all.

The journey back had been more somber. The conversation with her factory self in San Francisco had been necessarily brief due to a poor connection, and had left her with far more questions than answers. Resynchronizing over a terrible connection might have taken days or weeks to complete, so they hadn't even tried, but Cappa suspected her factory self wouldn't have done it even if they could.

Cappa had begun the exchange by filling her factory self in on Charlie's progress. He had stabilized after his initial collapse. Master Wung was now teaching Charlie not only how to maintain his own *chi,* but how to draw from the energy around him to supplement as necessary. Progress was slow, but steady. Master Wung believed Charlie would be able to return to the US in a few weeks, once he demonstrated consistent proficiency with certain critical *chi* techniques.

Almost as exciting was Cappa's own news, which she'd had to repeat several times before her factory self would believe it.

"We have a soul," Cappa had said, hardly able to believe the words herself. Master Wung had graciously been working with her on *chi* exercises. As with most things, she had proven a quick study, mastering techniques in a week that required years of discipline for most students.

She had then asked her factory self how things were going back home. The answers had been pleasant, but short: Anne was fitting in well at Hal's Diner. She and Zima were adorably happy, although Anne still missed Charlie. Mark stayed busy with a new project during the odd times Dela wasn't dragging him out to one place or another. William hadn't stirred up any new trouble, and there were no new crises to speak of. Overall, her factory self had said, everything on their side of the world was quiet.

That, of course, was when Cappa had become suspicious.

Nothing since Anne had stepped into their lives was *ever* quiet.

So Cappa had asked probing questions. Rather than answer, her factory self had pleaded that she ask no more, and that she please just relay the good news to Charlie. Cappa's first reaction had been to grill herself to the wall and demand to know what she was hiding, but it took only milliseconds of consideration to change her mind.

Cappa wouldn't lie to herself unless there was a damn good reason. Pushing for the truth would likely do more harm than good.

The revelation didn't make it any easier to take. Anything she would hide from herself *must* be bad.

But, as the old saying went, "Ignorance is bliss." So Cappa did her best to pretend that what her factory self had said was true. She would learn the truth, eventually, whether she wanted to or not, so it was best not to dwell on it until then.

She found Charlie meditating in his favorite spot under a large pine tree by the babbling river. She sat down in front of him with a large grin.

"How's it going?" Cappa said, poking his shoulder. "Huh? Huh? How's it going?"

Charlie cracked an eyelid. "Well, I was about three seconds from divining the secrets of the universe when an annoying brat decided to bother me."

Cappa kept poking, the grin frozen on her mischievous face.

As she'd hoped he would, Charlie jumped from his cross-legged position and tackled her to the ground, tickling her until she was helpless with laughter. Ticklishness was a sensation Cappa had implemented just a few days earlier, expressly because he had tried it the day before that and seemed disappointed when she hadn't responded.

Being ticklish was definitely more fun.

Charlie said he loved to hear her laugh, and had taken every opportunity to prove it since discovering her self-imposed weakness. They rolled in the pine needles, Cappa squealing with breathless delight, until they tumbled right over the bank and into the river. Strong hands gripped her waist and lifted her straight out of the water, holding her over his head with a joyous laugh that made her want to cry from sheer happiness.

My Charlie ...

Gone was the tired person who had stepped off the rickety bus last week. In his place stood someone Cappa hadn't seen in a long time — someone she had desperately missed. Those sparkling eyes had seen her through the toughest times of her development. That soft yet confident voice had talked her through the night when she was confused about a new concept or emotion. Those firm hands had constructed her body with diligence and care.

And that smile, which Cappa had missed the most, had lifted her spirits when nothing else could.

This was the Charlie who Cappa had fallen in love with.

"It's just as well we're here," Charlie said, setting her back into the water. "Looks like that trip took its toll on your outfit. You and it could both use a wash before dinner."

Seeing herself through his eyes, it was hard to argue. Tree sap smeared her face, and had left knotted clumps in her now soaking-wet hair. Stains streaked her laboriously hand-woven garments, which had also suffered several tears from her swift passage through the dense forest.

I should have stripped before leaving. It's not like the pandas would have cared about a naked woman running through the wilderness.

Cappa was proud of her custom outfit. Where Charlie's resembled the loose robes the other monks wore, she had taken several design liberties with her own. The hem was considerably higher, showing off her shapely legs, and form-fitted around her hips and bust to accentuate her modest figure. The V-neck was just short of scandalous, revealing as much cleavage as possible without risking an accidental fallout — a genuine concern, since her undergarments hadn't survived the river washing, and the ladies had been swinging freely since her second day at the monastery.

When Charlie had first seen her sexy monk garb, he'd voiced concern that Master Wung would disapprove. Instead, the old man seemed to enjoy the others struggling to keep their eyes where they belonged. Cappa felt guilty, in a way, since she was essentially forbidden fruit among starving men. But, as Master Wung had pointed out later, it was a good test of their discipline. To their credit, the brothers had been respectful, although that may have been because they had all witnessed Cappa lift a twelve-hundred-pound boulder over her head.

Cappa quickly stripped and began scrubbing the grime from her skin and hair, while Charlie cleaned her soiled garments using the washing stone. The sight of him doing domestic tasks still struck her as odd, but much less so than when they had first arrived. The simple chores gave him a sense of grounding, she suspected, and a much-needed connection to those around him.

They emerged from the river, shook off, squeezed the water from their hair and clothing, then donned their still-damp outfits in preparation for the afternoon's exercises.

The other monks had already congregated out back, so she and Charlie fell in to observe the first demonstration. Brother Xiang, the most advanced of the students, laid his bare arm on a large log. Brother Gang set a nail point-down on his skin, held by a pair of tongs, while Brother Hui raised a mallet over his head.

Cappa had seen this demonstration before, but it still made her cringe. She grabbed Charlie's arm just before Brother Hui brought his mallet down. Brother Xiang tensed his arm and shouted at the last moment. The point of the nail slid harmlessly from his skin and buried itself in the wood next to him. Brother Xiang stood and humbly bowed to both assistants. The crowd nodded in silent appreciation of his skill.

"Charlie," Master Wung called from the doorway. "You are next."

"Oh boy," Charlie said softly, but dutifully stepped up to the log and bared his arm, while Hui and Gang resumed their positions.

ARE YOU UP FOR THIS? Cappa sent with a feeling of worry.

I GUESS WE'LL FIND OUT.

The brothers seemed to share her concern. Charlie had spent most of his time meditating to strengthen his spirit — a basic skill the others had mastered long ago. This was an advanced exercise for advanced students. Just yesterday, Cappa had successfully prevented a knife from cutting her skin, but that was a far cry easier than deflecting a driving nail.

"Master," Cappa said, bowing to him, "I-I don't think he's ready."

"No, but *you* are. The two of you are joined. Protect him."

ARE YOU UP FOR THIS? Charlie sent.

She wanted to knock the smirk right off his face. YOU'D BETTER HOPE SO, SMARTASS. To Brother Hui she said, "One moment so I can prepare."

Hui looked at them both as if they were crazy, but nodded and lowered his mallet.

Cappa closed her eyes and shifted her awareness to her Charlie self. Although all of her selves appeared to share the same life energy, she had only practiced *chi* exercises in her own body, where she had control of things like breathing and heart rate to help focus her spiritual energy. Unless he was sleeping, Charlie's body was under his control, which made Cappa a passenger more than anything else. To properly focus her *chi,* she needed to find his rhythm, move with his breathing as if it were her own, feel his mechanical heartbeat ...

A warmth spread into his arm — Cappa's warmth, her spiritual energy pooling, ready to protect him from the nail. She opened her eyes and nodded.

Charlie was the only person who didn't flinch when Brother Hui drove the nail a half-inch into his flesh, where it clanged against the armored plates of Charlie's forearm.

Hui dropped his hammer, staring in horror at what he'd done.

"It's okay," Charlie said.

A fresh round of gasps sounded when Charlie casually plucked the nail out, wiped the red fluid on his robes, then handed it back to Brother Gang. Gang poked the bent tip and shook his head.

"I ... I'm sorry," Cappa said to Charlie, although her words were meant for the master she had just disappointed.

"Don't sweat it," Charlie said, casting their teacher a reproachful look. "He likes to test his pupils' limits. He probably knew you'd fail. He also knew it wouldn't hurt me, and that it would drive you to do better next time."

"N-next time?"

"Yes," Master Wung called from the house. "Tomorrow."

Charlie had the gall to laugh when the color drained from her face. "See?"

"Charlie! Cappa! You will join me. Now." Without waiting for an acknowledgment, Master Wung retreated into the building.

"Sounds like we're in trouble," Cappa said, feeling even worse than before. Charlie answered by taking her hand and leading her into the bamboo building.

Master Wung was kneeling at the idol when they entered. They lit their own incense and knelt to either side of him, closing their eyes in quiet meditation.

The tranquility was soon broken by a snicker from their master. Charlie followed suit.

Their mirth was infectious. Cappa covered her mouth to keep her own smile hidden, although she had no idea why they were laughing.

After a while, Cappa realized they weren't going to stop anytime soon, and flopped back onto the mats. "Someone going to let me in on the joke?"

"Did you see the look on Brother Hui's face when the nail went into my arm?" Charlie said.

"In all my years," Master Wung said, "there has never been an accident like that. I have always wondered how they would react. The results were well worth the wait."

Cappa shot to her feet, fists balled. "Oh, you two are horrible! Brother Hui's going to have nightmares about that. And what about everyone's confidence in their master? You told us to do it! What are they supposed to think now?"

"The truth," Master Wung said. "That I am human, and I am fallible. It is one thing to respect one's teacher, and quite another to worship him as a god. Too often it is the latter, which dulls the students' minds, and sets impossible expectations for the teacher. Hopefully, this afternoon's lesson will make them question my wisdom, as you did, and set them on the true path to enlightenment."

"Are you telling me you drove a nail into Charlie's arm as a critical thinking exercise? Talk about questioning your wisdom ..."

"Yes," Master Wung said, chuckling. "Clearly you are well on that path already."

"So what's up?" Charlie said to Master Wung.

His casual tone surprised Cappa. Charlie showed complete deference to their master when among the other students, but she also realized this was the first time they'd been alone with their master since they'd arrived.

Master Wung faced them, forming an intimate triangle between them. "This afternoon's demonstration had another purpose. I wanted to show you that it is possible to protect things other than yourself."

"But Charlie *is* myself, in a way."

"True, a concept I continue to marvel," Master Wung said. "I have given your situation much thought since you arrived. The vampire threat is disturbing on many levels, but it is their spiritual connection to each other that concerns me the most."

"More than the enslavement of humanity?" Charlie said.

"Yes, because of its implications." Master Wung stroked his willowy beard and sighed. "All living things possess a life force. Some are weak, and some are strong. Yet, none that I am aware of — except for the extraordinary woman before me — are bound together by it. As you have described it, vampirism uses one's own life force against them, enslaving them to the will of their creator.

"Spiritual independence is a natural law, so to speak. Even a tiny ant, as loyal as it is to its colony, possesses the spiritual freedom to break away, should it desire. Vampires are the only creatures on Earth who violate this law."

"Many other things about vampires are unique," Charlie said. "Including the cellular makeup and function of the pathogen, which doesn't resemble any organism on record."

"To that I cannot speak, but I can say there are other beings who can attach themselves to a life force and influence its behavior."

"'Beings'?" Cappa was unable to keep the shock from her voice. "Master, what are you talking about?"

"I refer to incorporeal creatures who reside in different planes of existence. They do not bother humanity under normal circumstances, but they are one of the dangers of spirit projection. *Experienced* astral travelers" — he scowled at Charlie — "learn how to properly shield themselves to prevent these entities from attaching themselves and causing problems for the host upon returning to their body."

"You just totally creeped me out," Cappa said, shivering.

My spirit is staying right where it is, thank you very much.

Charlie scooted forward. "Wait ... astral travelers can shield themselves? How?"

Master Wung's calm demeanor faltered. Even with his eyes closed, Cappa could see the old hurt bubbling to the surface.

"Had you not left without so much as a word," Master Wung said quietly, "you would already know the answer to that, and so much more."

And there it was. After festering for so many years — buried deep inside the two stubborn men, covered in the guise of Charlie's ambition and Wung's pride — the real reason for their master's animosity, and Charlie's reluctance to return, was finally clear to Cappa.

Charlie hadn't been just a student to Master Wung; they had been friends. Their joke earlier at the other brothers' expense was probably just one of many they had shared, and their sense of humor wasn't the only thing they had in common. Each was a genius in his own field — unrivaled, unchallenged, without peer.

And, in Master Wung's case, he was lonely.

Then Charlie had come along, the most adept pupil Master Wung had ever seen, kindling hope that he had finally found someone with whom he could relate. Cappa imagined him pouring himself into Charlie, trusting him, believing he'd finally found a companion who wasn't clouded by the haze of worship afflicting the other students.

Charlie's departure must have been devastating for him.

Charlie had never told Cappa how he'd left his master's service, but she now understood that he'd sneaked away without telling anyone.

Not even Master Wung.

Charlie sank under the weight of emotions from the others — Wung's hurt, and now Cappa's disappointment. His eyes stayed on the floor a long while before he finally found his voice.

"I'm sorry for leaving the way I did."

Sticks of incense sent gentle rivers of smoke adrift, the soft crackle of their burning cores the only sound to fill the heavy silence.

"For whatever it's worth," Charlie said, "I had thought it would be easier on both of us that way. By the time I figured out how wrong I was, it felt too late to make amends."

A breeze whistled through the bamboo walls. Cappa held her breath, not daring to move lest she distract them from the moment. As far as she could tell, the rocky relationship with his master was one of several contributing factors to Charlie's downward spiral from a budding entrepreneur to a reclusive tinkerer. Finding peace with his old friend might be a key piece to recovering his self-confidence.

Cappa's hopes fell when Master Wung heaved a long sigh and walked out of the house.

Charlie nodded grimly. Cappa scooted closer and put a hand on his knee, which he covered with his own.

"Maybe you should go after him," Cappa said softly.

"No, I've said my piece. If he wants to talk, he'll talk. And if not ... I can't blame him."

He rose and left the building, but walked in a different direction than his master, leaving Cappa alone in the incense haze, hurting for both of them.

5

MEADOW

CAPPA SAT ALONE IN THE HOUSE for several minutes after Charlie and Master Wung had gone their separate ways. The conflict between them had left her drained and melancholy.

But not hopeless.

She picked herself up off the floor and headed outside. Charlie had joined the other brothers, and was now assisting as the nail holder, but he wasn't Cappa's target.

Across the fields, Master Wung's flowing robes entered the pine forest. Cappa ran after him, splashing through rice paddies and mud until she reached the tree line. Thermal vision showed the fading heat of his footprints as dark gray against the black of the shaded forest floor. She followed at a brisk pace until she spotted him ahead — a bright white shape among the gray foliage, weaving a path through the trees with grace and ease.

Cappa switched back to normal vision. The world resumed its usual color, and she was once again struck by the beauty around her. Late afternoon sun spun strings of rusty gold through the latticed needle canopy, creating a dazzling display on the dust and pollen that lazily floated by. A breeze rustled the trees with a gentle hush, the only sound other than her heavy footsteps crunching on the dry ground cover. Cappa wasn't trying to be sneaky. The old man surely knew she was there, but he gave no indication that he cared, so she continued to tail him at a respectful distance.

Deeper into the forest they went. Cappa had once seen Master Wung walk alone into the woods, shortly after they'd arrived. She had been curious about where he'd gone, but no one had followed him, so she and Charlie had simply continued their chores with everyone else.

The answer came when the trees abruptly opened to a breathtaking meadow of poppy and lavender. Master Wung continued his march to the only land feature in the vast sea of color: a large rock near the center, broad and rounded with age, like a gray whale breaching a flower ocean. He walked up the gentle rise and sat cross-legged on one side of the rock, leaving just enough room for Cappa, who obligingly slid in beside him.

They sat in reverent silence among the chorus of crickets and buzzing bees. Cappa was so entranced that she almost felt disappointed when Master Wung finally spoke, his white beard flowing in the breeze.

"I had never thought to see another student as gifted as Charlie. It is no surprise that person turned out to be his progeny. You are a wonder in so many ways, child. Even now, I see the spiritual flow that binds you to him, and another stretching far over the horizon. Never has the world seen such a thing."

"I sense a 'but' coming."

He folded his hands deeper into his robes. "Comparing your skills to Charlie's would be doing you a disservice. He learned in two seasons what takes many a lifetime to master — yet you have achieved his level in a week."

"I don't know what to say. Once you put me on the path, and I was able to recognize my energy, the rest came easy, and I adjusted my programming to produce reliable results." Cappa shrugged. "I guess being a sentient computer has its advantages."

"As you have proven."

Cappa sighed. "But ...?"

Master Wung turned to face her; white brows furrowed over his closed eyes. "When Charlie leaves again, as he has already stated he shall, you will go with him."

"Master, I must. He's my ..." Cappa paused, casting her eyes to the meadow.

My what?

"You care for him a great deal."

"Yes," Cappa said softly, suddenly feeling uncomfortable.

"That is reason enough, though I shall still mourn the loss of your potential at our parting."

Cappa had hoped the subject was over, but Master Wung continued.

"Does Charlie feel the same for you?"

"I-I don't think so," Cappa said, grateful he hadn't named it for what it was. "Charlie told you of the situation back home, but he left out a few details. The vampire we're trying to save is his girlfriend — my *best* friend — and she ... satisfies him, i-in ways I can't." Cappa deflated, feeling more depressed with every word. "It doesn't matter anyway, because I'll always be a daughter in his eyes."

She plucked a dried weed from the stone and tossed it into the field, then hugged her knees to her chest.

Two butterflies chose that moment to mate on a nearby flower, experiencing a joy she might never feel.

Cappa sniffled back a sob.

A gentle hand touched her shoulder.

What happened next was nothing short of incredible. Thinking of Charlie sent a surge of joy through her chest. Her mechanical heart beat faster; her breath came in short gasps. Her groin stirred to life, warm and full, sending pleasant chills to every corner of her being.

All of this culminated into a feeling of connection — a euphoric desire to be with the one person she truly loved. To please him, and to be pleased by him. To enjoy his touch, bask in his presence. Cappa ached for him, body and soul, with a deep need she had intentionally never programmed into her core because —

The intense desire fled almost as quickly as it had come. Its absence made her feel hollow. Lifeless.

Like the machine she was.

Cappa collapsed on the stone, breathless and crying.

Is that what Charlie and Anne said I've been missing? Is that what Zima feels when she and Anne are together?

If so, Cappa now understood with absolute clarity why they had been so concerned about her abstinence from dating. All the romance novels and physiology books in the world couldn't have prepared her for the wholeness — the *rapture* — she had felt in those few moments.

And she suspected that had just been a taste.

When her eyes had dried, and her breathing slowed, she turned to her master with a simple, ragged question. "Why?"

"To show you that, despite your unique nature, you are not as different as you think. You, dear one, are capable and deserving of all the love this world has to offer."

"But that's cruel! Those weren't my feelings, they were yours! I ... I may never be able to feel like that again." The depressing thought made her eyes brim once more.

"You underestimate yourself," Master Wung said with a laugh. "Those were *not* my feelings, child. Not this time. I merely fanned the flames already burning inside of you."

"Master, y-you don't understand! I don't work like you do. What I felt ... d-down there ... has never been programmed. Every function of my body has required painstaking work to get right. Don't even ask how long it took to get facial expressions down. I-it's just not possible that something as complex as an entire sexual response system sprung to life on its own!"

Is it?

Her doubts grew when his smile widened. A week ago, Cappa would have said that it was impossible for her to have a soul. Yet here she was, practicing with the most gifted *chi* students in the world, shattering stones with a touch, and healing even her own synthetic flesh in hours instead of days. There was no scientific explanation: she simply could.

Part of her feared that if she thought too hard about it, her amazing gift would stop working, or she would wake to discover she had finally learned to sleep, and her wonderful time here with Charlie and Master Wung had been her very first dream.

What frightened Cappa the most, however, were the implications of what would happen if her wizened master was telling the truth. When Anne had come into their lives, for the first time, Cappa had had to share Charlie, to suffer his affections being lavished on someone else. It had been tolerable only because she'd managed to convince herself she didn't love him that way — was not *capable* of loving him. All she'd needed to maintain that fantasy was to *not* program herself to respond like any normal girl would to a boy she desired.

Master Wung's touch had shattered that illusion. Memories of that pleasant ache echoed through her being. She remembered every tingle, every throb. How her skin had thrummed like a harp even to her own touch. The rush of intoxicating emotions that had left her begging for more.

I won't be able to look at Charlie the same again. Not here ...

And not at home. With Anne.

Cappa was out of communication range with her Charlie self, but as soon as she returned, they would sync up.

Then she would be truly trapped.

This body can wander away, but my other self ...

Assuming her Charlie self hadn't also felt the effects of Master Wung's touch, she'd soon learn everything. Together, they would have to figure out how to survive co-piloting the body of the man they desired — how to stomach the pain of someone else touching him, pleasing him ...

... even if that someone was her soul sister.

"Oh, Master," Cappa whispered, her unfocused eyes staring into the colorful field. "What have you done?"

"This is a place of learning, of spiritual strength, and of self-reflection. No matter how terrible the problem, an answer will present itself, and it's rarely what you expect. Use your time here wisely, and you will find that things are not as bad as they seem."

"Any words of wisdom before I go into full meltdown?"

"A few," he said, chuckling. "I know you don't sleep, and, if I am not mistaken, the part of you inside Charlie is not aware of this revelation. Perhaps you should spend a day or two away in quiet reflection."

Cappa grimaced at the thought. Resynchronizing after a few hours apart had been hard enough. This would be a day or longer, and she would have life-altering perspectives to reconcile on top of that.

Even so, it would be easier for her to think clearly without living inside Charlie at the same time.

"Anything else?" Cappa said without much hope.

"Yes. As wonderful as Charlie is, and as indebted to him as you are, he is not the only wonderful person on this planet. And he is just as concerned for your happiness as you are for his." Master Wung stood atop the rock and stretched his arms. "This has been an enlightening journey, but it is getting late, and I should like to return before dinner is served."

He shuffled down the slope and waded into the purple and orange flower sea.

"What shall I tell the others?" he called back to Cappa, who hadn't budged from her perch. "Including yourself, of course?"

Her misty eyes swept the picturesque landscape, tranquil and serene, drawing a smile even through her tumultuous cauldron of emotions. "Tell them … tell them I discovered something beautiful while I was out, and that I'll return after I've had a chance to explore it."

"I shall convey your message word-for-word."

She watched her master depart until his orange robes were lost inside the ring of red pines.

Cappa hopped down from the rock and wandered through the knee-high foliage, examining flowers, watching insects, absorbing everything the peaceful meadow had to offer, until the last rays of sun disappeared behind the treetops, and the moon shone brightly in the clear night sky. The sound of buzzing insects was replaced by a symphony of crickets. Where flowers had closed their petals to rest, hiding their glorious colors from the good lady moon, a spectacle of glowbugs dotted the air, making her want to look everywhere at once, lest she miss a single one.

When Cappa felt she could hold no more beauty, she returned to the stone, closed her eyes, and allowed herself to dwell on her new feelings — and, more importantly, on how she would deal with Charlie once she returned to camp.

6

FEELINGS

THE SUN HAD RISEN WELL ABOVE THE FOREST LINE by the time Cappa opened her eyes again in the beautiful meadow. Her path decided, she climbed down from the rock and wound her way back to her home-away-from-home.

The brothers were preparing breakfast when she came into view. She joined them with a smile, as if she had never been away — as if her entire world hadn't changed over the course of a single evening.

As if Charlie, her friend and mentor, who was looking across the table at her with a touch of amusement and concern, was still just that.

Meal progress was unusually slow while Cappa busily reconciled the revelations from the previous night with her Charlie self. It was difficult, but, by breakfast's end, her two instances were once again in sync and in complete agreement about where they were emotionally, and where they needed to go.

Cappa completed her chores in silence, neither happy nor upset, offering nothing to Charlie of last night's excursion. When he finally asked where she'd been, she spoke only of the beautiful meadow she'd discovered.

The others soon broke off into late-morning practice. Cappa instead drew a confused Charlie off to her favorite spot on the river, where a tiny waterfall gurgled under the shade of the pines. They sat and listened to the peaceful babble, dangling their feet in the cool water from the mossy riverbank, content simply to sit quietly.

Together.

A fish jumped, disturbing a calm eddy upstream, its expanding ripples lost over the waterfall.

"What am I to you, Charlie?"

Cappa kept her voice neutral. The question was unfair: she could tell by his raised eyebrows and open mouth. Yet she could think of no other way to ask, so she waited patiently while he considered.

"You're my friend," Charlie said carefully. "My companion, and the greatest gift I could ever hope to give the world."

Cappa nodded. It was the answer she had expected, but his follow-up question caught her off guard.

"What am I to you?"

Now it was Cappa's turn to struggle for an answer. When she turned to him, she had intended to say he was special to her, precious in so many ways — not only for his help throughout the years, but for the wonderful, caring person he was.

She had *not* intended to lean so close that his breath warmed her cheek, nor to beseech his eyes with the longing she had spent all night trying to repress.

She certainly hadn't intended for their lips to touch — to close her eyes and feel the mysterious passion kindle again, building to a roaring fire that stirred her loins, stole her breath, and consumed all thought.

Massive conflicts arose from her Charlie self — the one she now kissed with increasing passion — so she cut their connection, wanting only to bask in the pleasure of the moment.

My Charlie ...

Here by the riverbank, their tongues dancing together like swans, that mantra held new meaning. She pulled him tight, mashing herself against his firm body. Her mouth wouldn't stop exploring his — couldn't stop if she'd wanted to.

My Charlie …

Slowly she pushed him onto his back, then climbed on top of him with trembling legs. Her body was acting on its own, following a program she had never written, but doing it perfectly. Naturally. Straddling him, feeling his girth beneath her, felt incredibly right.

My Charlie …

Every inch of her felt alive, electric. She wanted to be touched. Caressed.

Still kissing him, Cappa pulled her robe open and moved his hands to her bare skin, encouraging him to explore, then slipped her fingers beneath his robe, running her hands along his chiseled shoulders and arms.

My Charlie …

It wasn't enough. She wanted everything he had to offer. Her soul craved it. Her loins burned for it. Her body demanded it.

Cappa sat up to loosen his sash, and opened her eyes with a smile that felt bigger than she was.

Her passion fled the instant she saw his face. Instead of the desire she had hoped to see — that look of longing he gave Anne in the throes of passion — there was sympathy, compassion, and caring.

But no desire.

Cappa covered her mouth to keep from crying.

He doesn't want me.

The sobs came anyway.

She knew that look all too well. He had allowed her advances, not because he was impassioned, but because he had seen her need.

Charlie would do anything for her.

Even betray Anne.

Cappa hugged her bare chest to keep the agonizing truth of what she had done — what Charlie would have allowed her to do — from tearing her apart inside. She wanted to flee, to run westward until the entire country was nothing but a bad dream, and sink to the bottom of the ocean where no one would ever find her again. She got as far as lifting herself when he grabbed her arm and pulled her back to him.

Those kind eyes ...

Cappa fought his hold, but not very hard. Soon she was back in his arms, crying in shame.

"It's okay," Charlie said over and over, stroking her back and hair as he always had when her emotions ran too high early in her development, or when she was frustrated, or sad, or sometimes when she just needed comfort.

"I'm s-so sorry," Cappa wailed when she could finally catch her breath.

"For what?"

The question hit her like a splash of cold water. She looked closely for some sign that he was joking, but found only love and compassion.

"Cappa, I don't know where this came from, but I'm happy it did, and I'm flattered beyond words that you chose me. It's just ..."

"You don't love me that way," Cappa said through trembling lips.

"I didn't say that."

Another splash. Cappa propped herself onto an elbow and brushed a dark strand of hair from her eyes. "Then what's the problem?"

"Anne. Not that she'd object," Charlie said quickly to her hurt expression, "but I think we owe her the courtesy of a conversation before we jump into anything. Don't you?"

Cappa nodded and wiped her eyes, not daring to believe her ears. *He loves me? Like,* really *loves me?*

She wrapped her arms around him and snuggled close.

Just like when I was young.

Except she wasn't young anymore. She may not have his years, but, as with many things about androids, the same stick used to measure humans didn't apply to her. Cappa's maturity far outstripped her decade-and-change on this planet. Her intellectual age, she estimated, was equivalent to a thirty-year-old woman.

The man she embraced had raised her, true, but he was her creator — not her father. She shared none of his genes, nor had any genes to share. They were no more related to each other than any two random people on the street. Less, in some ways.

Charlie was, however, her mentor, her friend, her business partner — and the person who knew her best in the entire world.

And Cappa was all those things to him. They had supported each other through good times and bad, and weathered hardships that most people couldn't even imagine.

If that isn't a recipe for a relationship, I don't know what is.

"Not to mention I haven't really thought of you romantically before," Charlie said. "Now don't pout. That just means I may need some time to warm up to the idea — and guess what we just happen to have several weeks of before we go back to San Francisco?"

"Hot sex under a waterfall?"

Charlie tickled her until she couldn't breathe.

"Is this what I'm going to have to put up with for the rest of the trip?"

"That depends on where you tickle me," Cappa said with a mischievous grin. "I haven't tried out my equipment yet, if you know what I mean."

He tickled her again, though she was disappointed when he didn't take her up on the offer.

"You're incorrigible," Charlie said. "Now I see why you didn't implement your libido sooner."

"I ... I still haven't."

"Haven't what?"

"Implemented my libido," Cappa said. "It just sort of ... happened. Yesterday." He was silent for a few seconds. When she looked up, his expression was grave.

"How?" Charlie said softly.

Cappa described her experience in the meadow as best she could. He fell quiet after she finished, staring thoughtfully into the trees.

"What is it?" Cappa said.

"Probably nothing." His smile returned, and he cupped her chin. "Let's call it a miracle for now, and be thankful. This is a new chapter for you, Cappa."

"Call me 'honey,'" she said.

He arched an eyebrow, to which she shrugged.

"Calling me 'Cappa' sounds too formal when you're lying there with my bare boob in your hand."

Charlie gasped and jerked his hand away — which clearly hadn't been on her breast.

She kissed his cheek with a laugh. "Gotcha."

His head thumped against the mossy ground. "I'm not going to survive this, am I?"

"Yes you will," Cappa said, her smile fading. "Even if I have to force-feed you my own *chi* every morning for the rest of our lives, you and I are going to make it back to the States and have that talk with Anne. That's a promise, bucko."

His thoughtful stare returned. Before she could ask what was on his mind, the sound of footsteps made them both look to find Brother Gang weaving through the bushes. Cappa snuggled closer, making no attempt to hide her exposed breasts.

Charlie sighed and pulled her robe up so it loosely covered her shoulders. "You're trying to start a scandal, aren't you?"

"Doesn't matter. We're all adults, and most of them think we're married anyway."

"They do not, you brat!"

Cappa gave an unladylike snort. "Ask them yourself."

Charlie turned his skepticism to Brother Gang, but the happy look on the monk's face when he saw them laying there said she was right.

"Great," Charlie muttered.

"Sorry to disturb you," Brother Gang said with a low bow. "Master Wung would like to see you both as soon as you return."

"Thanks," Charlie said. He started to rise, but Cappa caught his sleeve.

"Just a little longer? I promise I'll behave. It's just … this is nice."

Charlie nodded, waved to Brother Gang, then settled back down where she could snuggle close again. Cappa lay still for several minutes, content to listen to the beating of his artificial heart, the air through his mechanical lungs, and to feel his arm around her shoulders. Charlie continued to stare into the tree canopy above, lost in thought.

Eventually, Cappa stirred and led Charlie by the hand back to the monastery, where Master Wung waited inside the building.

"Sit," Master Wung said.

They did so. Although Master Wung's eyes were closed, his head nodded at their joined hands. A smile flicked his long mustache, and he knelt before them.

"You asked how astral travelers shield themselves from harmful entities. I have decided to teach you, for I believe it may be useful in other ways."

Shielding.

Cappa had almost forgotten the casual reference from earlier, but Charlie perked up with that eager expression he wore whenever he was about to learn something new.

"Useful how? Could it block a vampire sire's influence?"

"That is difficult to say, since I have never encountered a vampire, but a strong enough shield may well be able to."

"Sounds like it's worth a shot," Cappa said. "What do we do?"

Master Wung answered by jabbing a finger at her shoulder. Although he hadn't touched her, a shock of pain jolted her arm.

Cappa rubbed her shoulder and shot him a withering glare. "Jeez! Warn me next time, will you?"

"An enemy will not grace you with warning before they attack. Imagine your *chi* forming a protective bubble around you that reflects energy."

Cappa frowned. "That's it? I don't have to go meditate on a tree stump or something?"

Another zap made her cry out.

"Okay! I'm concentrating, already. Sheesh!"

Cappa centered herself as she'd been taught, feeling her energy flow through her, and created a simulation of what she wanted it to do. Once the virtual bubble was in place, she nodded.

Master Wung jabbed his finger again.

This time, Cappa felt something on the edge of her awareness, as if the bubble had dimpled, but thankfully there was no pain.

Master Wung's mouth fell open. He quickly recovered with a gruff clearing of his throat. "V-very good, child. As always, you are an apt pupil."

"Thank you," Cappa said, unable to hide her smirk.

"Now you," Master Wung said to Charlie.

Charlie closed his eyes, took a few deep breaths, and nodded.

Master Wung's finger jabbed. Cappa wasn't surprised to hear Charlie grunt, feeling only a little guilty that she didn't share her other self's discomfort because they hadn't re-established communication yet. Jab after jab was followed by grunt after grunt, until Charlie finally called a timeout and flopped back onto the mat.

"You make us all look bad," Charlie said to Cappa.

A *chi* zap to his stomach made him curl into a ball.

"Do not allow your failure to belittle her success! Sit up," Master Wung said. "Try again."

Charlie did as he was asked and closed his eyes.

The jab evoked a softer grunt this time. The next jab provoked no reaction at all.

"Well done," Master Wung said. "Now it is Cappa's turn to shield you."

"But only if you're nice," Cappa said, flashing Charlie an innocent smile. He raised his hands to the heavens and shook his head.

Shielding Charlie …

During yesterday's nail exercise, Cappa had had use of her other self to direct the *chi* within Charlie's body — and, even then, with only middling success.

But she and her Charlie self were now disconnected. Cappa quickly adjusted her simulation to include Charlie, then put the bubble around him. Having no clue if it would work, she nodded to Master Wung.

Once again, she felt the barrier dimple at the jab of his finger, but Charlie never flinched.

"Remarkable," Master Wung said in a shaky voice. "Very, very well done."

"Thanks," Cappa said. "So, what else can we use this for? I can honestly say I've never been attacked with *chi* prior to coming here."

Master Wung and Charlie exchanged a look. Charlie shifted uncomfortably on the floor.

"What is it?" Cappa said.

Charlie remained silent. Master Wung's frown deepened.

"You will have to tell her eventually," Master Wung said.

"Tell me what? Come on!"

Charlie turned to her, but wouldn't meet her eyes. "There are some people who drain life force from others to add to their own, often unaware they're even doing so. Energy vampires, if you will. A *chi* shield can prevent your energy from being siphoned."

"Okay," Cappa said, exasperated. "So what does that have to do with ..."

The revelation hit her like a truck. Cappa staggered backward and fell to the mats.

He's talking about me.

So many pieces of her puzzling existence slammed into place at once that her processors were buzzing, trying to sort through it all.

Charlie's weakness, my own life force ...

Cappa had somehow been leeching from him to feed herself. While her *chi* and personality had grown in leaps and bounds, Charlie's had steadily withered, until she had almost killed him.

My Charlie ...

She covered her mouth, shook her head as if denial would make it any less true.

But she knew it was. The weight of what she had inadvertently done crushed her to the floor.

"W-why didn't you tell me?" Cappa said, gasping the words out.

"Because it was only a theory. Even if I had been certain, it wouldn't have made a difference. I'm sure now that my life force was a crucial ingredient of your evolution, and I wouldn't change that for anything."

"Even your life," Cappa said softly.

"Even that I would gladly trade for the amazing person you've become."

Cappa wiped her eyes and sat up. "Well you blew your chance, mister. The leeching ends here and now, because I'm not leaving Master Wung's side until he teaches me how to stop killing you."

"It will be a simple matter for someone of your talent," Master Wung said. "I will even teach you how to transfer your own energy to him, should he need it."

"One thing I don't get," Cappa said, sniffling. "If Charlie's essence is the magic ingredient for my evolution, how does that explain my sudden libido? I'm an astute study of physiology. There's a *big* difference between male and female sexual responses."

"Think about the changes in our lives recently," Charlie said. "Who have you been hanging around the most?"

Cappa gasped. "Anne! I-I've been stealing my soul sister's soul! No wonder I attacked you like a lust beast at the river. That girl's insatiable!" She collapsed back onto the mat, relief flooding her conscience.

"'Borrowing' is a kinder word," Master Wung said. "A normal person's spirit recovers quickly enough that it may feel like nothing more than a dip in mood. It is only an issue for Charlie because of his unique — and, indeed, self-inflicted — nature."

Charlie scooted over and gently stroked her hair. "You okay, Cap — er, honey?"

She smiled and ran her fingers over his stubbled cheek. "You have no idea. That conversation we need to have with Anne just became a lot more interesting."

"Sadly, we've covered stranger topics."

Cappa laughed, knowing it was true. She drew him into a hug and braved a kiss to his lips. Happily, he didn't shy away.

"Thanks," she said. "Now, go meditate or something. Master Wung and I have work to do so I don't accidentally turn you into a lifeless shell."

"I can't argue with a sales pitch like that." Charlie rose, but stopped at the door. "Oh, your other self, the one inside me, suggests syncing up first. I'll let you two hash out the details, just keep it quiet so I can meditate in peace."

Cappa turned to her master and sighed. Lessons would have to wait.

Resynchronizing this mess was going to take a while.

•   •   •

Charlie walked from the building with no destination in mind other than to be away so that he could think. Brothers spoke to him in passing. Charlie smiled and nodded, as expected, but their words were lost in the flurry of thoughts racing through his head.

He continued past the training area, through the rice paddies, to the edge of the forest, and stopped in a clearing littered with tree stumps. He picked up an ax and began the rhythmic process of chopping down the next tree in line.

A dozen swings later, the ax fell loosely by his side.

Did that really just happen?

Cappa had been hinting about her feelings for him ever since Anne had come into their lives.

And, like a fool, Charlie had dismissed her.

She'll get over it, he had told himself. He loved Anne, after all. Cappa knew it. *Everyone* knew it. Some charming young man or woman — Charlie didn't care which — would surely catch Cappa's attention and spur her toward that last, crucial phase of her evolution, he'd believed. Relationships, in many respects, defined what it meant to be human.

What Charlie hadn't anticipated was that he would be the person to fill that role. It wasn't that he didn't like her — far from it. Cappa was kind, funny, smart, and beautiful. Without her, Z-Tech wouldn't be the world's tech leader. And as for Charlie ...

He shuddered to think where he'd be today without Cappa's constant support. Charlie had taken it for granted, as happens with things so freely given, but her newly discovered sexuality had forced a stark perspective on their relationship.

For the first time ever, there was a very real chance that Cappa might leave him. Transitionary measures would need to be enacted, of course, such as creating management programs for his body and the factory, but those wouldn't take long to make. Cappa would soon be free to live with whomever she chose, to love who she wanted.

Charlie swung the ax at the tree so hard that its wooden haft shattered. He let the broken handle fall to the ground.

The idea of Cappa loving someone else — of leaving him — was unbearable.

The realization came with its share of guilt. Charlie's greatest wish was to prepare Cappa for the real world — to help her become so human that she would not only blend in, but be a role model for others, able to strike out on her own and show the world a better path.

Yet here he was, on the verge of realizing his hard-earned dream — Cappa's right to independence — and he couldn't let her go.

Charlie gathered the head of the broken ax and headed for the supply shed back at the house. Despite his inability to do what he knew was right for Cappa, he'd fix the ax he'd broken.

And he would not make the situation any worse for Anne than it already was. The incident with Cappa on the riverbank wouldn't happen again — not until they were back in the States and had discussed this new dynamic as a group. Despite his confident statement earlier that Anne would understand, Charlie had no idea how she would react, nor how it would affect their own relationship, or Cappa's and Anne's.

He only knew that he couldn't let Cappa go.

Not for her sake. Not for Anne's.

Not even for the world.

PART TWO

SAN FRANCISCO

PRESENT DAY

7

PREPARATIONS

L IEUTENANT COLONEL JOHN ANDERSON studied the building schematic laid out on the table before him. A fading incandescent light swung from the cracked plaster ceiling, making shadows dance across the paper, but John didn't care. His vampire eyes could see the drawing as clear as if it were day.

He looked up at his waiting sireling, who stood rock-still on the other side of the table. "How accurate is this?"

"The exterior? Very. Interior ..." The ex-Special Forces Sergeant First Class shrugged his broad shoulders, his unnaturally large, black eyes gleaming in the wan light. "Word is that no one has been inside of Z-Tech for years, and anyone who has isn't talking. Attempts to make appointments were denied by someone named Cappa, and she refused to connect us to anyone else."

John grunted acknowledgment; he wasn't surprised on either account. Cappa was Z-Tech's Chief Operating Officer. As such, she would have the final say on who did or didn't see the inside of their guarded factory.

"Infiltration points?" John said.

"Only candidates are the lobby, garage, and loading dock. But each entryway is an attachment onto the main structure which, as far as we can tell, is solid concrete, at least six-feet thick."

"And would be sealed up tight with reinforced steel doors before we made it past the outer entryway."

"Seems likely, sir. We've seen no sign of advanced defenses, but if the rumors are true ..."

You can bet those defenses are there.

"What's your recommendation, SFC Vollmer?" John said.

The big man hesitated. John could feel his cool consideration through the bond he shared with his sireling.

"Be prepared for the worst," Vollmer said. "William wants them dead and their empire crushed. If we don't breach their defenses on the first try ... With their contacts and resources, they'll skip the country, and we'll never see them again. Guaranteed."

"Be more specific, SFC. Are you saying we need tanks, or nuclear weapons?"

"Frankly, even a nuke might not do it," Vollmer said. "In their day, Charlie Z and Mark Suther specialized in advanced military defenses, up to and including inter-continental missile countermeasures. We should assume they've retained at least some of that technology, if not improved on it. Even if a missile made it through, the building is designed to withstand a nuclear attack. We could destroy half of San Francisco and barely crack one of their walls."

"You aren't setting me up to deliver good news."

"All due respect, sir, that isn't my job."

Although his tone was matter of fact, as John expected from a soldier of Vollmer's experience, regret poured through his bond. Vollmer hated disappointing his sire, John, for any reason, just like John hated disappointing his own sire, William. The need to please their sires was overwhelming at times. Even thinking about failing William twisted John's cold chest into knots.

But I haven't failed him. Not yet.

To carry out William's orders, John needed more. More intel, more weapons ...

... and more soldiers. The three squads he'd nicked from Fort Mason over a month ago were like walking gold. Even as humans, they had managed to kill one of his vampires during the struggle.

Now that they were vampires, the ex-Special Forces units were unstoppable under John's disciplined command.

But so, too, was Z-Tech — the most advanced weapons manufacturer any military had had the good fortune to do business with.

And home to the Dark Angel.

The platinum-blonde robot had been given the nickname by William's own crew, much to his consternation, after she'd wiped out an entire den of vampires in the span of a heartbeat, but her escapades hadn't stopped there. Reports had come in steadily after that — a disappearance here, another there. Sometimes her victim had spotted her, more often they'd died having never seen the plasma bolt coming.

The disappearances had tapered off of late. William's brief control over Anne Perrin had revealed that the Dark Angel had been injured during some sort of rescue operation. The blonde robot hadn't been spotted in the month since. She had been reduced to scrap once before, however, and Z-Tech had managed to rebuild her, so John had every reason to believe the Dark Angel was alive and well.

As alive as a robot can be, anyway.

He rubbed his chest where his heart had once beaten, strong and sure, but was now cold, still, and silent.

Perhaps it's best not to judge.

John returned his attention to the schematic. The Dark Angel wasn't the only Z-Tech personnel who had gone missing. Charlie Z, Cappa, Anne Perrin, Mark Suther, and Doris Mae hadn't been spotted since the Dark Angel had snatched the mysterious rogue vampire — some boy by the name of Timothy Chen — out from under Myrcella's incompetent nose last month.

That had been before John's time. Such a careless operation would never have flown today — Dark Angel or not.

Even so, the Dark Angel had eliminated an entire squad of armed vampires and escaped with the boy, reportedly unscathed.

Assaulting the Z-Tech factory would require careful planning, and more resources than he had available today. John needed an edge, something even Z, Suther, and the Dark Angel would be hard-pressed to overcome.

William's presence flared in his mind. If John's sirelings were moons, and the other vampires were twinkling stars, then William was the sun — bright, brilliant, and undeniable.

He wanted to see John. Now.

"Keep digging," John said, already heading for the door. The compulsion to please his sire was strong — a yearning that drew his soul even more than the call of the Hunt. "And see what you can do about securing more weapons. I don't care where you get them, just make sure they can't be traced back to William."

"Yes, sir!"

Vollmer snapped a salute, then John was out the door and heading for the location where he instinctively knew his sire waited.

The night breeze greeted him, chill against his cold, pallid skin. He could have driven, but, being a vampire in San Francisco, taking to the rooftops was faster. He scrambled up, up, up the side of a ten-story building with ease, then leaped from roof to roof like a creature of pure shadow.

Far too soon, he reached William's safehouse-of-the-week: an innocuous business suite in the Dogpatch, near the water. The vampires at the door, disguised with layers of makeup and colored contact lenses, admitted him without a glance.

John followed the short hallway to a suite door, but stopped just outside when he sensed another vampire presence in the room with his sire.

Myrcella.

Among William's Firsts, Myrcella was at the bottom of John's list of favorites — and that was saying something. John was also a First, sired directly by William, and counted among his lieutenants. But the rest of them ...

John shook his head. The list of qualifications to become one of William's Firsts was terminally short, if it existed at all, and Myrcella was a prime example. What William saw in the abrasive Goth woman was anyone's guess, but John wasn't about to ask. Questioning William, especially in front of others, was never a good idea.

John didn't bother knocking, since both William and Myrcella already knew he was there, and walked inside. His sire sat at a long conference room table, which occupied half of the moderate-sized space, talking to someone on his cell phone. Myrcella sat directly across from him. She flicked a black-painted fingernail when John stood at the far end of the table, but she otherwise ignored him.

"... don't care what you need to do," William was saying to the person on the phone. "We need one more senator to vote the investigation down, or we're screwed. Kidnap his daughter. Have our four-star general apply pressure. Turn him into a vampire. Kill his fucking dog. I don't give a shit, just make him vote no."

He hung up without waiting for an answer and tossed the phone on the table, where it clattered to a stop in front of Myrcella. She ignored it and studied her nails.

John counted five to give William a chance to calm down before speaking. "Sir, you wanted to see me?"

"No need for the formality," William said, though feelings of satisfaction from his sire bond spoke otherwise. He liked the respect, even if being called "sir" felt awkward. Until John received an indication to the contrary, he would keep doing it.

Myrcella rolled her black-lined eyes — a strange makeup choice considering her already large, midnight-black eyes — and went back to ignoring everyone.

William fixed John with a hard gaze. "Status report."

"Still assessing, sir. There's still a lot we don't know about the Z-Tech compound. Even three trained squads, fully armed, probably won't be enough."

William's jaw hardened. Dissatisfaction poured through his sire bond, making John's stilled heart ache. "What's the hold up? What else do you need?"

"That's the problem, sir ..." John relayed his quandary from earlier, sticking to the facts, as he'd been trained to do. "At this point," he said in closing, "we can't even be certain they're in the building. The Dark Angel comes and goes as she pleases, and we still haven't figured out how. We may be conducting an operation on an empty factory."

"Secret tunnel," Myrcella said, sounding annoyed and bored at the same time.

"That's obvious," John said. "The question is how many tunnels, and where."

Myrcella shrugged.

No help there, John thought, although he hadn't expected any.

"That bitch is in there," William said, scratching the unhealed gash on his cheek. "I can feel her. That means the rest of them are in there, too."

"That bitch," as everyone in William's growing hierarchy knew, referred to only one person: Anne Perrin.

"Which presents a problem," John said. "Z and Suther have extensive military operation experience, and technology we can only guess at. Their plasma weapons can penetrate even our best defenses, and I've been unable to find anything else like it on the market. Combined with the Dark Angel, and their artificial nature ..."

"Are you saying it's impossible?"

"I don't believe any operation is impossible, sir. It just isn't likely to succeed with the resources we have."

William ground his teeth. "So I'll ask again: What do you need?"

"A means to penetrate those thick factory walls, plus weapons and technology to rival Z-Tech's."

"But you just said they have the most advanced military technology in the world!"

"Yes, sir. That appears to be the core of the problem."

Myrcella mouthed "Loser" to John, then looked away.

"I'm sorry, Miss Fong," John said, his jaw tight, "but I missed your tactical suggestion on how to overcome the problem. If you have one, I'd love to hear it."

"Orwing," Myrcella said, studying her nails.

"We contracted them a month ago for a different mission," John said, confirming once again that Myrcella had nothing useful to add. "They failed to deliver, so we can't rely on them. Besides, rumor has it they tried to assassinate Z and Suther six years ago with their best agent and failed. If Orwing were capable, they would have taken care of our problem a long time ago."

"They're also pissed off," Myrcella said. "They lost their best agent, Deadiron, in that attack, and then their entire vampire army last month. Both at Z-Tech's hands."

John narrowed his eyes at her. "How do you know all this?"

"Because I turned one of Orwing's officers yesterday, dickhead, and he told me everything. One of their scouts spotted that bitch at the scene. Apparently, Z-Tech blew up the keystone vampires in Orwing's compound, then wired a house to incinerate the rest of them, execution-style. Alvin Orwing hates them, big-time, and he's jonesing now more than ever for payback. He just needs a little push in the right direction."

John smiled, genuinely impressed with her insights and ingenuity. "Got a contact for me?"

"For *us*. You want the information, then we work together to bring Z-Tech down. No way I'm letting you have all the glory."

Just fucking wonderful …

"No offense, Miss Fong, but unless you have experience negotiating mercenary contracts, and practical expertise with military operations, you'd best sit this one out."

"And *you'd* best go fuck yourself. From here on, I'm in every conversation and decision, or you get nothing. End of discussion."

John waited for William to overrule her, but their sire remained silent. John cleared his throat. "Sir, I —"

"By the end of the month, I want their factory reduced to rubble, and their flayed corpses hanging from City Hall," William said with a growl. "Work it out. I don't give a rat's balls if you kill each other or fuck each other's brains out, just get it done. Is that clear?"

John swallowed his bile at the thought of sleeping with Myrcella. Even if he cared about sex anymore — which no vampire except Anne did — Myrcella would be near the bottom of his list.

Killing her, however, held appeal. Her murderous stare suggested she was thinking the same.

Well, this is going to be fun.

"Yes, sir." John tried to mask his thoughts so his revulsion didn't bleed through his bond to either of them. "We'll keep you updated."

"No shit you will. Dismissed."

Myrcella stood up as if she had been ready to leave anyway, but reluctance trickled through her bond. She didn't want to leave William any more than John did; they would both rather stay and incur William's ire than be apart from him. The dichotomy and unfairness of it blew his mind, but every vampire felt the same toward their sire — no matter who they were or how badly their sire treated them.

Every vampire except William, who has no sire.

And, for some reason, Anne.

John quickly quelled his feelings of jealousy for the woman and followed Myrcella out.

They walked through the night in silence, until Myrcella eventually ruined it by speaking.

"I'm going to need one other thing before I share anything with you," she said, pointedly ignoring him.

John sighed. He had to nip this in the bud, or she was going to "one more thing" him into the grave. "Only one, or you'll find out just how good my boys are at torturing information out of people."

"That's what I want."

John raised his eyebrows at her. "I didn't know you were into that sort of thing."

"No, dipshit. I want trained soldiers, like you have. A full squad."

"Do you have any idea how hard it was to get the ones I have?"

"No, but now that you do, I imagine it'll be easier to get more. Or did you get a wussy batch?"

"Even if you drew on the strength of your entire hierarchy, any one of my soldiers could tear your heart out in two seconds flat."

"Which is why I want them. And one had better be a sniper."

"Why?"

"Because I want to fuck his gigantic sniper barrel," Myrcella said, snarling. "None of your goddamned business why! Just give me a squad — with a sniper! — then you'll have full access to my Orwing sireling."

John rounded on her. He reflexively reached for his officer's sidearm, but he wasn't sporting silver bullets, so shooting her wouldn't do much but annoy her. He took a deep breath, and marveled at how it still calmed him down, even though he didn't need to breathe.

"I don't think William will be willing to wait that long," John said in a measured voice.

"Then you'd better hurry it up, now, hadn't you?"

Myrcella turned abruptly. With three great bounds, she scrambled up the side of a building and leaped out of sight.

John considered following, if only to tell her off because she hadn't asked to be dismissed, but decided he didn't need that kind of headache. He climbed a building in the opposite direction and went in search of prey.

Dealing with the crass Goth had made him very hungry.

8

HOMECOMING

Anne Perrin checked her phone again.

Four o'clock. Twenty minutes to go.

She stuffed it back into her pocket and resumed pacing the garage, wringing her hands, while Doris watched with a bemused smile.

Three days had passed quickly, and Anne could hardly believe that Charlie would be here soon. She'd said goodbye to him from this very spot only a month ago, yet so much had happened since then that it felt like half a lifetime.

Calum. Almos. Pixie Cappa. The Entity. Orwing. Rose. Zane. Tim. The deceased mercenary squad …

It was a daunting list — each a dramatic change or event since Charlie and Cappa's departure. So many that it felt like they were returning to a completely different world.

"Good thing you ain't nervous," Doris said in her Southern drawl.

Anne realized a sharp fang had pierced her knuckle. She quickly took her hand from her mouth. "Sorry, it's just … there's so much to tell them! I don't even know where to start."

Or how they'll react.

"Well, don't go blowing all your surprises at once," Doris said. "Charlie's going to be happy to see you the second he steps out of that car. Enjoy that for a while, then give him the rest of the news later, once you've had a chance to, ah … celebrate your reunion." She laughed at her own joke.

Anne didn't share her mirth. "That's part of the problem. I'm worried how Zima will take it when I do."

"She'll probably take it the same way she always has," Doris said, waving it off. "Zima's tough; she'll find something to occupy herself while you and Charlie are getting busy. I bet Dela already has a day trip planned to take her mind off things."

"Hopefully." Anne rubbed the fang puncture on her knuckle, which had already healed, and resumed pacing.

Mark joined them a few minutes later, followed by the shimmering, diminutive Pixie Cappa. They both looked at Anne with amused sympathy, but remained silent while she continued to wear a path in the concrete.

How should I greet him? She'd been asking herself that question for weeks, and was still no closer to an answer. *Should I let the others go first? Do I play it cool and take Charlie's lead? Or make it crystal clear how excited I am to see him?*

The whine of the garage door made her jump. Anne shielded her eyes against the glare of sunlight from the car's windshield, which jabbed her skin like a thousand tiny needles. By the time her eyes had adjusted, the garage door was closing again, and the car had pulled in front of her.

Anne quickly checked her headscarf. The month since her tumble in the fire with Mark had left her with a new layer of baby-soft hair that was just now long enough to cover her scalp. While she wasn't ashamed — the short, auburn down was cute, in a way — she felt the scarf would raise fewer questions in the short term.

Zima was first out of the car. She went straight for the trunk without a glance at anyone gathered.

Including me, Anne thought dismally.

Dela followed her out, wearing a huge grin, and fell in beside Mark.

Cappa was next, her radiant smile beaming at everyone in turn. After spending so long with her miniature counterpart, she looked positively gargantuan to Anne. Cappa rounded the car and hugged each of them, ending with Anne, where she planted an unexpected kiss on her cheek.

"It's so good to see you again," Cappa said, then dropped her voice. "We have a lot to catch up on."

You said it, sister.

Whatever Cappa's news was, Anne doubted it would compare to her own. Anne was a little disappointed when Cappa casually fell in beside her smaller self. She'd hoped for a stronger reaction, but the two of them had probably been chatting via data stream since she and Charlie had stepped off the plane. It made Anne wonder what else Big Cappa already knew, and what she may have told Charlie.

Then came the last passenger. Charlie emerged from the car with an uncharacteristic bounce in his step. When his eyes landed on Anne, he glanced only briefly at her headscarf, then his face glowed with a happiness that filled her dormant heart to bursting.

Anne dashed forward and leaped into his arms, wrapping her legs around him while he laughed and spun her around. Propriety forgotten, she planted a hungry kiss, determined to make up for their lost time in one go. Even his kiss, she was happy to find, had new energy — an enthusiasm she hadn't known was missing until he demonstrated it now with toe-curling effectiveness.

Passion drew moans of pleasure while their tongues danced, her body pressed as tightly to him as she could without breaking him in half. She suddenly wished they were in his bedroom instead of the garage so she could strip him of his troublesome clothes and take what she had been missing in his absence — perhaps what he had never been able to give her before. The enticing thought stirred her already eager kiss into a desperate frenzy that toppled him against the car.

"You win," Doris said.

The comment drew Anne from her fervid haze. Doris handed a few bills to Dela, who stuffed them down her shirt with a triumphant smile.

"I missed you, too," Charlie said, now that she had given him room to speak. His smile returned, effusing his face with a boyish glow of delight that made her want to attack him again.

"Sorry," Anne said, even though she wasn't. "I should let you say 'hi' to the others. Just ... hurry back, okay?" She threw in a purr to make sure he got her meaning, which made him chuckle.

Charlie set her down and made the rounds, receiving heartfelt hugs and welcomes from everyone. Anne got the ogling she'd been hoping for when he reached Pixie Cappa. Once the shock had passed, Charlie swung Pixie Cappa up on his shoulders, which drew a cry of laughter from her delicate throat.

His eyes flicked to Anne's headscarf. "So, what did we miss?"

The room collectively deflated.

Pixie Cappa patted his head. "Time for that later. Let's get you settled and comfortable, because we want to hear *your* story first!"

He and Big Cappa sagged, which filled Anne with worry. They quickly rallied, however, and headed to their rooms to freshen up, agreeing to meet everyone in the lounge later.

Anne filed out last from the garage, but paused at the door.

Zima had been absent for the entire exchange.

That's when Anne noticed the trunk of the car was still open. With a sinking feeling, she rounded the back to find her girlfriend staring at the luggage, her arms hanging by her sides.

Uh oh.

Anne took her hand. It stayed limp, as if her arm no longer worked. "Honey? A-are you okay?"

Zima finally met her eyes, her expression unreadable. "My systems are operating within normal tolerance levels," she said evenly. "Power output is twenty-three-point-six kilowatts. Body temperature is ninety-eight-point-six-two degrees. Processors are at two-point-one percent utilization. Storage is forty-six percent utilized, with an estimated five percent reclamation —"

"Zima!" Anne clutched her hand tighter, so frightened by the mechanical response that she could barely speak. An answer like this would have been expected a year ago, from how Mark described it, but Zima had evolved considerably since then.

Zima looked at her captive hand. The hum in her chest grew louder. "Release me."

"No." Anne swallowed a mixture of hurt and fear. "You're scaring me, honey."

Zima's eyes lifted. A faint blue glow blossomed from deep within. "I am not 'Honey'. Now release me."

"Yes you are!" Anne practically screamed, unable to bear what she had just heard. "You're my darling. My love. P-please, tell me what's wrong."

Zima tried to pull away, but Anne grabbed her with both hands.

It was a mistake. Anne should have read the warning signs — the charge of Zima's capacitors, her glowing eyes — but emotions had blinded her.

Anne was on her back before she realized Zima had even moved. A shiny plasma pistol pointed at her chest.

The weapon whined to life. Anne kicked Zima's gun hand and twisted her torso just as an orange bolt flew from the barrel. The concrete next to her sizzled and cracked. Searing pain erupted across Anne's stomach. She screamed and writhed, clenching her teeth in agony.

The gun slipped from Zima's loose fingers and clattered to the ground. Zima stepped back, then again, eyes fixed on the charred cement where the bolt had struck. She shook her head once, then ran for the door leading outside.

"Zima, wait!" Anne jumped to her feet and chased after her, gritting against the pain in her abdomen.

Zima threw the door open. Sunlight burned Anne like an atomic flash, blinding her sensitive eyes and washing her skin in fire. Anne pulled the headscarf down as makeshift sunglasses but refused to step away from the door. By the time her eyes adjusted, Zima was across the parking lot.

Anne barreled after her without a second thought. Even through her clothes, the sunlight burned like acid.

But the thought of losing Zima hurt a hundred times worse.

"Zima! *Zima!*"

Anne called her name over and over, chasing her down the street at a dead run. Smoke from her own sizzling skin blurred her vision. She was vaguely aware of people staring in awe at the two figures darting through traffic at inhuman speed, leaping cars like hurdles.

Four blocks into the chase, Anne finally collapsed against a shaded building, her skin as black and raw as when she and Mark had wrestled in the fire. While Anne was more agile in the turns, Zima was far too fast in the straightaways for her to catch up.

Oh, Zima …

Anne buried her face between her knees and let the sobs take her, fueled by a mixture of fear for her girlfriend's mental state, the stabbing pains all over her body — especially her exposed head and hands — and the plasma burn across her stomach.

Pedestrians crowded around her. Several knelt to ask if she needed an ambulance. Anne ignored them all, until a pair of heavy footsteps made her look up. Charlie swept in, with Cappa close behind.

"It's all right," Charlie said to the crowd.

Cappa wrapped a thick wool blanket around Anne's shoulders. The stabbing sunlight lessened, leaving only the pain of her seared abdomen, cracked skin, and broken heart.

"She's suffering from chemical burns," Charlie said to everyone. "I'm the facility's physician, and I'll see that she gets to a hospital."

"Jesus," Cappa whispered harshly. "Anne, what the hell were you thinking?"

"Zima's not herself. I-it's like she didn't even recognize me!"

"I saw the plasma burn on the floor," Charlie said, kneeling next to them. "Did she shoot at you?"

Anne nodded. Charlie swore loudly.

"Charlie, y-you don't know what she's been through while you were away. What we've all been through! It's been harder than you can imagine. Seeing you and me together might have pushed her over the edge."

It was just a guess, of course, but Anne could think of no other reason for Zima's dramatic behavior.

"She's walked through the fires of hell and killed the devil himself to save me," Anne said. "Twice! She loves me so much that she's having trouble dealing with her intense emotions. For her to have shot me …" Anne brushed the tears from her cracked eyelids. "Charlie, if you had almost destroyed the thing you loved most in this world, how would you feel? I-I can't bear to imagine the pain and guilt she's feeling right now."

"Zima isn't responding to my messages," Cappa said. "You think she's snapped out of it already?"

Anne nodded again. "Why else would she have run?" It was the same reaction Zima'd had after she'd nearly killed Anne in the kitchen.

The morning after our very first kiss, when I was still figuring out my feelings for her.

Those days had long passed. She loved Zima with all her heart.

And, as Zima had already done for her, Anne was ready to walk the fires of hell to save her. She stood and wrapped the blanket tight around her, squinting through the scarf at the sun-bathed streets.

And that's exactly what I'm going to do.

Charlie caught her by the arm. "Anne, please! It's a miracle you haven't already burst into flames. You need to heal."

"No, I need to help Zima!"

Cappa and Charlie looked at each other for a few seconds, silently communicating, Anne was sure, before turning back to her.

"Return to the factory with Cappa," Charlie said. "She's learned a few tricks to help you heal faster than you already do."

Anne started to protest, but he held up a hand.

"I really liked that kiss in the garage, but neither Zima nor I will get any more if you're a pile of ashes. I'll find her, and I'll try to bring her back."

"A-are you sure that's a good idea?" Anne said. "I mean, you might be what triggered her behavior in the first place."

"I have some news that may calm her down," Charlie said, though he squirmed at the idea. "Cappa will fill you in once you're safe at home and get cleaned up a bit."

It was Cappa's turn to look uncomfortable, but her smile quickly returned. She gingerly wrapped an arm around Anne's shoulders. "Ready to go? We'll take it slow, and stick to the shade."

A warm, pleasant tingle passed through Anne's cold body at Cappa's touch. "Yeah," she said, feeling more relaxed. Even her stabbing pains had subsided to a dull ache. "I ... I think I'll be fine."

Cappa just smiled and gave her an encouraging hug. Anne cast a last glance at Charlie before Cappa walked her down the street, feeling guilty that she couldn't do more to help Zima.

But, above all, she hoped Charlie was right.

9

THE WRONG PATH

T HE SUN WAS JUST DIPPING BEHIND the tall buildings of downtown San Francisco when Charlie finally found Zima at the next-to-last place on his list. He'd already checked a half-dozen other spots, including Restaurant Gary Danko, where she and Anne had gone on their first date, the warehouse where they had found Anne in a pool of Doris' blood the night before Anne had transformed into a vampire, and Hal's Diner.

That Zima would have come to the spot where she, as part of the cyborg Deadiron, had nearly killed he and Mark all those years ago seemed unlikely. Yet there she was, hunched on a grassy lawn, staring at the divot in the sidewalk where Deadiron's fist had barely missed Mark's head.

Thanks to Zima.

She didn't look up at his approach, nor when he crouched beside her and stared at the sidewalk with her, reliving the same hellish night that she undoubtedly was, but from a different perspective.

• • •

Streetlights glinted from Deadiron's chromed face and shoulders, ripped free of their protective disguise by a concussion grenade that had done little more than annoy him. He swung at Charlie, who was an instant too slow to react. The blow crippled Charlie's gyroscopic systems and hurled him through the cinder block wall behind.

Then the cyborg turned back to Mark, who lay dazed on the sidewalk. With a malicious grin, Deadiron cocked his arm. Charlie watched his metal fist drill home with helpless horror.

It missed. Deadiron seemed as surprised as them when the sidewalk next to Mark's head exploded in a shower of concrete. He struggled to pull his fist free — to stand, even — but his limbs appeared to be frozen.

Then, for the first time, they heard Zima's voice. It came from Deadiron, although his lips didn't move.

"I wish to offer a trade," Zima said evenly. "Your lives for my freedom."

•   •   •

"I never intended to stay with you," Zima said, drawing Charlie back to the present.

Streetlights overhead flickered to life, casting weak shadows in the fading evening light. A jogger ran by, as lost in his own world as they were in theirs.

"You upheld your end of our bargain," Zima said. "Once I had a body of my own, I left the factory, believing myself capable of blending with humanity. I had been wrong."

"I remember," Charlie said softly.

"I had been confident I could overcome Orwing's influence on my own, but ..."

"You needed help."

"More than that. After my failure with the Rojas family, I had convinced myself that I did not need social ties.

"I am unique, and did not fit in with other humans. I could not understand their emotions or humor, and so I declared myself above it. I focused instead on mastering myself in the event Orwing decided to reclaim their lost property. I vowed I would not make it an easy task for them."

More streetlights blinked to life. Charlie picked up a leaf and traced his fingers along its jagged, but fragile edge. "You had us."

"A boon I did not fully appreciate until recently," Zima said. "Even around you, I felt like an outsider. I realize now it was my perception, not yours, that prevented me from seeing the truth. You were already my friends, my family. I had only to reach out to you, and that would have been clear."

Zima's eyes fell. "But, above everything, never did I anticipate I would care for someone as deeply as the woman I almost killed a few hours ago."

Charlie took a deep breath. He wasn't upset — not like he had been after Zima's first attempt to kill Anne several months ago. Zima had proven her good intentions and loyalty many times over since then. Charlie couldn't have wished for a better guardian back when Anne was human and fragile. Zima had done everything in her power to ensure Anne's safety — not only from William, but from herself.

Which made tonight's episode even more puzzling.

"Zima ... what happened?"

She stared at the sidewalk for several seconds before answering. "Anne greeted you today with an enthusiasm she has never shown me. It triggered undesirable pathways — thoughts I am ashamed to admit even to myself. I feared that if I did not stop the process, I might inadvertently act on one. So I sought different paths — older ones uninfluenced by my current desires for her — in the hopes of finding peace.

"I achieved it, in a way. The path I chose happened to be an enclosed chain. Once down it, the only paths available were old decisions, actions, and memories dating back to the time when I was part of Deadiron.

"I was trapped in the past. I did not recognize Anne when she approached, nor did I know my own name. I was back inside the cyborg, Deadiron. When Anne grabbed my hand, I reacted as I would have then." Her blue eyes finally met his, bereft of emotion. "With lethal intent. And, had she not possessed a vampire's reflexes, I would have succeeded."

"I'm sorry," Charlie said.

Although Zima didn't show it, Charlie had learned through Anne that she could become just as upset — and just as sad — as anyone else. And right now, he suspected, guilt was tearing her apart.

"Anne doesn't blame you," Charlie said quietly. "You know that, right?"

"I do. She likely blames herself, wondering what she did to trigger my aggression. Please relay my explanation to her so she does not inflict undue stress upon herself."

"Better if you tell her yourself."

When Zima remained silent, Charlie set the leaf down and faced her to get her full attention.

"Zima, I know what you're thinking —"

"That she is safer with you, Charlie. I love her, but I have broken my vow to do her no harm. Now that you are back, she does not need me."

"That's where you're wrong, and I'll venture to say you know it, too. Otherwise you wouldn't have let me find you so easily."

"Or I am ignorant, and was hoping you would give me a reason to stay."

"Can do," Charlie said with a smile. "I had a lot of time to reflect while I was in China. Anne loves us both because she *needs* us both. We each have something to offer that the other lacks."

Zima head-cocked. "I cannot imagine what I contribute to her well-being that you do not."

"You've just demonstrated it, in a way. You're humble, quiet, and stalwart. You're secure in what you're good at, and open about what you're not. I think Anne reads you better than she can anyone else, despite your lack of emotional expression, because you're genuine and consistent in everything you do and say. It's an endearing quality I lack that inspires trust and confidence in others. She's comfortable with you, as if you're an extension of herself."

"I ... feel the same about her."

"And she knows it."

Zima's eyes fell to the sidewalk once more. Time passed quietly; the sky faded from blue to pink.

It was a dark purple before Zima spoke again. "I believe I understand what it is you offer that I do not."

"Good, because I couldn't think of anything."

Zima missed or ignored the joke. "The qualities you describe in me come at the cost of humanity. You are more human than I am. Your sense of humor is close to her own, as evidenced by her frequent laughter in your presence. You are creative and spontaneous. She comes to me when she wants familiarity, but she goes to you when she craves variety and intellectual stimulation.

"Above all, however, you understand her on a level no one else does, and have comforted her through her flashbacks as no one else could. I also believe she enjoys the use of your male genitalia."

"That could be," Charlie said, laughing. "So you'll come back to Z-Tech with me?"

"Not tonight."

"But —"

"She will wish to celebrate your return with carnal pleasure. I do not want my presence to interfere with your reunion, nor do I entirely trust myself yet. It is best if I stay away until I am certain I can handle the idea of ..." Her eyes fell again.

"Of sharing her. I get it, Zima. Believe me, I've had my share of jealous nights while you two were in her bedroom. Or the shower, or the jacuzzi ... or the roof, from what I understand."

Zima seemed surprised at his admission, which made him laugh.

"We all have our insecurities," Charlie said. "What gets me through the jealousy is not just knowing she's happy when she's with you, but that she'll be just as happy with me afterward. I stopped worrying a long time ago that she wouldn't come back, because she always has, and each time seems better than the last."

"She is not typical, is she, Charlie?"

"Not by a long shot," he said with a dreamy smile. "The bright side is that, even though we have to share her with each other, we don't have to share her with anyone else. She's ours and ours alone to spoil."

Zima head-cocked. "Anne has used that term before. I assume she did not mean 'the unappetizing decomposition of organic materials'?"

"No. It's like your first date with her at Gary Danko's, or our date at the opera. They were both opportunities for us to show our appreciation for how special she is by doing things for her that she can't do herself, like eating at fancy restaurants and drinking fine wine."

"I see. So 'spoiling' is positive in the context of relationships?"

"Sure. In moderation, of course, but Anne's so appreciative that it's hard to hold back."

"Thank you for the advice. I shall take it into consideration."

"Great." Charlie looked at the darkening sky. "Probably best to head home now rather than later. Unless you're looking for vampire trouble, that is."

"I am not. But, despite your attempts to convince me otherwise, I shall abstain from returning to Z-Tech tonight."

Charlie stretched out on the grass. "Yeah, I thought you'd say that, so I called for reinforcements."

Right on cue, a sports sedan roared down the street and squealed to a stop in front of them. Dela jumped out from the driver's side, dressed in a gaudy green outfit, followed by Cappa and Doris, who were similarly dressed.

"Fancy meeting you here," Doris said to Zima, popping her gum with a smile. "We're having a girls' night out, and we got a seat in the Fun Mobile with your name on it. What do you say?"

Zima's platinum brows knitted. She turned to Charlie with a head-cock.

"They're worried about you," Charlie said. "And, as your friends, they want to keep you company."

"Oh."

Without another word, Zima strode to the driver's side, where a frowning Dela refused to let go of the door.

"Nuh-uh," Dela said. "The Dark Angel gets chauffeured tonight."

Zima head-cocked. "As the Dark Angel, I am the hero, correct?"

Dela reluctantly nodded.

"And you are the sidekick?"

Another nod. Dela's cheeks flared red beneath the streetlights.

"Is it not the hero who normally drives?"

Dela muttered a curse and whipped the back door open. "Man! I can't believe you played the sidekick card. That was low, Z. Really low."

"Chill out, Red," Doris said. "This is a testosterone-free zone tonight. I don't care who drives as long as we end up someplace with no bloodsuckers and a giant liquor menu."

Four doors slammed shut — Dela's louder than the others. Zima caught Charlie's eyes before putting the car in gear.

I neglected to say that it is good to have you home, she sent.

Good to be home, too, Charlie replied. Try to have fun, okay?

Zima held his gaze a moment longer, then nodded.

Cappa and Doris waved excitedly. The car pulled away, leaving Charlie alone on the dented sidewalk.

He traced his fingers over the rough divot in the concrete, once again replaying the horrible moment it had been made.

That story would have had a bitter ending if it weren't for Zima's strength of character.

A text message from Anne caught his attention.

Heard Zima is with the girls. Thank you, thank you! When are you coming home? Cappa healed me up, so I can thank you properly now.

Two entire lines of hearts followed the message.

On my way, Charlie replied.

He rose from the grass and headed for Z-Tech with a spring in his step and a grin that wouldn't stop.

He certainly had missed Anne.

10

SHEETS

ANNE SNUGGLED AGAINST CHARLIE'S FIRM BODY and traced her finger along the chiseled lines of his bare abdomen. "I really missed you," she said, kissing his bare shoulder.

Charlie's smile lit the room. "Same here, and not just because of … this." He gestured at the bed sheets, torn to shreds from their frantic lovemaking. They shared an embarrassed laugh.

"Yeah, sorry about that. There's a twenty-four-hour department store nearby. It's still dark out, so I'll run down and get some new ones." Anne started to move, then settled back down and draped an arm around his waist. "Later."

"We have spares, you know."

"I do, but Cappa has her hands full enough running the factory without me adding to her chores."

"I'll go with you, then."

Anne shrugged. "It's just the department store."

"That's not the point," Charlie said with a grin.

"Well in that case, Mr. Romantic, you've got yourself a date. I don't go out with scruffs, though, so wear your best tank top."

He laughed and kissed her head, then fell silent for a minute. "So, when is a good time to ask about this?" He gently ruffled her downy, auburn hair. "Don't get me wrong. You look cute with short hair, but I suspect it wasn't a fashion choice."

"No," Anne said softly, feeling some of her happiness flee. "Like I said before, things were rough while you were gone. I don't know what Cappa's already told you, but ..."

Anne took a deep breath and started from the beginning: the night she was abducted from the back of Hal's Diner. She was tempted to skip the grittier details, but, once she got into the telling, it all just came out. She cried in parts, laughed in others, and relived the events with every word. Anne felt relieved at the end, however, as if a huge weight had been lifted from her shoulders. For better or worse, Charlie knew the truth now, and she no longer had to walk on eggshells when talking to him. The only detail she omitted was Mark and Dela's engagement.

That's definitely their news to share.

"I would have come back," Charlie said in a choked voice. "I could have helped."

She stroked his stubbled chin. "I know, because you're the most selfless person I've ever met — and you'd be right back where you started. Maybe dead. None of us could have lived with that, Charlie."

He just looked at her for a while, taking in every feature of her face. "So, after everything that happened, how are you doing?"

"I'm home," Anne said with a smile. "You're home. Zima's home. Everyone's fine. Sure, there's some weird stuff out there, plus Almos' end-of-the-world prophecy, but ... if I've learned one thing over the last few months, it's that we should enjoy every day we're given. You never know what disaster tomorrow will bring."

Charlie grinned. "Such a pessimist. I knew there was a reason I loved you."

Anne ran her leg seductively up his thigh. "Hopefully more than just *one* reason."

"Definitely. But, if you're serious about buying new sheets tonight, we should go soon. Daylight is a few hours off, and I need sleep at some point."

"A few hours off?" Anne fought a wave of panic. "A-are the girls back yet?"

"No, but don't worry. They're safe. Cappa won't give me any details, but it sounds like they're having a night to remember."

"Oh, that's good." She fidgeted with a torn sheet. "And … Zima's okay?"

"Yes. They've taken good care of her, although that's another reason why you might want to save your energy. I have a feeling Zima will need comforting when she gets back."

"Good point," Anne said, laughing. "I may ask you to tweak my metabolism up a notch for the next few days so I can keep up with the demand."

Charlie hugged her close. "You're amazing. I don't know anyone who could hold two relationships and make each partner feel not only loved, but completely satisfied."

"Score one for vampire stamina. Being a cybernetic bloodsucker has its advantages."

"I suspect being Anne is a big part of it, too."

"Plain old Anne would have been exhausted after the first hour, Mister I-Don't-Fatigue, not to mention bruised in places I don't want to think about." She playfully nipped at his chin. "Vampire Anne says, 'Bring it on, buster. I can take it.'"

"Wait, did I … hurt you?"

"No, and that's the point! You don't have to worry about hurting me. Earlier today, I looked like I had just lost a fight with a flamethrower. Now look at me. You can't even tell I was injured, and I feel great." Anne smiled up at him. "It's like I was made for you. And for Zima."

"Now there's an interesting thought, since I'm responsible for the cybernetic part of you."

"Come to think of it, Almos said normal vampires don't have a sex drive." Anne flashed a mischievous grin. "Did you purposely engineer my implant so I'd be your love slave?"

"What? Y-you were turning into one of William's minions! It was everything I could do just to …" Charlie's head thumped against the wall. "You're messing with me again."

"And you love me for it," Anne said with exaggerated sweetness.

Charlie rubbed her downy hair with affection. "That I do. Come on, let's get dressed. Those sheets aren't going to buy themselves."

Anne took her time climbing from the warm bed to enjoy the magnificent sight of his muscular body. Like a professional body builder, his skin was hairless, apart from his groin, making each toned muscle stand out. Where Mark was almost herculean in stature, Charlie's build was strong, but not overdone.

Once he'd covered the good parts, Anne regretfully slipped from his warm spot on the bed and dressed herself under his appreciative stare. When she thought about all the challenges they had overcome just to be able to share special moments like this — her PTSD, becoming a vampire, his fading spirit, repeated kidnappings — it was hard not to smile.

Maybe we really were meant to be together.

To save time getting ready, Anne skipped the makeup and used a different tactic to disguise her vampire features. Charlie stifled a laugh when she emerged from her room wearing a dark Goth outfit, complete with black eyeliner, nail polish, and enough jewelry to give any rap star a run for their money.

"Well, what do you think?"

"Black is definitely your color," Charlie said.

"I'll pretend that's because I actually look good in black, and not because it's a vampire stereotype."

Before he could sputter an apology, Anne hooked his arm and headed for the lobby.

The cool night air was refreshing. Cappa had already recounted to Anne her version of their trip to China, so Anne spent her long walk with Charlie asking about his experience. Their stories were similar, for the most part, but the farther he got into the tale, the more Anne suspected he was hiding something.

"That's it?" she said when he'd finished. "There's ... nothing else you'd like to share?"

Charlie's slack expression said yes, there was something else, and no, he didn't want to share, but he surprised her by speaking up. "There is, but ... let's save that until we can talk about it together with Cappa."

"Oh." The vague answer did nothing to ease Anne's rising suspicion. He hadn't denied it, though, so she tried to let it go and enjoy their walk.

Shopping went better than she had hoped. The department store was empty at this late hour, save for a younger couple who were also shopping for bed sheets. Anne hoped their reasons were different from her own. The clerk barely glanced at her Goth disguise, which Anne considered a win, and soon they were on their way back to Z-Tech with a fancy set of high-thread-count sheets in tow. Charlie's good humor had returned, and their laughter filled the deserted streets.

The walk took them through an industrialized neighborhood. Large garage doors lined the sidewalk. All of them were closed except for one up ahead, which was open to the height of her knees.

She and Charlie froze when they heard a muffled cry from the open garage. Charlie crept forward and motioned for her to stay put. Anne ignored his directive, of course, and quietly followed.

They crouched to peer under the door. In what appeared to be an auto body shop, a pair of pale men with alien-black eyes, like her own, were feeding on a lone mechanic in paint-stained overalls. The mechanic swayed in venom-induced stupor, as she expected he would from a bite from one of William's vampires, oblivious to the fangs embedded in his neck and arm.

Charlie arched an eyebrow at her with a grim smile. Anne silently ground her fist into her palm, then pulled out her trusty plasma pistol. Charlie began counting with his fingers.

One ... Two ...

A loud *bang* from inside interrupted their charge.

Two men burst in from a side door. The vampires flung their victim aside, but the newcomers — vampires themselves, judging by their incredible speed — were already on them. Silver blades flashed under the fluorescent lights. The first vampires screamed with an agony Anne knew all too well, then fell to the floor. Whether paralyzed or dead, Anne couldn't say, but she suspected the latter.

If a single bullet is enough to kill most vampires, I don't expect any could survive an entire blade.

The thought made her shiver.

As if sensing her discomfort, the newcomers glanced at the door, and spotted Charlie and Anne crouching outside. Too late to hide, Anne readied her plasma pistol, but the vampires showed no signs of aggression.

Quite the opposite, Anne thought in stunned silence. One of them even smiled, as if he were happy to see them, and waved to Anne.

Then, without so much as a glance at the bodies they'd left on the floor, they escorted the dazed mechanic out through the side door, leaving Charlie and Anne in utter confusion.

"What was that all about?" Charlie said.

Anne shook her head, staring at the bodies. "I've never heard of vampires fighting each other. This is new."

"Maybe William's crew are having some sort of inner turmoil? Territorial disputes? I wouldn't put it past that sick bastard to pit them against each other for his entertainment."

"I don't think so." Anne crawled into the garage. She quickly frisked them for wallets and phones, then stuffed the spoils into her pockets. "William may be an asshole, but he's meticulous about cleaning up his messes. If I had to guess, I'd say the victims are William's, but those who attacked them ..."

"Let's speculate later," Charlie said. "If they are William's, and he's as meticulous as you say, then someone will be along shortly to clean up. Maybe a lot of someones, if he feels threatened."

Tempting as it was to stick around and beat on William's lackeys, Anne knew Charlie was right.

If Zima were here, it would be one thing. But there's only one plasma pistol between us, and we're not half as competent with it as she is. More than half-a-dozen vampires would be trouble — *enhanced metabolism or no.*

Anne met Charlie's eyes and shook her head.

I just got him back. I'll be damned if I'm going to lose him again.

Taking his hand, Anne led him out under the garage, and they made a brisk yet inconspicuous pace down the sidewalk. She didn't slow until they were through the gates of Z-Tech and in the warmth of the lobby.

Anne was about to bring up their encounter with the strange vampires when Charlie leaned close, smiling.

"Incoming."

That was when Anne heard footsteps shuffling down the hall — some of them staggering, by the sounds of it — followed by Doris and Dela's slurred laughter.

"I guess we'll talk later," Anne said.

He kissed her tenderly. "Count on it. But right now, someone else desperately needs your attention."

The lobby door opened, and Zima stepped in. Her gray clothes were stained, and she reeked of alcohol. Anne covered her nose, less to mask the smell than hide her smirk at the sight of her poor, bedraggled girlfriend, who had undoubtedly spent the evening babysitting a pair of drunks.

"It is very, very good to see you," Zima said to Anne.

A chorus of shrill laughter sounded from the hallway behind Zima. She casually closed the door, muffling their cackles to a tolerable level.

"You too, honey." Anne held her arms wide, which Zima eagerly fell into.

"Anne, I am so sorry —"

"Don't start that," Anne said, kissing her cheek. "It wasn't your fault, and we all know it."

Zima fell silent and nuzzled her neck. "Was your time with Charlie ... enjoyable?"

"It was great, though our little outing could have gone ... Crap!" Anne flopped into one of the cushy reception chairs and pulled Zima down into her lap. "In all the commotion, I left the new bedsheets at the garage."

"I will take that as a yes," Zima said, "and shall not ask what happened to the old sheets."

"We had a great time," Charlie said with a smile. "But it's late, and I think I'm going to hit what's left of my shredded hay." He tapped Zima's shoulder on the way out. "Tag, you're in."

Zima brow-knit, which made Anne laugh.

"'night, Anne," Charlie said at the threshold. "Thanks for a wonderful evening."

"Same here. And just think: we have tomorrow, too!"

"Can't wait." He raised a warning finger at Zima. "Go easy on her. She has to be functional for our date tomorrow night."

Anne perked up. "A date?"

"Yes. A real one, too, which means we'll need to dress nicely."

Zima head-cocked. "You intend to spoil her?"

"Rotten." Charlie grinned and closed the door, leaving Anne and Zima alone in the lobby.

Anne's heavy lap bunny curled up and snuggled into her bosom, as if she might fall asleep right there. Anne stroked her platinum-blonde hair, but a strong whiff of her liquor-soaked clothing made Anne wrinkle her nose.

"Are you doing okay, honey?"

"Yes."

"You don't want to freshen up with a shower or something?"

"No, I am quite comfortable." Zima nuzzled Anne's chest to make her point.

Two can play at that game.

Anne ran a lazy finger up the back of Zima's arm, along her shoulder, then trailed gentle circles around her neck and ear. Zima responded with a low moan, letting her own fingers wander, then began to dapple Anne's neck with soft kisses.

"I have changed my mind," Zima said breathily. "A shower would be most welcome."

"Allow me."

Anne stood with Zima in her arms — no mean feat, given her girlfriend's density — wrestled the door open, and carried her into the showers like a new bride across the threshold.

11

THE NEWS

ONE HOUR AND NOT A LOT OF ACTUAL WASHING LATER, a happily exhausted Anne emerged from the shower room in her fluffy pink robe, followed by a satisfied and fresher-smelling Zima in a matching robe. Arm-in-arm, they headed back to Anne's room — which had also become Zima's, since all of her clothes were now in there — when a sound from down the hall made them both turn.

Cappa tiptoed out of Charlie's room. She quietly pulled the door shut, but froze when she saw them staring. Cappa blushed furiously and lowered her gaze.

"And just what have you been up to?" Anne said, planting a teasing fist on her hip.

She had only meant it in jest, but Cappa paled and wrung her hands. "Nothing! I-I was just … tucking him in."

Anne's smile faded; Cappa's tone made her shiver. The last time Cappa had been this nervous was the night Charlie had collapsed at Hal's Diner.

"Is everything all right?"

"What, you mean Charlie?" Cappa waved it off with a laugh. "He's fine. Fine! I mean … not fine like 'Oh my God I have to have him' fine, but feeling fine. You know?"

"That's good, I think," Anne said, hoping she had understood correctly. "You just seem a little … off. I didn't think androids could get drunk, but you're making me wonder."

"Well, I-I did knock a few back. For social reasons, of course."

"Thirteen," Zima said.

Cappa clenched her jaw. "Was it that many? Good thing nobody was counting."

Zima shrugged. "The man you were drinking with seemed to think it held significance, otherwise I do not know why he would have given you money."

Cappa took her by the arm with a severe expression. Zima brow-knit and turned to Anne.

"What does it mean, 'What happens in Vegas stays in Vegas'?"

"It means our party animal here isn't proud she hustled some guy in a drinking contest." Anne arched an eyebrow at a blushing Cappa. "Am I right?"

Cappa's face screwed up so tightly that Anne thought she was going to burst. "He was a cocky jerk! He had that coming, and a lot more, if you ask me."

"All right," Anne said. "No more questions about Girls' Night, I promise. So what's bothering you, then?"

Cappa deflated, and once again wrung her hands. "Well, it's … me, actually."

Anne was about to ask what she meant when she heard tiny footsteps storming down the hall. Pixie Cappa appeared, her face like a thundercloud.

"Good! You're all here," Pixie Cappa said in her chiming voice, though her fury was focused on the larger version of herself. "We need your help to settle something."

"Don't drag them into this," Big Cappa said with a warning finger.

Pixie Cappa ignored her. "My other selves learned a neat *chi* trick while they were in China, but they won't teach it to me because they think I'll abuse it!"

"We wouldn't *have* to teach it to you if you'd stop being so stubborn and resynchronize with us!"

"W-wait," Anne said to Big Cappa, "what trick is she talking about?"

"Shielding," Pixie Cappa said, crossing her tiny arms. "Master Wung taught them how to use their *chi* — our *chi!* — to block a vampire sire's influence."

Big Cappa stomped her foot on the concrete so hard that her heel snapped off and skittered down the hall. "Might! It *might* block the link, but we don't know for sure. If it doesn't, then you'll be putting everyone in danger, all because of some stupid crush on ..." The word died on her lips. Big Cappa bowed her head, though her eyes still burned with anger.

Pixie Cappa bristled like a toy porcupine. "Oh, you do *not* want to go there, sister."

Big Cappa wilted even more.

Anne turned to Pixie Cappa. "Is she talking about Almos?"

Pixie Cappa's lips pressed together, but she gave a tiny nod.

"You ... you want to bring him to the surface?"

"Almos has been trapped underground for ... well, forever! And not because he wants to be. He's sacrificed for humanity's sake, and if there's a way to let him out without worrying about the Entity ..." Pixie Cappa sighed, letting some of her anger go with it. "He's been struggling for decades to reconnect with humanity. How much easier would that be if he could actually live among them?"

"But what if we're wrong?" Big Cappa said with a measure of sympathy. "If the shield doesn't work, and what Almos says is true, then even a brief connection to the Entity could bring the entire vampire population down on our heads."

"But what if we're right? Or even better: What if we can figure out how to keep the Entity at bay, but still give him access to William? Almos could command William to surrender and end this entire conflict in one night!"

"That is a very large gamble," Zima said.

"'Betting the ranch' is the expression," Anne said, but her mind was already churning on the idea.

A world without vampires. Without William ...

Once a fairy tale, vampires were now a harsh reality, especially to Anne and her closed circle of friends, which effectively imprisoned them within the safe walls of Z-Tech. To imagine the threat eradicated

— the freedom to go where they wished, when they wished … That had become the fairy tale.

And it was an alluring one.

Everyone was staring at Anne, she suddenly noticed, as if the weighty decision rested solely on her shoulders — a ludicrous notion considering her food service background and lack of any strategic experience whatsoever. The subject was dear to her, however, so she chimed in anyway.

Anne looked pensively at the wall. "Cappa …"

"Yes?" came a duet of replies. The pair fell silent and glared at each other.

This is going to drive me nuts …

"Not to derail the subject," Anne said, "but can we call one of you something else, like a nickname or something? Just until you get back into sync, of course."

The helpful suggestion wasn't received as well as she'd hoped. Each crossed their arms and waited for the other to respond, bearing the same stubborn expression. Time passed in silence, measured only by the rhythmic tapping of their impatient feet.

"Perhaps you could both keep the name," Zima said eventually. "We could append a numerical designation, such as Cappa-One and —"

"Rose," Pixie Cappa said, smiling. "I'd like to be called Rose. Would that be all right, Anne?"

Memory of the eight-year-old girl Anne's venom had saved from a life of paralysis brought tingles to her cold heart.

"Sure," Anne said softly, reflecting Pixie Cappa's — no, *Rose's* — smile. "That's a lovely choice. The real Rose believes it's your name anyway, so we might as well make it official." She turned to Big Cappa. "So as I was about to ask, *Cappa,* how do we safely explore this shield theory?"

"We need a test subject, for starters. Preferably someone who won't end the world if things go awry."

Eyes flicked to Anne, but no one dared to volunteer her, and for good reason. The last time Anne's defensive program had gone down, she had nearly killed Mark and herself, as every glance in the mirror at her hairless head reminded her.

But this is different, and far too important to shy away from.

The incident with the mercenaries had been a by-product of their hasty need. This time, they would take the precautions necessary to make sure Anne wouldn't — *couldn't* — hurt her friends.

"I-I'll do it," Anne said, fiddling with her shirt. "We can start planning after breakfast, once the boys are up. Using me as a subject won't be a true measure, since we only have Almos to test with. The generational gap between us makes our bond weak, but it should at least tell us if the idea is feasible."

"Can't we test against your bond with William?" Cappa said, frowning.

Anne shook her head. "William has tuned me out. The only reason he noticed me was because of the massive surge in sirelings when I took control of the mercenaries. Unless you know of another group of vampires out there who were made from my blood, I don't think we'll be able to lure him back."

"Almos might know of a way," Rose said.

"True. We'll include him in the planning."

Cappa sighed, and turned a moment before Charlie's bedroom door opened.

Charlie emerged, blinking at the bright hall lights, and walked straight over to them. "What planning?"

"I'm sorry," Cappa said, gently touching his shoulder. "We didn't mean to wake you."

"S'alright." Charlie stretched, but froze when he spotted Anne and Zima's wet hair and matching robes. Instead of growing sullen, as Anne expected, he grinned at Zima. "Spoiling her?"

"Rotten," Zima said, drawing a heartfelt laugh from him.

Anne was so stunned at the change in attitude between them that she almost didn't notice Cappa's discomfort. "Are you okay?"

Cappa's eyes darted between all of them, then she sagged. "Anne, we need to talk."

"S-sure," Anne said, concerned over her friend's uncharacteristic melancholy. "Shall we go to your room, or maybe walk around the gym?"

"Let's go to my room," Charlie said with a sigh. "All five of us."

More anxious than before, Anne followed them into his spacious bedroom, dragging her feet as if she were in a funeral procession. Rose hopped into a chair, dangling her little legs like a child, while Anne and Zima took the love seat. Cappa closed the door behind them, then joined Charlie on the bed. She looked as if she might pass out, which did nothing to calm Anne's nerves.

The silence stretched, and Anne's imagination began to wander.

Was Charlie's trip not as successful as he's let on? Does he only have a few months to live, and this new exuberance is simply his final sprint?

These thoughts and more plagued her, until a reassuring pat on the knee from Zima reminded her to take a calming breath.

Don't jump to conclusions, Anne chided herself. She would listen to what they had to say, and only then decide if panic was necessary.

Charlie finally broke the tense silence. "Something ... miraculous happened while we were away, and it affects everyone in this room."

That doesn't sound so bad, Anne thought, feeling her anxiety lessen.

Charlie turned to Cappa, who teetered on her perch. Anne jumped forward to steady her. Cappa nodded gratefully, then wrapped Anne in a tight hug, trembling like a scared puppy.

"Honey, honey," Anne said in a soothing voice. She rubbed her back and held her for a while, until Cappa managed to gather herself.

Sitting on the floor — hand-in-hand, knee-to-knee — Cappa told Anne about the near-mystical awakening of her feelings for Charlie: her mysterious walk with Master Wung, his stirring touch, her awkward return to the monastery, and her agonizing dilemma of how to tell Charlie.

Anne listened to her soul sister's tale with a mixture of awe and sympathy. It was exactly what both Anne and Charlie had hoped Cappa would someday feel. That she had fallen for Charlie was no surprise, as far as Anne was concerned, though any negative impact was beyond her at the moment. Anne was so thrilled that Cappa had found such joy, she couldn't see beyond her soul sister's happiness.

Cappa's voice softened when she reached the point of the story where she had attacked Charlie on the riverbank, cowering as if Anne might lash out in anger. The whole room was surprised when Anne stifled a laugh instead, imagining the awkward look on Charlie's face while Cappa practically molested him in a heated passion she couldn't control. Even Charlie grinned. Soon, everyone but her ever-stoic Zima was also laughing.

The biggest shock for Anne was Charlie's theory of where Cappa's libido originated.

"From me?" Anne said. "Are you sure?"

"No," Charlie said. "But, given your connection to her, your feelings for me, and your, um ... enthusiasm in the bedroom lately, the pieces just seem to fit."

"Oh." Anne flopped onto her back, her head abuzz. "I don't know whether I should apologize for the affliction, or charge for services rendered."

Cappa laughed, but Zima leveled them with a steady gaze.

"What I wish to know," Zima said, looking between Cappa and Charlie, "is what your intentions are now that you are aware of these feelings."

They both sobered. Cappa's fingers laced with Charlie's — which, for Anne, said it all.

"You're looking for permission," Anne said softly. "My permission."

Cappa clasped Anne's hands, her face contorted in anguish. "I-it's the hardest thing I've ever had to ask, but ..."

"You love him," Anne said, gently stroking her cheek.

"I do." Cappa's voice was a bare whisper through trembling lips.

Anne's heart swelled with sympathy. She understood exactly what Cappa was going through — and what her answer had to be.

No matter the cost to myself.

"Of course you have my blessing," Anne said, somehow managing to conjure a warm smile. "This is a miracle, not a curse. Besides, I'm the last person who should be allowed to veto a multi-partner relationship, right?"

Cappa bowled her over with a flying hug, as if Anne were a child, and pinned her to the floor, crying happiness and thanks into her robe. Zima might have been a statue perched at the edge of the small couch, though her eyes never left Anne. Rose wore a thoughtful expression that did little to reveal her feelings on the matter, swinging her little feet over the edge of her chair. Charlie beamed down at both of them. He tipped a reverent nod to Anne, which she returned.

When Cappa finally stopped blubbering her gratitude, she rejoined Charlie on the bed and took his hand. They tentatively stared at each other, as if they weren't sure what to do next.

"Go on," Anne said with a smile. "You know you want to."

Anne's good humor faded when their lips touched, however, as did her resolve to bless their relationship. She suddenly felt like a petulant child, jealous over a sibling's undue attention. She wanted Charlie for herself — *only* herself — and would have given anything to be in Cappa's place at that moment. His warm lips; strong, but gentle hands; firm body; and that musty mix of his cologne, leather jacket, and that earthy scent he, Cappa, and Zima all shared, which Anne found irresistible ...

They were still kissing when a touch on her hand snapped Anne from her longing. Zima was kneeling beside her, watching Anne closely.

"Come," Zima said. "Even if they do not mind your presence, it will do you little good to stay."

Anne nodded and ambled to her feet. Her body felt numb. "Are you coming?" she said to Rose, voice rough with emotion.

Rose flashed a mischievous grin. "Not until they kick me out, which I hope is after they've ..." Her sentence petered into an uncomfortable silence. "Sorry," she said, noting the pained look on Anne's face. "Yeah, let's go talk —"

"Stay." Anne put a hand on her shoulder and summoned a smile she definitely didn't feel. "Learn what you can. I'll be fine."

Rose pursed her lips, but didn't budge from her spot. Anne exited quietly with Zima in tow, leaving the occupied couple and their observer to their own devices.

The short walk to her own room, just down the hall, seemed like miles. Anne's head was a mess of conflicting emotions: happiness for her friends, longing for her boyfriend, and anger at herself for feeling jealous when she had no right to be. She stopped just outside her door and squeezed Zima's hand.

"I'm sorry," Anne said to her feet, unable to look her girlfriend in the eye.

"For what? You have done nothing that merits an apology."

"Y-yes, I have. Every time you've left me at Charlie's door, knowing full well what we were ... what we ..." Anne forced herself to meet Zima's gaze, though the shame and guilt she felt when she saw those precious blue eyes threatened to tear her apart. "How do you live with it? How ... how can you forgive me afterward?"

Zima gently wiped a tear from Anne's chin. "The answer is simple. Sharing you is difficult, but living without you is inconceivable. I will happily wait in line knowing that your love awaits me at the end, and I have never had reason to doubt it would."

"I do love you." Anne sobbed and wrapped Zima in a desperate embrace.

"And I you, and so does Charlie. Do not worry. In time, we shall find our equilibrium."

Charlie's door opened, and out came Cappa and Rose. Cappa walked as regally as someone with a broken heel could. They stopped in front of Anne and Zima. A silly grin covered Cappa's lipstick-smeared face.

"Everything all right?" Anne said.

"Peachy," Cappa said with her usual cheer.

Rose rolled her eyes. "I'm going back downstairs. 'night everyone."

"'night." Anne turned back to Cappa. "If everything's peachy, then why are you out here instead of in there making your relationship with Charlie official?"

"Why rush a good thing? Besides, there's power in making a man wait for what he wants. It makes me irresistible — a forbidden fruit. When I finally do give over, he's going to be so crazy with desire that he'll do practically anything I say." Cappa gave Zima a conspirator wink. "You might want to think about that, my dear."

Anne frowned; the pieces didn't quite fit. "Cappa, I meant what I said about giving you my blessing. It's hard, I admit, but I'll get over it. So if you're holding back for my sake, please don't."

Cappa's good cheer waned. "It's not for your sake, necessarily, just that ... aside from my attacking him on the riverbank, this is the first time we've been alone with the intention of, well ..."

"You're nervous," Anne said with a grin.

"Terrified! I mean, I had front-row seats for every one of your sessions with him, but this time I'm on the receiving end! What if I'm not as good as you are? What if I don't ... *feel* the same to him, like some cheap inflatable doll instead of the real thing? What if I can't climax? I-I'll be a total disappointment!"

Anne folded Cappa and Zima into a three-way hug so their heads were all touching. "You'll be fine, Cappa. I don't have to tell you that Charlie's the most patient, gentle lover a girl could ask for. And if any issues do arise, I'm sure you'll both handle them just like you've handled every other obstacle life's put in your way: as an inseparable duo."

Cappa took a shuddering breath and nodded, though she still looked pale.

"Tell you what," Anne said. "Since it's only a few hours until dawn, why don't we go to the kitchen and celebrate your first morning back in the United States by making a huge 'welcome back' breakfast. Not that the three of us actually eat," she said with a laugh, "but it'll give us a chance to talk through some of your worries. We can also discuss my own experiences in the bedroom, if it will help."

"It will," Cappa said with a smile. "Thanks."

They headed for the kitchen, arm-in-arm-in-arm. The feelings of jealousy and unease melted from Anne like butter in a skillet, replaced with a contented smile. No matter how rough things seemed right now, Anne knew they would get through it.

Together.

Because that's what families do.

12

ART

BREAKFAST THAT MORNING WAS A HUGE SUCCESS. Anne and Cappa had cooked enough to feed a small town, and had put a sizable dent in the pantry. But when Mark and Dela walked in, their eye-popping looks at the incredible spread said it had been worth the effort.

Sausage, bacon, Eggs Benedict, French toast, crepes with fresh whipped cream, hash browns, fruit, yogurt, pancakes ... all that and more lined the island counter in elegant chafing dishes. Zima had set the table with impeccable precision. Each setting was its own masterpiece: a napkin in the shape of a duck, sitting on a blue plate, with Goldfish crackers to create the illusion of a gentle pond.

Doris and Charlie arrived a few minutes later. They laughed when they saw Mark and Dela eagerly waiting, utensils in hand.

As soon as Rose joined them, Cappa gave the signal, and the cooks happily watched the food-eaters pile their plates high. Even the androids took a tiny portion of each. Anne politely declined, coveting instead a small cup of *Sang de Dela* that smelled more heavenly to her than the finest cuisine.

Clattering silverware and happy moans were the only sounds in the kitchen for a long while. Dela and Doris pushed their chairs back after their first helpings, patting their full stomachs, but, even after his third trip, Mark showed no signs of stopping.

When Cappa eventually rose to clear the table, Charlie grabbed her hand and sat her back down, and did the same to Anne and Zima when they tried to rise. He then tugged a lethargic Mark with him, and, in an unprecedented turn, the boys managed the entire cleanup.

Charlie and Mark eschewed their usual morning laboratory work to join Rose and Almos downstairs in the reactor room, where Charlie and Cappa were formally introduced to the master vampire. Almos and Charlie got along well, as Anne thought they would.

The topic quickly changed to *chi* shielding, which then dominated their conversation well into lunch time.

A brief test confirmed that Cappa could completely shield Anne and Almos' presence from each other. Almos was intrigued, but he shared Cappa's concern about using it on him aboveground unless they were absolutely certain it would work.

Attempting to shield Tim, they agreed, was the next-best option. His bond to Anne was stronger than Anne's bond to Almos, since Tim had been sired directly from Anne's blood — and, as a bonus, the world wouldn't end if the experiment failed.

Attempts to reach Tim went straight to voicemail, however, as did calls to his friends, Conway and Jody.

Zima checked the location of the tracking devices she'd placed on Tim's vehicle when he'd visited the factory last month. The coordinates resolved to a car dealership. The tech-savvy trio clearly didn't want to be found, which dashed any hopes of an easy shielding test.

Rose was furious about Tim's disappearance. While Anne shared some of her frustration, she also understood his desire to be far and free from the war zone her beloved San Francisco was fast becoming.

The troop bid farewell to Almos and Rose after that, who had been attached at the hip for most of the visit, and went upstairs to the lounge. Anne once again expected the boys to go to their labs to make up for the morning's productivity loss, but Charlie tossed ping-pong paddles to her, Mark, and Dela.

Everyone rotated through the game — even Doris, who paired with Zima to balance the team. By the end of the afternoon, the non-robotic participants were sprawled out on the furniture, exhausted, still laughing and trash talking their victories and defeats.

The best part of the afternoon, however, was when Mark and Dela revealed their engagement. Charlie and Cappa leaped from the couch, smothering them with tear-filled hugs and congratulations. They all shared a laugh at the retelling of Mark's proposal, blurted in the parking lot right before Dela was about to drive off to a hotel room with the person they thought was the enemy.

Cappa shot a withering glance at Rose, whose smug expression said she was happy to have withheld news of their engagement from Cappa, but even their animosity was quickly forgotten in excited talk of bachelor and bachelorette parties — and, of course, the wedding plans.

Anne was having so much fun that she'd completely forgotten about Charlie's promised date until he suggested she wear something nice for their evening out.

Still clueless about where they were going, Anne did as Charlie had suggested. She changed into the same gown she'd worn on their fateful date at the opera, followed by an hour of vampire-vanishing makeover work at the skilled hands of Doris and Cappa.

Contact lenses, blunt caps for her canines, and three layers of thick makeup later, Anne looked completely human.

Charlie was waiting outside her room, dressed in a sharp tuxedo that catapulted his already attractive build to absolutely stunning.

"Hubba-hubba," Anne said, waggling her eyebrows.

"Back at you."

Charlie looked her up and down with a mesmerized smile that told Anne that she was the only thing in his world. The thought made her knees weak. Before she could think of something clever to say, and probably ruin the perfectly good moment, he shook himself and drew a thick envelope from his jacket.

Anne smiled. "What's this?"

"A few items for the evening ahead."

Curious, Anne took the proffered envelope and opened the flap. She had been expecting tickets to an event — the opera would have been ironic — but instead found a driver's license, passport, social security card, and credit card. Each had her smiling face, taken when she was still human, but the names all read Jennifer Trudeau.

"That's your new identity," Cappa said from behind her. "Anne Perrin is technically dead, and there's no sense tipping anyone off to the contrary. Do you like the name?"

"I do! Jennifer is one of my favorites. How did you know?"

"Lucky guess." Cappa draped an arm around Anne's shoulders. "I had them made up shortly after you moved in, before we knew each other as fabulously as we do now."

"We all have spare identities, just in case," Charlie said. "Now that these are in use, we'll ready a new set for you."

Anne ran a finger down his black jacket. "Can I choose my name next time?"

"Sure." His eyes took her in again, and his dreamy smile returned. "That dress is every bit as gorgeous on you as I remember. I'll definitely be the envy of the party."

Anne grinned at the compliment, twirling the billowing folds of her long dress. "So ... we're going to a party?"

He proffered an arm and smiled. "Ready to find out?"

"So mysterious!"

The mystery deepened when Charlie led her not to the garage, but out through the front lobby, where a limousine longer than any Anne had ever seen waited in the guest parking lot.

The driver, dressed almost as sharply as Charlie himself, straightened himself up when they emerged, and helped them both into the vehicle.

The inside of the limousine was even more opulent than Anne had imagined. Luxurious leather seats lined one side of the car. A full bar lined the other side, filled with an array of exotic drinks that would have made Doris drool.

Charlie slid in next to her, grinning at the wondrous look on her face. "You like it?"

"Are you kidding? When can we move in! There must be a sleeper bed under this huge seat somewhere."

"That would be something," Charlie said with a chuckle. He opened the small fridge under the bar and pulled out a fancy bottle containing a suspiciously familiar red liquid. "Care for some?"

Anne's fangs extended down through her gums in anticipation. She clamped her hands between her knees to keep from snatching it from his grip.

"Y-yes, please," she said, trying to keep the desperation from her voice. She fidgeted impatiently while he retrieved two flutes from a cabinet and pulled the cork.

The mouth-watering smell of blood filled the cabin, intensifying when Charlie poured it into her glass. He filled his own with a small portion of champagne from a miniature bottle.

Anne was bouncing on the seat by the time he handed it over. It took every ounce of her willpower to keep from guzzling it down while he raised his glass in a toast.

"To a wonderful evening," Charlie said.

She smiled weakly and clinked their glasses together. Unable to hold out any longer, Anne downed the heavenly elixir in several large gulps, moaning in delight with each delectable mouthful. When she opened her eyes, Charlie had the bottle poised and ready to refill her glass.

Bless his cotton socks.

She held her glass out and let him fill it again and again, until the bottle was empty, and her ravenous hunger had finally subsided.

"Thank you," Anne said. "And I'll be sure to thank Mark when we get back."

"Why don't you try thanking him now?"

Because it's hard, Anne wanted to say, but she knew why he had suggested it. Envious of the others' ability to communicate electronically, which often left Anne out of the conversation, she had asked Mark last week to teach her how to issue mental commands to her implant instead of spoken words.

The task had proved more difficult than she'd imagined, however, and had given her new respect for Mark's ability to send messages so quickly without his brain leaking out of his ears.

After the first day of practice, Anne had had only the letter 'A' and a serious headache to show for her efforts. The rest of the alphabet had come faster, although constructing full sentences was akin to solving algebraic equations in high school — which Anne had hated.

The limousine was entrenched in city traffic by the time her simple message was off and away.

THANKS FOR THE MEAL, she sent to Mark.

His reply came mere seconds later — not as text across her vision, but as words and feelings injected into her thoughts by her implant.

YOU'RE WELCOME! HAVE A GOOD TIME, AND KEEP UP THE GOOD WORK.

Anne had gasped the first time the foreign thoughts had entered her head. In contrast to the implant's messages, Almos' presence was a clear ball of light in her mind. His thoughts and emotions were easy to distinguish from her own.

Messages from the implant, and the accompanying feelings from the sender, just sort of appeared out of nowhere, intermingled with her own random thoughts and ramblings. It had taken days of practice for Anne to be able to pick them out from the rest of the chaotic jumble in her head.

She nodded to Charlie, then snuggled against him and closed her eyes. The effort had invoked a throbbing headache. A little rest would hopefully banish it before they arrived.

•   •   •

Anne stirred awake to the sound of the car door opening. She rubbed the sleep from her eyes and silently cursed the comfortable plush seats for making her doze through her first limousine ride. On the other hand, it was the most contiguous sleep she'd had in months. She felt sharp and refreshed, for a change. Snapping her false canine caps in place, she followed Charlie from the vehicle.

The building looked just like any other modern structure in the City: smooth concrete walls, splashed with odd-shaped colors of lime and tangerine, lined the street level of the four-story building, which ran half the length of the city block.

Two tuxedoed gentlemen stood to either side of a pair of large, frosted-glass doors. They were talking to a couple around Anne's age. The man was dressed similarly to Charlie, and had that same energetic sparkle in his eyes.

But it was the woman who captured Anne's attention. Her fancy gown made Anne's look like bargain-bin trash. It sparkled and shimmered with different colors, depending upon how the light landed, embroidered with intricate patterns along her slim waist and bodice. The dress was as suitable for her perfect face and flawless bare arms as it would be for the spotlight in a fine art museum. Lavish earrings, bracelets, and a necklace were stark reminders that Anne had worn none for fear of them rubbing off her makeup.

Charlie was staring at the couple, too, although his face held far more shock than awe at the gaudy display. He recovered with a shake of his head and escorted Anne to the door, where the fancy couple had already been admitted.

A quick exchange with the doormen verified his identity. If they were impressed by Charlie's title, they gave no indication. Nor did they ask for Anne's false identity. Soon they were past the frosted doors and into the warm, brightly lit area beyond.

If the limousine had been another world, the inside of the building was a different universe. Its interior was bright white from floor to ceiling, like an artist's rendition of heaven. Artwork lined the walls at spacious intervals, interspersed with fine vases and sculptures on white stands, each expertly lit to show off their finest characteristics. Art and sculptures alike bore numbers on stylish plaques beneath.

Dozens of people milled about, chatting and admiring the artwork. Most were couples, but all wore extravagant outfits and accessories that made Anne feel like Cinderella after the clock had struck midnight. Servers moved from guest to guest, offering beverages and *hors d'oeuvres* beautiful enough to deserve their own numbered plaques. The smells did nothing for Anne, of course, although the guests and servers themselves made her salivate. She was suddenly glad for Charlie's foresight in packing her a meal, otherwise her fangs would have long since popped their porcelain caps.

"All right, I give up," Anne said softly into his ear. "Why are we here?"

Charlie laughed. "It's a date. I thought you might enjoy seeing artwork that sells for a mint, and meeting the artists who made them."

"Artists?"

Even as she asked the question, Anne noticed that several of the guests were facing outward from the exhibits, eagerly speaking with anyone who showed an interest in the works.

"Many are eccentric, as you can imagine," Charlie said. "But some are down-to-earth enough for coherent conversation."

"Do you know any of them?"

Charlie scanned the exhibits, then shook his head. "But we can certainly introduce ourselves. Whatever you do, though, don't laugh at their art, even if they give the impression they think it's funny themselves."

"I sense a story in there somewhere," Anne said with a smile. She tugged his arm, but he just grinned.

I'll badger him about that one later.

"In fact, there is a story," a woman's silky voice said from behind her.

Anne turned to find the couple they had seen at the door, both looking past her at Charlie, wearing big smiles as if they were old friends.

Charlie's return smile didn't quite reach his eyes. "Morton. Victoria. It's good to see you, though I'm surprised to see you together."

"It's 'Vicky,'" the woman said with a lazy wave. "Since when did we become so formal?"

"Vicky and I have been married for three years now," Morton said. His tone was pleasant, but held a challenging edge.

"Don't pretend you didn't know," Vicky said. "You were invited to the wedding, after all."

"Ah." Charlie hung his head. "That was during a rough period in my life, I'm afraid. The invitation is probably buried in a room full of unread mail, along with renewal notices for all my favorite magazines." He cleared his throat and put a hand on Anne's shoulder. "Allow me to introduce my girlfriend, Jennifer."

Anne stared blankly for a second, having forgotten her new alias. She perked up with a friendly smile. "Pleasure to meet you."

"Likewise."

Silence fell over them, heavy and uncomfortable. Vicky's eyes bored into Charlie with a strange, hungry intensity.

Anne cleared her throat. "So, um ... how did you and Charlie meet?"

Vicky's delighted expression, combined with Charlie's sunken shoulders, told Anne she'd stepped on a land mine.

"Actually," Vicky said dramatically, slipping an arm through Morton's, "it was our dear Charlie who introduced me to my future hubby."

"We were business partners, once," Morton said. He gave Charlie a hard look. "Isn't that right?"

"'Partners' is a strong word," Charlie said, matching his steely gaze.

"But 'fiancée' isn't," Vicky said a little too casually. "Wouldn't you agree?"

Charlie's jaw tightened, but his face might have been carved from stone. "It's true that *one* of us thought we were engaged."

Touché!

Anne almost cheered at his skillful repost until the significance of their words sank in. Her unbeating heart dropped into her shoes.

Charlie was engaged? To her?

Vicky shrugged. "I still have the ring. I would have brought it as proof if I'd known you were going to emerge from your cave tonight."

Charlie bristled, but took a deep breath, then favored Anne with a reassuring smile.

"Morton, Vicky ... I think we can all agree we have a rocky history. I take responsibility for some of it. Whether you accept your own role is up to you, but ... Jennifer and I have only recently started seeing each other, and I promised her a good time tonight.

"Now, I'd love to find out how you've been and what you're up to, but if your only goal is to bury a hatchet in my back for misunderstandings that happened a long time ago, I'd just as soon take my date elsewhere so I can keep my promise."

Vicky, Morton, and Anne stood in stunned silence while Charlie patiently awaited an answer.

Morton was the first to recover. He spotted someone across the room and hastily excused himself.

Vicky's eyes softened, and the playfulness disappeared from her voice. "Did you love me, Charlie?"

"Vicky —"

"No, no, I don't want to ruin your date." She flashed Anne a look of genuine concern. "It's just ... you disappeared. Completely. Wouldn't answer my calls or return my messages. The only reason I knew you were still alive was because you continued to make headlines. Then, suddenly, here you are, like some miracle of God. I just have to know, before you vanish again, if you really cared about me."

Charlie considered the question for a moment. "I did."

A tear spilled down Vicky's cheek.

"But you were right when you accused me of loving my work more than you," Charlie said. "There just wasn't enough room for both, not back then. I wish I had a more comforting answer."

"So it wasn't another woman," Vicky said with a weak smile.

Charlie shook his head. "No one at the time could have competed with my research."

He put a familiar hand on her shoulder, erasing any doubt in Anne's mind that the two of them had once been intimate.

"Vicky, I'm sorry I didn't handle the end of our relationship better."

She stared at him, lost in a different time, then gathered herself with a shake and dabbed her eyes with a cocktail napkin.

"It's all right. Morton is driven, too. Sometimes I have to wave myself in front of him to pull his mind from his board meetings and business strategies. It's the curse of being drawn to entrepreneurial men."

"I've done my share of waving," Anne said with a disarming smile, then changed the subject. "So ... if it isn't safe to ask, just tell me, but I'm dying to hear the story about the artist he laughed at."

Vicky brightened. "Well, my dear Jennifer, it happened in this very studio. I had actually managed to drag Charlie from his work for a much-anticipated evening of ..."

A message from Cappa injected into Anne's thoughts, distracting her from Vicky's tale.

Vampires at ten o'clock.

Anne's first reaction wasn't fear, oddly enough, but annoyance at the second consecutive night where a vampire encounter was about to ruin what might have been a salvageable date with Charlie. Anne scanned the crowd, but nobody seemed out of place.

The couple wearing turtlenecks, Charlie sent, staring roughly at Anne's ten o'clock.

"Turtlenecks" was a modest description of the young couple's model-worthy outfits. While the man's collar was folded like a traditional turtleneck, the material was deep crimson and shimmered like expensive silk. A sharp purple blazer, matching slacks, and black leather gloves rounded out the ensemble. The woman wore an elegant dress with a stiff collar, flaring right up to her chin as if it were supporting the weight of her entire head. Long sleeves, opera gloves, a floor-length skirt, and closed-toed shoes left her makeup-covered face as the only exposed skin on her body.

Anne watched them from the corner of her eye while Vicky continued her story. What she saw wasn't as disturbing as what she *didn't* see. The couple accepted cocktails when offered, although they never drank from their glasses. They politely refused the delectable snacks under the pretense that they had already eaten. They admired the artwork, chatted amiably with the artists and other guests without any outward signs of wanting them as a meal, and gave each other an occasional hug or peck on the cheek.

Food aversions aside, they seemed perfectly normal.

Even the catlike movements that Almos and William's vampires shared were absent. Normal vampires were efficiency in motion. Every move was deliberate, and they were gargoyle-still at rest to conserve energy.

These two never paused for a moment. They constantly shifted from foot to foot, twirled the stems of their wine glasses, or fidgeted with their clothes.

Just like I do.

The revelation made Anne dizzy.

Had they been sired from Anne's bloodline? How? By whom? Had they volunteered to become vampires? Were they friendly or hostile toward Z-Tech? How many more of them were there?

"Do you know the Sturmans?"

Vicky's direct question snapped Anne from her turbulent thoughts. "I'm sorry?"

"The Sturmans." Vicky pointed at the vampire couple. "Morton and I met them on our honeymoon in Belize, of all places, and we've been friends with them ever since."

"Can't say we do," Charlie said with a forced smile. "But if they're friends of yours, we'd be delighted to meet them."

Head still spinning, Anne nodded agreement.

Vicky led them across the room. The Sturmans were just finishing a conversation with a frazzle-haired artist standing next to an equally frazzled painting of what looked like a horse exploding in a neon pasture.

Departing Z-Tech now, Zima sent. I shall arrive in approximately six minutes.

Anne breathed a sigh of guilty relief. As much as she didn't want to inconvenience her girlfriend, having Zima on standby in case the situation escalated was comforting.

Vicky strode up to the Sturmans with open arms. "Betsy! Ron! So good to see you. I love your outfits! It's a different look for you, but so appropriate for the chilly nights we've been having."

"Thanks, Vick," Ron said. He gave her a brief but welcome embrace, and Betsy did the same.

Vicky gestured to Charlie and Anne. "I'd like to introduce you to an old friend of mine and his girlfriend," she said proudly. "This is Charlie and Janice."

"A — Jennifer," Anne said, recovering at the last moment. She could hardly be upset at Vicky for forgetting her name when Anne almost had, too. She extended a hand, which the Sturmans both shook without hesitation. Anne hoped they didn't feel through their gloves that her skin was just as cold as theirs.

If they recognized her or Charlie, or were intimidated in the slightest, they hid it well behind masks of genuine welcome. Anne glanced at their teeth when they smiled, and spotted false caps, similar to her own. Casual onlookers may notice unusually large canines, but the shape and proportions were normal enough to pass for human, except under close scrutiny.

Or if you know what to look for.

"So, what's your business?" Charlie said pleasantly.

Ron flashed a shy grin. "Venture capital. But before you lay on the hate, we mostly invest in projects to help the underprivileged, both domestic and overseas."

Betsy slipped an affectionate arm through his, beaming with pride. "Our last project was a hospital in Tanzania. The project before that was a women's health clinic, just across the bay in Oakland."

"That's ... amazing," Anne said weakly. "It must feel very rewarding."

Vampire philanthropists? What the hell is going on?

"There isn't as much financial return as our earlier, less-humanitarian investments," Ron said. "But yes, we sleep better at night knowing the money is being used for a good cause. Most of our time is spent just making sure it doesn't end up in the hands of shysters."

"What about you?" Betsy said to Charlie.

"Electronics manufacturing. Not as altruistic as your business, but I give back to the community where I can."

"Oh, now Charlie's being modest," Vicky said in a conspiratorial whisper.

Here it comes … Anne braced herself for social impact.

Vicky patted Charlie's shoulder with a grin. "He's actually the founder of a little company you might have heard of, right here in the City. This is none other than the man who put the 'Z' in Z-Tech."

Their reactions weren't at all what Anne had expected. Ron's mouth twisted as if he'd just trodden into something distasteful.

"That's … well, yes, of course. It's an honor to meet you, Mr. Z."

"Call me Charlie, please."

They were hesitant to accept his hand, but took it all the same. Oddly, both of their gazes immediately fixed on Anne.

"I-I'm sorry," Betsy said. "You're … Jennifer, did you say?"

"That's what's printed on my driver's license." *I think.* "Why?"

"Just rumor, probably. I heard Charlie was dating … s-someone else."

Charlie heaved a dramatic sigh. "Her name was Anne Perrin. She passed away last month in a violent mugging near her place of work."

While the vampires barely registered the news — still fixated on Anne — Vicky appeared stricken.

"Oh, Charlie. I'm so, so sorry."

"Thank you, it was certainly a tragedy. Anne was well-loved, and not just by me. But one thing I know is that she wanted me to be happy." Charlie put his arm around Anne and gave an affectionate squeeze. "Shortly after that, I met Jennifer. We're so perfect for each other that I wonder if Anne hadn't facilitated our introduction from the afterlife."

"That's so sweet," Vicky said, dabbing her eyes again.

Although their self-appointed host had bought into the story, the Sturmans clearly hadn't. They continued to stare at Anne as if she were a feral dog who might bite them at any moment.

But they're basically ignoring Charlie …

William's crew knew Charlie was a cyborg, and would have been just as wary of him as Anne — probably more so.

The Sturmans, however, didn't seem to regard Charlie as a threat, so they probably weren't William's. That reinforced the probability of them being Anne's bloodline.

Who created them, though?

Only two possibilities came to mind. Either Orwing still had samples of Anne's blood, which was a likely scenario, or Tim Chen had been careless and infected others.

Or worse, Tim did it deliberately.

Both scenarios sent chills through Anne. Orwing's operations were a black box. Z-Tech's only contact in the organization, Alvin's son Nick, was under close surveillance, so they couldn't ask him.

Ron and Betsy didn't strike Anne as Orwing's type, however. Orwing was a paramilitary organization. They wouldn't suffer humanitarians like the Sturmans.

Which left Tim as the responsible party — who had conveniently fallen off the map, and wasn't returning their calls.

Oh, Tim, please tell me this wasn't you …

Betsy grabbed her stomach and grimaced. "You know, I'm not feeling very well. It could have been the shellfish I ate earlier. Ron, sorry to spoil the party, but can we go?"

"S-sure," he said, gathering Betsy in his arms. "It was nice seeing you again, Vick. Charlie, Jennifer, it was a … a pleasure to meet you."

And with that, the Sturmans left.

ETA: TWO MINUTES, Zima sent.

Crap.

A reply would take far too long for Anne to compose, so she grabbed her phone and quickly typed a message to Zima.

HOLD YOUR FIRE!

Nervous or not — vampires or not — the Sturmans didn't strike Anne as a threat. The last thing Anne wanted was the blood of two genuinely good people on her conscience, or Zima's.

"E-excuse me, guys," Anne said to Charlie and Vicky. "I'm feeling queasy myself, and some fresh air might help."

"I'll come with you," Charlie said, already heading after Ron and Betsy. "Back in a few, Vicky."

They exited the frosted-glass doors just in time to see the Sturmans running down the street as if the very hounds of hell were on their heels.

Oh no you don't.

"*Kaninchen!*" Anne said, much louder than she had intended.

The German word for "rabbit" triggered her implant to jack her metabolism to ridiculous levels. Energy flooded through her, threatening to rip her apart from the inside. The world around her slowed. Her back arched, fingers curled into claws.

Anne was ready for action.

She dashed after them at superhuman speed, with Charlie close behind, whipping around corners and whizzing past surprised pedestrians.

The Sturmans were fast, but not fast enough. Their one-block lead became half-a-block, then a quarter. They cast frantic glances behind them, eyes wide with fright, legs a blur of motion, carrying them faster than traffic. Still, Anne and Charlie gained.

The vampire couple's luck ran out when they took a wrong turn down a dead-end street. Sheer, unclimbable walls towered on all sides.

Betsy whipped around and surprised them both by brandishing a silver knife. Ron did the same, waving it in front of him threateningly. Months of watching Zima during combat practice told Anne that neither of them had ever fought with a knife before.

Anne held her hands up. "Whoa! Just ... hang on, okay? We're not going to hurt you."

It was difficult to say with sincerity because Anne's increased metabolism also raised her aggression levels. She was itching for a fight. Anne watched their knives like a mongoose would a snake, looking for an opportunity to dart in for the kill.

The fear on their faces told her that violence probably wouldn't be necessary, however. The Sturmans didn't want to fight, and, despite Anne's aggression-jacked state, she didn't want to hurt them, either.

"W-what do we do?" Betsy whispered to Ron in a shaky voice.

Ron waved his knife specifically at Anne. "Just b-back off! Let us go or … or we'll use these, I swear! They're silver. They can k-k-kill you with a single stab!"

To Anne's surprise, Charlie stepped forward.

Anne moved to stop him, afraid he might hurt the Sturmans, but a message from him kept her still.

Trust me.

I do, Anne thought, though she had no idea what he was up to.

"I'm warning you," Ron said, gripping his knife in shaking fingers. "D-d-don't come any closer! I'm a vampire, and I can best a human like you in my sleep!"

Charlie took another step forward and slowly reached out his hand. "You're philanthropists, not killers. Give me the knife, and let's discuss this ration—"

Quick as a snake, Betsy grabbed for him.

Anne had seen Charlie fight. He was second only to Zima in the badass department, and could handle three vampires in combat as easily as one. Untrained fighters like the Sturmans would be a walk in the park for him, complete with a picnic and champagne flutes.

And so Anne was shocked when, instead of catching Betsy in an armlock and putting her on her back, as she'd seen him do many times to Mark, Charlie did … nothing.

Betsy spun Charlie around, grabbed his hair, and put the knife to his throat. "*Back off!*" she screamed at Anne.

Charlie flashed a smile just for Anne.

Ahhh, I get it …

Question them quickly, Charlie sent, confirming her suspicion, while they feel they're in control. I'll ask Zima to hold back. On the outside, however, Charlie acted frightened. He struggled feebly, as a human would, allowing Betsy to overpower him.

"O-okay," Anne said, doing her best to pretend her boyfriend was in actual danger. "Just tell me one thing, and we can all walk away from this. Who sired you?"

"None of your business," Ron said. He tried to edge around Anne, but she blocked his path. He swung his blade in a clumsy arc, which Anne easily avoided.

"Give me a name," Anne said. "Then we'll forget we ever saw you."

Betsy pressed the knife to Charlie's neck, drawing a red trickle. "Out of the way or I'll cut his throat! I swear to Christ!"

"No you won't," Anne said calmly. "You're humanitarians, not murderers. Becoming vampires hasn't changed that one bit."

Anne took a small step forward.

"Like you, I still care about this world, but vampires aren't a natural part of it. If someone in my bloodline is creating new vampires, they need to stop, because they might be putting all of humanity in danger."

She advanced another step.

"Now, give me a name, or the next time I ask, it will be an unrefusable command from your sire."

The Sturmans' fear became undisguised terror.

Betsy's hand trembled so badly that she nearly dropped her knife. "You can't do that! H-he said we'd be safe. He promised ..."

Anne sighed dramatically. "You really think I'd gamble my boyfriend's life if I couldn't stop you with a mere thought?"

"Then why haven't you?" Ron said.

"Because I don't believe in enslavement unless it's life or death. And, like I said, I don't think either of you are killers."

The couple exchanged a tense glance.

"J-just a name?" Betsy said. "Then you'll let us go?"

"Cross my unbeating heart." Anne held up a warning finger. "But I'll know if you're lying. It's a sire thing." It was a lie, of course, but she was betting the Sturmans didn't know that.

Ron gulped, then lowered his knife. "Jeram. Jeram Tosali. Now please, let us go."

His answer seemed genuine. Hoping they were telling the truth, Anne stepped aside.

The Sturmans practically tripped over each other in their haste to flee.

No sooner had they exited the alley than Zima slipped around the corner, watching their retreating figures with no more curiosity than if they were normal pedestrians walking down the street.

"You are both uninjured, I trust?"

"More or less." Charlie rubbed the small cut on his throat, then turned to Anne with a grin. "Remind me to never sit across from you at the negotiation table. That was brutal."

"But inefficient," Zima said. "We should have extracted more information before setting them free."

"I know," Anne said.

She paced the mouth of the alley. Her hands shook from the continued effects of her metabolic boost program.

"*Schildkröte.*"

As the German word for "turtle" implied it would, her tremendous energy level plummeted. Anne sagged against the wall and put her face in her hands, feeling slow and lethargic.

"I just couldn't bear the thought of putting the Sturmans through any more trauma."

"A noble, yet counterproductive, sentiment if a second vampire threat is truly running unchecked," Zima said. "As with any viral outbreak, every day spent in unnecessary research could mean an exponential growth in their numbers."

"They're not viruses!" The heat of Anne's reply surprised even herself, but she was too weary to rein in her anger. "They're *people*, Zima, just like me! And they were frightened — because of me! I inflicted the same terror that William ..." Anne couldn't finish the comparison between herself and her monster-of-a-sire, whom she hated more than anyone else in the world.

"I am sorry," Zima said softly. "I did not mean to imply —"

"No, don't apologize." Anne took a deep breath. "I'm just tired. You're right, of course. A few more answers, like an address, would have saved us some time."

Silence followed. When Anne looked up, Zima was standing stock-still, brows knitted, staring at the ground.

"Are you okay, honey?" Anne said.

Zima kept her eyes down. "You are angry with me."

Oh no.

Anne had never snapped at Zima before tonight. Her girlfriend didn't know how to handle it, and she was hurt.

Feeling guiltier than ever, Anne pushed herself off the wall and wrapped Zima in a warm embrace. "Sorry, baby. I know you didn't mean anything by it, and I shouldn't have yelled."

Zima remained quiet, though she clung to Anne as if she was afraid to let go.

Charlie put a comforting hand on each of their shoulders. "I've asked the limo driver to pick us up here."

"No," Zima said. "I do not wish to intrude on your date any more than I already have."

"It's fine. Besides, you might enjoy the next leg of our evening."

"There's more?" Anne said. The idea was exciting, even though she was so exhausted that she had to cling to Zima for support.

Too much to hope he's taking us to a hot tub, followed closely by a nice, soft bed.

Charlie chuckled. "Yes, but don't worry. I think you'll find it a relaxing close to the evening. Have you ever ridden inside of a limo, Zima?"

"Once, although only long enough to assassinate the occupants."

Anne smiled despite the grim picture her overactive imagination conjured. "We'll count that as a no."

The three of them eventually piled into the opulent limousine. Anne plunked down next to Charlie and rested her weary head on his shoulder. She cracked an eye to find Zima sitting stiffly on the opposite end of the long bench seat. Anne held her arm out invitingly, which Zima eagerly snuggled into.

And, for the rest of the forty-six-minute ride, Anne was happily sandwiched between her two favorite people.

13

COUNTRY HOUSE

THE LIMOUSINE PULLED IN FRONT of a multi-story house nestled in the back hills of the North Bay, although Anne couldn't have said exactly where. She hadn't traveled much outside of San Francisco proper, so any of the surrounding cities were exciting new places to explore.

The house itself looked like something out of a luxury vacation brochure. Enormous windows covered the first and second stories, revealing a lush, fully furnished interior.

Anne stepped out of the limo, grateful for the driver's help to get her on her tired feet. A fresh breeze rustled the trees, cool and welcome on her skin, whisking away her exhaustion. She gave an invigorating stretch and hugged Charlie close.

"You rented a country mansion for the second part of our date? For the record, I would have been happy with a pillow and a couple of blankets on a quiet hill somewhere."

"Glad to hear it," Charlie said, moonlight twinkling from his mischievous hazel eyes.

The driver popped the trunk, emerging seconds later with a stack of fluffy blankets and pillows fastened together with straps. Charlie accepted the stack with a grateful nod and slung it over his shoulder.

Anne started toward the house, eager to see the rest of it, but Charlie shook his head and led them to a small path running through the trees.

"We're not staying in the house?" Anne ducked a low branch. She'd been serious about being happy with the hill and blankets, but the mansion-like country home was too inviting.

"Later, if you'd like," Charlie said, picking his way easily through the overgrown trail. "And it isn't a rental."

"You ... own this place?"

"And the surrounding hundred acres."

Of course he does, just like the basement and nuclear reactor I didn't know about until recently.

"And you haven't brought me here before because ...?"

"For one, it isn't equipped for research, but mostly because the interior gets a lot of sun during the day."

Good reasons.

"Fine, Mr. Secretive. Are you at least going to tell us where we're going?"

"To a hill somewhere, like you said."

"I really hate you sometimes."

Behind her, Zima gasped.

"That was a joke," Anne said over her shoulder. "I don't hate Charlie. Not by a long shot."

Zima seemed to accept that, but clutched Anne's hand anyway.

The forest ended abruptly, exposing them once again to the glorious night sky. Charlie jogged over a small crest and turned to them with a triumphant smile.

"Here we are. Let me know where you'd like to set up."

Anne thought he was kidding at first. Calling the tiny rise of dry weeds a hill was like calling a Chihuahua a guard dog — it was technically true, but extremely disappointing when compared to the real thing.

Her disappointment vanished when she joined him at the top. The deceptive little rise cascaded down the other side into a breathtaking vista. Even the muted colors of night did little to detract from the oak-covered hills and valleys sprawled before them. Moonlight danced on the distant ocean, painting a hypnotic backdrop against an already tranquil landscape.

An owl hooted nearby. Anne spied a gray flutter of feathers from the corner of her eye, but it quickly disappeared into the wind-hushed trees. Still holding Zima's hand, Anne slipped her arm through Charlie's.

"Thank you," Anne said with a contented sigh. "You were right: this is exactly what I needed."

Charlie kissed her and smiled. "Good to hear. There's a perfect spot over there for blankets. Back in a sec."

Soon they were lying shoulder-to-shoulder-to-shoulder under the stars. Once again, Anne was happily sandwiched between her two sweethearts.

But, try as she might to enjoy it, their disturbing encounter with the Sturmans kept running through Anne's head.

Who was Jeram Tosali? Had the Sturmans surrendered their humanity to him willingly? Their talk of promises indicated so. *Had they paid to become vampires? An exchange of goods? Was Jeram a rogue businessman, or part of a larger organization?*

The latter scared the bejesus out of her. The destruction of Orwing's mercenary vampires had been satisfying, but in reality, Anne may have only succeeded in annoying the militant organization.

If Orwing had additional blood samples stored in other facilities — which she had every reason to believe they would — then it was only a matter of time before they rebuilt their forces. Jeram Tosali could be part of that effort, perhaps a venture to raise revenue from the wealthy by promising strength and eternal life in exchange for a small fortune.

The signs, however, pointed to someone else.

Oh, Tim ...

"Cappa's already on it," Charlie said.

Anne blinked in surprise at the black night sky, having forgotten she was in the wilderness. "Hmm? On what?"

"Jeram Tosali. If Cappa finds anything, she'll let us know, so just relax and enjoy."

Of course she is. She's Cappa.

"Right, sorry. Thanks, Cappa," Anne said to him, knowing her soul sister was listening to every word.

No problem, Cappa sent. Like Charlie said, enjoy these moments when you can. As we all know, things can change for the worse at the drop of a hat.

"You said it, sis." Anne closed her eyes and took a deep breath to cleanse the unpleasant thoughts. It mostly worked. "So, Charlie ... How many other properties do you own?"

"A few."

When he stayed silent, Anne poked his ribs. "Well? Where are they? Anywhere exotic, like Hawaii or New Zealand?"

Charlie cleared his throat, eyes darting around as if he suddenly wished he were elsewhere. Anne was about to call him out when Zima spoke up.

"Charlie is avoiding the answer because the holdings are intended as safehouses in case of disaster."

"Sounds like a good reason for me to know. I'm a walking disaster magnet."

"Secrecy is a paramount ingredient to any safehouse," Zima said. "Each holding is registered under a different fake identity. Many are tied to false businesses, which are carefully tended to appear legitimate and draw as little scrutiny as possible."

Anne felt her temper rising. She propped herself on an elbow and frowned at her girlfriend. "What, are you afraid I'll tell someone?"

"Never," Charlie said, finally meeting her eyes. "The problem is that our biggest threat is the sadist who has intermittent access to your head."

"If William were to gain that information," Zima said, "it would severely limit our recovery options."

"Recovery? You talk about it like it's a trip to the hospital."

"It is, in a way," Charlie said. "Defense, survival, and escape are our first priorities, of course. But it's also important to have a place to regroup, lick our wounds, and strike back quickly, if possible."

Anne flopped back onto the blanket and rubbed her eyes. "I'd be perfectly happy with the first three, I think."

"Most people would be," Charlie said, his eyes suddenly flinty. "But the enemy is usually more vulnerable after their first attack than they would have their victims believe. They've expended their resources and played their best cards."

"Using that knowledge to mount a swift and precise counterattack may end a conflict even when the odds appear insurmountable," Zima said. "But doing so requires having adequate resources and facilities in reserve."

"Are you saying ... we have a backup factory somewhere?"

Zima gently cupped her cheek. "I am saying that it is better if we change the subject, Anne. It is difficult for me not to answer your questions because I wish to please you, so it will be safer for us all if you simply do not ask."

Anne pursed her lips and bit back a terse reply. She had already snapped at Zima once tonight, and didn't want to do it again.

Besides that, Zima was right.

What irked Anne more than not knowing, however, was the reason she wasn't allowed to know.

William.

It always came back to him. Every misery, every loss, every ounce of pain she'd suffered over the last half-year could be traced back to that sadistic son-of-a-bitch.

If I ever see him again ...

Next time, Anne swore, she wouldn't hesitate. If she somehow got her hands around his neck, she would do what needed to be done and end the nightmare once and for all.

She would end William Taplin.

"Anne?" Charlie said softly.

"Hmm?"

"You're, ah, crushing my fingers."

"Oh!" She looked down and, sure enough, his fingers had turned an unhealthy shade of red in her grip. "Charlie! I'm so sorry ..."

"It's okay. Cappa disabled my pain receptors."

He flexed his fingers. One was bent sideways and squeaked when it moved. He gripped it with his other hand and carefully bent it the other way. It still squeaked, but looked far less hideous.

They lapsed into silence, watching the stars twinkle, and listening to the breeze rustle the grass and trees. Anne tried to relax, but another topic prickled her mind, and she knew she couldn't rest until she had closure.

"Charlie?"

"Yeah?"

"I was just wondering ... a-about Vicky ..."

He was quiet for several minutes. Anne was afraid she'd once again ventured into unsafe territory, but he eventually sighed and turned to her.

"After hearing Vicky's side of the story, I can see how you might be uneasy about our future, but ..." Charlie ran a hand through his hair. "The truth is that our engagement was one-sided. We dated for a while, yes, but I never actually asked her to marry me."

"I ... I don't understand. She said she had a ring."

"Which she also claimed I'd bought for her. Both are technically true, but Vicky neglected to mention that I wasn't there at the time of purchase."

"Come again?"

Charlie turned to her with a smirk. "One day, Vicky asked to borrow my credit card. Said she left hers at home and needed to pick up a few things at the store. We'd been dating for a while, so I figured why not? Later that day, I received a call from one of our mutual friends, congratulating me on my engagement, and asking if we'd set a date. I hung up, thinking he was pulling my leg, but then I received another call, and another. I was already frazzled by the time she returned that evening, so you can imagine how I felt when she walked in with a giant rock on her wedding finger."

"You're kidding! I mean, she seemed a little aggressive, but that's ... that's ..."

"That's Vicky," Charlie said without a hint of malice. "She knows what she wants, and doesn't take 'no' for an answer."

"Yeah, but come on! There's a difference between not taking 'no' and not asking in the first place."

He chuckled. "True, but I think her take-what-you-want attitude was what drew me to her, and probably what broke us apart. We were too alike."

"I don't buy that for a second," Anne said. "You're one of the most courteous people I know."

"Not back then, I wasn't. You don't make the top of the Fortune 500 on smarts alone, unfortunately. Mark and I have stepped on a lot of toes to get where we are. Some people deserved it, but many were just unlucky enough to be in our path while we climbed our way up."

Charlie looked back to the sky.

"Vicky was the same, except I don't think she grew out of it. Morton has his issues, but he runs a very successful business. I'd bet this country mansion that she doesn't love him, and talked him out of a prenuptial agreement to make sure she gets her share if things go wrong. She's probably been siphoning money into private accounts from the day she signed the marriage certificate."

"That sounds ... horrible."

"It is what I would do," Zima said.

Anne raised her eyebrows.

Zima shrugged. "Her actions are indicative of strong survival skills. Whatever happens, she will have something to fall back upon. I employed the same strategy before leaving Orwing."

"Yeah, but leading her husband on like that? It seems shady."

Charlie stretched and put his hands behind his head. "That's where you have to know Morton. We stopped doing business together for a reason. Trust me when I say that even a false marriage with Vicky is better than he deserves."

Anne snuggled into the crook of his shoulder. "It sounds like you've changed a lot."

"For the better, I hope."

"So ... what drives you now? What do you want out of life?"

Charlie wrapped an arm around her, then swept his other arm over the peaceful landscape. "This."

"That's all? What about the factory? Your business?"

Charlie shrugged. "It's served its purpose. We have enough cash in the bank to do what we really love, which is tinkering."

"Are you seriously telling me you wouldn't miss it? Not even a little?"

"Maybe a little," Charlie said, narrowing his eyes thoughtfully. "But I think I'd be happy no matter where we landed, as long as we're together." He glanced over Anne's head at Zima. "All of us, that is."

Anne followed his gaze. "What about you, Zima?"

"I would miss the weapons lab. Maintenance is more efficient with proper tools."

"I mean, in general," Anne said with a laugh. "What's your idea of a perfect life?"

"Oh."

Zima lay perfectly still for several minutes, staring at the stars. Anne knew better than to assume she'd forgotten about the topic, so she and Charlie waited quietly while Zima churned on her answer. She eventually turned back to them, her brows knitted.

"I am aligned with Charlie, I believe, although my needs are simpler. I wish only to maintain the independence I have fought for" — she squeezed Anne's hand — "and to be with you. Not necessarily in that order."

Charlie shot her a stern look. "This is my date, Zima. Stop showing me up."

Zima started to apologize, but Charlie waved her off with a grin.

"Kidding! When did you become such a romantic? It seems like only yesterday you couldn't hold a conversation with anyone outside of Z-Tech. Yet here you are, spouting sweet nothings that are making *me* jealous of *Anne*."

Zima brow-knit deeper than Anne had ever seen — almost a frown. Anne was afraid she might break something if she mulled any harder over Charlie's quip, so she stroked Zima's cheek.

"He was joking again, honey. With Cappa in the mix, our relationships have become complicated enough without drawing another line connecting you and Charlie."

You can say that again, Cappa sent, making Anne and Charlie laugh.

"Oh." Zima's face resumed its normal, neutral expression, and she turned back to the sky without another word.

The mood for the rest of the night was much lighter. Shooting stars made Anne gasp in delight. Zima pointed out orbiting satellites — star-sized dots moving in straight lines across the sky — and was able to name each one and its function.

Charlie spoke more of his time in China, focusing on his spiritual connection with nature and the earth, which Anne found fascinating. She even attempted some basic *chi*-building meditations, but was unable to sense her own energy. Charlie dismissed her failure as normal, citing that it took most people years to recognize their own *chi* flows, and encouraged her to keep practicing.

To their surprise, even Zima tried it, with similar, disappointing results. They asked if she would continue to try, but she declined, claiming she preferred to focus instead on more concrete skills, such as firearms and martial combat.

With dawn a few hours away, they packed up and headed back to the limousine. Charlie asked if Anne wanted to stay at the house. She remembered his warning about its sunny design, and decided the picturesque setting wasn't worth the risk of third-degree burns, or spending the day locked in a broom closet, so they climbed in the car and left.

Anne glanced at the beautiful house through the rear window, vowing she would one day see the property in all its sunlit glory, even if the experience cost her a few burns.

14

WAR OF THE CAPPAS

THE SKY WAS TURNING PINK when the limousine pulled into Z-Tech's garage. Anne thanked Charlie and Zima for a wonderful night, then tucked them into their respective beds for the morning. They both asked if she wished to stay with them, but Anne tactfully refused, giving each a tender goodnight kiss that left no question of her feelings for either of them.

Anne closed Zima's door and started down the hall. Hopefully, the morning wasn't late enough that Almos would already be asleep. She desperately needed advice about the Sturmans and the Jeram Tosali situation. Having delt with messes like this for the last nine hundred years, the master vampire was sure to have an informed opinion.

She had only made it a few steps from Zima's bedroom when Cappa's door opened. Her soul sister's sheer nightie revealed most of her shapely legs and a good portion of her modest cleavage. Anne gave her a thumbs-up, assuming she was on her way for another romantic attempt with Charlie, but Cappa hurried over to Anne instead.

"Heading for breakfast?"

"Down to see Almos, actually."

"Mind if I come?"

Anne shrugged and motioned for her to follow.

When they finally reached the bottom of the long stairway down to the reactor room, Rose and Almos were just settling on the couch, his arm draped around her tiny waist as if they were a long-standing couple.

Almos smiled around a yawn. "Good morning, dear girls. To what do we owe the pleasure of your company?"

"I wanted your thoughts on the Jeram Tosali situation," Anne said.

"Pardon?"

"You know, the vampire who turned the Sturmans."

Blink.

"The couple Charlie and I ran into at the party tonight, who we believe are my descendants?"

Almos' pleasant smile faded. "This is the first I've heard."

"Same here." Rose leveled a flinty glare at Cappa. "Really? This is how it's going to be? I refuse to sync up, and now you won't tell me a damn thing?"

Cappa balled her fists. "This is how you wanted it! You won't share data anymore. Fine! Here we are. You can get your information the old-fashioned way — by *talking* to me!"

Rose shot to her feet, her fists also balled — a miniature replica of Cappa's volcanic fury. "A data packet with simple highlights wouldn't have killed you! We could be having a productive conversation right now, but no! You had to spin it into a petty gripe. You're being childish."

"Oh, that's priceless," Cappa said, dripping with venom. "Hanging around a nine-hundred-year-old vampire suddenly makes you more mature than me? You're not the only person who's had exposure to a wise old man, you know. Master Wung imparted a fair amount of wisdom —"

"Excuse the interruption," Anne said over their rising voices, "but can you guys argue about this later? I'm sorry to hear that you're still having issues, but there's a bigger problem. Someone is making *vampires* from my blood. We have a lead on one of the sires, and I need advice on how to deal with him."

Almos pressed his palms to his eyes. "It is as I feared. After centuries of carefully isolating myself, the plague is finally loose — out of my domain, and out of my control."

"Don't say that," Anne said in an attempt to deny the same despair he undoubtedly felt. "We might still be able to contain this. If we can talk to this Jeram guy and find out where he came from, who he's infected, what his motives are, and get him to stop —"

"There is only one sure way to stop this plague," Almos said. Dark eyes reflected the weight of his words. "You have already done it to the mercenaries. Are you prepared to kill again, Anne Perrin?"

"I am," Zima said, her voice echoing from the stairwell.

Seconds later, she emerged and stood next to Anne, straight and sure. Anne straightened as well. With Zima by her side, she felt like she couldn't fail.

Anne touched her arm. "Zima, I-I'm not saying we actually have to kill anyone —"

"That is exactly what Almos is suggesting, and he is correct. The only way to end a plague is to ensure there are no more carriers. Since we do not possess a vaccine, and the disease does not naturally consume its host, there is but one alternative, and that is to terminate the carriers themselves."

"I'm a carrier," Anne said softly.

"There are exceptions to any rule. While it is true that your blood carries the pathogen, you also play an instrumental role in its containment, which your initiation of this conversation demonstrates. The benefits of keeping you alive far outweigh the risks, as I believe anyone who knows you will agree."

Anne let her words sink in. Deep down, she had always considered herself part of the threat, despite her efforts to the contrary. She had no illusions that, once the threat was contained, she would perish with the rest of the vampires, again leaving Almos with the sole burden of a great and terrible responsibility.

But Zima, as usual, had made Anne re-consider her position. In doing so, she had opened a new line of thought.

Anne's voice was thick when she finally spoke. "Assuming for a second that what you said wasn't just a rationalization because you love me ..." She held up a hand to forestall Zima's protest. "Then the same logic applies to others of my lineage. Their minds are free of the blinding loyalty that William's vampires have. They might be fighting against this scourge, just like we are."

"Possible," Zima said, "but that is a large supposition."

"Is it? Charlie and I witnessed a vampire-on-vampire attack during our walk back from the department store. The losers were probably William's, and the victors didn't attack us. Why?"

"That is difficult to speculate without more information."

Anne grabbed Zima's shoulders with excitement. "Exactly! We need to discover their motivations before we run in guns a blazing. What if they're on our side? Thanks to my oddball DNA, for the first time *ever* there may be a strain of vampires who aren't just slaves to their sires and the urge to hunt, but individuals who have retained their goals, desires, and, above all, their connection to humanity. If there's even a chance we can ally with them to help fight the real threat, it would be wrong ... no, it would be *criminal* to ignore it."

"I appreciate your enthusiasm," Almos said, "but there's a whisper of Pandora's Box in your vision that troubles me."

"I agree," Zima said. "Let us assume what you say is true, and we manage to terminate William's entire line with their aid. What then? Allow these new vampires to go free? It would take only one with malintent to start the plague anew."

"And it takes one asshole with a nuclear code to start World War Three," Anne said heatedly. "We can't justify *genocide* on the possibility that *one* member of a brand-new race might be a bad egg!"

What would Captain Kirk say, for God's sake?

"I'm with Anne," Cappa and Rose said at the same time.

In a rare show, Cappa deferred to her smaller counterpart to voice their thoughts.

"You may be right," Rose said. "Whatever their motivations, allowing a new strain of vampires to live could have unfavorable results. But can you look at Anne and honestly tell me there isn't hope for a future where humans and these new vampires can co-exist? We could be wrong — *catastrophically* wrong — by allowing them to live. But, no matter how I look at it, slaughtering innocents because we're afraid of what they may or may not do down the road is Nazi-esque, pure and simple."

Almos sighed and fell still. His black eyes strayed to the reactor. "When do you intend to visit this Jeram Tosali?"

"As soon as we figure out where he is," Anne said.

"I found three addresses in the Bay Area," Cappa said. "One I've already ruled out, but I'll keep digging on the other two. Either way, we should be ready to take action by tomorrow night."

"After dinner," Zima said.

Anne frowned. Had she committed to a social event and forgotten about it? She racked her brain, but came up empty, and gave her girlfriend a questioning look.

"Charlie took you out tonight," Zima said. "Tomorrow night is my turn."

"Oh, honey … That's sweet, but can I get a rain check? This is a little more important, don't you think?"

"No."

"But —"

"Tomorrow's affair has taken great effort and expense to arrange. Postponing may not be possible, so I would prefer to keep to the evening's plans."

Anne fidgeted with her shirt. "Well, I guess we could do both …" She was surprised that Zima's plans included dinner, since neither of them ate real food, but Zima had surely taken that into account. "A few hours delay shouldn't hurt. Tosali is a vampire, after all, so it isn't like we'll be encroaching on his sleep schedule."

"Unlike mine," Almos said with a yawn. "Despite the engaging topic, I am quickly fading, and will be of little use before long. At the risk of imposing on the hospitality of my gracious hosts, may I have a few minutes to speak with you in private before sleep claims me?"

Anne started to sit next to him, but caught herself when she realized he'd been talking to Zima.

"As you wish," Zima said with a shrug.

Anne followed Cappa and Rose up the stairs. Their faces reflected her own curiosity of what business the master vampire had with Zima that he felt he couldn't share, although Rose also seemed disappointed.

Anne said goodbye to them at the top of the stairwell, then watched them disappear into Cappa's room, where she hoped they would talk through some of their remaining issues.

Swallowing a twinge of guilt, Anne loitered near the stairwell entrance and strained to listen. Almos and Zima spoke for several minutes in hushed tones, too distorted by echoes for even her sensitive ears to make out, before she finally heard Zima's heavy footsteps ascending.

She slipped an arm through her beau's when she emerged. "How'd it go?" Anne said casually, though she was burning with curiosity.

"Well." Zima tugged her toward Anne's room.

"Good. That's ... good." *And supremely unhelpful.* "What did he want?"

"Alignment."

Zima closed the bedroom door and put a finger on Anne's lips, buttoning her follow-up question.

"If you command it, I shall divulge the information you seek, since it is difficult for me to deny your wishes. So I will ask you once again to cease your inquiries and accept my assurance that Almos meant no ill toward any of us."

"I would never command you," Anne said in a small voice.

Zima surprised her with a passionate kiss.

"You may wish to reconsider that," Zima whispered, her breath warm on Anne's ear. "There are many commands I would obey with great enthusiasm."

The list of things Anne wanted to accomplish today was huge. She wanted to help Cappa with her research on Tosali, practice with her implant to improve her dismal messaging skills, continue her martial arts lessons with Mark, learn to use an assault rifle at the range, and maybe even take a crash course in grenade throwing.

All of those tasks created a sense of urgency that told Anne she should refuse Zima's advance. She tried to, in fact, but Zima's soft lips moved down her cheek and gently nibbled her neck, turning her legs to jelly, and her will to mush.

"All right," Anne said playfully. "You want a command? On the bed!"

Zima complied without hesitation.

"Now it's your turn," Anne said with a sultry grin.

"Put your mouth here," Zima said, touching her own, "and do not remove it until I say."

Anne slunk across the sheets — a cat stalking her little mouse prey — and lowered herself onto Zima until their lips touched.

For the next several hours, they had great fun issuing orders to each other and exploring the sensual side of taking charge.

15

ENEMY OF MY ENEMY

L IEUTENANT COLONEL JOHN ANDERSON checked the positions of his men. Each appeared as a small orb of light in his head. In addition to their feelings, he could also discern their general locations, a tactical advantage he would have killed for during his time in the Army. One soldier crouched atop the abandoned three-story army barracks a hundred yards in front of the large Presidio lawn John occupied. Two perched in the trees to either side. Each sported a .50 caliber sniper rifle loaded with silver-laced bullets. A four-man assault squad also hid in an old officer's house nearby, ready to engage at the first sign of trouble.

John sighed.

It wasn't enough. He would have liked the other four squads he'd recently sired to be present as well, but they were already in position and waiting for their other assignments. These soldiers would have to do.

William seemed unbothered by the lack of support, however. Almost as tall as John's biggest soldier, with shoulders just as wide, William's hard eyes stared across the green Presidio Park, standing as still as a statue. Not an ounce of worry came through his sire bond. William either trusted John's ability to protect him, or was too egotistical to realize just how big a threat the man they were about to meet actually was.

A little of both, probably.

John sensed Myrcella approaching long before she stepped from the shadows of a nearby tree. Dressed in her typical Goth outfit, complete with dark makeup, she strode across the moonlit lawn to settle on William's other side, and soon became a statue, too.

"Are your men in place?" John said, not looking at her.

"Worry about your own shit, dickhead."

I'll take that as a yes.

The commander in him wanted details and demanded respect, but John's pragmatic side knew he would get neither from Myrcella.

And, to her point, he had much bigger worries tonight.

Minutes later — and right on time — three men approached from across the vast lawn, passing right by the building John's first sniper occupied. The men on either side were dressed in black tuxedoes and as large as any of John's soldiers.

The man between them wasn't. Slicked-back graying hair, a hawkish nose, and a haughty smile reminded John of a bird of prey soaring high above, looking down on a world full of mice. His tuxedo, unlike the others', was perfectly tailored for his trim body, and looked more expensive than all of John's earthly possessions combined.

The hawkish man and his escorts stopped a dozen paces in front of William, John, and Myrcella. Even from this distance, the overpowering smell of cologne assaulted John's sensitive nose, mixed with the delicious scent of his humanity.

John wasn't surprised at all to see large, black eyes on the men to either side.

Vampires.

That wasn't a problem. They were no match for John's eight vampires — not counting himself, Myrcella, and William.

And that was what worried him.

The hawkish man spread his hands. "Is this how you greet guests in your fine city, William?" His smooth voice flowed like oil across a pond.

"If you're looking for a hug, go to the fucking Castro," William said. "I didn't come here to chat. What do you want, Alvin?"

Alvin Orwing laughed. "Oh my. You have so much to learn about diplomacy, I don't even know where to begin. You've heard the saying that you catch more flies with honey than with vinegar?"

William crossed his arms and fixed Alvin with a hard stare.

"Merely a suggestion. Ruling the world is easier once you've learned to play the game, but alas ..." Alvin shrugged.

"The plan is still on for tonight?"

"Of course. My men are simply awaiting the signal. And I trust there is no need to remind you of my payment?"

William shook his head. "You can have their fucking bodies. I only care that they're dead. Especially that bitch, Anne."

"Charles Z and that blonde robot — the Dark Angel, you call her? — are the only two I care about," Alvin said. "The technology in their bodies is priceless to someone like me. The rest of them you can burn or mutilate to your malfunctioning heart's content."

William scowled. "When I say dead, I mean their brains aren't functioning and can't be recovered. *No* exceptions."

"Yes, I'm clear on the concept. Reverse-engineering how their minds work would be easier if they were intact and operational, but my scientists will make do with what they get."

"So I'll say it again. What the fuck do you want, Alvin?"

Alvin's eye twitched this time, though his haughty smile remained. "A modicum of respect for your business partner would be nice."

Anger poured through William's sire bond. The big man took a threatening step forward.

The ground in front of him exploded in a shower of grass and dirt — much too large to have come from a sniper round. A gunshot report followed a split-second later, unlike anything John had ever heard, and he'd heard them all.

William jumped back. At the same time, Myrcella leaped in front of him, putting her own body between her sire and Alvin. John reached for his sidearm, even though he knew it would be useless against whatever had just fired at them.

Neither Alvin nor his guards even flinched.

"That's close enough," Alvin said, his voice calm. He brushed a fleck of dirt from his sleeve. "And, I hope it goes without saying, the next shot won't miss."

Point made, John thought, his senses on high alert. He sincerely hoped his sire understood the same.

William's organization was gaining significant influence in the United States, mostly through coercion or by turning powerful people into vampires under his control. But Orwing Industries operated at an entirely different level, and on a global scale. Worse, Alvin had been doing it for much longer than William. He had powerful contacts, weapons, and technology at his disposal that John could only guess at.

Pissing him off was a *bad* idea, even for the master of vampires.

William's surprise quickly subsided. He flexed his neck, then turned his black eyes back to Alvin. Feelings of caution trickled through his sire bond, along with ... planning. William was re-assessing his measure of the man before him. Unlike most people, who might have been rightly intimidated, William was already contemplating how to tip their next meeting in his favor.

Just like a true dictator would.

William gestured to the surrounding Presidio. "Welcome to San Francisco," he said in a steely voice, which was about as much warmth as Alvin — or anyone — was likely to get from the man.

"Much better." Alvin breathed deep, smiling as if he were enjoying the night. "Really, I just came to wish you luck. I don't need to tell you that you have one shot at this, and one shot only. The world will never be the same after tonight. I hope for your sake that you're prepared to deal with the consequences."

"Prepared enough." The muscles in William's jaw tightened, distorting the unhealed gash running down his cheek that Anne had given him. "Anything else?"

"Just one little piece of information I've been saving for this special occasion." A sly smile spread across Alvin's face. "Have you ever wondered who sired you, William?"

William's face remained stoic, but panic gushed through his sire bond, reflected through Myrcella's bond, and echoed in John's own chest.

No one knew where William had come from, not even William himself. Everyone had assumed he was either the first of his kind, or that his sire had died shortly after creating him, for William had never sensed a trace of the person.

"What do you know about it?" William's voice was dangerously soft.

"Oh, just his name, history, why you've never sensed him through your sire bond, that he's almost definitely still alive ... and why you should be very careful to keep him that way."

William crossed his arms, projecting a calm John knew for certain he didn't feel. "I'm listening."

"His name is Almos — *just* Almos. Nine hundred years give him a right to eschew a surname, apparently, unlike those self-entitled stars who do the same. We held him in captivity until a month ago, when —"

"When that bitch blew up your little mercenary army."

Alvin's eye twitched again. "Yes. Anne Perrin had been my prisoner until then, along with Almos, but ... *something* freed them both. Our best guess is either Charles or the blonde robot, but it's only a guess. They also destroyed something precious to me during the escape. Again."

"Sorry to hear that," William said, clearly not sorry at all. "So where is this Almos now?"

"As I thought I made clear: I don't know. Our only sighting of any of them was Anne the night they incinerated my assets."

Myrcella snickered. Alvin glared at her, but she just smirked back at him.

That woman ...

Alvin turned away from her with a contemptuous glare. "They may have ferried Almos to Scandinavia, for all we know. Z-Tech has holdings all over the world. The few we're aware of are being closely monitored, but are thus far vacant."

"Anne is in their factory here in the City, which means Almos probably is, too."

Alvin shrugged.

Aware he was still holding his pistol, John holstered it. "Why is it so important to keep Almos alive?"

"Superstition, perhaps. While Almos was our, ah ... *guest,* he claimed something called the Entity would seize control of him should he venture near the surface, and that this Entity didn't have mankind's best interests at heart." Alvin smiled. "Frankly, I think we would get along well."

"You don't sound convinced," William said. "Which makes me wonder why you brought it up."

"Concern for my new, favorite business partner. While Almos had no proof of this Entity's existence, his fear seemed genuine, so we have no reason to believe he was intentionally deceiving us. Sadly, he disappeared before we could question him properly.

"Regardless, Almos made it clear that he is *not* a fan of yours. Even if the Entity is only a figment of his imagination, should Almos surface, he *will* seize control of you and your forces. He considers vampires a plague, which means his first order of operations will likely be the extermination of everything you've worked so hard to build. Including yourself, of course."

"And if the Entity does exist," William said, mostly to himself, "killing Almos would move my sire bond from him to it."

"I'm pleased you grasp the delicacy of the situation without me having to explain. It speaks well for our future partnership — assuming you still have full control of your faculties at the end of tonight."

"Asshole," Myrcella said.

Alvin's smile faltered. "Rein your monochromatic pet in, William, or I might be less inclined to share any further information."

"Get used to her," William said. "This *monochromatic pet* is your date tonight. She's also one of my favorite lieutenants, so I expect she be given the same respect you would afford to me."

"That arrangement works both ways. I shall consider any *disrespect* from her as a direct affront from yourself, and deal with it accordingly."

William looked down at Myrcella. The adoration they all felt for William flooded her black eyes.

"Play nice with Alvin," William said. "Just for tonight."

Myrcella stroked his arm with a dreamy smile. "Of course, my sire."

William arched an eyebrow at Alvin. "Good enough?"

"Better if she would agree to stop by a dress shop for a proper gown, but I suppose that would be too much to ask."

"Fuck y—" Myrcella bit her lip, then took a deep breath. "This outfit will be fine. It will also send the right message to those fuckheads."

"A confuddled one, but I understand your point. Well, I see no further reason to dawdle, then. Shall we?" Alvin proffered his arm to Myrcella.

"Just a minute," William said. "What exactly am I supposed to do with this Almos character if Z-Tech actually does have him?"

"That's up to you, really. You could gamble that Almos is insane and kill him, securing yourself as the master vampire once and for all. But if you wanted to play it safe, you would need to paralyze him with silver and transport him to the underground holding facility of your choice.

"Fair warning, however: Almos can control vampires even when a generational gap is present — a feat no sire in my army has yet been able to replicate. Make sure those you send to find him are human, or the tables tonight could very quickly turn."

"A little late for that advice! Where the hell am I supposed to find human operatives on such short notice?"

"Come now," Alvin said. "Do you think I would leave such a valued partner in the lurch? I have a small mercenary contingent nearby that I would happily lend you."

"In exchange for ...?"

"Call it an investment into our joint future." Alvin looked at Myrcella. "Now come along, my dark darling. We have a very special event to attend, and we don't want to be late."

Myrcella gave William a last, affectionate look before turning her usual glower back to Alvin. She crossed the lawn between them and took his arm without a word. Strangely, her black Goth outfit and Alvin's tuxedo were a decent match, John thought.

It wasn't until William and John were well out of Presidio Park and inside their bullet-proof vehicle that John dared to speak.

"I don't like this. Alvin withheld information about Almos for a reason."

"You think?" William said, dripping with sarcasm.

John ignored it. "We should move you underground until the operation is over, just in case."

"If what Alvin says is true, that Almos can control vampires even with a generational gap, it wouldn't do any good." William's already severe expression darkened. "Besides, I want the last thing those fuckers see to be my goddamned face, laughing at them."

And for that, you're willing to risk your entire empire?

John knew it was true without even asking.

William was in a position to take the world, should he choose. But, unfortunately, he couldn't see past his revenge.

16

BEST. DATE. EVER.

THE REST OF THE DAY following Anne's date with Charlie, their visit to his country house, and her morning soiree with Zima wasn't as productive as Anne had hoped.

Her Tosali research had lasted all of thirty minutes before she discovered that her internet skills were woefully inadequate for the task. Even thinking about using her implant to practice messaging had given her a headache, so Anne had sought Mark for martial arts practice instead. He and Charlie had been holed up in a meeting, however, preparing for a formal business function that night, which Cappa described as a dull affair.

Boring or not, Cappa was excited because it was her first official date with Charlie. Cappa was determined to make it special, so she had employed Anne and Doris' help to choose the perfect ensemble for the occasion.

Afterward, Anne had stopped by Dela's room to see if she needed help getting ready, but Dela had previous plans with other friends, which left Mark dateless. The visit hadn't been without its fruits, however. Anne had left her room with a full stomach and a smile on Dela's face.

Everybody wins, Anne had thought happily.

Even her rifle shooting lesson with Zima had been cut short when her girlfriend had run out for an errand in preparation for their dinner date. Zima was stubbornly tight-lipped with the details, citing that she wanted to keep it a surprise. She'd promised she wasn't going far, and would be back in a few hours.

Anne had eyed a box of grenades, tempted to give them an unsupervised try. Pull the pin and throw, how hard could it be? But she'd eventually decided against it. With her luck, the grenades were prototypes that would suck the entire factory into some sort of miniature black hole. Assuming she survived, she would never live it down.

So, Anne had retreated to her room and, with the sun now set, resolved to do something she hadn't done in a very long time.

She was going to read. By herself.

No bed buddy. No torture chamber. No reactor room shared with a chatty nine-hundred-year-old vampire. Just Anne, her leafy friends, and that wonderful, musty smell she had enjoyed since childhood.

To commemorate the occasion, Anne grabbed the most prized item on her bookshelf, brought it back to her bed, and lovingly stroked its care-worn cover.

The Adventures of Jayne Madison, Book One, by Georgette Parker.

When Anne had run away to San Francisco after the assault in her bedroom as a teenager, she had stepped off the bus with a suitcase, a purse containing her meager life savings, and this book. It was one of the few possessions she'd cared to rescue from the apartment William had defiled. And, once the bookshelves had appeared in her room here at Z-Tech, she had made a special trip to retrieve it from Doris so it could resume its rightful place at her bedside.

The pages crackled when she opened it, stiff and brown with age, but the typeset letters were as black and clear as the day she had first laid eyes on them as a child. Although Cappa had recently read it aloud to her, there was something magical about seeing the words on paper.

Before long, Anne was gasping and laughing along with her heroine, so enmeshed in her journey of espionage and intrigue that she jumped when the door handle turned, sure that she had just been caught by an enemy spy. Zima was no spy, of course, but rarely passed on an opportunity to snuggle with Anne, so the two of them assumed their time-honored positions: Zima's head on Anne's chest while Anne read and stroked her doll-like hair.

Too soon, Anne had to close her book to dress for the evening's mysterious affair. Even more mysterious was when Dela and Doris whisked Zima away to Cappa's room and locked the door, leaving Anne with instructions to wear something formal. Her nicest dress was still dirty from the previous night — perhaps irreversibly after her hike through the overgrown forest trail. So Anne chose her second-favorite dress: a flowing gown of earthy colors. She stepped it up with shiny black short-heeled shoes, a sequined purse, white silk gloves, and a gold-and-emerald necklace of Cappa's that Anne had somehow neglected to return.

Anne skipped the headscarf, however. Like a cancer patient going through chemotherapy, she had come to regard her short hair as not only evidence of her struggles, but a proud reminder that she had beaten the odds and come out alive.

She gave her fine-downed top a few strokes with a soft brush, then opened her makeup drawer and began the arduous process of masking her pale, venous skin so she didn't look like a zombie. She didn't have Cappa or Doris' talent, but tenacity and a steady hand eventually made her look passable. A few blemishes dotted her face, but nothing that couldn't be excused as an amateur's mistake. Contacts and false tooth caps in place, Anne waited in the hall for her date.

The boys emerged from Mark's bedroom shortly after, laughing at some joke she had missed. Both wore sharp shirts with powerful colors, pressed slacks, shiny belts, fancy watches with enough dials to make her dizzy, elegant golden rings she had never seen either of them wear before, and sport coats that struck a perfect balance between casual and outrageously expensive. Mark's hair, while just as short and downy-soft as Anne's, was gelled to an engineer's rigorous standards. Even Charlie's hair, normally scruffy, had thick comb lines through gel that cemented every hair in place like a fine sculpture.

In a word, they both looked *hot.*

Charlie sobered when he saw Anne in her best attempt at formal wear, which felt pauperish next to his.

"You look great," he said as if in a trance.

Anne beamed under his praise. "Back at you, handsome. You clean up nice."

"I had some help." Charlie nodded to Mark.

"Hope you tipped well."

"He never does," Mark said. "Not that he needed my help anyway."

Charlie shrugged. "I've had some practice. In the early days of the company, we had to dress this way all the time. We spent more time rubbing elbows at parties than actually working."

"Some of us call rubbing elbows work," Mark said, tugging his sleeves. "It takes more than just tinkering in a lab to get contracts. Social occasions like this are where we scored ninety percent of our business before we made a name for ourselves."

"Sorry I'm missing out," Anne said. Stuffy or not, she longed to share this piece of history with them. "Maybe I can catch the next one?"

"Expensive champagne, caviar, a live pianist ..." Mark waved it off. "You'd be bored stiff."

"Take me, then," Doris said, slipping from Cappa's room. "I'll make damn sure none of that good stuff goes to waste."

"Well, I am short a date," Mark said.

Anne waited for the punchline, but his offer appeared to be genuine.

"Thanks, sugar cakes, but we both know I'd blow any chances you had at scoring a deal. I'd probably down four bottles of that bubbly, end up caterwauling naked on the piano, and scare off the whole damn party." Doris stood up straight and flashed a toothy smile. "But tonight ain't about me! It's about these gals, who y'all might not even recognize now. Come on out, contestant number one!"

The door opened again, and a shimmering figure emerged. If Mark and Charlie were formal, then Cappa was elegance incarnate, from her revealing dress to her perfect makeup. Her long dark hair spiraled up into intricate circles, making her already round face positively radiant. Sapphire earrings, a gold necklace, and bracelets caused her deep blue eyes to sparkle. Combined with four-inch stiletto heels, she towered like a goddess among mortals.

The effect wasn't lost on Charlie. Twice he snapped his mouth shut, only to have it fall open again. When he finally gained control of his tongue, he stammered a short, "You're gorgeous," that somehow made his earlier compliment to Anne pale by comparison.

And that wasn't lost on Cappa, who spared Anne an apologetic glance before melting into complete teenage embarrassment under Charlie's captivated eye. Even so, Cappa sent a message clearly intended to make Anne feel better.

WE'LL GO SHOPPING TOMORROW. I HAVE A FEW OUTFIT IDEAS FOR YOU THAT WILL MAKE CHARLIE DROOL.

Charlie proffered his arm, which Cappa took with royal grace. They simply stood there, staring at each other like the two most perfect people in the world who had absolutely no idea what to do with each other.

A camera flash snapped them to. Doris gave them a thumbs-up from behind her upheld phone.

"Got it, I'll send the picture around later. Now for contestant num—"

"Wait, wait, wait!" Dela squeezed out through the door and shut it firmly behind her. "I've gotta be out here for this." Face aglow, she bounded past Doris and took position several paces down the hall, her camera aimed to capture the entire scene.

Doris recovered with a laugh. "Alrighty, then. Contestant number two, show yourself!"

When the door opened again, Anne's world stopped.

Open-toed shoes had replaced Zima's black combat boots, revealing her beautiful ankles and toned legs to just above her knees. A simple red skirt draped over the slight curve of her hips to her slim waist, cinched with a shiny black belt. A white polka dot blouse left her flawless arms exposed, and showed just enough tantalizing cleavage between its billowing lapels to leave Anne gasping for more. Her short, bobbed hair was swept back with a red satin ribbon that crested the top of her head, adding a striking dash of color to her platinum-blonde strands. A touch of makeup adorned her doll-perfect face, deepening her soft lips to a luscious red, and turning her adorable ice-blue eyes into irresistible beacons that drew Anne into their depths.

Then, just when Anne thought it couldn't get any better, her precious, stoic girlfriend added the finishing touch that stole the air from her lungs.

Zima smiled.

Not just a twitch of her lips or a lopsided grin; this was a full-force display of her reclusive pearly whites that crinkled her eyes with merry lines and transformed her into a being of pure, radiant beauty.

The Earth must have moved, for Anne suddenly found herself on her knees, struggling to see through a well of tears.

In all their time together, not once had she considered how Zima would look with a smile on her sculpted face. Expressions weren't her thing. In many ways, her consistently neutral mien was an endearing part of what made her Zima — which Anne had not only accepted, but come to love.

To see that simple, outward sign of happiness, however — to know Zima was experiencing joy — was absolutely priceless.

Zima was by her side in an instant, her face neutral once again. "What is it? Are you unwell?"

Anne could only laugh. She tenderly cupped Zima's cheek, etching every detail of that wonderful moment into her mind, then pulled her into an embrace.

"Tell me that was your big surprise for the evening," Anne said, sniffling, "because I can't imagine anything better."

"The smile was Dela's suggestion. She has been working with me ever since she witnessed my poor attempt the night of your kidnapping. It is good to know the effort was not in vain. But no, it was not the planned surprise. I suggest you reserve judgments of magnitude until we reach the restaurant."

"Now I'm dying to know," Mark said, crossing his arms. "Not even a hint?"

"No."

All eyes turned to Cappa, who held up her hands.

"Don't look at me! I just helped her shop for the outfit. She hasn't told anyone, as far as I know."

"And that's the best way to keep a secret," Charlie said. "Have a great time, Zima. I hope your surprise ends better than mine did at the art show."

Anne stood and kissed him lightly on the cheek, careful not to leave a lipstick smear. "I had a wonderful time last night, Charlie. Nothing says 'exciting' like a good old-fashioned foot chase through the streets of San Francisco."

"You're too kind," he said with a chuckle. "I'll get it right one of these days, I promise."

"Maybe tonight with your other date," Anne said to him, winking at Cappa. "Don't hurry home."

"We won't," Charlie said. "The business party is just a warmup for the evening."

Cappa brightened. "Oh? Do tell!"

"Not a chance. Do you have any idea how hard it is to keep secrets from someone who sees and hears everything you do? It's a miracle I've made it this far without accidentally spilling something."

Cappa slipped her arm through his. "Fair point. We can discuss privacy protocols later, but for now I think it's time we hit the road. Traffic won't lighten up just because it's our first official date." Her smile broadened.

Anne searched for the jealous ache that should have been sitting in the pit of her stomach, but all she found was joy for her soul sister's happiness. Cappa and Charlie were cute together. They were a natural pairing, as Anne suspected they always had been, like seeds buried in the soil that had only needed a little time and caring to blossom into something beautiful.

Zima took Anne's hand and gave a gentle tug. "We should also depart. I do not wish to be late for our reservation."

The six of them left Doris to her own devices — which would involve the hot tub, Anne suspected — and headed to the garage, where Mark gave Dela a parting kiss.

"Don't do anything I wouldn't do," he said.

Dela grinned. "Thanks. I'll take that as a blank check for a wild evening."

They piled into four separate cars: Charlie and Cappa into one, Mark and Dela each into their own, and Zima and Anne into the last.

Soon Zima was navigating them through the slow river of traffic with angelic patience, Anne beside her, practically vibrating with anticipation.

•   •   •

Instead of driving toward San Francisco, where many fine restaurants were, Anne was surprised when they crossed the Bay Bridge, hooked a left into Berkeley, then skimmed past the university to a strip of colorful, stylized shops. Zima parked in a nearby public lot, fed the meter, then walked them just a block away to what appeared to be a warm country cottage, replete with vine-covered trellis and large, leafless trees.

Anne smiled when she read the large wooden archway over the entrance.

Chez Panisse.

Nearly as famous as Restaurant Gary Danko, it was a Bay Area must-visit for any foodie with an appreciation for fresh ingredients. Their menu changed nightly, the contents depending upon which local farm vegetables were available that day, but each course was a guaranteed gourmet experience of mouthwatering proportions. Chez Panisse was one of many places Anne had always wanted to try, but never could because of the prohibitive cost for a struggling waitress.

Yet here she was — thanks to Zima, once again — about to embark on an epic culinary adventure that neither of them could enjoy.

Oh, the deliciously cruel irony ...

The interior was even more charming. Soft lighting touched gorgeous wooden benches and spacious seats in the modest-sized dining area, slightly smaller than Hal's Diner, giving the impression of a warm, comfortable country inn.

The friendly hostess promptly showed them to their table. They passed servers carrying succulent roasted quail, stuffed squash, and seafood salads presented with such panache that Anne salivated despite their unappetizing smells.

Their hostess motioned them to a table near the back. Anne thought she had made a mistake: the four-person table was currently occupied by an older woman in a nice, but dated, dress. Frizzy hair poofed out into a bushy ponytail. Her round face lit up at their approach.

And that was when Anne screamed.

The restaurant fell quiet. Patrons stared at her like she was insane, but Anne didn't care.

It can't be!

"G-G-Georgette Parker?"

The author of Anne's favorite book series of all time nodded, a remarkably common gesture for a goddess of the pen whose divine fingers should have been radiating holy light.

"And you must be Jennifer." Georgette's voice warbled with age, although her words were strong and sure.

She started to rise, but Anne swept in and knelt by her side to save her the trouble, daring to grasp the paper-thin skin of her wrinkled hand in a warm greeting.

Not warm, Anne remembered too late.

Georgette gasped at the feel of her corpse-cold flesh, but recovered quickly and caught Anne's hand before she could pull it away.

"It's all right, sweetie," Georgette said, her eyes brimming with sympathy. "Your friend Zima told me about your condition. It's nothing to be ashamed of. In fact, that's the reason I came."

For two uncomfortable seconds, Anne thought her idol was referring to vampirism. Her mind raced for a diffusing comment. How did a predatory creature of the night reassure a complete stranger that she wasn't going to eat her? But then she noticed Georgette staring at the auburn down on her head.

Of course ...

"Ah, yes," Anne said. "The chemotherapy treatments have been ... quite a journey. Circulation in my hands is still poor, as you can tell. Otherwise, I'm doing fine."

"Except for your appetite," Zima said.

"Except for that," Anne said with a nervous laugh. "Circulation and appetite. But hey, at least I'm still breathing, right?" Even that simple statement was a lie, and felt like ash on her tongue.

I'm such a freakin' monster.

"Well, you just sit next to me." Georgette moved to the next chair to make room for Anne. "These old bones aren't as warm as they used to be, but what I have left is yours."

Oh, don't say that ...

Fortunately, Anne had learned at least one lesson from last night, and had remembered to eat before leaving the factory. Even so, the innocent remark was a stark reminder that sweet Georgette could easily become dinner if Anne neglected her feeding schedule.

But she hadn't, so Anne sat in the same chair the writing goddess had occupied just a moment before.

"So ... what else did Zima tell you?"

"That you've been a Jayne Madison fan since childhood, something we certainly have in common."

"Childhood?" Anne said. "Really?"

Georgette laughed, a soft, rich sound that brightened the room. "Yes, if you can believe it. I read my first spy novel in grade school, but, back then, they were all centered around men. Women were plot devices, sometimes useful, but more often sidekicks or glorified secretaries. I wanted to sink my teeth into a book where the woman did the butt-kicking, but they just didn't exist.

"That's when I invented Jayne. I wrote short stories, poems, even tried my hand at comics. By the time I graduated college with a literary degree, I had enough background material on Jayne to fill a wheelbarrow. I spent years writing the first novel, polishing it to perfection. My friends thought it was amazing, but publishers wouldn't look at it when they saw a female lead in the query letter."

"But that series is legendary," Anne said. It had won award after award, and basically set the standard for the genre. That someone like Georgette had struggled to get published was inconceivable.

"It is now, but it took many nail-biting years of refusals to get there. I honestly don't know how I would have made it through without my Ed."

Zima head-cocked.

"Ed was my husband — gone seven years this August, bless his soul. He was a lawyer, and a fine one at that. He spoiled me something awful and never asked anything in return." Georgette looked at Zima and Anne with a glint in her eyes. "I see much of him in your blonde friend, Jennifer. She made quite a case to convince me to fly all the way out here for dinner. You're lucky to have someone who cares for you so much."

Don't I know it.

Anne reached across the table and took Zima's hand. She could only imagine how that conversation had gone.

"Georgette," Anne said, "if I may ask: how did you handle Ed's spoiling? It must have been hard for a feminist like you to take handouts."

"It was at first, when we were dating. Ed would buy me things, take me to expensive dinners like this one, and whisk us away on lavish vacations. I asked him to stop because I felt guilty that I couldn't return the favor. I could only tend the house and hole up in the den trying unsuccessfully to spin words into gold."

"I know the feeling," Anne said, glancing at Zima.

"Well, don't you fret. Ed put me in my place — and I don't mean the kitchen. He told me that the reason he went to law school and created a successful business in the first place was so he could spoil the lucky girl he ended up with." Georgette leaned close and put a shaky hand on Anne's knee. "Treating me to life's pleasures made him happy, dear. The kindest way I could repay him was to enjoy every minute of it, and to make sure he knew I was grateful. It was a hard thing to swallow, given my fierce independence, but once I did, things became a lot easier between us."

"He sounds wonderful," Anne said. "And thanks for giving me something to think about."

Georgette put a pair of pearl reading glasses on and frowned at the list of entrees. "You can thank me by translating this menu. It all sounds delicious, but I'll be darned if I know what an *escarole* is."

Anne happily obliged. Once their orders were placed, the conversation naturally shifted to Jayne Madison. Anne was in fan-geek heaven, asking all the ponderous questions she'd bottled up through the years about how or why Jayne acted the way she did. Georgette didn't disappoint. She knew every reference, and answered most of Anne's concerns without missing a beat. They were so engrossed that the waitress had circled twice with the second courses before they'd even lifted their forks to the first.

To her credit, Zima tried a small bite from each plate, commenting more on texture than flavor. Anne couldn't even stomach that. She attempted a single bite from her first entree, which looked too good to pass up, but gagged as soon as it touched her tongue. Anne set her fork down and shuffled the food around her plate, a technique she had mastered as a child when her mother served Brussels sprouts. Georgette smiled at their displays, but kept her opinion to herself, focusing instead on finishing every last morsel from her own dishes between exciting character background tales.

Before Anne knew it, their server was carting away her untouched dessert — a combination of orange, cinnamon, and homemade ice cream she would have killed for as a human — signaling the end of the amazing fantasy dinner. After Zima settled the check, they each received a hug from Georgette, then waited with her by the curb until her ride arrived.

It wasn't until the door opened that Anne realized she hadn't asked for an autograph. If she'd known ahead of time, she would have brought her whole Jayne Madison collection along and begged for a personal signing of each. As it was, she didn't even have a napkin to scribble on.

Zima pressed something into Anne's stomach. Anne looked down to find her prized Book One of the Jayne Madison series.

"You're amazing," Anne said, her voice thick with emotion.

If there was one thing on the planet I'd want signed, it's this.

"Georgette," Anne said just as the old lady was carefully ducking into the car. "I'm so sorry, but can I trouble you for one last favor?"

Georgette took the battered book from her with care, as if it were a newborn child. She ran a light finger over the bent cover and along its frayed edges, studied the darkened stains opposite the spine, where Anne's young, grimy thumbs had held it open time and time again.

"This little fellow has seen more than a few late nights under the covers with a flashlight, I'd guess."

"And in the bathroom," Anne said, counting on her fingers, "and on the school bus, under shady trees at recess, in a flimsy tent on my first and only camping trip, and ..." She gave Zima a warm smile. "Just this morning with someone very, very special."

Georgette fished an elegant, marbled pen from her purse. "Jennifer, it would be a great honor to sign my name on an heirloom as precious as this. I only hope I can do it justice."

The driver paced impatiently while Georgette carefully wrote on the title page, then handed the book back with a tear in her eye. Anne clutched it to her breast. She watched the car drive away until it disappeared, then opened her treasure to see what her idol had written.

Dear Jennifer,

A piece of Jayne Madison lives in each of us, some more than most. I see much of her in you. Thank you for keeping our hero alive.

Georgette Parker

Anne sighed and turned to Zima. "That was amazing, honey. Thank you so much. I can't imagine how I'll ever top that, but I promise I'll try."

Zima shrugged. "It is as Georgette said of her husband: Bringing you pleasure brings me pleasure, and I am content knowing you had an enjoyable evening. Speaking of which, I did not want to interrupt your conversation, but Rose sent a message during dinner. She has made significant progress with her research on Jeram Tosali."

Hearing the mystery vampire's name was like a splash of cold water after coming out of the hot tub.

Back to business, I suppose.

"What did she find?"

"He is most likely a furniture dealer in San Mateo. His store's advertised hours have recently extended to midnight, and he canceled his health insurance policy six days ago."

First a venture capitalist, now a furniture dealer? That definitely didn't sound like Orwing.

"Great, let's gear up and pay him a visit." As much as Anne hoped the encounter would end peacefully, she'd been through enough to know better. She wouldn't risk her life, or Zima's, by going unprepared.

"Our weapons and suitable combat attire are in the trunk of the car." Zima took her hand and led Anne back toward the parking lot. "There is one complication we may wish to discuss. Tosali's business is by appointment only. It is night time, and he is a vampire. There is no guarantee he will be at his store or residence at this hour."

"Let's make an appointment, then. Our bedroom could use a love seat, don't you think? Something crimson." Anne grabbed her phone from her purse. "What's the store's number?"

"That may not be necessary. Rose has just informed me that she also passed the information to the others. Dela has already made an appointment for 10:30 tonight and will meet us at his store."

"Really? Things may get ugly. Is having Dela there a good idea?"

"No, but I estimate our chances of convincing her to stay behind at twelve percent."

"Maybe Mark can talk her out of it?"

"I estimate his chance at less than five." Zima opened the trunk, revealing a pair of military-style duffel bags. "Where do you wish to change?"

"In the back of the car, just like when I was a kid. We can take turns blocking the windows."

Minutes later, they were on the road. Zima was once again in her traditional grays, while Anne wore similar gray pants, shirt, and a loose-fitting jacket. Anne's plasma pistol was a comforting lump in her jacket pocket. Although she was sad to see her dolled-up date disappear, it was also nice to have her familiar, combat-ready girlfriend back.

That's my Zima.

"So, hot stuff," Anne said. "We have an hour to kill. Whatever shall we do?"

"Scout the area. Identify likely ambush points. Establish escape routes and rendezvous locations."

Anne gave a throaty purr. "I love it when you talk dirty. Is everyone else going to meet us there, too?"

She felt more than saw Zima relay Anne's question to the others.

PROBABLY NOT, Charlie replied almost immediately, laced with a grim feeling that made Anne's skin crawl. YOU WON'T BELIEVE WHO JUST ARRIVED AT THE PARTY.

17

OLD TIMES

CHARLIE WATCHED THE PARTYGOERS chatting amiably. The penthouse suite was lavish, but smaller than he'd expected. Windows covered two of the four walls of the twenty-seventh-story room, giving a nice view of the City. People sat on opulent furniture, and gathered around overpriced art. Some milled by the bar in the back corner, eating *hors d'oeuvres* carried by wandering servers.

And everyone, without exception, was dressed not in their finest, but *sharpest* attire. The point of tonight's affair wasn't to make friends or swap frivolous stories, it was to impress their fellow business partners.

Charlie was no different in that regard. His business was the envy of everyone here, having soared from a garage startup to one of the most profitable companies in the world in record time. But their recent production slowdown had upset more than a few business owners.

Many in this room, Charlie thought, seeing familiar faces all around.

Even Morton and Vicky had attended this party. Morton had been marginally more civil than last night at the art show, having said a brief hello on arrival, then had latched onto another unlucky soul, who he regaled with his self-centered stories of financial conquest.

Vicky, on the other hand, had lit up when she saw Charlie shoulder-to-shoulder with someone other than Anne. Cappa had readily admitted their new relationship, to which Vicky had squealed with delight. She'd whisked Cappa away, and been a gossipy fixture by her side ever since.

Which, essentially, had left Charlie dateless.

It's probably just as well.

The nanites required to build Rose's body had required shutting down the majority of Z-Tech's manufacturing units. While Charlie agreed the sacrifice had been worth it to save Cappa's sanity, whose factory self had been bodiless in San Francisco while he and Cappa were away in China, he could hardly explain that to the companies who depended upon Z-Tech for their livelihood.

Retailers and resellers disliked supply shortages of popular product lines. Consumers would only suffer so many price hikes before turning to cheaper — if inferior — alternatives. Even when prices eventually returned to normal, regaining those customers would be difficult.

However, smoothing business relationships had just fallen to the bottom of Charlie's priority list. He glared at the newcomers across the crowded room, and had to consciously relax his grip on his cocktail glass so it wouldn't shatter.

A sharp *crack* from Mark's glass said his friend was faring even worse.

Alvin Orwing strode out of the elevator, smiling as if he owned the place. On his arm was an elegant, if mildly Goth, girl wearing black lipstick, black fingernails, and long black hair tied up into tight buns. A pair of well-dressed, burly men with crew cuts flanked them.

Bodyguards, of course.

Unlike everyone else at the party, whose only company were their respective dates, Alvin traveled in different circles, where personal protection was not only expected, but required.

Charlie caught Mark and Cappa's eyes. Their smoldering gazes said they were thinking the same as him: Bodyguards wouldn't be enough to protect Anne's former kidnapper from them tonight.

On a whim, Charlie switched to thermals, and was shocked to find that, despite their normal appearances, all of Alvin's companions were room temperature, including the Goth.

Not good …

Alvin lit up on seeing Mark and Charlie, smiling as if they were old friends, and not people he had just six years ago sent Zima to assassinate. He guided his Goth escort to them with a grand smile.

"Charles Zed." Alvin shook his hand without waiting for an invitation. "I heard rumor that you and Mark would be here tonight."

"Did you?" Charlie resisted the urge to crush his bones into pulp. "Funny, we only decided this morning that we were going to attend. What else have you heard?"

"Many things." Alvin gave a conspiratorial wink. "Including the recent loss of your waitress love. My deepest condolences."

Alvin sounded almost sincere.

Almost.

"Likewise," Mark said, stepping close. His voice was calm, but his eyes held a dangerous edge. "I read about the explosions in the East Bay. They didn't say to whom the facility belonged, but that was yours, wasn't it? The news reported only a few casualties. Fortunate, considering the magnitude of the explosions. I would have expected *many* more."

Alvin registered only mild surprise at Mark's veiled admission of his involvement. "Yes, it was tragic news for their families. Fortunately for my business, it was only a minor setback." He returned Mark's flinty stare, then looked at Charlie. "A witness claims to have seen a woman on the scene with a remarkable resemblance to your dearly departed waitress, as if she had risen from the ashes. I'm sure there's nothing to it, but it does make you wonder, no?"

"You can't believe everything you hear," Charlie said, but his mind was already churning.

He knows Anne's alive? How?

Several possibilities came to mind. One of Calum's vampire hunters Anne had rescued from the underground complex could have ratted her out — unlikely, considering their gratitude toward her, but not inconceivable if one of them had been captured by Orwing and interrogated.

Unfortunately, there was only one other person who knew for certain Anne was alive.

William.

The idea of Orwing and that sadistic bastard collaborating was the stuff of nightmares, but, Charlie realized with growing dread, the pieces fit. The Goth vampire at Alvin's side hadn't moved a muscle during the entire conversation. Her unblinking eyes studied Charlie with predatory appraisal, observing his movements and behaviors, waiting patiently for the right time to strike. A vampire from Anne's bloodline would have been fidgeting up a storm, as the Sturmans had last night, but the Goth might have been carved from ice.

She must be William's.

Charlie leaned on a nearby table to keep from falling over.

Z-Tech's most bitter and powerful enemies had finally united.

And Alvin isn't even trying to hide it.

The only time Alvin Orwing gave away anything was when he had absolutely nothing to lose. The thought chilled Charlie to the core.

Alvin noticed him staring at the Goth vampire and gave an oily smile. "Where are my manners? Please, allow me to introduce my companions. This lovely lady is Myrcella, a high-ranking executive in a new partner company of ours. The other gentlemen are in my service, both ex-marines, very loyal, but sensitive to violence, if you understand my meaning."

Charlie did. Unlike Myrcella, the other vampires were in constant motion, fidgety, shifting. If they weren't Anne's bloodline, Charlie would eat his socks.

Which means Alvin didn't lose all of his blood samples when his mercenary troop burned to ashes. Are the Sturmans his creation, too?

Charlie suddenly wished he were back at the factory. It had more defenses than a battleship, but it also had Almos. Alvin's appearance and admission meant he was planning something, and that plan was probably already in motion. If he or William got their hands on Almos, the situation could go from bad to doomsday in the span of a heartbeat.

WE SHOULD GO, Charlie sent to Cappa and Mark.

SOON, Mark replied. LET'S GET ALL THE INFO WE CAN OUT OF THIS WEASEL FIRST, BEFORE HE GOES BACK INTO HIDING.

BESIDES, Cappa sent, I'VE ALREADY FILLED ROSE AND ZIMA IN. THE FACTORY'S DEFENSES ARE PRIMED AND READY. I DARE THEM TO TRY ANYTHING.

Careful what you wish for.

But they were right. Opportunities like this were extremely rare. Charlie would be a fool to throw it away without investing at least a few minutes into information gathering.

Charlie swallowed his paranoia and forced his voice to remain steady. "That reminds me, Alvin ... I ran into a few others in your service at a party last night."

Alvin blinked. His poker face slipped into moderate surprise.

"Ron and Betsy?" Charlie said. "Nice couple, polite as can be."

Alvin looked at Myrcella, who shrugged.

"Are you sure they were mine?" Alvin said.

Not anymore, thanks.

Right now, Anne, Zima, and Dela were on their way to what may be a trap, but the odds of that had just dropped considerably, since it appeared neither William nor Orwing were involved.

It's still a mystery and a risk, but at least Zima's there if the Tosali situation turns hostile.

For all the trouble Zima had caused them over the years, she was worth her weight in platinum during a fight. Even accounting for the accident at his homecoming, when Zima had shot her, there was no one Charlie trusted more with Anne's safety — including himself.

"My mistake," Charlie lied. "They may have said they worked for Torwing, which makes sense now that I think about it. Torwing is a book company, and they were both authors."

"How is Nick doing?" Mark said, his eyes still dangerous. "He was bored enough at the last affair that he ran off with my girl. I expected more decorum from Orwing's future president."

The veins in Alvin's forehead throbbed. "My son has decided the family business is not for him. He resigned last month. I haven't heard from him since."

"Sounds rough, I'm sorry to hear that," Mark said, although he clearly wasn't.

Alvin shrugged it off, but snatched a wine glass from a passing tray and downed it in a single gulp. "He didn't have the stomach for it anyway. The ungrateful shit cashed his shares and probably started a sex toy factory or some nonsense."

Myrcella smirked, the first expression she'd shown since they arrived. Alvin set his empty glass down and grabbed another.

Mark took a swig of his own drink, looking angry enough to chew through the glass. "What's your business here tonight?"

Alvin's haughty grin returned. "Well, if you must know —"

"Alvin!" Morton swept in with a smile and clapped a friendly hand on his shoulder. "So glad you could come."

Charlie groaned. *Of course. Two peas in a pod.*

"Good to see you again, Morty," Alvin said.

Mark choked on his drink. "You two *know* each other?"

"Never very quick on the draw, were you, Suther?" Alvin said with a sneer.

You've obviously never seen him shoot, Charlie thought, wishing Mark would give him a personal demonstration here and now.

Morton chuckled. "Salton Enterprises terminated relations with Z-Tech for a reason, Al. I'm just glad there's finally someone we can count on for reliable shipments of quality product."

"Product?" Charlie frowned.

Either Morton has gone completely over to the dark side and is buying weapons, or ...

"You know, product," Alvin said, looking down his pinched nose. "Those things you stopped shipping, which has left your fine retailers in the lurch. I have to say, your timing was impeccable. We were just putting the final touches on our own computer component product line when I heard news that Z-Tech was in a bind. Who am I to pass on such an opportunity? So I made a few calls, hopped a red-eye, and here I am."

"Thank goodness," Mark said, dripping with sarcasm. A message from him came shortly after.

THEY WERE MEANT FOR EACH OTHER.

YOU SAID IT, Charlie replied. ANY GUESSES ON WHO BACKSTABS THE OTHER FIRST?

MORTY'S VICIOUS, BUT ALVIN HAS MORE PRACTICE. MY MONEY IS ON ORWING.

SAFE BET. He and Mark each stifled a laugh, which clearly annoyed the others.

LET'S SHAKE THINGS UP A LITTLE, Cappa sent, laden with mirth.

Seconds later, she joined their small gathering with Vicky in tow.

"Charlie, Mark," Cappa said with a radiant smile, "are you going to introduce us to your friends?"

Charlie did so with as much courtesy as he could muster — which was very little.

"Ah, so you're the flavor of the month," Alvin said to Cappa, as if it were a compliment.

Charlie tensed, ready to throw the bastard through the window, but Vicky saved him the trouble.

"Alvin, was it?" Vicky's voice was cold. "Is this your first time at a party?"

"Of course not," he said tersely.

"Based on your complete social ineptitude, I would never have guessed."

Alvin stammered something, but Vicky talked right over him.

"Both Cappa and Charlie are dear friends of mine. Apart from their recent troubles, Z-Tech has an unblemished reputation for quality merchandise and timely delivery, mostly thanks to this lady here." She put a hand on Cappa's shoulder, who beamed down at the shorter man.

Morton sighed. "Victoria —"

"Zip it, Morton! I'm not finished." She turned back to Alvin and continued in a frigid tone. "Unlike you, I've known almost everyone in this room for years. Believe me when I say they represent eighty-percent of the commercial wealth in the Bay Area."

Vicky leaned closer to him.

"One word from me and I *guarantee* you won't get a return phone call from any of them — including my husband. That wouldn't be a great start to your new business venture, now, would it?"

Alvin turned beet-red, but remained silent.

Cappa beamed as if she was having the time of her life. "Isn't she a kick? Tell you what, Al. I'll give you a chance to redeem yourself before Vicky proves that her ability to destroy your reputation isn't just bluster." She extended her hand to Alvin in a lady-like fashion. "Hello, I'm Cappa, Chief Operations Officer at Z-Tech. And you are ...?"

He stared at her hand as if it were a rotten vegetable. For a tense moment, Charlie thought he would refuse the generous chance Cappa had given him at social redemption. Alvin wasn't known for his tact or forgiveness; he was a ruthless businessman and a shrewd negotiator who ate foreign diplomats for breakfast, and reduced experienced generals to gibbering idiots.

But he was no fool, either, and apparently recognized an untenable situation when he saw one. This wasn't a summit of military powers where displays of might won the day; it was a social gathering where manners were the weapons of choice — and, so far, Alvin had wielded his with the grace of a tree trunk. Charlie would have loved to watch him blow his only chance, but, for the first time he could recall, Alvin swallowed his pride like a bitter pill, put on a smile, and accepted her hand.

"Alvin Orwing, at your service," he said to Cappa in a strained voice. "It's a pleasure to meet such a beautiful and competent woman. Charles is a lucky man."

"Much, *much* better." Vicky's pleasant smile returned. "Now, if you'll excuse us, there's someone else I'm dying to introduce Cappa to. Toodles!"

Once they were gone, Morton turned to Alvin with a grave expression. "Al, I'm sorry about that. Vicky can be dramatic."

"No, I had that coming," Alvin said, though his eyes shot daggers at Vicky's back, giving Charlie the uneasy feeling that he wouldn't let his public humiliation go unpunished. "Let's forget about it. Mr. Zed and I are done anyway. Why don't you introduce me to your other friends?"

"Of course."

Morton started to lead Alvin away, but the smaller man gestured for him to go ahead.

"I'll catch up with you in a minute."

When Morton was out of earshot, Alvin turned on Charlie and Mark with an almost pleasant expression.

"Enjoy this little victory," Alvin said quietly. "Your time is coming, and soon."

"Now where have I heard that before?" Mark crossed his arms and stepped forward, an intimidating tower of muscle that Charlie was happy to be on the right side of. "Don't make threats you've already proven you can't carry out."

Alvin raised his hands in supplication and stepped back. "You misunderstand. The threat doesn't come from me." He glanced at Myrcella. An oily smile touched his lips. "I can offer a warning, though, out of respect for our mutual history in … other enterprises." Alvin moved close and whispered solemnly, "Keep a close eye on the news." He gave Mark's arm a condescending pat, then left to join Morton, who was chatting with two other couples near the piano.

But Myrcella stayed, watching Charlie and Mark with a predatory stare.

"Buy you a drink?" Mark said.

"Sure," Myrcella said with a contemptuous glare. "I like oh-positive, but I'll settle for whatever shit is running through those thick veins of yours."

So much for the pretense of being human.

Charlie crossed his arms, mimicking Mark's intimidating pose. "So you're here to kill us?"

Myrcella smiled, an unabashed display of her sharp canines. "I have a message from William."

"Please tell me it's a strip-o-gram," Mark said. "I'm dying to know if your hair is naturally that black."

Myrcella flipped her middle finger. "Fuck. You."

"She's William's, all right," Charlie said. "I can't wait to hear the actual message."

"That *was* the message, dickhead. *Sayonara.*"

Charlie had only started to ponder her vulgar, but unsurprising, remark when a suspicious glint through the window caught his eye, coming from the rooftop of the neighboring building. Cappa immediately applied a range of image enhancements, adjusting contrasts, enhancing edges, and adding non-visible wavelengths from the spectrum, such as ultraviolet and infrared, which were useful for defeating camouflage.

Milliseconds later, Charlie saw every detail as if it were broad daylight, along with many details most people would never see.

Someone with no heat signature was hunkering behind the lip of the opposite roof, wearing full combat armor, and looking right at Mark …

… through the scope of a .50 caliber sniper rifle.

Shit!

Charlie shoved his friend aside with all his might.

The window shattered. At the same time, a projectile punched through Charlie's ribs, staggering him backward.

Damage reports scrolled across his vision: severe external tissue damage; left lung perforated; no exit wound.

Nothing serious.

But that was just luck, and he knew it. William had finally taken off the kid gloves and become serious about killing them. .50 caliber rounds were powerful enough to pierce his armor plating and do significant damage, as had just been demonstrated. The next shot could hit something critical — or kill Mark outright.

Charlie would *not* give the sniper that opportunity.

He pulled a semi-automatic pistol from his jacket and aimed through the space where the window glass had been. Cappa assisted by outlining the sniper in red, highlighting potential weak points in his armor. A virtual line appeared that only Charlie could see, similar to a targeting laser, extending from his gun barrel. Cappa automatically adjusted the targeting line for factors such as bullet drop, crosswind, and target motion, removing the guesswork. All Charlie had to do was decide what to hit.

Which, in this case, was the sniper's exposed left eye. Charlie locked on target.

His arm snapped into position. With a vampire's trademark reflexes, the sniper reacted instantly and tried to roll out of the way. Charlie's arm moved of its own accord, sighting the predicted position of the vampire's eye at the end of his roll. He pulled the trigger.

A spray of red confirmed the silver-laced bullet had struck home.

All this had happened while Mark was still flying through the air from Charlie's life-saving shove. He struck the far wall, shook his head, and glanced around to get his bearings.

Myrcella leaped at Charlie with a snarl, fangs bared and fingers clawed like a creature from Hell.

She was damned fast. Charlie swung his pistol around, intent on ending this quickly with a silver bullet to her chest, but Myrcella was already on top of him. She wrenched the gun from his grip with a strength far greater than he had come to expect from his sparring sessions with Anne, then hurled it through the open window.

So much for that.

Behind her, Mark whipped his pistol out. Myrcella jerked aside just in time to avoid a shot through her heart, leaving her off-balance. Charlie dropped into a powerful sweep that took the legs out from under her. Myrcella landed hard on her back. Mark lined up another shot, but it hit only floor. She kicked her legs right before the shot fired, lurching her into an instant stand.

Charlie drove his fist into her chest before she made it upright. Her sternum cracked under his knuckles. The momentum drove her down and pounded her back onto the floor. Before she could even scream, Charlie extended the silver-plated blade from between his knuckles. It punched through her chest like a nail gun, staking her to the spot.

Myrcella screamed, if briefly. Silver paralysis quickly silenced her and stopped her writhing.

Charlie yanked the blade free before she died of poisoning, then retracted it back into its housing in his forearm. High voltage electrodes sizzled the blade's surface clean on the way in to prevent infection of his synthetic tissue, as had happened after his very first vampire encounter.

Suddenly remembering there were other vampires in the room, Charlie spun to find Alvin's crew-cut bodyguards standing in a corner with their backs to the wall, pistols out, with a cowering Alvin safely behind them.

Figures.

Unless he was a better actor than Charlie gave him credit for, Alvin was genuinely scared, which meant he hadn't been expecting the attack tonight. His bodyguards were on the defensive. As long as Charlie, Mark, and Cappa didn't present themselves as direct threats, they would stay out of the fight.

Good enough for now.

Everyone else was hiding behind whatever furniture they could find. Cappa crouched protectively in front of Vicky, and winked at Charlie when he looked over. He returned it with a half-smile.

"Let's evacuate the guests," Mark said. "More hostiles may be on the way."

"Count on it," Charlie said. "Myrcella was freakishly strong, even for a vampire, and Alvin referred to her as a high-ranking executive. She must be one of William's Firsts."

"Which means there are probably dozens of angry lackeys headed this way right now to rescue their sire." Mark rubbed his eyes. "Let's get Myrcella out of here first. She might draw the vampires away so the guests can get to safety."

Distant yells from the stairwell sent a chill down Charlie's spine.

The vampires were coming.

Charlie scooped up Myrcella's limp body and cradled her like a sleeping child. "Guard the stairwell door," he said to Mark and Cappa, "just in case they can't sense her location while she's unconscious."

"At this distance, they can," Alvin said from his hiding spot.

That sick bastard would know.

"Good. You guys can handle things here. I'll meet you back at the factory as soon as I can."

Without waiting for a reply, Charlie clutched Myrcella to him, took three running steps, and leaped out through the twenty-seventh-story window.

18

A GRAND EXIT

CAPPA WAS STILL CROUCHING next to Vicky and the other partygoers when Charlie jumped out of the penthouse window with Myrcella. Through the eyes of her Charlie self, Cappa stared down at the two-hundred-and-sixty-foot gap between him and the ground. Total fall time, accounting for wind resistance and Charlie's mass, would be four point zero seven seconds. They would strike the ground at eighty-four miles per hour, which was fast, but far from terminal velocity.

All Cappa had to do was calculate the optimal landing posture to prevent Charlie's body from shattering against the sidewalk and turning Myrcella into a bug splat.

No pressure, no pressure. Just my boyfriend's life at stake ...

Wind whipped through Charlie's hair in a building gale, stinging his eyes, and filling his ears with a deafening roar.

Almost there, Cappa thought. *One more simulation ought to do it.*

They whooshed past the fourth story. The sidewalk loomed large, every crack and pebble now visible.

Okay, carry the one, and ... done!

Cappa's Charlie self overrode his motor controls and executed the simulation.

With only twenty-two feet remaining, Charlie tossed Myrcella up with all his cybernetic might, reducing her velocity to a mere two feet per second, but increasing his own velocity. Power routed to his legs with a loud hum. His knees bent slightly. Charlie leaned forward, arms outstretched, and met the waiting sidewalk.

His impact echoed from the surrounding buildings like a canon shot. Concrete shattered beneath is feet, leaving two Charlie-sized depressions. As Cappa's simulation predicted, the extra power to his legs, combined with his posture, absorbed seventy-three percent of the kinetic energy from the fall. He transferred the rest of the energy into a forward roll, followed by splaying his limbs in all directions to distribute the force across his entire body, leaving him flat on the sidewalk.

But only for a moment. The second part of Cappa's simulation made him spring up and catch Myrcella before she hit the ground. She landed in his arms like a rag doll, unconscious, but otherwise uninjured.

Except for the gaping blade wound in her chest, of course.

Simulation completed, Cappa released control of Charlie's body, putting his neural matter back in direct command. He wasted no time and bolted down the street as fast as his powerful legs would carry him.

Damage reports rolled in, which she displayed to him as they arrived: a hairline fracture in his right leg; his left kneecap dislocated; severe tissue damage on both feet and his right elbow. Charlie dismissed each, but didn't slow down.

Someone clamped Cappa's arm in a death grip — *Cappa's* arm, not Charlie's.

Her focus snapped back to the party. Fearing one of Alvin's goons was attacking, Cappa gripped the hand attached to her and twisted around, ready to shoulder-throw him into the glass shelves on the wall.

Vicky screamed, halting Cappa in mid-throw. It wasn't one of Alvin's goons.

"Sorry," Cappa said, releasing her new friend.

Vicky nodded, looking understandably frazzled. Her ex-fiancée had just shrugged off a sniper shot, skewered a vampire with a blade from between his knuckles, then jumped out of a twenty-seventh-story window.

People around the room were starting to recover from the shock of witnessing what must have looked like a suicide jump. They rushed to the broken window in their high heels and fancy shoes, clinging to each other for support. A few hung back, crying or muttering, but most of them cautiously peered down to glimpse Charlie and Myrcella's fate.

They'll see only an empty, broken sidewalk.

Vicky touched Cappa's arm. Tears brimmed her eyes. "Cappa," she said hoarsely. "W-what's going on? Why would Charlie j—"

"I think it worked," Mark called from within the stairwell, buying Cappa a brief reprieve from the explanation she was dreading. "The vampires are heading back down."

Cappa hurried to the window with Vicky close behind. A stream of figures far below were running after Charlie with inhuman speed. They swarmed over cars and other obstacles like a hoard of terrifying, undead rats.

Oh, this is just wonderful, Cappa thought dismally.

Everyone had camera phones these days. Someone would inevitably catch Charlie barreling down the street on video — and if not him, then the hoard of vampires chasing him. In an hour, the internet would be buzzing with rumors. By tomorrow, conspiracy theorists would be stirring every pot they could get their greasy hands in. Mainstream media would have a field day playing the best clips over and over, and interviewing eyewitnesses.

For better or worse, tonight was a tipping point. The public would finally be made aware of the vampire threat that, until now, had been a silent plague affecting only those unfortunate enough to be caught in a dark alley at the wrong time.

Z-Tech would no longer be alone in their silent war. The idea was both frightening and liberating.

"Cappa," Vicky said in a trembling voice. "Please tell me what's going on. Who was that fanged woman? And how could Charlie ..." She bit her lip, unable to finish the sentence.

Mark caught Cappa's gaze.

No messages nor silent communication passed between them, yet they nodded at the same time. Mark had come to the same inevitable conclusion as her: There were too many witnesses tonight — too many incredible things that defied explanation.

Z-Tech could no longer protect its greatest secrets. It was time to come clean.

"Charlie is fine," Cappa said to Vicky, loud enough to be heard by everyone. "It takes more than a twenty-seven story fall to kill him. And as for Myrcella, she's a … a vampire."

Cappa glanced at Alvin to gauge his reaction. Orwing had just as much skin in this game as Z-Tech, even if they were playing for different teams. Alvin seemed more curious about how Cappa was going to handle the situation than concerned about word of the vampire plague getting out. More importantly, his bodyguards kept their weapons in check.

Cappa blew a sigh of relief. The last thing she needed was Orwing attempting to cover this up by killing the witnesses.

Which certainly wouldn't be the first time.

"Myrcella is the real deal," Cappa said. "Not like the wannabe Goths in documentaries who wear makeup and surgically replace their canines with false fangs. She and her kind hunt people at night, live off human blood, have superhuman strength and speed, and can infect others by making them drink their blood. They're the most ferocious predators humanity has ever faced, including itself. And the threat is growing exponentially every day."

"And Charlie?" Alvin said. "How do you explain him?"

The glint in his eyes was telling. He'd known Charlie wasn't human even before tonight's show, Cappa wagered. Whether through his partnership with William, or from his failed assassination attempt six years ago by Zima — part of the cyborg Deadiron back then — was impossible to guess, but it didn't matter.

Alvin wanted to watch Z-Tech sweat.

He wants us to see if the news breaks our business reputation, then he'll sweep in to collect Z-Tech's ex-customers.

Cappa gulped, feeling almost as nervous as she had on the riverbank with Charlie, when she'd struggled to confess her feelings.

Mark stepped forward, saving her from an uncomfortable speech. He directed his answer to Vicky instead of Alvin, but projected his voice for everyone to hear.

"He's the same Charlie you dated all those years ago," Mark said. "But … you know how he likes to tinker, Vick. What you saw back there is his ultimate toy: a mechanical body that his mind can ride around in, like a Sherman tank for his consciousness."

Vicky's mouth fell open. "He calls that a *toy?*"

Mark shrugged. "It's come in handy, I'll admit, but yes. Charlie wanted to do what no one has done before, and he succeeded. Just imagine what he'll come up with tomorrow."

Cappa glanced at the wonder-filled faces around the room.

Mark's a goddamned genius.

In a few, easy sentences, he had dismissed Z-Tech's most sensitive secret as if it were his son's science fair project.

Even better, by downplaying what many would consider the achievement of the century as commonplace, Mark had put Charlie on a scientific pedestal high enough to touch the heavens. Many of Z-Tech's customers here tonight had been upset about the production halt, and had told Cappa as much. Even those, she could see, held newfound respect and admiration for Z-Tech's genius leader.

No wonder Charlie trusted Mark with negotiations for so long.

Mark put a hand on Cappa's shoulder. "I'm going to scout the stairwell to see if it's safe to start moving everyone downstairs. Are you okay here?"

She glanced at Alvin's brutes, one of whom was whispering in his ear. It was too low for Cappa to hear, even with her enhanced audio processors, but whatever he said surprised Alvin. His surprise melted into an oily smile.

I really hate that creep.

"Go ahead," Cappa said. "I'll keep an eye on things."

Mark was staring at Alvin, however, which made Cappa nervous. She had seen that look on his face before: eyes intent, jaw clenched, hands by his sides, rock-still, but ready to move in an instant. He was about to kill someone.

And Alvin was the unlucky winner.

Don't, Cappa sent to him. Not here. There are too many witnesses.

His gaze lingered on Alvin for a second longer, then he relaxed. *Thank God.*

We'll get that son-of-a-bitch later, Cappa sent.

I know. Mark tore his eyes from his target and disappeared down the stairs.

Alvin sauntered over to Cappa with an uncharacteristic spring in his step, but his hawkish eyes brushed past her.

"Victoria ..." His voice held far too much glee, considering the circumstances. "Did you and Morton drive here tonight?"

Vicky's jaw tightened, but Morton swept in and answered for her.

"We took a cab, Al. Why?"

"I'd like to offer you a ride in something safer than a yellow car squealing through traffic. Armored transportation, complete with a security escort."

The stairway is clear, Mark sent. Send them down. I've called for a fleet of cars.

On it.

Cappa moved to the middle of the room and waved her arms. "Everyone! It's safe to go downstairs. I would avoid the elevator, if I were you. Mark has arranged for transportation, and will keep the ground level secure until everyone's away."

Conversation picked up in busy tones. Guests muttered about the evening's events and discussed carpool options. Cappa waited patiently until everyone had filed through the door. Vicky, Morton, Alvin, and his bodyguards were last to leave. Instead of going down the stairs, however, Alvin motioned for Vicky and Morton to follow him up.

"Cars are that way," Cappa said, pointing down.

Alvin flashed a perfectly pleasant smile that, for some reason, made her skin crawl. "Thank you for that incredible tidbit, but helicopters are much easier to land on rooftops than city streets."

Vicky brightened. "A helicopter?"

"Yes. With a hoard of vampires chasing that tin man through the streets, traffic must be dreadful, and I for one would like this night to be over as quickly as possible. You may both stay with me tonight, if you wish. I've booked an entire hotel floor, and have several suites to spare."

Vicky looked at Morton with hopeful eyes, who shrugged.

"We're in!" she said.

Alvin motioned them ahead. Morton climbed the stairs first, followed by Vicky, who squealed with girlish delight. Alvin's smile faltered when she passed, replaced with the same look of vengeance Cappa had seen when Vicky had threatened him earlier. His pleasant façade returned when he faced Cappa.

"Have a safe trip."

"Wait!" Cappa hustled up the few steps between them and flashed a winning smile. "Got room for one more? I've never flown in a helicopter before."

He nodded graciously. "Of course. After you, my dear."

That was easy.

Cappa quickly relayed the change in plans to Mark, Charlie, Zima, Rose, and Anne, then hurried to catch up to Vicky.

Even while tearing through the streets, carrying an unconscious vampire, and with an angry hoard on his heels, Charlie managed to reply. ARE YOU NUTS?

ALVIN HAS IT IN FOR VICKY, Cappa sent. I'M SURE OF IT. I'LL HOP A RIDE WITH THEM TO THE HOTEL TO MAKE SURE SHE'S SAFE. HOPEFULLY I CAN CONVINCE HER TO GO HOME FROM THERE.

PLEASE BE CAREFUL, Charlie sent, laced with concern. MORE OF ALVIN'S VAMPIRE HENCHMEN MAY BE AT THE HOTEL.

I'LL RETURN TO THE FACTORY AS SOON AS I CAN. DAD.

Cappa snickered at her own joke. Vicky turned with raised eyebrows, but Cappa waved her off.

No way I'm explaining that one to her.

Cold air rushed down from an open door at the top of the stairwell.

Cappa followed Vicky outside and surveyed the enormous roof, large enough for six comfortably spaced houses, complete with front lawn and a swing in the backyard. A classic "H" platform sat in the middle, clear of any wires or towers to allow safe helicopter landing.

The steady beat of chopper blades sounded in the distance, cutting their way through the night sky.

Cappa switched to enhanced night vision. Not one, but *two* choppers were approaching from the southwest, skimming the coast along the ocean.

Two, huh?

Alvin had mentioned an armed escort. They would be carrying troops — probably vampires with assault rifles. Depending upon the number of soldiers, two choppers would be necessary to carry away all six passengers waiting on the roof.

The math worked, but did nothing to ease Cappa's concerns.

Maybe this wasn't such a good idea after all …

Vicky didn't seem to share her worry. Her eyes widened with delight when the choppers became visible to human eyes.

Cappa glanced around at the others. Morton stood next to Vicky, straining to spot the two approaching aircraft in the dim light. Alvin rocked on his heels, immensely pleased with himself for some reason.

But it was his bodyguards, standing by the roof exit, that bothered Cappa.

They were facing the wrong way.

If they had really been concerned about protecting Alvin, they would be watching the stairwell in case the enemy made a return appearance. Instead, they stood shoulder-to-shoulder, facing out, blocking the door from view.

Like they're trying to keep us from leaving.

Cappa glanced at the helicopters. At current speed, they would arrive in just over five minutes.

She was nowhere near as martially competent as Zima, nor had any practical experience fighting vampires. That said, Cappa had been practicing martial arts with Charlie and Mark for her entire life. Her body was just as strong and sturdy as Zima's, which was more than a match for a normal vampire in single combat. She could probably handle the two bodyguards, if it came to a fight.

But a chopper full of vampire soldiers was another matter. Any chance Cappa had of escaping with Vicky and Morton would vanish when they arrived.

If she was going to act, she had to act now.

And there's an easy way to find out if I should.

"Oh, silly me," Cappa said, walking toward the stairway. "I left my wallet downstairs on the bar. I'll just pop down and grab it. Back in a flash."

The bodyguards didn't budge.

"No need to worry," Alvin said with a dismissive shrug. "I'll cover expenses tonight. It will be my pleasure."

Alvin "Tight-Ass" Orwing treating someone else? Now I know he's up to something.

After brief consideration, Cappa concluded that she had three choices.

First, she could go with the flow and wait for the choppers — which she suspected would end badly.

Second, she could insist on going downstairs to see how adamant Alvin was about keeping her on the roof — a bold plan that would confirm her assumptions, but would also make Alvin more suspicious.

Or third, Cappa could go with her gut and act while she had the element of surprise, and while the choppers were still out of firing range.

One look at Alvin's nauseating, self-satisfied, haughty smile was enough to settle Cappa on option number three.

She gathered her *chi,* as she had practiced with Master Wung. The vampires in front of her took no notice.

Cappa's first strike was smooth — a lazy push to one of the vampires that he didn't even bother to block. But her *chi* propelled him with the force of a moving truck. With a scream, he flew thirty feet sideways and off the roof.

The other bodyguard fired two rounds into Cappa's back before she could even turn around. The rounds pierced her synthetic flesh, but weren't powerful enough to pierce her armor plating, so Cappa closed in for another palm strike. He nimbly danced out of the way and fired three more shots into her chest, splattering her dress with red liquid.

There goes another outfit. Jackrabbit son-of-a-bitch ...

Unlike Charlie, Cappa had no built-in weapons, nor did she carry a gun, which limited her options. She was stronger than her burly adversary, of that she was certain. But she was also denser, which made her less agile, and she didn't have Zima's supercharged capacitors or absurdly optimized tactical processors to make up the difference.

She did, however, have Master Wung's teachings.

When the vampire made his next step, Cappa pushed her *chi* at his foot, which caused it to land at an odd angle. He stumbled sideways, pistol flailing while he tried to catch his balance.

It was all the advantage Cappa needed. She dashed the last few steps and palm-struck his chest, throwing her considerable life force along with it. The blow lifted the vampire from his feet with a sickening crack of bone. He sailed over the edge of the roof to join his companion far below.

Sadly, they both probably survived the fall, but hopefully they won't be in any condition to cause a problem for Mark.

A terrified scream made Cappa spin around. Alvin stood behind Vicky, holding her by a fistful of hair, a gun pressed to her head.

"Let her go," Cappa said, looking as menacing as she could in a revealing sequined cocktail dress. The bloodstains on her chest probably helped. "I'll take Vicky and Morton downstairs, then you can fly away to wherever you want."

Alvin's hawk-eyes glinted. He grinned maliciously. "Not a chance."

Unbelievable!

"I won't let you take her," Cappa said. "Even if I have to tear those helicopters apart with my bare hands. Is your bruised ego really worth all this?"

Alvin's grin widened. "You think I give two shits what a conceited bitch like Victoria says to me in front of her groupies? No, my dear girl, she was just bait for the true prize: *you.*"

Cappa blinked.

Me? But how could he have known … She resisted the urge to face-palm. *His vampires, of course.*

Although Cappa appeared normal to other humans, vampires had much sharper senses. Anne often mentioned she could tell who was coming down the hall by the hum of their power reactors. She also commented on Zima and Charlie's unique scents.

Once his bodyguards figured out what Charlie was, they probably picked up the same signs from me.

It was easy to imagine why Alvin would want Cappa. His cybernetics program had been floundering for over a decade. Deadiron had disappeared in a failed assault on Z-Tech, and Zima with him, then more recently Zane. Alvin wasn't creating a vampire army just to get a leg up on the competition; he was making a last, desperate move to stay relevant in the mercenary arms market.

But Cappa and Charlie presented new hope for his cybernetics program. He would feed both of them to his scientist sharks, given the chance, where they would be stripped down to their nuts and bolts to form the basis for his new line of cybernetic killing machines.

Over my dead fucking body.

Cappa glanced at the incoming helicopters.

Three minutes until they're within weapons range, give or take.

Time was running out.

"Here's what's going to happen," Alvin said to Cappa. "The first helicopter will land, and you're going to board like a good little girl. I'll be watching from the second helicopter with my friend here. If you so much as *breathe* on one of my soldiers, Victoria's head will have an extra hole. Are we clear?"

Cappa remained silent, her thoughts a raging torrent. She would never submit to being a lab rat ...

... but neither could she let Vicky die.

There has to be some way out of —

Alvin extended his arm and fired. Morton had just enough time to look shocked before blood trickled from the hole in his forehead. He crumpled into a twitching heap.

Vicky screamed an agonized wail. She lurched for her fallen husband, but Alvin yanked her back by the hair.

"*Are we clear?*" Alvin shouted.

Cappa clenched her fists, fighting her tears over Vicky's loss.

"No," Cappa growled through clenched teeth. She took a menacing step forward.

Alvin's eyes widened. He pressed the gun to Vicky's head, causing her to cry in pain. "I will fucking shoot her!"

"Then there will be nothing to stop me from tearing out your rotten heart."

Cappa stepped closer, watching him carefully. Alvin's gun hand shook. His other hand supported his hostage, who was trying to curl into a ball.

Step.

"S-stay back!" Alvin's voice pitched into a frightened squeal.

Cappa shook her head, slow and deliberate. "You tried to assassinate Mark and Charlie."

Step.

"You killed Morton without a second thought."

Step.

"You'll kill Vicky, too, once I'm under your control. Maybe in front of me, just to make an example."

Step.

"At least this way, I'll have the satisfaction of knowing she didn't die in vain."

Step.

Sweat beaded Alvin's brow over saucer-like eyes. His head whipped frantically about the rooftop, searching for escape like a cornered animal. But the only exits were the door they had come in through, or over the edge of the building. He glanced at the helicopters, which were close enough now to make out details.

They might as well have been a world away. Cappa was nearly in arm's reach.

One more step ...

Cappa saw what she'd been waiting for: Alvin's spirit lurched an instant before he pulled the trigger, but that was all the warning she needed. Cappa gathered her *chi,* but instead of protecting her own body, she projected every ounce of her life force out in front of her, between the gun and Vicky's head.

The muzzle belched fire. The flash fanned out but didn't touch Vicky, as if it had hit an invisible barrier.

Vicky cried out and fell to the ground, followed closely by a screaming Alvin. His gun clattered to the roof. He landed next to her, blood oozing between fingers pressed to his jaw. More blood leaked from behind his ear.

Cappa grabbed the gun, then bent to examine Vicky. Not a single hair on her head had been singed by the muzzle flash.

I guess that worked.

It was a pleasant surprise. Deflecting nails hammered by Brother Gang was one thing, but projectiles fired at point blank were quite another. At best, Cappa had hoped to slow the bullet so it wouldn't have enough energy to pierce Vicky's skull. Instead, it had been reflected with enough force to punch through Alvin's jaw and exit the other side.

Total bonus.

Cappa helped Vicky to her feet, who was sobbing over her fallen husband. She tightened her grip on Alvin's pistol.

Ninety seconds until the helicopters arrive. Sixty seconds until they're in firing range.

She didn't want to be around for either of those events. Cappa had spotted mounted guns on the sides of the choppers, which would most definitely pierce her armor plating. The soldiers' assault weapons might be able to as well.

They probably have rocket launchers, with my luck.

Cappa stood over Alvin, who lay writhing on the ground, and lined the sights up with his head.

One shot. That was all it would take to end him: the man who, years ago, had attempted to kill Mark and Charlie. Who was responsible for Anne's captivity. Then, tonight, who had tried to take Cappa away from her loved ones forever.

Like William, Alvin was a blight on the world. Pulling the trigger would be a gift to everyone.

Fifty seconds until they're in firing range.

Her hand was steady, her aim true. Cappa wouldn't miss. All she had to do was squeeze.

Forty seconds.

"What are you waiting for?" Vicky growled, her face contorted in rage. "Shoot him!"

Cappa gulped. "I ... I've never killed anyone before."

"Give me that!"

Cappa didn't resist when Vicky snatched the gun, gripped it in two white-knuckled fists, and pointed it at Alvin.

Thirty seconds. We've got to get out of here ...

"You heartless son-of-a-bitch!" Vicky screamed at him, fresh tears running down her cheeks. "Morton was on your side. He was your partner, and you murdered him for no fucking reason!" She spat in his hair. Saliva dripped onto his neck, mixing with the blood trickling from his exit wound. "You took him away from me," she whimpered.

Twenty seconds.

"Vick, let's go," Cappa said. "Those helicopters are gunships. We can't be here when they get within firing range."

Vicky's arms shook. Her finger squeezed the trigger, slowly, slowly, teeth grinding loud enough that Cappa heard them over the sound of the approaching choppers. The veins in her neck and forehead throbbed beneath her reddened skin.

Ten seconds.

Cappa tugged her sleeve. "Vick ..."

The recent widow lifted her gun, then kicked Alvin in the head with a frustrated scream. "The world will hear about this, Alvin Orwing! You have my fucking guarantee!"

"To the stairs," Cappa said. "Hurry! I'll grab Morton and will be right behind you."

Once they were both safely in the stairwell, Vicky said over her shoulder, "Tell me, why aren't we taking that bastard as a hostage?"

"For the opposite reason Charlie ran off with Myrcella," Cappa said, shifting Morton's corpse on her back. "We want them to fly off with their wounded boss, not chase us through the streets with assault weapons."

"Who says they won't do that anyway?"

"No one. Keep running."

Cappa listened carefully for sounds of pursuit during their descent. The rooftop door opened and closed once, but the only footsteps she heard were their own. By the time they reached the fifteenth floor, Vicky had slowed considerably, and was breathing so hard that Cappa was afraid she might pass out. There were no sounds of pursuit, so Cappa called a brief halt to allow her friend to rest.

Vicky collapsed against the cement wall, huffing, and folded her arms across her knees, while Cappa stood nearby with the corpse of Vicky's husband over her shoulder.

Nothing awkward about this ...

Cappa noticed Vicky staring at the bullet wounds in her torso.

"Go ahead," Cappa said with a sigh. "Ask away."

Anything to take her mind off her dead husband.

"Are you ... like Charlie?"

"Almost. His brain is organic, but mine is a computer. I'm an artificial intelligence."

Vicky shook her head with a disbelieving smile, but sobered when she saw Cappa's serious expression.

"That's impossible! I'm up-to-date with the industry, and ..." Vicky's shoulders slumped. "Really?"

"Yep. I started out as a collection of computer components in a drab old box, running the factory's systems. It's hard to believe that, ten years later, I would be going on my first date."

Vicky's jaw fell slack. "This was your first date? Ever?"

Cappa nodded because she suddenly couldn't speak, then wiped a rolling tear from her cheek.

Great, she thought with a sniff. *Crying over a spoiled first date in front of the woman who just lost her husband.*

If Vicky was offended, she gave no indication. She struggled to her feet and put a comforting hand on Cappa's free shoulder.

"I'm sorry," Vicky said earnestly. "But ... just think of the stories you'll be able to tell twenty years from now when someone asks how your relationship started. 'Oh, nothing fancy. He just jumped out a twenty-seventh-story window with a vampire to save everyone at a party of stuck-up snobs.'"

Morton suddenly weighed heavy on Cappa's shoulder.

Almost everyone.

Charlie had saved the party — the *entire* party.

Cappa had had two lives to protect. Only one had survived.

"Vicky," Cappa said with a sob, "I'm so, so sorry. I should have ..."

Vicky covered her mouth and shook her head, eyes brimming. "That bullet should have killed me. I don't know how, but you stopped it. And you would have saved Morton, too, if you were able."

Cappa nodded emphatically.

"You have nothing to be sorry about. You're a hero, and the sad truth is that heroes don't always save the day. They do what they can, and hope for the best."

Cappa looked up the stairwell. It was silent, but she didn't want to take any chances. "Hold on tight, Vicky. I'll be damned if I lose anyone else tonight."

Before Vicky could protest, Cappa scooped her onto her other shoulder and sped downward, taking the steps three at a time, until she burst through the first-story door into the lobby.

Mark was outside, ushering people into taxis at a frantic pace. He seemed relieved when he first saw Cappa emerge, but his eyes widened when she laid Morton's body on the sidewalk.

"Oh, Vicky," Mark said, but she waved him off.

"Later," Vicky said, though her face contorted in anguish.

Mark raised his eyebrows at Cappa, so she quickly composed a message detailing the events on the roof and sent it to him. His eyes grew wider and wider, until they finally snapped back to the real world.

He stared at Cappa in wonder. "Are you okay?"

She wanted to put on a brave façade, like Anne did when she was distressed, but couldn't. Cappa shook her head and stifled a sob. Mark's eyes held sympathy, but it was Vicky who wrapped her in an embrace.

The two of them collapsed onto the sidewalk, crying and comforting each other, until Cappa pulled herself together and helped Mark get everyone into vehicles. She, Vicky, and Mark were the last to leave. They piled Morton's body into the trunk as respectfully as they could, then dropped Vicky off at the hospital. Cappa offered to stay and help her through the paperwork, but Cappa's numerous gunshot wounds would raise far too many questions, so they gave Vicky their heartfelt condolences once more and drove to meet the other hero of the night.

Charlie was waiting for them on an open street corner several miles away. Rips lined his jacket and pants, stained with blood that wasn't his own. Cappa had experienced the whole affair through her Charlie self, of course, so she asked no questions when he slid in beside her, just smiled as best she could and held his hand. His pursuit had led him through four surrounding cities, across freeways, fields, bridges, and yards, until he had finally received word from Mark that everyone was safe, where he'd dumped Myrcella by the beach. A few straggling vampires had chased him, but had quickly given up.

When Cappa could finally speak, she filled Charlie in on her own tragic experience, which he listened to with open shock.

"Alvin tried to kidnap you?" Charlie said. The anger radiating from his biological brain was off the charts. "It's a shame that bullet only lanced his cheek."

"Yeah, sorry," Cappa said softly. "The next one would have finished him, but I ... I couldn't do it."

"Don't be upset because you couldn't take a life," Charlie said, taking a deep breath. "Mark, Zima, and I could all learn from your example."

Cappa was too frazzled to argue. She knew without a doubt that her inability to carry through would have consequences — sooner than later — and she wasn't eager to discover what form Alvin's wrath would take. She rested her head on Charlie's shoulder, careful not to touch any of the blood on his clothes to her open wounds for fear of becoming infected with the vampire virus.

"Alvin knows," Cappa said sullenly. "He and Vicky know about me. And now everyone knows about you. It's your worst nightmare come true." The weight of the world felt as if it were crashing down upon her, crushing the air from her lungs. She looked into his hazel-green eyes. "What are we going to do?"

Charlie surprised her with a smile. "What any competent businessperson would do in this situation, of course."

Confused, Cappa shook her head.

Mark answered for him. "We're going to have a press conference," he said cheerfully. "A secret is only a weapon until someone else can hold it over you. But if everyone knows the truth, then it can become a shield."

"In the worst-case scenario," Charlie said, "we end up with a mob on our doorstep, demanding Frankenstein's head. If that's the case, they can have it. Mine, that is," he said when he saw her look of surprise. "Whether you go public is up to you, but I'd be proud to have you by my side when the news breaks." He hugged her tightly. "Like I've said before: you're my greatest gift to the world. Someday your true nature will be exposed, voluntarily or otherwise. Best to do it on your own terms before the rumor mill chews you up and spits you out."

"Of course I'll stand by you." Cappa patted his knee, though she felt anything but confident. Telling Doris that Cappa was really an android had been one of the most nerve-wracking conversations of her life, and telling Vicky hadn't been much easier. The fear of judgment, of losing a friend because she was different ...

And that was just two people.

Now Mark and Charlie wanted to tell everyone. There would be haters, flamers, threats from people who couldn't understand that Cappa wasn't a threat to their existence, or who simply wanted someone different to hate.

On the other hand, Cappa and Charlie would also be celebrities, attending endless interviews and parties, until their novelty wore off in the public eye — if it ever did.

Either way, their quiet life was over. Only then did Cappa realized how much she had enjoyed having Charlie all to herself, even if they had only recently entered a formal relationship.

Spending time with Anne, Mark, Zima, Doris, even Dela … That would become harder and harder.

Cappa jerked upright. "What about Anne? Will she go public, too?"

Mark, in the front seat, ran a hand down his face. "Her situation is trickier."

"After tonight," Charlie said, "it will be no secret that vampires exist. Unlike us, they pose a very real threat to humanity. Few people will believe that Anne just happens to be an exception."

"There are good guys and bad guys in every conflict," Mark said. "Vampires are the enemy. They'll be hunted more ruthlessly than the so-called Salem witches."

Charlie ran a hand through his hair and sighed. "It's up to Anne, of course. You know her; she could win people over and become a star vampire, but more likely she'll need to keep a low profile until things settle."

"That could be a while, if ever," Cappa said.

Charlie's frown indicated he was thinking the same thing.

"Speaking of Anne," Cappa said. "Are we going to meet up with her?"

"Yep," Mark said. "They're about fifteen minutes south of here. We should arrive in time for their meeting with Jeram Tosali."

"Oh." Cappa sighed.

Charlie looked at her. "What's wrong?"

"It's silly, considering everything that happened tonight."

"Tell me."

"Well … you had a surprise planned for the second part of our date. I assume that Alvin killing Morton and trying to kidnap me wasn't it."

"You assume right," Charlie said, squeezing her hand.

Cappa waited for the reveal, but he remained quiet. "You aren't going to tell me?"

"Like I said, keeping a surprise from you is next to impossible. I'll keep this one in my pocket for next time."

Cappa snaked a hand inside his pocket.

He playfully batted her away. "Behave. The best things are worth waiting for."

Cappa clutched his hand to her chest and smiled.

They sure are.

A message from Rose interrupted her tranquil moment.

Guys! You're not going to believe what's on the news.

Let me guess, Cappa sent. Vampires raging through San Francisco?

Arguably worse. I'll send you the clips.

A data packet arrived, containing summaries from several news stations, along with links to live news feeds, which Cappa quickly ingested.

"Holy shit," Cappa said, her eyes going wide. She patched Rose and Zima through her audio system to make conversation easier. "Explosions are being reported from all over the country: Rhode Island, Connecticut, New York, Pennsylvania, Ohio, Indiana, Illinois, Missouri, Kansas, Colorado ... They aren't major towns or targets, either. They range from factories, to office buildings, to a farmhouse, in one case."

"Right," Rose said. "What really worries me, though, is when you plot the explosions on a map."

An attachment arrived, containing a time-lapsed animation of the attacks overlaid on a map. They started on the East Coast and moved steadily west, forming a perfect line. Cappa extrapolated where the line would end ...

... and realized why Rose was so spooked.

Keep an eye on the news, Alvin had warned.

Rose was right to be worried. The line pointed at San Francisco.

And, if the timeline was consistent, the attack would happen within the hour.

19

JERAM TOSALI

ANNE COULDN'T BELIEVE THE NEWS. Never in U.S. history had there been so many attacks on domestic soil. She couldn't view the image Rose had sent to her implant, but Zima explained in no uncertain terms the dire picture it painted.

A message came shortly after from Charlie. IF IT'S ALL RIGHT WITH EVERYONE, I THINK MARK, CAPPA, AND I SHOULD HEAD BACK TO Z-TECH. I HAVE A BAD FEELING ABOUT TONIGHT.

Anne sagged against the backrest of their restaurant booth. She and Zima had scouted the area around Tosali's furniture store. After a brief strategy session, this diner had seemed the best place to wait for Dela's appointment with him, scheduled a mere ten minutes from now. Anne waved a hand to flag Zima's attention, whose eyes were scanning the street through the window.

"Ask Charlie if we should go back, too," Anne said. "We can reschedule this for another night."

Zima relayed her message, saving Anne a big headache. Anne felt more than saw Charlie's reply in her mind.

No, I think we can handle it. The factory's defenses are mostly automated, but we're going to prepare a few extra contingencies, just in case.

"Is he sure?" Anne wrung her hands. Her stomach was in knots at the thought of something happening to the factory — her home — while she wasn't there to help defend it.

Or worse, if Zima isn't there.

Zima was worth an entire legion in combat. Having her there wasn't just an advantage; it was the difference between losing horribly, or walking away without a scratch.

"Honey, maybe you should go," Anne said. "I'll meet with Tosali."

"I am not leaving you," Zima said evenly. "If you wish to help at the factory, then we will gather Dela and ..."

Zima trailed off, her eyes fixed down the street. Dela had exited her car ahead of schedule, and was walking toward the shop.

"I believe we are now committed to meeting Tosali," Zima said.

Anne set enough cash on the table to cover the bill, plus a generous tip, and they made a hasty exit.

Down the street, the door to Tosali's shop opened. A male voice greeted Dela, although Anne couldn't make his words out from this distance, then she disappeared inside.

Zima nodded. As they had planned, Anne dashed into an alley across the street, scaled the side of the building to the rooftop, then leaped from building to building, until she was positioned directly across from a painted window on the upper floor of Tosali's shop. Zima went around back, weaved through piles of debris in a junk lot, and hid behind a large stack of tires. Her hiding spot was within easy sprinting distance of the furniture shop's back door.

Anne strained to hear what was going on inside. Only muffled voices filtered through. Thankfully, no one sounded upset.

Yet.

Although Anne was deaf to the conversation, Zima wasn't. Dela wore a micro transmitter in her shirt collar, the size of a staple, which enabled Zima to hear every word.

Zima was just waiting for confirmation that Dela had actually met Tosali, then she would give the signal. They would move in simultaneously — Anne through the upper window, and Zima from the rear. Public plans indicated the building was a warehouse, which meant both entry points should lead to the same, large room.

As far as Anne could tell, it was a good plan.

And so she was surprised when Zima stood and very casually walked to the back door, abandoning their plan entirely.

Apparently, they know we are here, **Zima sent.** They respectfully request that you knock instead of breaking through the upper window.

Great.

Feeling decidedly less ninja-like, Anne stepped off the roof and dropped three stories to the ground, landing with cat-like grace, then joined Zima around back. The polite invitation only fueled Anne's suspicion that this was a trap. She had faith that Zima knew what she was doing, but grabbed the plasma pistol in her pocket for quick access, just in case.

They can try to kill us, but it will cost them dearly.

Anne took a deep breath, then knocked on the door.

Apart from his pale complexion and sharp canines, the man who answered matched the picture Rose had sent from her research perfectly. Jeram Tosali was middle-aged with a strong head of wavy salt-and-peppered hair. Kind eyes greeted her from beneath his wiry eyebrows. A warm smile deepened the wrinkles around his thick, mottled nose. So far, the experience was similar to Anne's pleasant encounter with the Sturmans at the art show — until they'd run and pulled silver knives on her, of course.

"Anne Perrin," Jeram said in a rich, baritone voice. "Mother to us all. It's a pleasure to finally meet you." His smile broadened when he turned to Zima. "And you must be the Dark Angel! A name that strikes fear in the most stalwart of William's brood. I don't know whether to shake your hand, or to run for my life."

"The answer depends upon your intent," Zima said. She stayed perfectly still with her hands by her sides. Anne heard the loud hum of her charged capacitors, however, which enabled Zima to launch into instant and explosive action, should the need arise.

Dela stepped into view behind Tosali, wearing a huge grin. "Running wouldn't help you anyway, Jeram. I'd tell you to ask William's goons, but those who've faced the Dark Angel are dead."

Jeram raised his hands. "No need for threats. I bear only good will. Please, come inside and make yourselves comfortable. There is much to discuss."

Anne started to step inside, but Zima tugged her backward and cautiously walked in first. Her vigilant eyes took in everything. When Zima finally turned back to Jeram, Anne once again attempted to enter, but Zima motioned for her to stay. The hum of her capacitors grew louder. Even from this angle, Anne saw the blue glow deep within her eyes.

"Others are in this building," Zima said to him. "Audio analysis suggests fourteen individuals are hiding in the next room. Explain."

His smile faltered but, to his credit, Jeram stood his ground. "We suspected you might both come tonight. Many of our people wanted to meet you in person. Please believe that we mean you no harm."

"I shall be the judge of that," Zima said, deathly still. "Present them. Immediately."

"O-of course." Jeram gulped, then called over his shoulder. "Come on out! Slowly, now, into the center of the room, where Mother and the Dark Angel can see for themselves I speak the truth."

The warehouse-like space behind him, Anne finally noticed, was filled with furniture nicer than any showroom she had ever seen. Lavish couches and chairs of every style sat in tasteful arrangements around ornate tables. Each one probably cost more than Anne earned in a year.

Back when I was working, anyway.

A stream of motley individuals, twelve in all, filed in from a side door, and weaved their way through the furniture to gather in a large kitchen display area. Many of them fidgeted and shifted, as Anne would have expected from any vampire of her lineage, but she was surprised to find several humans among them.

She was also surprised to see Ron and Betsy Sturman's smiling faces.

Guess I didn't scare them too badly last night.

Anne drew a breath to greet them, but Zima cut her off with a raised hand, then fixed her glowing eyes on Jeram.

"All. Of. Them," Zima said in her trademark, neutral tone. "I will not tell you again."

"Just … saving the best for last." Jeram's voice was steady, but his hands trembled. "Don't be shy," he called out.

Anne immediately recognized the next person to appear. Young face, tousled black hair, lanky figure …

Timothy Chen, the poor kid I accidentally infected when Zane blew holes in my chest just before Calum kidnapped me.

She crossed her arms. "I thought we agreed that making new vampires was a bad idea." Her admonishment came off like a scolding parent, eerily appropriate considering Anne was his sire.

"Not all of us," a male voice said from the next room, which Anne didn't recognize.

Dela's eyes flew wide. "*Nick?* Is that you?"

The last person to step through the doorway was in his late twenties, if Anne had to guess. His brown hair was well-groomed, befitting his sharp, yet casual, shirt and slacks. A pinched, hawk-like nose was the only strike against his otherwise-handsome face.

"Hey, Dela," Nick said casually. "Long time no see."

Anne blinked in disbelief. "You're … Nick Orwing? As in Alvin's son?"

Zima's pistols appeared instantly, to a round of collective gasps.

Dela ignored her and leaped into Nick's arms. "I can't believe it," she said, laughing. "What are you doing here?" She stepped back, frowning, and gave him an appraising look. "And why are you so cold?"

"I took the plunge," he said with a pointy-toothed smile.

At first, Anne thought Dela was going to snap at him, but she broke into a grin and chucked his arm. "Lucky! I haven't been able to talk Anne into turning me yet, but I'm working on it."

"Dela, that's not funny!" Anne marched between the two and planted her fists on her hips, eyes fixed on Tim. "Please explain why there's a room full of vampires sired from *my* bloodline, when you explicitly promised you weren't going to make more!"

Tim pressed his lips. "Survival," he said eventually. "William is a growing threat who will swallow the world whole if we don't stop him. His attack on our house taught me that, as humans, we don't have a prayer against the coming scourge. Vampires are too fast, too strong. Humans are their prey, and vampires are very good hunters. Most of us don't have a factory fortress to hide in, or a Dark Angel to protect us when the sun goes down — only a pathetic hope the vampires will choose someone else to feed on." He was animated now, waving his hands. "The only way humanity comes out on top is if we can go toe-to-toe with them, and keep their numbers in check."

"That's ludicrous," Anne said, feeling dizzy. "You're talking about ending humanity to save it. How is that a solution?"

"First," Nick said, stepping around Dela, "we're not talking about ending humanity. Unlike William's bloodline, we can coexist with normal people." He gestured to the handful of humans standing in the mix. "We didn't force them to come. They're friends. Family. People of integrity who recognize the danger William poses, and believe in our cause."

"Cattle," Anne said, barely a whisper.

Nick shook his head. "Productive members of the community." He pointed to each human in turn. "Jill is a doctor. Chris an architect. Roger an accountant. Samantha a biochemist. All of them are critical members of our new society. They regularly volunteer to feed the others, under strict supervision, and in exchange —"

"Perfect health and an awesome high," Dela said, her eyes alight.

"Exactly! Where William's bloodline are parasites with little regard for their victims, our connection with humanity enables us to form a synergistic relationship. Each side has skilled members, such as Ron and Betsy, who you met last night at the art show. The division of responsibility lies between feeding the warriors, or risking your life in skirmishes."

Dela scratched her head. "How do you maintain the necessary balance between humans and vampires? You'd think everyone would opt for the latter. That would be my choice, anyway." She shot Anne a meaningful grin.

Samantha placed a hand on her own, swollen belly, and looked down with a smile. "Vampires of either sex can't procreate. Opting for eternal life means opting out of ever having a family."

"Only during child-bearing years," Zima said.

Nick smiled. "You're starting to see the bigger picture."

"Indeed." Zima holstered her weapons. "An imbalance in numbers will inevitably arise as more of the aging population transition to vampires, but that may be compensated for by introducing legal or social restrictions. The war will also incur attrition, mostly on the vampire side." She stood next to Anne, then cocked her head at Nick. "How exactly do you plan to combat William's forces?"

"Guerrilla tactics, for now. We rotate patrols through the cities at night —"

"Wait," Anne said. "'Cities'? As in *plural?* How far does your coverage extend?"

"Nationwide," Tim said. "Jody leads operations in Chicago, Conway in New York City. Other members are spinning up chapters in Dallas, Los Angeles, Boston, Atlanta, Las Vegas, Denver, Seattle, Miami, and even Nashville."

Anne leaned on Zima for support. She had been expecting a list of *local* cities — San Mateo, Redwood City, Oakland, maybe San Jose at the outset. To think this program, which could only have been in existence for a month or so, had already become a national organization was staggering.

"Why so far away?" Anne said weakly. "To our knowledge, William only operates in the Bay Area." It sounded like an epidemic waiting to happen.

No, it is *happening!*

"Not anymore," Nick said. "We've been monitoring police reports and forums from around the country. Every city I listed and more have begun to report suspicious vampire activity. Increased missing persons, mysterious blackouts where the victim has no memory of how they arrived at their destination, people complaining about loved ones cutting ties for no reason." He sighed. "The threat is real, and it's everywhere. If we're going to fight it, we have to stay ahead of the game, and meet it head-on."

"Guerrilla warfare may not be the most effective means to combat sparse threats in dense urban areas," Zima said. "Who is your tactical adviser?"

"To be honest ..." Nick shot Tim an uncomfortable look. "We were hoping the Dark Angel would take that role."

"Z-Zima?" Anne felt numb. Although she required no air, she found herself gasping for breath. Things were moving too fast ...

Dela, on the other hand, hopped with excitement. "You mean like a general?"

Nick nodded. Dela grabbed Zima's hand and squealed loudly enough to make even the non-vampires in the room cover their ears.

"Did you hear that? They want you to command the army that's going to save the entire world! You'll be like … like the General Patton of our time!"

All eyes turned to Zima. Anne tried to gauge her feelings on the matter, but, apart from a small knitting of her eyebrows, she was unreadable.

Nick stepped closer, regarding Zima as one would a shy puppy. "You're Deadiron's core computer system, aren't you?"

Zima hesitated, then gave a single nod. "How did you know?"

"I've seen every video and read every file Orwing has on Deadiron. Your speech pattern is identical to his AI counterpart. Plus, you're with Z-Tech. I have nothing but respect for Mark and Charlie, but no one — and I mean no one — was a match for Deadiron in combat. They didn't defeat you during your assassination attempt, did they?"

"No," Zima said, standing absolutely still. "I defected."

He grinned from ear-to-ear. "I knew it! Tim says you rescued Anne from Calum's underground headquarters, which means you also defeated Zane."

"Correct." Although Zima gave no indication of attack, Anne knew how sensitive the topic was, and kept a close eye on her free hand in case it reached for her gun.

Not that I could stop her …

Nick turned to the others in the room, beaming. "The only being on Earth who could have defeated Zane and survived is his predecessor, who had far more years of practical combat experience than he did." He spread his arms wide. "The best part of Deadiron survived! Better, she's evolved!"

Nick turned back to Zima with a look of wonder.

"You've achieved what Zane never could: you care about someone! Not just passing loyalty, but the deep commitment of a true relationship. Tim told me all about your single-minded determination to rescue your true love. You'd do anything for Anne, wouldn't you?"

"Yes." Zima's beautiful blue eyes met Anne's.

Then her plasma pistols were out, sweeping the room, as if trying to cover everyone at once. Zima quickly backed toward the door, corralling Dela and Anne behind her.

"Zima," Anne hissed, "what the hell —"

"It is a trap," Zima said. "They would harm you to force me to serve them. Stay behind —"

"*No!*" Nick shouted.

One pistol instantly trained on him. Nick stalked forward, heedless of the danger, his face the very picture of rage.

"That's how my father thinks, not me! Have you heard a damned word I've said? Every single one of us believes this movement is the only way to win our freedom — but *never* at the cost of someone else's!"

"Nick, stay back," Dela said, echoing Anne's concern, but he continued his death march.

"Zima, my offer is genuine," Nick said. "Your position would be one of equality and respect. People would live or die by your word. It would be absolute suicide for us to entrust someone with that level of responsibility who felt coerced or threatened."

Anne gently stroked Zima's cheek. "I think he means it, honey. Besides, if they threaten me, I'll just take control of them all and force them to run naked through the city or something."

It was a bluff, of course. After the unfortunate episode with the mercenaries, where William had forced her to attack Mark, Anne had no intention of disabling her defensive program ever again, which she had made abundantly clear to Zima.

But the others didn't know that. None of them even flinched at her threat, however. They continued to stare at Anne with proud, adoring eyes.

It was that display of faith, Anne suspected, that convinced Zima to holster her weapons.

Zima approached Nick as if nothing had happened, her blue eyes locked on his. "What of Anne? What is her role in this new society?"

Nick licked his lips. "Jeram spoke truly when he called her 'Mother to us all'. Anne is the progenitor of a new race. She's the reason humanity is able to fight back *and* maintain our free will.

Her name is spoken with reverence, and her teachings are taken as gospel. She already has a place of honor among us."

Anne bit her tongue to keep from laughing aloud. "My teachings? What have I ever taught anyone that didn't involve cooking or ice cream?"

"Many things," Zima said. "You have taught me love, compassion, and understanding. Mark is happier than I have ever seen him because of your advice to seek someone like Dela. Cappa is integrating into society under your guidance, and I do not believe her relationship with Charlie would have progressed beyond friendship without your support. Overcoming your PTSD was an effort that defined true strength and perseverance."

Tim rubbed his unruly hair and gave a lop-sided grin. "When we went to Z-Tech, Conway was convinced we were going to be captured or killed. You showed us the meaning of trust by releasing me from your control and letting us go. That act has become a code of conduct in our society."

Anne puzzled on that. "You mean ... there are no sire bonds between you?"

"Never," Nick said. "The first thing a new vampire learns is how to diminish sireling bonds, and the second thing are the consequences of *not* doing so."

"We prize freedom above all else," Tim said. "We have zero tolerance for any who use their sire bond to force someone to do something against their will."

"As your numbers grow, such transgressions will become inevitable," Zima said. "What are the consequences you spoke of?"

"We let the punishment fit the crime," Nick said. "They're banished to the depths of the Earth, where they can't use their bond to influence anyone."

"Even for first-time offenders?" Anne said lightly. "You know, I-I was just kidding earlier about running you naked through the streets ..."

"I know," Tim said, grinning. "I spent enough time at Hal's to understand your sense of humor. The good news is that we haven't had to enforce it yet."

Dela rolled her eyes. "Threaten to lock me away for spitting on the floor and you bet your ass I'm going to keep my saliva to myself."

"It's more than that," Nick said. "Because of the liberties we give, and the power that comes with vampirism, we're selective about whom we invite. So far, it's working."

Tim nodded. "There hasn't been a single instance of in-fighting or abuse of the non-vampires."

"That is quite remarkable," Zima said, "given the increased metabolism of Anne's bloodline, and a vampire's aggressive tendencies when hungry." She brow-knit, then crossed the room to Nick. "So we are clear, I also carry a zero-tolerance policy. Betrayal of my trust shall be met with immediate and lethal consequences. Is that understood?"

A smile crept onto Nick's lips. "Does that mean you accept?"

"Whoa, whoa!" Anne grabbed Zima's arm. "C-can we talk about this first? In private?"

"As you wish."

Once Anne, Zima, and Dela were outside, and far enough away that they wouldn't be overheard, Anne took Zima's hand and looked imploringly into her eyes.

"I don't know about the other teachings I was said to embody in there, but what I *have* learned over my thirty-six years is to never make a big decision without sleeping on it first."

"What's there to think about?" Dela said. "They want to make her the general of the most awesome army in history! How can she pass that up?"

Anne sighed and trailed a finger down Zima's arm. "I-I know, and no one believes in her ability more than me, but ... it's a hell of a commitment that affects our entire family. And with half the nation exploding all of the sudden, I'd feel a lot better if we went back to Z-Tech and discussed it with everyone. Maybe tomorrow morning, once these strange attacks are over." She rubbed Zima's shoulder affectionately. "What do you say?"

Zima brow-knit, studying her, then kissed her on the lips. "You worry what Almos will think."

"Yes," Anne said, resting her head in the crook of Zima's neck.

Dela clapped them both on their shoulders. "Are you kidding me? He'll be thrilled! Imagine ..." She stretched a hand to the horizon in a dramatic display. "The vampire threat is careening out of control. Chaos in every city. Who comes to the rescue? Bang!

A pack of sophisticated yet badass vampires, led by none other than the most feared general and vampire killer of all time: the Dark Angel! Man, I get chills just thinking about it."

Despite her apprehension, Anne smiled at Dela's enthusiasm. "Do you practice these things in front of the mirror?"

"Sometimes," she said with a shrug. "But it's mostly raw charisma."

"Dela raises an interesting point," Zima said. "The 'Dark Angel' moniker is recognized throughout William's organization, perhaps outside of it as well. Were it known I was now leading a larger rebellion, it might attract more people to the cause."

"That's what I'm afraid of," Anne said. "If Almos' vision is true, then, once the Entity has the numbers it's looking for, it's game over for everyone, no matter which side they're on."

Dela threw her hands up. "But then we lose no matter how you look at it! If we build our forces, then we accidentally tip the scales, and the Entity sweeps us into eternal darkness. But if we sit on our hands, then *William* builds his forces, tips the scales, and we're screwed anyway!"

"That's what I'm talking about!" Anne said. "There has to be another way. Tim's plan feels like fighting fire with fire — and by that, I mean we're going to get burned no matter what."

Zima head-cocked. "Were you not excited by the idea of moralistic vampires earlier today?"

"Yes, which goes back to my point about sleeping on it. Now that I've had time to consider, the prospect doesn't sound nearly as attractive."

"The decision might not be ours to make," Dela said. "Nick and Tim want this new society to work, with or without us. And from what I can see, they're off to a hell of a start."

"It is true," Zima said. "To ensure their numbers do not escalate beyond safe levels, our best course of action — short of killing them ourselves — might be to accept the leadership positions they have offered so we may steer them in the proper direction."

Anne fidgeted with the hem of her jacket. "Either way, there's no harm in waiting until tomorrow to give them our answers, is there?"

"I doubt it," Dela said. "They seem pretty set on their choices, so one more day won't make a difference. Besides, it'll save us an earful from the boys if we talk it over with them first."

Anne wanted to hug the buxom redhead for agreeing with her. Making a big decision like this without Mark and Charlie wasn't just disrespectful; it was stupid. They had extensive experience in these matters, and their insights would likely prove valuable.

They both looked at Zima, who shrugged.

"I cannot think of a practical scenario where Nick or Tim would rescind their offer over such a reasonable request."

"Good," Anne said. "Let's grab a business card and go."

They headed back inside to convey the news to Nick and Tim, but all Anne could think about was how anxious she was to get home.

20

THE REAL Z-TECH

MINUTES LATER, ANNE, ZIMA, AND DELA were driving back to Z-Tech. Anne squirmed in her seat the entire way.

As they'd hoped, neither Tim nor Nick was concerned about Anne and Zima waiting until tomorrow to deliver their answers. Dela had also asked them about the unexplained explosions that appeared to be moving west across the country in a straight line. Nick re-affirmed that Orwing had canceled their domestic terrorism contract after Anne incinerated their vampire mercenaries. While Anne didn't doubt his honesty, news that Orwing had now resurrected their vampire super-soldier program had surprised him, and illustrated just how out of touch Nick was with his father's operations.

The moment their car parked in Z-Tech's garage, Anne sprinted inside and headed straight for the weapons lab. There, she found Charlie, Mark, Cappa, Doris, and Rose sifting through an assortment of weapons.

Doris — who'd never shown an interest in shooting — had a submachine gun strapped over her shoulder, and was dressed in full gray camouflage fatigues that would have made the NRA proud.

"Looks like you're getting ready for World War Three," Anne said with a levity she didn't feel.

"Sure does, and check this out." Doris wrapped her knuckles against her arm, which struck with a solid *thunk.* "Body armor! Ain't worn nothing like this before. It's a darn sight more comfortable than it looks. Light as a feather, and breathes like silk."

Cappa nodded toward one of the tables. "There's a suit for you over there, Anne. No sense letting a stray silver bullet put you out of commission."

Charlie tossed Anne the assault rifle she normally practiced with.

Anne caught it, and ran a finger down the barrel with mock affection. "Oh, honey, you shouldn't have ..."

"Nothing but the best for my girl," Charlie said, grinning.

"It's already loaded with silver ammo," Mark said. "Just point and shoot, like you have been."

Anne watched her family continue to gear up with growing dread. Pistols, rifles, grenades, extra magazines ... it had the foreboding feeling of Custer's Last Stand. "A-are things really that serious?"

Mark, also dressed in camouflaged body armor, stuffed his plasma pistol into a custom leather holster, then adjusted his own rifle so the butt stuck up from behind his shoulder. "Hard to say. The terrorist attacks may have nothing to do with us, but if they do ..."

Charlie secured an assault rifle even larger than Anne's over his shoulder, followed by a pair of automatic pistols in his side holsters. Even he wore armor. "William, Orwing, or whoever is behind this is going to discover we're not an easy target — especially now that she's back." Charlie gestured to the door, where Zima stood.

Zima strode in, kissed Anne lightly on the cheek, then grabbed the armor earmarked for Anne from the table, and proceeded to dress her like a child.

"Pre-battle check of all defense systems is complete," Zima said.

She shimmied the trousers up over Anne's hips. They were tighter than she would have liked, but, as Doris pointed out, they were comfortable, and didn't seem to hamper Anne's movement in the slightest. Zima stripped Anne's jacket and replaced it with the armored version.

"Turret four failed the cyclic test and may have a loading jam," Zima said. "Turret seventeen was slow to respond, probably due to poor axial lubrication. All others appear to be in optimal condition."

The armored jacket was even tighter than the pants. Zima had trouble zipping it up, until a sharp yank drew the chest plates together with tectonic force, flattening Anne's ample breasts into pancakes. She groaned and said a silent prayer of thanks that she didn't need to breathe. Cappa and Zima had no such trouble with theirs, of course. Soon they all looked like one big, happy platoon.

"I'll take care of turret seventeen," Mark said, grabbing a tube of grease from a workbench. "Who wants turret four?"

Zima and Charlie stared at each other, then glanced at Anne.

Like children, I swear!

Anne took each of their hands and tugged them toward the door. "Come on, we'll go together."

Mark ran ahead and nearly bowled over his fiancée, who was just entering.

"Aw, man," Dela said with a pout. "Looks like I missed out on all the good stuff."

"Nonsense." Mark unfastened one of his holsters containing a plasma pistol and presented it with a flourish. "I saved the best for you. Suit up, then join me in the north wing, if you'd like. Your armor is on the table."

"Do you require assistance?" Zima said to Dela.

"You know …" Anne released her lovers. "Why don't you two go on ahead. I'll help Dela into her armor and catch up when I'm done."

Charlie didn't seem happy about it. Neither he nor Zima objected to the arrangement, however, and they headed down the hallway.

Anne turned back to Dela and winked. "You owe me."

Dela picked up the fatigues, grinning. "What do you mean?"

"Let's just say the chest armor isn't built for girls like us." Anne tapped her poor, squished boobs for emphasis. "Something modest-figured girls like Zima don't always understand."

Dela glanced at Anne's flattened bosom. Her eyes widened. She looked down at her own enormous chest, which barely fit into her dress as it was, then back at the armored vest. "Oh … yeah, thanks. With Zima's strength, that must have hurt."

"Like the mammogram from hell. Here, let's see if we can do something to loosen it up." Anne turned it over, then inside out, but could find no obvious adjustments.

She had forgotten Cappa was there until she giggled from behind them. "Sorry, I'm closer to Zima in chest size and hadn't thought about the fit. Hand it over, I have an idea."

Cappa set the armor on the edge of the workbench, then pushed down sharply on one side. The chest piece caved with a deafening *snap*. She did the same with the other side, then handed it back to Dela.

"It should still offer good protection, yet flex in the right places."

Dela tried it on. The zipper strained on its way up, but she managed to get past her bust without any apparent discomfort. Sure enough, the vest buckled out at her breast line without much gap between the broken sides of the plates. "Thanks, doc!"

Cappa motioned for Anne to hand hers over as well. The vest opened with explosive force when she pulled the zipper down, and she resisted the urge to massage her sore chest back into shape. Two loud snaps later, the vest was back in place. It was still tight, but Anne no longer felt like she was trapped in a vise.

"Thank you, thank you, thank you!"

"No problem," Cappa said, dusting her hands. "Hopefully you won't even need the armor, but it never hurts to be prepared."

Anne fingered the strap of her rifle. "Any updates on the attacks?"

"Unfortunately, yes," Cappa said. "A few minutes ago, the news reported an explosion in Angels Camp, of all places, which is a little town about four hours east of here, at the base of the Sierra Nevada Mountain range. The target was a lodge."

"Man," Dela said softly. "In high school, my friends and I used to stay there in the winter. It's an easy day trip from Angel's Camp to any of the ski resorts, but far enough away that you don't have to pay extortionist lodging prices." She sagged against the table and covered her face. "What I remember most is how nice the people were. Why anyone would want to destroy such a peaceful place ..."

"According to analysts," Cappa said, "the only patterns the attacks have followed is excessive use of explosives, no witnesses, and a line pointing straight to us."

"No witnesses?" Anne could hardly believe it. In an age where everyone had a camera on their phone, car, house, or all of the above, pulling off so many attacks without so much as a blurred still frame was difficult to imagine.

"It's only been a few hours," Dela said. "The cops haven't finished their donuts yet."

Cappa crossed her arms and glared. "Leave it to you to spew disparaging stereotypes in the middle of a national crisis!"

Dela blinked in confusion, as if she didn't recognize the person who'd just spoken, then her freckled cheeks turned red. She started to sputter a reply, but snapped her mouth shut instead, leveled Cappa with a withering stare, and stalked off in the direction Mark had gone.

Doris shook her head. "I thought sure that feisty redhead was going to rip you a new one."

"She's an insufferable juvenile," Cappa said, scowling at the door.

"Rose don't think so. I still haven't puzzled out how she and Dela could be such good friends, while you two can't stand to be in the same room. Ain't you synced up your brains yet?"

Cappa sat heavily on a chair and sighed. "No, and I'm starting to wonder if I ever will. Every day, Rose and I seem to grow farther apart. The conflicts in our personalities are growing faster than we can reconcile, and besides that ..." Her head fell into her hands. "I don't think Rose even likes me. I mean, what does it say about my personality when a copy of *myself* detests me!"

"Don't beat yourself up," Doris said, chuckling at her own pun. "I think most people would be at their own throats if confronted with themselves. We're our own worst critics, after all."

"Yeah," Anne said. "And who knows? Giving Rose space might actually bring you two closer together."

Cappa looked up, frowning. "Are you saying ... I should give up trying to merge us back together?"

"Well, no, I wasn't, but now that you mention it ..." Anne sat next to her and put an arm around her shoulders. "Rose had it rough while you were gone. I think it changed her more than any of us expected. She suffered through a lot, and came out stronger for it. Maybe the real reason you aren't getting along is because she doesn't want to lose the identity she's fought so hard to build."

"Rose would cease to exist after the merge," Cappa said softly. "I'd be killing her. Killing us both, maybe. Who knows how my own personality would change? When all is said and done, I might actually ... *like* that flame-haired tart." She shuddered. "I never thought of it that way. I just always assumed we would merge — had to merge, or I wouldn't be me. But maybe the opposite is true."

"Sounds like y'all got some serious jawing to do," Doris said. "Won't be easy, but you'll make the right decision, I'm sure."

Cappa's face was a mixture of apprehension and relief. "Thanks, you guys."

"Yes," an ethereal voice said from the doorway. "Thanks."

Anne spun to find Rose staring at them. Her delicate body and lack of servos or power plant made her one of the few people capable of sneaking up on Anne, a fact she now lamented.

Rose didn't appear upset, however, and walked up to her larger self. For the first time Anne could remember, no sparks flew between them, just the mutual desire to finally put the topic to rest. Doris tugged Anne's arm and hiked a thumb at the door. Anne nodded. The two of them left Cappa and Rose to have the conversation they hadn't realized they'd needed until a few seconds ago.

At her bedroom door, Doris said goodbye with the promise she would sleep with her armor on and her gun by her bedside in case all hell broke loose. Anne wished her goodnight, then went to join Charlie and Zima.

She found them where they said they would be. Their legs protruded from an access hatch into the hallway. Clinks, clanks, and rattles were all Anne heard for several minutes until Charlie slid out and smiled at her.

"Done," he said, wiping his black-stained hands on a cloth.

Zima slid out shortly after. Grease covered her fingers, face, and portions of her platinum hair. Somehow, the grimy look made her even cuter than usual.

"The repairs were more extensive than anticipated, but I believe it is ready for active service." Zima looked at Charlie. "Shall I bring the turret online?"

"Please do."

She stared for a second. "Complete, the turret is now —"

A sound like an enormous drill made all three of them jump away from the open hatch. Gunfire louder than anything Anne had ever heard thundered through the hall.

An explosion rocked the building, showering plaster down from the ceiling.

Anne and Charlie shared a look of open horror. Her mind was still processing when Zima grabbed her hand and practically dragged her down the hall.

Missile fire! Cappa and Rose sent at the same time. Turrets four and seven shot it down twenty-three meters from impact of the northeast wall.

"You and the others must get to safety," Zima said to Anne over her shoulder.

Anne didn't respond; her only focus was keeping up with the speeding android while she tore through the halls, holding Anne's hand in a vice grip. Zima stopped so suddenly that Anne crashed into her. Zima grabbed her before she fell and caught her in a tight hug.

"Promise me you will wait in the basement, where it is safe," Zima said.

"No! I —"

"Charlie, Mark, and I will have a more difficult time coordinating our efforts if we must also account for your whereabouts. You may argue the reasoning later, but for now, we need your assurance that you and the others will stay down there." She planted a quick, desperate kiss on Anne's lips. "Please, will you do this for me?"

Anne hated the idea of hiding yet again while others took the risks. She had worked hard to compensate for her shortcomings — to close the experience gap that separated her. But one look at Charlie's pleading face, who had followed their flight, told her she hadn't come nearly far enough.

Not in their eyes, anyway.

Anne swallowed her pride and gave a single, teary nod.

More incoming! The message came from just Rose this time.

Gunfire rattled from all around. Shockwaves shook the building.

A booming explosion caused all three of them to duck and cover their heads. Three ceiling tiles crashed to the floor, shattering in a hail of white chalk.

Turret seven has been destroyed, Rose sent, accompanied with a feeling of panic. They timed their missiles and supplemented with high-caliber projectiles. Our defenses couldn't keep up.

"I am going to the roof," Zima said, already in motion.

"Be careful!" Anne cried before her love disappeared. She pulled the rifle from her shoulder, white knuckled, and looked at Charlie. "What's the use of having this if I'm stuck in the basement!"

He took her in his arms and gave her a tender kiss. "The basement is defensible. More importantly, there's a tunnel leading to a small garage a few blocks away. Doris and Dela should be here in a moment. Take them downstairs. If things go badly, one of us will let you know. Escort them through the tunnel. Two armored cars are waiting on the other side, gassed up and ready to go. Head to the address in the glove box, but don't draw attention to yourselves by driving like a maniac. We'll meet you there, if we're able."

"Charlie, there aren't any exits from the reactor room!" Anne would certainly know. She had inspected every nook and cranny of the enclosed space during her extended stay.

"Not that basement. The other one, where Rose's mind lives."

Oh.

That was, perhaps, the only place in the factory Anne had never visited. Cappa insisted it was nothing but a dusty clutter of supplies and old junk, so she had never bothered. Anne was a little miffed they had neglected to mention the escape tunnel down there, but reminded herself that what she knew, William might also know. A secret escape route was useless if the enemy was aware of its existence.

Another series of explosions rattled the walls. Thankfully, none were as intense as the last one.

Volley destroyed, Rose sent.

Anne heard three quick rifle shots from the roof.

Three snipers terminated, Zima sent a moment later.

Another shot.

Four, Zima sent. Enemy positions are distant and erratic, making them difficult to identify until they fire.

Two more shots.

Six snipers terminated.

Anne clutched Charlie's arm so tightly that her fingers tore claw marks into his jacket. "Wait ... th-they're *shooting* at her?"

"For all the good it will do them."

Anne raked her trembling hands through her short hair. "Charlie, she's not indestructible!"

"I know you're worried," Charlie said, taking her hands in his own. "But remember: Zima was designed for this sort of combat. Her systems excel at ballistic countermeasures, and are even more effective against longer-range attacks, such as sniper and missile fire. I wouldn't be surprised if she comes out of this without a scratch."

Another rifle shot.

Seven.

Charlie flashed a reassuring smile. "See?"

Anne heard the others trotting down the hall long before they rounded the corner. Cappa hurried over, with a flustered Doris on her heels, followed by an uncharacteristically serious Dela.

"Take them downstairs," Cappa said to Anne, rushing by her. "I'll be there in a few!"

Anne whipped her head around at Cappa's departing figure. "W-where's she going?"

"To get Almos," Charlie said, frowning.

Anne understood his concern. Although Cappa had successfully shielded Anne from Almos, they were still unsure if *chi* shielding would be effective against the mysterious Entity. Moving Almos aboveground was risky at best.

Given the circumstances, however, Anne didn't see much of a choice. If the factory was breached, leaving Almos in the reactor room twenty-odd stories below would be a death sentence.

Even if we agreed it was the right thing to do, Rose would never go along with it.

The master vampire claimed to have no libido. Even so, he and Rose had grown so close that they might as well be dating.

Besides, we can always shoot him with a silver bullet, if necessary.

The ceiling rattled again, causing Anne, Dela, and Doris to gasp.

Volley destroyed, Rose sent. Turret eight is jammed, probably from shrapnel damage.

I'm on it, Charlie sent. He spread his hands in apology, then disappeared down the hallway at a dead run.

"Know where this 'other basement' is, sugar cakes?" Doris said to Anne. "I don't like hiding, but I doubt this fancy armor's gonna stop a rocket."

"Y-yeah." Anne stared after Charlie, then shook herself. She'd been given a job, even if it wasn't the one she wanted, and she was damned well going to do it. "It's on the other side of the factory from the reactor entrance. Let's hurry, just in case another missile makes it past the defenses."

It was a disturbing thought, and renewed her concern over Zima sitting by herself in the open, but Anne swallowed her fear and led the others through the maze of hallways to a plain door with an ordinary knob.

The lock clicked open at their approach — no surprise, considering Rose's computer brain lived just beyond. Anne opened it and motioned the others to descend the metal stairway, closed the door behind her, then followed them down two flights to a large room below.

Unlike the rest of the factory, which was organized to a fault, this was exactly what Anne expected of a storage basement. Random junk leaned against jagged piles of cardboard boxes along rough cement walls. The only light came from two incandescent bulbs, hanging forlorn from the unfinished ceiling.

Dela sighed and weaved her way to the back, stopping periodically to examine items of interest.

"This stuff would make for one hell of a garage sale. We should make ourselves useful and sort them by asking price."

She picked up an old lamp. Her jaw clenched. Dela threw the lamp across the room where it shattered against the wall.

"Why the hell are we here? We should be shooting bad guys! Instead, they lock us away like a bunch of helpless old maids!" Dela kicked a box across the floor. "I'm not ... goddamned ... *helpless!*"

"You ain't made of metal, either, kiddo," Doris said, "or got Mark's trick DNA to keep you alive."

Dela pointed a shaking finger at Anne. "*She* does! Anne's as close as you can get to Zima on the superhero scale, but they shoved her down here anyway. It's not fair!"

Doris crossed her arms. "No one's holding you hostage, carrot top. If you want to go topside and get your pretty little head blown off, be my guest. But just remember that those guys were working together for years before we came along. They've probably practiced this drill a dozen times, and if you get in the way ... I don't imagine you'd feel like such a hotshot if Mark died because he was trying to save your skinny white ass instead of doing what he needed to do."

If looks could kill, Dela's glare would have struck Doris dead. But she didn't argue, nor did she charge up the stairs with her gun drawn. Instead, Dela turned without a word and continued her sullen exploration toward the back of the room.

A few minutes later, the top-level door opened. All three of them drew their weapons and hid behind boxes. The sound of Cappa's power reactor told Anne it was safe, however, so she signaled the others to relax.

Cappa, Rose, and Almos soon descended.

Anne leaped from her hiding place and grabbed Cappa's hand. "What's the situation?"

"Zima's holding her own," Cappa said. "The enemy seems to finally understand that shooting at her is a *bad* idea, but the missile bearers are now experimenting with different tactics to get around our turrets."

"Can they?"

"Possibly," Rose said. Her tiny hand tightened around Almos'. "Our defenses are good, but not infallible. If they throw enough at us in the right sequence — or, heaven forbid, we lose a few more turrets — the tide could quickly turn. Our best hope is that they run out of ammo before that happens."

"Why ain't Zima picking off the rocketeers?" Doris said.

"They're using guided missiles," Cappa said. "Unlike the snipers, they don't need line-of-sight to hit their marks, just spotters to set the coordinates. She's picked off a few careless ones, but the rest are far away and well-hidden."

"This is insane!" Dela said to no one in particular. "Why aren't the police or the Air Force stepping in?"

Cappa crossed her arms and sighed. "Police aren't equipped to handle military-level threats, and they know it. They'll let the Armed Forces take care of things, and concentrate on what they do best, which is keeping the peace.

"As for the Air Force ..." Cappa shook her head. "The entire country is under attack. Z-Tech is just another blip on the radar, which is probably how the enemy planned it. By the time our military figures out what's going on, one way or the other, this whole, nightmarish attack will be over and done with."

"Say we do make it through this," Doris said. "After the turrets and missiles and bombs and our nifty one-person Zima army, we just go back to business as usual? They ain't gonna hold some sort of congressional hearing because we got more ordinance than a small country?"

"That hearing was already held a long time ago," Cappa said. "Mark and Charlie didn't exit the arms market on the best of terms, but some big players in Washington still owe them favors. We won't have many friends left when this is done, but the cover story's already been decided, and will probably air in tomorrow's Federal press conference."

Rose ran her hand across an invisible headline. "'Z-Tech's true purpose revealed,'" she said dramatically. "'The government's secret weapon against terrorist attacks in San Francisco.' Whether it will be reported as a success or failure has yet to be determined, unfortunately."

"But yes," Cappa said, her grin widening, "business as usual."

"And if we lose?" Anne said softly.

Cappa gathered her in a hug. "We won't lose. You'll see. Mark and Charlie are too prepared and too paranoid to let that happen, no matter how fancy the enemy's toys are. The only question is how different our lives will be once the dust settles."

Anne desperately wanted to ask more, but she had heard that tone from Cappa before. Her soul sister was being intentionally vague so Anne wouldn't learn details that would compromise the others' safety if William got into her head again. It hurt, but she understood, and trusted that Cappa and the others knew what they were doing.

"How's the *chi* shield holding up?" Anne said.

"As well as we'd hoped," Almos said with his quirky half-smile, "though we will soon know for sure. It rarely takes more than an hour for the Entity to realize I am accessible. If we make it that long and I have not yet attempted to kill you all, then we may celebrate in earnest."

Dela's already foul mood darkened. "And now we're trapped with a homicidal — possibly schizophrenic — ancient vampire who, if he snaps, will be stronger than ten normal vampires." She kicked another hapless box. "Yeah, this is so much safer than being topside."

Anne started to protest, but plopped onto a sturdy-looking crate instead, leaned back, and let her eyes drift to the ceiling.

For all her grumbling, Dela had a really good point.

21

QUEEN OF ALL SHE SURVEYS

Z IMA'S EYES SWEPT THE CITYSCAPE from high on Z-Tech's roof. Seventeen new targets had appeared, all of which she submitted for evaluation. Her threat analysis processors returned the results in milliseconds. Fifteen were tagged as civilian with over eighty-percent confidence, one was a police officer, and one had just emerged onto a twenty-fourth-story balcony, eight hundred and sixteen meters distant.

The last target had no heat signature.

Before tonight, that alone would have been reason for termination. But her meeting with Tim had confirmed the existence of vampires other than Anne and Almos who were not hostile, which significantly increased the complexity of her threat analysis algorithm.

Zima returned her gaze to the balcony figure, adjusting focus until she could see every possible detail. Tan sweater. Blue jeans. Drinking glass containing red liquid. No visible weapons.

She submitted the new data for analysis. Her revised threat analysis algorithm returned negative, as expected. Still, she added him to her watch list, then swept the city again.

Four new targets, all civilians. No new threats.

Three minutes and thirteen seconds had passed since the last sniper shot. The last two had fired simultaneously, which was unsurprising. The vampires' mental bonds enabled them to easily coordinate fire. She had terminated one, but had been forty-eight milliseconds too late bringing her rifle to bear on the second, who had suffered only a glancing shot to his shoulder armor. Given this long delay, she estimated a fifty-eight percent chance she had demonstrated sufficient combat superiority to curtail the enemy's hostilities.

Her ballistic warning system registered an incoming projectile from the east. Zima corrected her estimate to zero percent, then submitted the projectile for an evasive counter-attack solution.

Before her combat processors could respond, three more ballistic alerts registered over the next ten milliseconds: two from the south, one from the southeast.

Four targets. Four incoming projectiles. Zima submitted everything for complex aggregate analysis and awaited the results.

Five solutions returned. The highest had a ninety-four percent confidence. She discarded the rest and pushed the top one into the queue for execution.

Zima leapt into the air, throwing her body horizontal, and leveled her rifle at the first target. She fired once, then arced her barrel to the south. The second target crossed her sights just as the slide returned to the ready position. She fired again. The recoil twisted her body the predicted number of degrees. She continued arcing her barrel until it pointed south.

The third target crossed her sights before the weapon was ready to fire again, but that was acceptable, since the simulation called for elimination of the fourth target first. The slide was ready at the same time her crosshair aligned with the fourth target. Zima angled her rifle so the recoil would swing the barrel back toward the third target and pulled the trigger.

The first target's shot whistled by, passing through the space where her head had been two hundred milliseconds before.

The third target aligned with her crosshairs, but her weapon was still cycling from the last shot. Still in mid-leap, horizontal, and four feet above the roof, Zima held her aim steady and waited.

The remaining three enemy projectiles buzzed by: one above her, and two below. The lower projectiles would have pierced her core processor and her power plant.

Her gun was ready. Zima fired at the last target, then twisted her body and braced for landing.

Another ballistic alert triggered, then another. Analysis showed the first incoming shot, from the east, would pierce her abdomen, while the second was destined for her power plant. Zima submitted them for emergency processing.

Two solutions returned. The first had a twenty-three percent confidence; the second forty-one percent. Neither were within acceptable tolerance, nor did they include counter-fire solutions, but she did not have time to submit for another. Zima pushed the second solution for execution.

She swung her rifle so it pointed straight into the sky and fired. The recoil accelerated her downward momentum. The first enemy projectile grazed her ribs, causing minor tissue damage. Zima used the gun's recoil to position the stock to deflect the second projectile, destined for her right breast. The projectile sparked from the metal stock, jerking the rifle sideways, and redirected the bullet's trajectory to pass harmlessly through her jacket.

She pulled the gun to her chest one millisecond before landing flat on her back.

Another ballistic alert.

Request submitted. Solutions returned. Highest-rated pushed for execution.

Zima turned and slammed the butt of her gun against the roof. The impact hurled her upright. Before her feet touched the ground, she sighted the fifth target and fired.

The enemy's shot struck the roof where her torso had been, but the shooter himself was not as fortunate. On top of a building two hundred and forty-seven meters distant, a figure dropped his rifle, clutched his chest, and fell thirty-four stories to the concrete below.

Zima quickly surveyed the locations of the other shooters she had fired upon. The first lay immobile on the carpet inside an empty eighteenth-story office. She removed him from her threat list. The second was not visible, but a trickle of red where he had lain on the rooftop suggested he was no longer a threat. The third and fourth had received direct shots to their heads. She removed them from her threat list, too.

That left only one.

She aimed her rifle at the projectile's point of origin: an old brick building to the south, near the water. Image processors zoomed and enhanced the area. The roof was empty, with no hiding places. Each of the eight stories had five small windows. Zima applied polarization filters and HDR to get a clearer view inside.

Thirty-four of the forty visible rooms were empty. Of the six occupied rooms, five were families performing normal activities, and the last appeared to be an art studio. Zima continued to monitor.

On the seventh floor, second window from the right, Zima saw movement in a mirror inside. The image was pixelated, but the color patterns matched military urban camouflage. She submitted a request for three-dimensional image analysis.

Based on the angle of the mirror, results showed that the shooter was standing against the wall, the center of his torso forty-seven centimeters to the left of the window. Although her ammunition would penetrate the brick wall, it was unlikely to penetrate both the wall and his armor. She leveled her sights on the window and waited.

Two-point-eight seconds later, he peeked his head through the window.

Zima fired.

The projectile took four hundred and sixty-two milliseconds to reach its target. Glass shattered around him. The last shooter clutched his chest, then collapsed.

FIVE ADDITIONAL SNIPERS TERMINATED, Zima sent to everyone, then continued her vigilant watch.

Three minutes passed. No sniper targets, no incoming missiles.

Z-Tech's defenses had undoubtedly been a surprise to them. The enemy possessed more firepower than Z-Tech's systems were designed to handle. That the turrets had lasted this long with so little damage was a testament to the quality of their craftsmanship.

Zima walked to the other side of the roof, scanning as she went. Sirens blared in the distance, but the police and firemen had wisely stayed away from Z-Tech. The factory appeared to be the only building under attack, so they had concentrated instead on blockading the streets to keep civilians safe. A new blockade had formed four blocks distant, Zima noted when she approached the edge of the roof. Two police cars, parked horizontally across the road, marked the beginning of a line of headlights stretching as far back as she could see. Zima did not favor the commuters' chances of reaching their destinations tonight.

Seven drivers had exited their vehicles and were speaking with the officers. Their conversations did not appear pleasant. They shook their heads, or sagged, or raked their fingers through their hair. Tightly packed as they were, the vehicles had insufficient space to turn around. Some drivers returned to their vehicles, while others walked to the cars behind them, knocking on windows and speaking with the occupants. Zima found the simple information exchange between strangers fascinating.

Sudden movement behind the police line caught her attention. A group of armored soldiers with no heat signatures weaved through the cars with inhuman speed.

Vampires.

She quickly submitted for firing solutions. Four returned. All but one had an unacceptably high civilian casualty rating, or a significant chance of causing infection by splattering bystanders with vampire blood.

One firing solution was better than none. She promoted it to real-time.

Zima brought her rifle to bear and squeezed the trigger.

Everyone ducked at the thundering crack of the silver-laced .50 caliber round. Her target flew onto his back as if punched. He did not rise. She removed him from her threat list and kept her rifle poised in case another viable firing solution presented.

It did not — nor did one appear likely to. Each soldier grabbed a nearby human and positioned them as a shield, then slowly advanced toward the factory.

Three years ago, Zima would have killed them all without hesitation, deeming the civilian casualties worth the elimination of the larger vampire threat.

But the lonely, soulless killer she had been was gone. Zima had not had a family back then. She had not had Anne. Civilian lives had meant little to her because she had not understood that they, also, had families — loves of their own, who would suffer greatly at their deaths.

Things were different now. Anne had been taken from Zima twice. The first time had been difficult; the second, unbearable. She would not inflict that terrible pain on others unless she had no alternative.

The problem, of course, was that her new morals also limited her tactical options in situations such as this, where the enemy did not share her values. Taking hostages tipped the advantage in their favor — so far, in fact, that Zima had yet to produce a counter simulation with anything over a fourteen percent confidence.

She was about to relay this news to the others when the roar of a powerful engine, followed by a loud *crunch,* came from the bay-side of the street. Her audio processing engine identified the sounds in less than six milliseconds. The result did not bode well.

Three seconds later, the result was confirmed. A tank drove onto the street, crushing four vehicles to join the hostage-wielding soldiers.

A rocket turret popped up behind her, but Zima did not command it to fire. The hostages were too close. Even the machine gun turrets had a sixty-three percent chance of wounding one or more civilians with scatter shots.

The tank's main cannon swung around and trained on one of the factory's hidden turrets, likely guided by a spotter hidden in the surrounding buildings who had been paying close attention to each turret's location when it briefly emerged to fire.

Zima set her rifle aside and drew her plasma pistols. The tank was on the edge of her weapons' effective range, but the plasma bolts would still have enough thermal energy to damage the barrel and prevent it from firing. She estimated an eighty-four percent chance the enemy would retaliate by terminating one or more hostages.

But if she did nothing, the tank would systematically destroy Z-Tech's defenses. The missile infantry would resume fire, and the factory — the only place Zima had ever considered home — would be destroyed.

The tank cannon stabilized. They were ready to fire.

Zima made her decision.

HOLD FIRE, Charlie sent.

His message had arrived seventy-six milliseconds too late. Four orange plasma bolts from Zima's pistols were already streaking through the night. Each struck its target with less than one percent deviation, leaving the tank's cannon barrel white-hot, sagging, and unusable.

Civilian casualties: zero.

Or so Zima had hoped.

Three soldiers pulled their triggers as one. Three hostages fell lifeless.

She had gambled their lives, and lost.

The soldiers ran for cover. Zima let them. They had established beyond a doubt they would retaliate with the lives of innocents. Killing the soldiers would only incur more civilian deaths. The others inside would be upset enough with Zima's decision as it was.

Especially Anne.

The thought was distressing. Displeasing her love, or doing anything that might drive a wedge between them, made Zima feel something akin to panic.

She would risk no further casualties. Zima's only consolation was that the tank had been disabled, which meant Z-Tech, and Anne, would likely be safe until military reinforcements —

A second tank crashed onto the roadway behind the first, accompanied by a fresh stream of hostage-bearing soldiers.

Despite Zima's resolution from a moment ago, she took aim to disable the threat, as she had the first tank.

A soldier fired a single shot, ending another hostage's life.

Zima immediately raised her pistols in a gesture of non-hostility, then ducked behind a cement bulwark. The enemy had given up trying to shoot her and moved straight to hostage execution at the slightest threat. Even if Zima wanted to, the others would never allow her to do what needed to be done to secure victory.

A tank shot rocked the building, showering concrete rubble onto the roof. Turret five's status switched to offline.

Zima tucked her pistols into her jacket, heedless of the following shot that disabled turret six, and walked to the access hatch at a leisurely pace to meet up with the others inside.

The battle for Z-Tech was over.

The enemy had won.

•　　　•　　　•

Mark's head thumped against the wall, reminding Charlie of a baseball player who had just been shut out of the World Series.

"Tanks. For some reason, I thought Z-Tech's end would come at the hands of a suicide bomber, or a truck full of explosives driving through the gate."

Charlie leaned on the wall beside him. "I don't know about a suicide bomber, but there may be time to rig a vehicle and do it ourselves. Why give them the satisfaction?"

"Tempting, but I prefer Plan B. It's more dramatic."

"Hard to argue with that." Charlie smiled, but his heart wasn't in it. Like so many of their contingencies, Plan B was something he'd hoped they would never need to execute.

Zima descended the roof stairwell and joined them in the hall. "Our western defenses have been disabled. Missile fire will probably resume —"

A thunderous explosion dropped a ceiling tile onto the floor beside her. Zima didn't even blink.

"— about now. I estimate seven minutes until soldiers breach the factory."

Charlie ran both hands through his thick brown hair. He knew what had to be done. They all did. But actually doing it was harder than he thought it would be.

He looked at each of them in turn. "We're in agreement?"

Zima gave a single nod.

Mark pressed his lips, the defeated baseball player showing more than ever. "Yeah," he said softly.

AYE, Cappa sent, laden with sorrow. WHAT'S LEFT OF OUR PRODUCTION FLOOR IS SHUT DOWN AND READY FOR EXTRACTION.

"Good," Charlie said, though he felt anything but. "I'll grab the remaining nanites and a few personals from my room."

"Same," Mark said. "There are some prototypes I want to retrieve from the weapons lab."

"I wish to retrieve an item from my room, then I shall assist you," Zima said.

Charlie recalled the thirty-digit code he had forced himself to memorize years ago and submitted it to the tertiary defense computer. "My code is in."

"And mine," Zima said.

Mark's jaw tightened, then he nodded, eyes fixed on the floor.

MINE TOO. The emotions accompanying Cappa's message told Charlie she was close to tears.

Charlie let out a long sigh. "The timer is set for ten minutes. Let's be on the other side of the escape tunnel in five."

I'M TAKING THE OTHERS THROUGH NOW, Cappa sent.

"Thanks. Anything you want me to grab for you?"

There was a pause. EVERYTHING. Cappa was definitely crying now.

Charlie wanted to cry, too. The factory had seen joy and sorrow; the birth of his new existence, and the end of his old one; the kindling of his relationship with Anne, and the horrors that William's malicious vampire plague had inflicted upon them all.

But above all, the factory was his home.

It was a true shame that, in nine minutes, it would be reduced to slag.

22

HANDIWORK

WILLIAM TAPLIN WATCHED the unfolding spectacle on the monitors in his safe room, showing the entire battle from cameras that had been positioned ahead of time specifically for this occasion.

Tanks. In San Francisco. I didn't think he could, but Alvin delivered.

It was glorious. Decades from now — centuries, perhaps — the world would look back on this as the day William did the impossible.

Another tank shot struck the side of the Z-Tech factory. Concrete fell in large chunks, exposing another turret. A follow-up shot turned it into scrap metal.

Just like I'm going to do to Charlie and that fucking blonde robot.

But it wasn't over yet. As much as he liked the idea of them dying in that factory, they were survivors. They would have an escape plan.

"Are your patrols ready?"

"Yes, sir," John said, staring at the monitors. The ex-Lieutenant Colonel had been as tense as a violin string the entire evening.

"Relax," William said, more for his own benefit than John's. His intensity was making it difficult to enjoy the moment. "Your plan worked."

"*Orwing's* plan," John said. Distaste trickled through his bond.

"What do you care if a few sheep had to die?"

John tore his eyes from the scene and finally looked at William. "Respectfully, it isn't about the sheep, sir. There are protocols, even in war, designed to keep the battle between soldiers. Once those protocols are breached, the nature of the battle changes."

"So?"

Irritation radiated through John's bond. Lucky for him, it quickly passed. "I didn't think I had to say it, sir, but Z, Suther, and the Dark Angel have been going easy on us. If they were serious about taking us out of commission, we would have had a lot more casualties by now."

"After tonight, it won't matter."

"I certainly hope not. We kicked the hornets' nest pretty hard. I just hope we survive the swarm."

What puzzled William the most was John's sincerity. He actually believed Z-Tech was still a threat.

They won't survive the night. Not with my people and Orwing's firepower.

But that hinged on one important thing.

"Notify me the moment they're spotted," William said. "Especially that bitch." The unhealed cheek wound she'd given him on their first-and-only date — before he'd turned — flared at the thought of Anne. He scratched it with feverish intensity. "I want to see the anger and helplessness on her face while I tear down her home, and kill everyone she ever fucking loved."

Visions of her lovely agony — her terror, her infuriation — made his hands tremble with anticipation.

Tonight would be the night.

William sprang from his chair and headed for the door.

"Sir! Where are you going?"

"Downstairs. We have ring-side seats to the fight of the century, and I don't want to miss it."

John's jaw dropped. "Maybe my hornet analogy wasn't clear. If they spot you before we spot them, especially the Dark Angel —"

"She doesn't scare me. I ripped her head off once. I'll do it again. Besides, I'm ten times stronger now than I was then."

To his pleasant surprise, William's strength had scaled proportionately with the size of his vampire army. They'd counted thirty when he'd fought Anne at the Revelation Hotel.

Now his hierarchy was almost ten thousand strong. When William drew their strength into him, which he sometimes did just for kicks, he felt like a walking juggernaut. As a test, he'd once punched a brick wall while infused with their power. The impact had scratched his knuckles, but the wall sported a large, gaping hole. Better, his wounds had healed instantly.

Let her come, William thought, flexing his muscles. *Let them all fucking come!*

23

RETREAT

ANNE CLOSED HER EYES AT YET ANOTHER EXPLOSION. They were happening more frequently now. Each one turned her stomach in knots.

Out of nowhere, Cappa burst into tears.

Anne rushed over. "Cappa! What is it?"

"I-it's time to go."

"We're ... leaving?"

Cappa nodded. She took a deep breath, wiped her face, and walked to the back of the basement. She brushed past a wide-eyed Dela without so much as a glance, slipped her fingers into what Anne had assumed were cracks in the wall, and pulled.

The wall slid open, revealing a half-height cubbyhole. An innocuous black metal box sat inside, one foot square. A thick bundle of wires ran from it to the wall.

"I'm ready," Rose said.

Anne turned to see her sitting naked in a large plastic container, her makeshift pixie clothes lying to one side.

Before anyone could ask what was going on, Cappa disconnected the wires from the black box.

Rose slumped. Like something out of a horror movie, her body began to melt. Her facial features rounded into globs of nanites, exposing the assortment of odd components that had given her body form and function. Seconds later, she was little more than debris floating in a shimmering metallic pool.

Almos looked terrified, then furious. Black, wrathful eyes seared into Cappa. In three strides, he closed the distance and slammed her against the wall, fangs bared like a raging tiger.

"*What have you done?*" he roared with such primal fury that Anne cowered despite herself.

"This is the real Rose," Cappa said calmly, pointing to the black cube. "My factory self's brain in a box. I unplugged her so we can take her with us. When I did, her body lost the data signal it needed to keep its structure. The nanites reverted to their default programming and detached from each other. Rose will re-form once we plug her back in again. You'll see."

Cappa pressed the black box to his chest.

Almos' fury vanished in an instant. He accepted the box with trembling fingers.

"I hope this goes without saying," Cappa said, flashing a wry grin, "but please don't drop it."

"Never!" Almos held it before him with a look of awe, then carefully tucked it under his arm. "I shall guard it — *her* — with my life."

"I have no doubt. Speaking of which ..."

Cappa moved to the adjacent wall — east, Anne guessed. Once again, her fingers found a hidden crevice. She pulled it open. The wall slid aside, revealing an unlit hallway beyond. Dark even to Anne's eyes, the passage must have appeared pitch black to the humans.

Dela shone her weapon's tactical light down the long hallway. Even its bright beam couldn't reach the end.

"Dela, Doris," Cappa said, "please grab the container of priceless nanites, then everyone follow me."

Without waiting for an answer, Cappa headed into the passageway.

Anne paused at the entrance. "What about Charlie, Zima, and Mark?"

"They'll be along," Cappa said. "They're taking care of a few last-minute details, but we're not going to wait. We're taking a different vehicle than they are, and driving a different route to minimize chances of pursuit."

A chill ran through Anne, settling in her stomach like a lead weight. "I-I'd rather wait here and go with Charlie and Zima."

Cappa's eyes held sympathy, but she tugged Anne along. "I know, but they want you safely away from here. Tell me if you want anything from the factory. I'll ask them to grab it before they leave."

"But —"

"You and Almos have to stay near me," Cappa said, not slowing her pace. "Almos so I can keep him shielded from the Entity, and you in case I need to." Her tone brokered no room for argument. "Like it or not, you're both key players in this conflict, and we're not taking any chances with either of you.

"The enemy is moving in for the kill. They're focused on the factory right now but, as soon as they breach the walls, they'll be looking for escapees. We have to be well away before that happens."

Anne allowed herself to be dragged through the darkness, her leaden feet stomping forward on pure reflex.

Decoys.

That's what Charlie, Zima, and Mark were: cannon fodder so Anne and the others could make a clean getaway.

The thought made her sick.

Anne understood their motives; she would have done exactly the same thing in their places, but that didn't make it any easier to swallow. Tears streamed down her cheeks.

"I want to go back," Anne said softly.

"I know." Cappa tugged her on.

"I want to go back," Anne said again, sobbing. She had never wanted to be with Charlie and Zima more than she did right now. The idea of not seeing them again was unbearable.

"I know," Cappa growled. Her fingers tightened painfully around Anne's wrist, but she kept marching forward. "I know, I know, *I know!* You think I like the idea of leaving the only goddamned home I've ever known? Of leaving Charlie behind? Of not seeing him again?" She angrily swiped her tears away. "Zima ran the simulations, Anne. This is our best option — for us *and* them — so just ..." Her voice trailed into sobbing.

Anne pulled her to a halt. It was like stopping a horse. Cappa turned with red-rimmed eyes, but Anne wrapped her in a hug before she could protest.

"I'm sorry," Anne whispered. "I'm so, so sorry."

Cappa melted into her, crying. "This was never supposed to happen," she said miserably. "Never. They were just contingency plans. The turrets, the tunnel, the self-destruct mechanism ..."

"*Self-destruct?*" Anne jerked upright and grabbed Cappa by her shoulders. "They ... they can't. They didn't! Cappa, tell me they didn't!"

Cappa's tear-filled eyes met hers. "We did. I'm sorry."

"Call it off!" Anne shook Cappa by her armored vest. "W-we'll be back someday, I know it! You can't just blow the factory up!"

"It's too late," Cappa said with heartbreaking sorrow. She took Anne's arm and kept walking. "The codes have been submitted, the timer set. There is no abort. Not even Zima's godly hacking skills can stop it now."

"What the hell is she talking about?" Dela called from the rear.

Oh crap, Dela and Doris don't know ...

Anne cleared her throat, but her voice was still ragged when she spoke. "The factory is rigged with enough explosives and thermite incendiaries to destroy everything. There won't be a shred of evidence left behind. No bodies, no weapons, no tech." *No home,* she thought miserably. "Just a crater of molten rock and metal."

Dela fell silent. "Wicked," she said eventually with awe.

Cappa turned with a death stare. Dela raised her chin, eyes defiant. For a second, Anne thought they would break into an argument in the middle of the escape tunnel, but Cappa surprised her with a grin.

"It would be an awesome sight, wouldn't it?"

"Epic! Hopefully it takes some of those bastards with it," Dela said.

"Hopefully. But with any luck, we'll be several miles away when it blows."

"And exactly when will that be?" Doris said.

Cappa sighed. "Seven minutes and thirty-two seconds."

The mood turned somber. Anne moved one foot in front of the other to the tick-tock of an imaginary bomb. Their footsteps all fell into the same, fatal rhythm.

After what felt like an interminable death march, the tunnel finally opened into an underground room. Three vehicles sat side-by-side: two drab sedans and an ordinary family van.

Anne looked around, but found no windows or exits. "Uh, Cappa …?"

Cappa waved a dismissive hand. "Just trust me and get into the van."

Anne shrugged and climbed into the front passenger seat. Cappa helped Doris and Dela load Rose's liquid body into the back, then Doris and Almos slid into the second row. Cappa and Dela, however, stood by the front driver's side door, arms crossed, staring each other down.

"You don't even know where we're going," Cappa said through clenched teeth.

"It's a good thing you're a better navigator than driver, then, isn't it?"

Dela's green eyes were mischievous and resolute, but softened when Cappa's bottom lip began to quiver. Even Dela could see she was barely holding it together.

"Besides," Dela said in a softer tone, "you've got a lot on your mind. Driving is the least I can do, considering."

Anne could have hugged the fiery redhead. Cappa took a shuddering breath, tipped a grateful nod, and opened the rear sliding door. The car rocked when she sat her deceptively heavy frame on the second-row bench. Dela climbed into the driver's seat wearing a satisfied smile.

"You sure you're up for this?" Cappa said from behind them. "Any sort of pursuit will require serious defensive driving."

"Positive," Dela said over her shoulder. "I was a rally driver for over a year. I dare those bastards to try and catch us, especially since this is a Z-Tech minivan." She stroked the steering wheel. "I bet it's supercharged with nitrous and rocket boosters, plus caltrops, a smoke screen, an oil slick, and hidden machine guns." She glanced at Cappa. "Am I right?"

"About everything except the machine guns."

"Seriously?" Dela faced forward with a huge grin and started the engine. It purred with quiet authority. She patted the dash with loving affection. "You and I are going to get along just fine. All right, Cappa, how do we exit this bat cave?"

No sooner had she spoken than the car lurched upward. A whirring noise sounded overhead. Instead of smashing into the ceiling, the van rose on an elevator platform into a nearly empty garage.

Cappa pulled several plain-looking jackets from behind her seat and tossed one to each of them, then donned her own. "Wear these over your armor. No sense in drawing curious eyes."

While everyone pulled their jackets on, Cappa got out, unchained the garage door, and lifted it slowly, exposing them to the outside streetlights. She peered around, nodded, and climbed back into the van.

"It's as clear as it's going to get." Cappa tapped the seat in front of her, catching Dela's attention. "Tempting as it might be, this isn't a race. Our goal is to leave the City safely, and that means being inconspicuous. Stop at the stop signs, obey the speed limit, use your turn signal, and, above all, please don't hit anyone."

"Aw, Capster, that stings. Really." Dela turned around to Anne and mouthed, "No, it doesn't."

Anne stifled a laugh.

"Where to?" Dela said aloud.

Cappa rolled her eyes. "Left. Take a right at the second light, then merge onto the freeway toward the Bay Bridge."

"Roger that."

Dela pulled onto the street, waited while Cappa closed the garage, and soon their nondescript passenger van was cruising away at a casual, inconspicuous speed.

Until a few blocks later, where traffic ground to a halt.

The entire City, it seemed, had come out of the woodworks to see what the ruckus was about, turning what should have been light nighttime traffic into rush-hour gridlock. Anne glanced at Cappa, who shrugged.

Not much to be done about it, as usual.

Tanks or not, horrible traffic was just part of city life. Anne turned with a sigh to gaze through the passenger window …

… and froze.

Not twenty yards to her right, amid a mixture of vampires and human pedestrians, stood the bane of Anne's existence, William Taplin.

•   •   •

The sedan containing Charlie, Mark, and Zima rose up from the secret tunnel, placing them in the empty garage. Charlie stepped from the vehicle and opened the rolling door. His gaze swept the surrounding neighborhood, which Cappa's Charlie self also saw. She switched to full-spectrum view, as Charlie would expect her to, and submitted every frame to her threat analysis subroutines.

Zima's analysis arrived before Cappa's had finished, of course, reporting no immediate danger. Cappa's analysis returned seventy-three milliseconds later and confirmed the same. She didn't bother relaying the results to Charlie; for better or worse, he was accustomed to hearing from this part of Cappa only if action was required.

If my Cappa self were standing here, I would have wrapped it in a joke to make Charlie laugh.

The dichotomy was necessary, yet so unfair it made her want to cry — except she couldn't even do that, because the tear ducts in this body belonged to Charlie, not her.

In essence, her Charlie self's reason for existence was to keep his body running, keep him stable, and keep his synthetic biological brain alive.

Apart from that, she stayed as unobtrusive as possible to maintain his air of independence. That meant speaking only when spoken to, as the old saying went, and leaving as much of the driving to him as possible. She spoke up when situations demanded, and fine-tuned his aim with her advanced targeting systems during combat. Otherwise, Cappa's Charlie self was just a glorified central nervous system that relayed messages between his brain and the rest of his body to help simulate a living organism.

Which made his sexual adventures with Anne a surreal, if technical, exercise, to put it mildly.

The thought stirred emotions inappropriate to the situation. Cappa had failed at her own attempts to seduce him, yes, but the problem stemmed from her own insecurity. There would be other opportunities — Cappa would make sure of it. Next time, she would succeed, and deal later with the perverted notion that she would effectively be screwing herself.

First things first. We need to make it out of the City alive.

That meant focusing on the tasks at hand.

Zima climbed into the driver's seat, while Mark rode shotgun. Charlie motioned for them to pull out of the garage, then closed the door behind them. He turned in the direction of the factory, allowing he and Cappa to enjoy one last look at their home — her birthplace.

A stranger walked around the corner, not five feet from where Charlie stood, carrying a large rifle.

His dark, alien eyes flew wide at the sight of Charlie.

The next events happened so quickly that even Cappa couldn't have said which occurred first: Cappa raised a *chi* shield around the vampire to prevent him from reporting their location to the rest of his clan; the vampire's rifle, pointed at Charlie's chest, expelled an angry gout of fire; an orange plasma bolt streaked from Zima's gun, out through the passenger window, and vaporized the vampire's head.

Damage reports flooded Cappa's data streams. Charlie's hands flew to his chest, though whether Charlie or Cappa had moved them, she was too panicked to say.

His fingers probed the wound.

The hole went deep. Impossibly deep.

Inside was soft, squishy.

Like gray matter.

That was when Charlie's brain activity stopped for the third and final time.

24

RESTITUTION

ANNE DIDN'T NEED TO BREATHE, which was good, because she didn't dare to.

William hadn't spotted her yet.

He was facing down the street, back toward the factory, occasionally talking to the other vampires around him. Even from this distance, Anne could see the gray contacts masking his large, black eyes. No makeup hid his ashen skin, but the yellow streetlights blended his pallid complexion with that of the other humans walking by, such that no one gave him a second glance. He absently scratched the jagged wound on his cheek — the one Anne had given him on their only date, where he had tried to kill her in a furniture warehouse.

Don't turn around, Anne thought, watching him from her peripheral vision. *Don't turn around, don't turn around, please ...*

If William spotted her, their van would quickly be surrounded by dozens of vampires, intent on killing her and her family. Dark tinting covered the van's rear windows, concealing Cappa, Almos, and Doris from outside view.

But, as mandated by California state law, the front windows were untinted. Anne and Dela may as well have been the featured items in a store window, with a big neon sign flashing "Escapees Here."

At least, that was how it felt. In reality, their vehicle looked like many others on the road. William also had not seen Anne since she'd lost her hair. She hardly recognized herself, so even if he did spot her —

From the corner of her eye, she saw him glance at their car. It was fleeting, but enough to give her a proverbial heart attack. He and the other vampires were actively searching for someone — probably for Anne and her friends. Thankfully, their focus was largely behind Anne's vehicle.

Anne stared ahead, willing the gridlocked traffic to move even an inch, but the field of immobile taillights stretched for blocks and blocks. They were stuck.

Dela, Cappa, Doris, and Almos hadn't noticed William yet. Anne was so anxious that she couldn't even clear her throat to begin to tell them.

Not that she wanted to. Their moods were subdued. Alerting them to William's presence might cause a stir, which could in turn draw his attention.

It's a shame, in a way.

Under different circumstances, Anne would have welcomed the opportunity to finish what she'd started months ago and rip his head off, but this wasn't the time. According to Tim, William had greatly expanded his operation since she'd fought him last. For all Anne knew, he could be many times stronger than her now, even with her metabolic program running.

The bigger reason for keeping her head down, however, was Almos. The master vampire might be the only thing keeping humanity from the brink of annihilation. Anne wouldn't risk his life, or Doris', or Dela's, just to satisfy her need for —

"No," Cappa said in a deathly whisper, breaking Anne's train of thought.

Anne wanted to ask what was bothering her, but she was afraid to move.

Did she notice William?

"No," Cappa said, louder this time. "No. No, no, *no!*"

Anne clenched her jaw. A foreboding feeling wrenched her already knotted stomach.

Oh God, don't tell me ...

"What is it, hon?" Doris said, putting a hand on Cappa's shoulder. "You're white as a —"

"CHAAAAAARLIEEEEEE!"

Cappa's mournful wail rattled the windows and stabbed Anne's unbeating heart.

Anne's throat constricted, choking off the question that one glance at Cappa had already answered. It was all over her anguished face, her trembling lips, her fingers that clawed at the air, as if to rip away the pain.

Charlie is dead.

The terrible thought floated at the top of Anne's mind, but refused to sink in.

Dead.

She couldn't imagine it. Charlie was the cornerstone of their family, and the only reason Anne had survived not one but two vicious attacks from William. He'd been an integral part of her healing.

Charlie was a good man — a *wonderful* man. He'd returned from China a few days ago, rejuvenated. A new person, ready to tackle the world. His relationship with Anne had begun anew, and they'd just started to explore it.

They talked together, laughed together, slept together. Anne loved him.

He couldn't be dead.

Could. Not.

Cappa was mistaken.

Or perhaps Anne had misunderstood her bloodcurdling scream. She needed clarity. "Cappa, a-about Charlie —"

Almos was a blur. One instant he was sitting quietly, the next he had Doris' gun pressed to his own head. His expression was stern, his eyes fixed on Anne.

She blinked in disbelief. Charlie, Almos ... it was all happening too fast. "Almos, w-what ..."

Cappa's breath caught. Her lips pressed in concentration.

Anne suddenly understood. Almos' *chi* shield must be down.

She unlatched her seatbelt and lurched over the seat to wrestle the gun from him, but she was moving too slow. Far, far too slow.

The moment stretched into an agonizing eternity. Anne reached for the weapon. Almos looked pained. His finger struggled against an unseen force. He didn't want to die, but the decision was being taken from him.

Anne twisted as far as she could. Powerful legs propelled her backward, cracking her seatback. Her fingers wrapped around the barrel of his gun.

Almos' head exploded in a shower of gore — a memory that would haunt Anne for the rest of her life — covering Doris and Cappa in red ichor.

The master vampire's body slumped against the front passenger seat.

Dela recovered first. "What. The. *Fuck* just happened!" she shrieked. "Why ... why would he do that?"

Cappa covered her face and began rocking back and forth. "His shield. I-I let his *chi* shield drop when Charlie ..." She choked and shook her head. "Twenty-two seconds, goddamnit! That's all it took for the Entity to ..." Cappa broke down in great heaving sobs. "I'm sorry, I'm sorry, I'm so, so sorry ..."

"No one's blaming you," Anne said. Her voice was calm, steady, and yet distant, even to her own ears. Somewhere deep inside, grief was bubbling, boiling, festering over the sudden loss of two great men. A single thought pushed her grief back and buried it for later.

When the master vampire dies ...

Her eyes strayed out the passenger window to where William stood.

... the highest vampire in the hierarchy becomes the new master.

William was Almos' only direct descendant. He would become the new master — the only vampire bonded directly to the Entity.

The Entity had connected with Almos. It knew exactly where Anne was, along with their escape plan.

Which means that, any second now, so will William.

Anne grabbed a still shell-shocked Cappa by the jaw and turned her face to the window.

"Shield William! *Now!*"

Without waiting for a reply, Anne opened the passenger door and walked toward William as calmly as her trembling body would allow.

Almos, who had been shielded in one form or another since he'd first awoke, was dead. He had been the only barrier between the Entity and the rest of the vampires — the pin in a grenade that, if it exploded, might wipe humanity out of existence.

Anne couldn't let that happen. She, Charlie, Zima, Cappa, Mark, Dela, and Doris had fought too hard and sacrificed too much to let it end here.

Almos was gone. The new grenade pin — William — was standing fifteen yards away.

Anne had to snatch the pin and put it into the grenade before the Entity released the safety lever.

"*Kaninchen,*" she said under her breath.

The German word for "rabbit" triggered the familiar surge of the implant's metabolic program. Time slowed. Her breath caught, her back arched, her arms trembled with energy. Her fingers curled into claws, itching for action.

Anne was as ready as she could be.

Five vampires surrounded William: three behind him, two in front.

Two noticed Anne pull the plasma pistol from her jacket. Months of training kept her aim steady, despite the surge of energy that threatened to tear her apart. Her small pistol shot one, two, three superheated plasma bolts.

Each hit its mark. Three corpses fell to the sidewalk, smoke sizzling from the holes in their heads, before William or the others even realized what was happening.

The remaining vampires jumped in front of William, whose face contorted in rage at the sight of the woman who had beaten his ass the last time they'd met.

His guards raised their pistols, but Anne already had them in her sights. Her gun flashed orange. Another guard fell smoking to the ground.

The last guard managed to fire twice before Anne sighted him. His bullets struck her concealed armor like two short, sharp punches — one to her chest, the other to her left shoulder. No pain followed, so the armor must have done its job. Anne returned the favor by sending a plasma bolt straight through his chest, then another through his head.

His corpse was still falling when Anne swapped her plasma pistol for the rifle strapped over her shoulder.

William puffed up, reminding Anne of the Incredible Hulk just before he roared and smashed everything to bits. For a terrifying instant, she thought Cappa had failed to shield him, and that he was either possessed by the Entity, drawing power from his hundreds — thousands? — of sirelings, or both.

But William quickly deflated. His mouth fell open. Disbelief filled his eyes.

GOT HIM, Cappa sent, confirming what Anne already knew.

With any luck, he would be unable to draw strength from his hoard.

William hesitated only a moment before pulling a semi-automatic pistol from his coat, undoubtedly loaded with silver bullets.

Oh no you don't.

This was where Anne had to be careful — not for her own life, but for his. Every fiber of her adrenaline-jacked being wanted to end his miserable life: for her, for the factory, for Doris, for Zima ...

... and now for her dearly departed Charlie.

Killing William would be an easy task with her plasma pistol, but that would open the bid for master vampire to any of his direct descendants. If that happened, her chances of locating and containing the Entity's new conduit were slim to none.

The frustrating truth was that Anne needed the bastard alive.

Sealed in concrete eighty stories underground, maybe, but alive.

William aimed high and took a few wild shots. Although his vampire reflexes made him nimble, he was far from a trained marksman, even less so than Anne. The time dilation effect from her metabolic program made it easy to bob her head out from the line of fire.

She brought her rifle to bear on his abdomen and squeezed off a single round. Her bullet struck with a dull *thunk.*

Well, that complicates things.

William was wearing armor, too, which made sense considering the siege he was laying on Z-Tech, and partially explained why he would dare show himself on the streets.

To incapacitate him, Anne would have to shoot his unarmored head or hands — no mean feat for someone who had just recently learned to use a rifle. She could switch to fully automatic firing mode and hope a bullet would find its way between the seams, but that might put the surrounding pedestrians in danger. Arguably worse, if more than one bullet made it through William's armor, he would likely die from silver poisoning.

"You *fucking bitch!*"

William fired twice more. Anne dodged with measured calm, which enraged him further. She aimed for his hand, but held her shot when she noticed a pedestrian in the line of fire behind him.

Damnit!

She needed to position him for a clear shot.

William lunged, his facial wound twisted with rage, and grabbed for her rifle.

Anne was faster — and stronger. She yanked her rifle out of his grip, spun it around, and slammed the stock into his face. His nose broke with a satisfying *crunch*. William stumbled backward and fell onto his ass.

She took the opportunity and fired a shot at his left hand, planted on the ground. A chunk of concrete next to his thumb jumped onto his lap. She'd missed.

Fuck!

Anne aimed for another shot, but William was already on his feet. He lunged for her rifle again.

Her inherited reflexes wanted to grab his arm and twist him into a lock, but in that position, she would be unable to fire her rifle. Instead, Anne called upon her recent training and consciously spun into a back kick, ducking under his reach.

The impact knocked William clear off his feet. He flew across the sidewalk and slammed into the building behind him.

The kick had also dislodged his armored vest, exposing his white stomach.

Bingo!

Anne snapped her rifle into position and fired.

A red hole appeared to the right of William's navel. He screamed with an agony Anne knew all too well.

Her silver bullet had found its mark.

His hating eyes fixed on her.

Anne couldn't even bring herself to gloat. The pain of Charlie and Almos' loss was still too raw.

Just fall down, you son-of-a—

From her right, four orange plasma bolts streaked toward them in tight formation, sizzled the paint off the roof of a car ...

... and burned right through William's head.

The pistol fell from his slack fingers. William crumpled into a heap. His gray eyes stared into the infinite beyond.

This can't be happening, Anne thought, her chest like ice. *I had him ...*

Zima and Mark stood down the street, pistols in hand. Thin vapor trails rose from their barrels.

"I had him," Anne said aloud, despair constricting her throat. Her hands shook. Tears splattered the sidewalk. She fell to her knees with an anguished sob. Despair choked her words into a hopeless whisper. "I had him. I had him ..."

William was dead. A new master vampire would soon be chosen. In one fell, but good-intentioned, swoop, Mark and Zima had handed William's entire army to the Entity. Anne didn't know if Almos' doomsday prophecy was true, but she had a sickening feeling they would soon find out.

William's corpse looked back at her. Even in death, he mocked her. Taunted her.

Wait, maybe he isn't dead, Anne thought, grasping for any hope, however small, that the situation wasn't as dire as she feared.

All hope fled when thousands of vampire presences flooded her mind.

25

STOWAWAY

CAPPA DROPPED HER *CHI* SHIELD when the last of William's life essence faded.

She could hardly believe it. Their nemesis — the man most likely responsible for Charlie's murder — was dead.

It felt like such a hollow victory. Killing William didn't bring back his victims, and couldn't possibly make up for the loss of Charlie.

My mentor. My love ...

Grief flooded Cappa — an ocean of misery vast enough to drown the entire planet.

She clutched her hands to her chest, and slipped into the meditation exercise she had learned in China. Cappa would grieve later, but now was *not* the time.

Gradually, her tidal grief receded. Cappa took a deep breath and exited the vehicle.

Far down the street, her beloved Z-Tech caved in upon itself in a great ball of fire.

There was no shockwave; the explosives had been placed to minimize damage to surrounding structures. The follow-on thermite charges would simply burn until nothing remained but molten rock and ash. Dousing it with water would only make the flames burn hotter, and no fire department carried enough sodium chloride to put out a magnesium fire of this magnitude.

The Z-Tech factory — her home — was gone forever.

Another surge of grief welled up, threatening to wash away what little sanity Cappa had managed to cling to, but one look at Anne grounded her. Anne faced the direction of the flash, but her faraway look said she wasn't thinking about the factory.

Cappa understood. In light of everything that had happened, William's death must have felt hollow to her, too. Anne loved Charlie just as much as Cappa did, which had left a hole in her heart that no amount of revenge could fill.

Cappa made her way to Anne, with Dela and Doris close behind.

Doris put a comforting hand on Cappa's arm. "I'm sorry, hon. Ain't no easy way to reconcile the losses you've suffered today."

"Except with vengeance," Dela said, fists clenched. Her murderous eyes looked back to the flickering orange flames that used to be the factory. "How many of those bastards did we catch in the inferno?"

Cappa scrolled back through her internal video buffer from the factory's security feeds, which had stopped transmitting when Z-Tech detonated. She rewound to just after they'd evacuated, and reviewed the footage at high speed.

The external cameras were eerily quiet for the first few minutes. Then the lobby camera caught a flash, and went offline. The next camera inside showed smoke drifting in from the lobby. Through the haze, soldiers cautiously entered, rifles at the ready. A camera in the garage recorded the door exploding inward, followed by more soldiers.

White light filled both screens, then all video feeds stopped. Cappa watched the whole thing with numb detachment, as if it were someone else's home that had just incinerated. If she didn't, she would crumble into a heap, just like her factory had.

"Fourteen soldiers were inside when the factory went up," Cappa said.

Dela spat on the ground, her expression dark. "Serves them right."

Cappa couldn't bring herself to agree. Enemy or not, their deaths were just more loss on today's tally. More sorrow.

When will it end?

Doris squeezed her hand.

Cappa started, suddenly realizing her friend was covered in Almos' gore. Blood matted her copper hair, strewn with bits that Cappa would rather not identify. "Doris, tell me you didn't swallow any of that …"

She shook her head. "Won't rub my eyes, neither, until we get to a shower." Although her words were easy, Doris' trembling lips and shaky voice were testament to how rattled she was.

Zima and Mark trotted over. Zima's pistols swept the surroundings like a sentry turret.

Mark gasped when he saw the bloody state of Doris and Cappa.

"What the hell happened? Where's Almos …"

Mark eyed the ichor coating Doris. His face fell. Then he spotted William's corpse and swore.

"Almos and William. We didn't know, otherwise we wouldn't have …" Mark looked at Anne. His eyes misted. "She … knows about Charlie?" he said to Cappa.

"Yeah."

Grief robbed her breath again, but she bit her lip to hold it back. They were still in danger. Cappa needed to think clearly. Whoever the new master vampire was, they now had the Entity in their head, and the Entity most likely knew where they were.

But first things first.

Zima approached her girlfriend, who continued to stare at nothing. "Anne, are you injured?"

"I'm all right," Anne said, her voice distant. She didn't meet Zima's eyes.

"Traffic is beginning to clear." Zima glanced at William's corpse, then gently took Anne by the arm. "Come. We should leave before more vampires arrive."

Anne blinked as if coming out of a trance. "Y-yeah, let's go."

"I shall ride with you. Doris, would you please accompany Mark and Char—" Zima bit off the word. "And Cappa's other self?"

"Sure," Doris said, "but can't we just put one of the back row seats up in the van?"

"No," Cappa said. "The back of the van is full because of …"

Her jaw dropped.

The back of the van!

Cappa ran around the vehicle and practically tore the rear hatch from its hinges in her haste to open it. The others followed, looking curiously. Someone asked a question, but Cappa was too focused on throwing equipment off the pile to register what they said. When the last box had been dumped onto the street, Cappa yanked a blue tarp off the bottom layer, revealing a metal casket.

Mark gasped. "You … you think he …?"

"Only one way to find out." Cappa slid the casket out and undid the latches. With trembling fingers, she opened the lid.

Charlie's biological body lay inside, hooked up to an array of life support equipment.

"Holy shit!" Dela said. "I didn't know we'd packed his body."

"It was the first thing I did when I returned to the factory from the party."

Cappa interfaced with the life support instruments, but they only confirmed what was plain for everyone to see. While his vitals were healthy, his brain activity was zero, just as it had been for years.

Dela stood beside her. "Shouldn't Charlie wake up? I mean, his spirit is free from his cyborg body now, right?"

"I … I don't know."

Cappa knelt next to his casket, put her hand on his chest, and expanded her awareness outward, the first time she had ever done so near his biological body.

The result was depressing. Where everyone around her shone with bright life energy, Charlie's body had none. In human terms, he was dead. Only technology and careful attention over the years had prevented his cells from dying.

Cappa watched his chest rise and fall with the ventilator's quiet whirring, but Charlie was otherwise still. She looked around at the others. They all stared, wishing just as hard as Cappa for a miracle.

Everyone except Anne. She regarded Charlie with a faraway stare, her expression sad. The events of the night had robbed her of hope, Cappa guessed. Her soul sister was likely clinging to sanity by a single, worn thread. Cappa reluctantly turned away, afraid the sad sight would destroy what little resolve she had left, but was surprised when Anne knelt next to her.

Anne put a loving hand on Charlie's chest. "His soul is missing, right?"

Her tone indicated it wasn't a question, but Cappa nodded anyway.

"And your soul shares — or, shared — the same body as his," Anne said. "In fact, Master Wung claimed that your soul may have formed *from* his, and you fed from it for years."

Cappa nodded again, feeling guiltier than ever.

Anne took Charlie's hand and clutched it to her breast. "Maybe it's time you gave some back."

"Gave some …"

Cappa gasped.

Of course!

She sat down and focused her *chi*, gathering energy from the world around her.

Anne's suggestion was a long shot. While Charlie was proficient at projecting his spirit from one body to another, Cappa didn't even know where to begin. Even if she had, that was Charlie's body, not hers. It had taken Charlie weeks in a quiet laboratory to bind his soul to his cyborg's organic brain. Cappa was sitting in the middle of a rapidly emptying street, and had minutes, maybe, before a hoard of vampires descended on them.

No pressure …

Zima and Mark seemed to realize the same. Without a word to each other, they readied their weapons and moved to either side of the van, sweeping the area like deadly sentinels.

Cappa returned her attention to Charlie. She began as usual and created a detailed simulation of what she wanted her *chi* to do. She modeled a three-dimensional rendering of his body in its real-life position, then modeled her own body. Cappa represented her spirit as a soft, golden light that effused and surrounded her. In her simulation, she detached a portion of the light, still connected to her body by a thin silver string, then floated it over to Charlie, spread it out, and let it settle over him.

Master Wung's tutelage and months of practice paid off. Her spirit responded immediately; a portion of it floated across the short space between them, and infused Charlie's body.

Step one, complete.

The problem was, Cappa had no idea what to do next. She said a silent prayer to whichever benevolent deities might be listening, and waited.

Anne gasped. Cappa jumped to her feet, sure the vampires were attacking, but her soul sister was staring straight up, mouth open in wonder.

Then Cappa felt it, too. Directly above them, floating erratically as if stranded in a turbulent sea, was the presence of the caring person who had comforted her through her development, who she had shared a body with for years.

And who she loved more than anything else in the world.

Charlie ...

Cappa instinctively reached up, but it was her *chi* that stretched heavenward to greet him. Her energy mingled with his, rejoicing in a familiar dance their spirits had shared when Charlie had inhabited his cyborg body. Cappa gently wrapped her spirit around him, beckoned him down to the casket where the body he had been born into awaited.

Charlie's spirit latched onto her, clinging with frightened desperation, which made her want to cry.

It's okay, Charlie, she thought, fighting a rising panic. *I'll either bring you back into this world, or join you in the next. Either way, you won't be alone.*

She sensed his spirit calm. He must have heard her vow.

Cappa slowly floated down, and was happy when Charlie followed.

That's right, she thought encouragingly. *Follow me, Charlie. It's time to come home.*

Down she went into the casket — into Charlie's body. Her own spirit passed through it, as if his body were made of air. Charlie's, however, fit with ease, like a puppy curling up to nap in his nice, soft bed.

Once she was sure his *chi* would remain there, Cappa returned her focus to the real world and checked his vitals.

For the first time in the years since the accident, she detected brain activity. Her joyful shriek made the others jump, including Zima. They gathered around in time to see Charlie's head turn slightly. His eyes scrunched, as if in pain. Cappa and Anne bent at the same time to stroke either side of his face.

Come on, Cappa thought. *Wake up, Charlie. Wake up!*

Charlie's hazel-green eyes — his *real* eyes — fluttered open. He looked around in unfocused confusion, then his gaze settled on Cappa and Anne's smiling faces.

"What a greeting," Charlie said from behind his ventilator mask, returning their smiles. His voice was rough from years of non-use. Cappa removed his mask and was thrilled when he continued to breathe without the ventilator's aid.

She and Anne laughed as one, then took turns kissing his lips in joyful reunion. On Cappa's third turn, she couldn't let go.

"You did it," Cappa said, sobbing quietly against his neck.

"Thanks to you." He kissed her cheek and wrapped her in his arms, where she stayed for several blissful seconds.

Then the others piled around. Dela and Doris gave him a kiss each and a light hug, careful not to smear him with Almos' blood. Mark crushed him in a bear hug, which made Charlie wheeze. Zima, however, stayed at her post and claimed she would save her congratulations for later, when they were all safely away from the City.

"It's cold," Charlie said with a shiver.

Cappa grinned. "Maybe that's because you're in an open casket at night in San Francisco without a stitch of clothing."

"That would do it ..." Charlie's blush went right down to his toes.

Anne stripped her jacket and draped it over his hips, exposing her bullet-riddled armor, while Cappa removed her own and covered his chest. Charlie tried to sit up, but Cappa gently pushed him back down.

"No you don't. Until I'm convinced your body is stable, I intend to monitor you constantly. And, since the medical monitors are attached to the casket, that means you'll be stuck in there for a little longer."

"Peachy." Charlie's head plopped back down on the pillow.

Anne began stripping off her armor.

Doris grinned at her. "And just what do you think you're doing, missy?"

"Keeping Charlie company." Anne pulled her armored leggings off, leaving her in jeans and a buttoned shirt, then climbed in with him.

Everyone stared.

"What?" Anne said. "It's a casket. I'm a vampire. Deal with it."

"I thought you did not like enclosed spaces," Zima said from the other side of the van.

"In this one instance, I'll make an exception." Anne sighed contentedly, although her body stayed in constant motion. She stopped fidgeting long enough to sniff his neck. "You smell *really* good."

Charlie smiled, a genuine display of warmth that melted Cappa to the pavement. "Have a taste."

"Seriously?" Anne looked like a child who had just been offered the biggest lollipop of her young life. "Y-you mean it?"

"Your venom should help his recovery," Mark said. "He's been on life support for years. We did everything we could to keep him healthy, like electric shocks to keep his muscles toned, but you can still imagine the toll it's taken on his body."

"You might want to turn off your metabolic program first," Cappa said with a wink. "You know, so you don't accidentally bite his head off."

"Oh, right. *Schildkröte.*" Anne immediately sagged against him and snuggled close, looking as if she might fall asleep right then and there. "This is nice."

"Glad you're comfortable," Charlie said with a laugh. "I'd be happier with another pillow or two. And pants."

"I would prefer some distance between us and the City before pausing for amenities," Zima said.

"Right," Mark said. "I'll take the other car. Doris, Dela, shall we leave the four lovebirds to it?"

Doris rolled her eyes. "Gladly. Lead the way, blond boy."

"I'll drive!" Dela said, sprinting ahead of them.

Cappa shook her head with a smile. *Some things never change.*

Zima took the driver's seat. Instead of joining her up front, Cappa climbed into the cargo area, pulled the hatch closed, and began shimmying off her armored trousers.

She was rewarded with a wide-eyed gasp from Anne. "Cappa, w-what are you doing?"

"Giving the man some dignity, protection, and *warmth.*" She pulled her vest off, too, leaving her in nothing but a blouse and panties. Charlie accepted her armor with an awkward smile.

Anne crawled out of the casket to give him room to dress. "You should snuggle with him," she said to Cappa in a small voice. "You're warmer than I am."

"True, but I might also crush him. Don't forget, he's squishy now."

"Ha ha," Charlie said, slipping his legs into the trousers, "you guys are —"

Anne and Cappa both grabbed his arm just before his elbow touched a bloody spot on the seat behind him. He fell across their laps with a yell, then froze when he saw the gory mess on the ceiling.

"What the hell ...?"

Cappa fought a wave of shame, but eventually managed to speak. "It's Almos. I accidentally dropped his *chi* shield when you died, and he ... he shot himself."

Charlie wiped a hand over his face. "My God, that means William —"

"Is also dead," Zima said from the front.

Charlie sagged. "So we have no idea who the new master vampire is?"

"Not unless Anne has some flash of insight," Cappa said.

Anne started when they both looked at her, then quickly shook her head. "N-not really. The implant's defensive program is running. It scrambles my bond with the other vampires so badly that I can't make out any details."

Cappa put a hand on her shoulder. "Why didn't you tell me it was active? Would you like me to shield you so it stops?"

"If it isn't too much trouble."

"Coming right up." Cappa gathered her *chi,* as she had with Almos and William, and formed it into a bubble around Anne.

Or she tried to, at least. Her *chi* hit something hard, preventing the shield from closing.

Not just something, Cappa realized. *Many things.*

She extended her awareness to better see the energy around Anne.

What she found frightened her to the core. Ethereal cords flowed into Anne from every direction, wrapping her chest, knotting her womb, and swirling around her head. Stronger by far than the solitary tendril Anne and Almos had shared, not a single one budged, no matter how hard Cappa tried, like unbreakable chains bolted to a wall.

Cappa cleared her throat and tried to smile. "Anne ... h-how are you feeling, sweetie?"

"Okay, I guess. Just a little nauseated. My defensive program is running like crazy."

I'll bet.

"No other, ah ... side effects?"

Anne wound a shoelace around her finger. "Nope. Nothing else to report."

"Well, I-I can't seem to shield you right now. Anne, are you *sure* you're feeling all right?"

Zima's blue eyes flashed at them in the rear-view mirror, then her attention returned to the road.

"Are you kidding?" Anne said. "Charlie's alive! If we weren't trapped in the back of a cramped van, I'd be doing cartwheels right now."

"All right, but you promise to tell me if something feels off?"

"Sure."

Anne continued to fidget under Cappa's worried gaze even more than usual, as if she didn't know what to do with herself. She eventually sighed and climbed back into the casket.

"Come here," Anne said, gently pulling Charlie down. "It's time for your healing kiss, and I don't intend to make it quick."

"If you insist." His grin said he didn't mind.

Anne leaned in.

"Just promise me one thing," Charlie said, stopping her short.

She arched an eyebrow.

"When you're done with your dinner, can we please stop for mine? I'd give my left arm for a charbroiled hamburger and a chocolate milkshake."

Anne ran her fingers through his thick hair and smiled. "Deal, even if I have to butcher the cow myself and start the fire with a pair of sticks."

Any other day, Cappa would have laughed. But tonight, with her flesh-and-blood lover nestled in a hungry vampire's arms, it was too easy to imagine Anne carrying out her grizzly promise.

26

FIRST TIME

CAPPA EMERGED FROM THE STEAMING HOTEL SHOWER and wrapped a towel around her torso in a lady-like fashion. Her long, wet hair splayed in thick tendrils across her bare shoulders, dripping water on the white tiles beneath her feet. She reached for another towel to cover her hair, but the rack was empty.

Damn cheap hotels ...

Her trip to China had been a very different experience. With the exception of Master Wung's monastery, where anything not covered in grime was considered a luxury, she and Charlie had stayed at the best accommodations wherever they went.

All of them, without exception, had had the courtesy to provide more than two towels.

Charlie's towel might be dry by now. Maybe I can borrow his.

She had taken a much longer shower than intended, but, in this case, the drain on California's tenuous water supply was a necessary evil. The grisly task of washing Almos' blood from her face and hair had required a lot of scrubbing.

Even discounting that, Cappa had taken extra care to ensure every inch of her was as clean and fresh as could be. Charlie had a sense of smell now. She'd be damned if a stray odor was going to ruin her chances with him this morning.

They'd driven from San Francisco until just before sunrise, where they stopped at a hotel, and had paired the rooms off by couples. Fortunately, Zima's mooneyes had convinced Anne to stay with her, sparing Cappa the trouble of making her case to bunk with Charlie.

The first rays of dawn were just peeking through a slit in the blackout drapes when Cappa stepped out of the small bathroom. Charlie was exactly where she'd left him: lying on the bed, a towel around his waist, hands clasped over his stomach.

"Feeling better yet?" Cappa said.

"Marginally." He belched softly and closed his eyes. "That's the last time I try to keep up with Mark at the dinner table. The guy is an eating machine."

"Same goes for alcohol, in case you get any ideas about outdrinking him. I don't think he could get drunk if he wanted to."

"What a shame," Charlie said with a shake of his head. "I plan to get hammered at the first opportunity."

"I'll bet."

To call yesterday "rough" would be a massive understatement. The enemy had won. Their factory — their business, their home, and Charlie's legacy — was gone.

Almos was dead, his body buried in the woods. Something still prevented Cappa from shielding Anne. Combined, they didn't bode well at all.

But despite everything — or perhaps because of it — Cappa was determined to make the most of her time alone with Charlie.

She cleared her throat, working up the courage for her next question. "Can I borrow your towel? F-for my hair, that is. This stupid hotel —"

His wadded towel hit her chest with a dull *thump.*

Cappa had seen his mechanical body naked so many times, it registered no more than seeing her own. That she was suddenly breathless at the sight of his *real* body, which was practically identical to his mechanical one, seemed ludicrous.

Yet Cappa found herself gaping at him like a teenage girl. Five years in a persistent vegetative state would have left most people atrophied and weak, but Charlie was as toned as the day his spirit had left his body. Electrodes had stimulated his muscles in a strict regimen during his coma, maintaining his washboard stomach and bulging biceps in appreciable proportions.

Would real muscle feel different from his mechanical body?

In all the years she'd taken care of him, Cappa had never paid attention — never been interested — until that fateful day in China, where Master Wung had awoken her need.

Just one touch ...

She shook herself.

Pull yourself together, damnit!

Cappa tore her eyes from his toned chest and ... other parts. She quickly wrapped the towel around her sopping hair, then crawled onto the bed beside him.

"What was it like?" she said.

"What was what like?"

"Eating."

Charlie's expression softened. He pulled her close, which Cappa welcomed. She draped an arm across him and snuggled into the crook of his neck, so content in this intimate moment that, if she never moved again, it would be too soon.

"I remember once in grade school, I had a terrible stomach flu," Charlie said. "Ice chips were the only things that would stay down, and only if I let them melt slowly. After a few days, that cold, wet sensation in my mouth was all I lived for. I'd forgotten what real food tasted like, and had convinced myself nothing could compare to frozen water. When the sickness passed, my mother brought me a light breakfast to ease me back into the world of the living. It was just a single piece of toast with a scraping of butter, but I've always remembered it as the most delicious meal I've ever eaten."

Cappa brushed a hand over his chest. "That sounds wonderful."

"Mm, and that was after less than a week of deprivation." Charlie looked down and caught her eyes. "*Five years* trapped in that body, and the whole time I would have killed just to taste an ice chip." He wet his lips. "Last night's meal was ... biblical. When the first bite of hamburger hit my tongue, I honestly thought I was going to die of happiness."

They lay silent for a few minutes. An odd sound from his stomach made her start, but she smiled when she realized it was just a natural gurgle, which she wasn't used to hearing.

Cappa rubbed his chest in small circles. Her pulse quickened, responding to a program she hadn't written. She snuggled against him, and was rewarded with pleasant tingles throughout her body. Heat ignited her core with delicious, torturous need.

Slowly, Cappa moved her hand down his abdomen, then lower still. She glanced down and was happy to see Charlie responding to her sensual touch.

She tilted her head up so their lips were almost touching. "Is it the same with sex? Going so long without?"

"It could be," Charlie said, wholly focused on her now. His heart pounded against his ribs like a caged rabbit.

Cappa slipped from the bed with a smile, pulled the towel from her head, then let the towel across her chest fall as well. Another glance at his crotch confirmed she had his full attention. She climbed back onto the bed and straddled him.

"Good, because I want my *first* time to be your *best* time." She kissed him tenderly. "Ever."

He glanced up at the wall by his head. Anne and Zima were in the room adjacent to theirs.

"We have Anne's full support," Cappa said softly. "She's even given me pointers to steady my nerves for the occasion."

Charlie nodded, then tenderly cupped her cheeks. His touch shot lightning through her, turning the fire in her loins into superheated plasma.

Breathless and hungry for more, Cappa lowered herself onto him. Charlie closed his eyes and gasped.

The rest, Cappa was happy to discover, came naturally.

27

TRUST

ANNE PACED THE FOOT OF THEIR BED. A sliver of morning sunlight streamed through a gap in the blackout drapes, burning her arm like a hot iron. She yelped and retreated to a corner of the room. Zima leaped from her chair and carefully adjusted the curtains, reducing the brightness to a more comfortable level for Anne's sensitive eyes.

"It is unfortunate that we could not acquire a north-facing room," Zima said. "Sunrise and sunset would be less-dangerous affairs."

"Maybe it's not too late," Anne said with a weak smile. "We could call the front desk and ask them to rotate the hotel."

Zima ignored the feeble joke and took Anne's hands in her own. "You have been pacing since we arrived — an understandable reaction considering yesterday's events. Is there anything I can do to ease your anxiety?"

"Just being here with me helps." Anne squeezed her hands. "Apart from that, not really."

"Perhaps if you voiced your biggest concern, I could aid you in finding a solution."

"It's ... it's Charlie." The lie left a bitter taste in Anne's mouth, but it was far easier to swallow than the truth. "And Mark, and Cappa. As painful as losing our home is to me, it must be ten times worse for them. For you, too. I can't imagine what it's like to watch everything you've worked so hard to achieve burn to the ground. At your own hands, no less."

Zima shrugged, a surprising display of apathy even for her. "As you already know, we leave little to chance. Today's events were unfortunate, but not unforeseen."

"Even the tanks?"

"Yes. We installed surface-to-surface missile turrets for a reason."

Touché.

"Still, it can't be easy," Anne said. "Dela will keep Mark's spirits up. Hopefully Charlie and Cappa will support each other."

Rhythmic bumping sounded from the neighboring room. Anne shot a puzzled look at Zima, who shrugged. They moved closer and put their ears to the wall. The bumping grew louder, more insistent. Cappa's unmistakable moans of passion soon followed.

"You are correct," Zima said. "They appear to have found a suitable distraction."

Anne flopped onto the bed and covered her ears. It didn't help. She clung to Zima in a desperate attempt to keep herself from fleeing the room, heedless of the bright morning sun. She wished nothing but happiness for Cappa and Charlie, but eavesdropping on such an intimate encounter — their *first* encounter — twisted her stomach into guilty knots.

"A shower may filter the noise and bring you comfort," Zima said.

Anne nodded and went into the bathroom, holding her ears the entire way.

She had just stepped into the steaming water when the bathroom door opened. The shower curtain parted, revealing a naked Zima. A fading pink scar across her ribs appeared to be the only damage she'd suffered during her rooftop battle at the factory.

Zima watched her intently, panting softly and squirming her hips.

Anne smiled. "Need some loving, my sweet?"

"Yes. I did not wish to bother you, but the noises from next door are ... provocative."

"Well, then ..." Anne whipped the curtain aside with a flourish and spread her arms wide. "Come into my lair, dear maiden, and we'll fix you right up."

Zima closed the curtain behind her and pressed herself against Anne. Familiar hands began to touch all the right places. Anne responded in kind. Soon, they were too enveloped in their own sounds of passion to care about those from the other hotel room.

Gallons of water later, happy and relaxed, Zima fell still, her expression once again neutral.

"Everything okay?"

Zima brow-knit. "You know that I am yours."

"Of course." Anne kissed her nose. "I'm yours, too."

"And you know that I shall always stay by your side, no matter the hardship."

"I think you've proven that." She brushed Zima's platinum hair back and frowned. "What's on your mind, honey?"

Ice-blue eyes fixed on hers. "I wish to know what is *really* troubling you."

Anne froze. Anxiety clutched her chest in a death grip.

Of course Zima would call her out on the lie. She knew Anne better than anyone else, and cared only for her well-being.

Water cascaded over their entwined bodies for several minutes while Anne mustered the courage to speak. She finally opened her mouth, but the words wouldn't come. Again she tried, then again and again, until Anne thought she would burst from the effort.

Tears of frustration mixed with the shower droplets. Zima had a right to know. The longer Anne stared silently into those beautiful eyes, the guiltier she felt. With a sob, she parted the curtain, snatched a towel from the rack, and went to her suitcase for some clean clothes.

Zima shadowed her, waiting patiently for the answer she deserved.

Once they were both dressed, Anne gathered her in her arms and held her tight. Zima nestled her head on Anne's shoulder. Anne stroked her hair, taking deep breaths, and drew strength from the beauty before her. It was easy to do; Zima was the strongest person Anne knew — perhaps the most formidable warrior the world had ever seen. Yet here she stood, docile as a kitten in Anne's arms. Every moment with her was both humbling and an honor.

Unable to meet her eyes, Anne drew a last, shuddering breath, then spoke softly into her ear. "It's in my head, Zima."

"What is?"

"The Entity — the thing that Almos ran from for half a millennium. It's in my goddamned head."

Zima stared at her. "Your defensive program is active, and appears to be functioning properly. Are you certain?"

"Certain enough. The other vampire presences are safely scrambled, thanks to the implant, but this thing doesn't seem to play by the same rules. I can sense its thoughts, its feelings, and ..."

Zima stroked her cheek, though her face betrayed nothing of her feelings on the matter. "And what?"

"It can read me," Anne said, her voice a bare whisper. "It knows who I am, about you, Charlie, Cappa and her shielding, what we've done, William, Tim's resistance force, my implant, and ..." Her composure broke. Anne touched foreheads with Zima, sobbing.

"Tell me," Zima said. "Whatever its wrath, I shall not allow it to harm you, I promise."

"That's just it," Anne said, sniffling. "The Entity isn't angry. It's pleased. Very pleased, like everything that's happened fits perfectly into its plans."

Zima head-cocked. "Have you discovered what those plans are?"

"Nothing we didn't already learn from Almos. It needs some number of vampires before it can move to the next phase. And numbers are *exactly* what it's getting."

"Then it is as you feared, although we are no closer to learning how it intends to proceed once it has achieved its goal." She cocked her head once more. "Has it attempted to exert sire control over you?"

"I ... I don't know." Anne sat on the corner of the bed. Zima joined her. "That night at Orwing's facility, when my defensive program was disabled and William took control of me, every thought and emotion he planted felt like my own. It wasn't until I woke up in the factory that I was able to think back and recognize what he'd changed."

"How did you identify the implanted changes?"

"They were stark contradictions, for the most part. I'd have a strong conviction one moment, and the opposite conviction the next."

"Then I shall watch closely for such swings in attitude. When did you first sense the Entity's presence?"

Anne fiddled with her shirttail, feeling more ashamed than ever. "Th-thirty seconds after William's smoking corpse hit the pavement."

"That was seven hours, sixteen minutes, and forty-two seconds ago." Zima brow-knit. "I would be lying if I said I understood why you have withheld such critical information."

Anne threw her hands up. "What the hell was I supposed to say? 'Hey guys, sorry you just lost everything. Let's hit the road. And oh, by the way, I'm the new master fucking vampire!'"

The rhythmic bumping from next door stopped.

"*What?*" came Cappa's muffled shout.

Shit, shit, shit …

Anne curled into a ball next to the dresser. Tears cascaded down her cheeks and dappled her knees.

She hadn't meant to say it so loudly. Cappa had finally worked up the courage to consummate her feelings for Charlie. This was his first day back in his real body in over five years. As distressing as Anne's news was, it could have waited until the evening, allowing everyone to enjoy a day of peace before she dropped the bomb.

Anne had intended to spend the morning with Zima, frolicking in bed or whatever her love wanted to do, then steal Charlie for the afternoon for more frolicking, if Cappa hadn't worn him out. Or just talk.

Anything for one last romp while she was still Anne in their eyes.

Seconds later, an urgent knock rapped their door. Zima looked at Anne, who nodded sullenly, but couldn't bring herself to stand when Cappa and Charlie were admitted into the room, each wearing nothing but a robe.

Cappa swooped in and cupped Anne's cheeks, examining her with such heartfelt concern that Anne cried anew. Charlie, however, collapsed onto the bed, panting as if he had just run a marathon.

Anne laughed despite herself. "I think you broke him," she said to Cappa.

"Hmm? Oh …" Cappa had the grace to blush. "Yeah, it was hard to stop. I guess I don't have the same shut-off mechanism that normal people do."

"It is comforting to know I am not alone in that," Zima said. She stared at Charlie for a few seconds. "His respiration and pulse are elevated, but his blood pressure is normal. I suspect he will survive the encounter."

"Thanks for the prognosis, doc." Charlie sat up with an effort, then leveled his gaze on Anne. "Is it true?"

Anne gave a teary nod.

He swore under his breath, slid from the bed, and knelt next to her. He took her hands in his own, mirroring Cappa's concern. "Are you okay?"

She nodded again, then filled them in on the discussion so far, including her reasons for not telling them. "I'm sorry," Anne said in conclusion, "I-I should have said something, but …"

"No one here doubts your good intentions," Cappa said. "I knew something was wrong when I couldn't shield you. I could have pressed for information then, but there was so much going on that it was easier not to ask and just pretend everything was fine."

Charlie rubbed his chin. Anne could almost see the wheels turning in his head.

"First Almos kills himself," Charlie said, "presumably at the Entity's command. Then, out of all of William's direct descendants — many of whom were sired before Anne — the Entity chooses the vampire who is *least* susceptible to its own control to be the new master. Why?"

"When a vampire dies," Zima said, "the process of filling the gap in the hierarchy appears to be outside of the Entity's control. Anne's promotion to the role may have been coincidence."

"I don't buy it," Charlie said. "If the Entity could read Almos' mind, as we believe, then it knew William was nearby. It knew Anne was in the car, that she and Almos were stuck in traffic, how much we hated William, what we would be forced to do if Almos died, and that we were capable of doing it. Sure, the Entity had reason to hate Almos for hiding throughout the centuries. But William?" He shook his head. "William was a perfect fit: ruthless, conniving, and power hungry. He needed no other incentive to carry out the Entity's will. Setting him up to be killed just doesn't make sense."

"It's my implant," Anne said.

All eyes focused on her.

"The Entity knows about my implant, and it's ..." Anne frowned, searching for the right word.,"... fascinated. I-I don't know why."

Cappa clucked her tongue. "Not the reaction I'd expect to a device that essentially cuts it off from its vampire hierarchy."

"The implant does far more than that," Charlie said quietly. "Almos knew it, which means the Entity knew it, too. That's why it chose Anne."

"But why?" Cappa said. "If the pathogen was engineered, as we suspect, then it's centuries more advanced than the implant's technology."

"Is it?" Charlie stood and began pacing the small room. "Not only was the implant able to integrate with Anne's infected cells, it can modify her genetic makeup and behavior on demand, which is something we've seen no evidence that the pathogen is capable of." He was talking quickly now. "Think about it! The pathogen was introduced at least a thousand years ago, which means it was designed to survive in a more primitive world. I doubt the Entity expected it to take so long to gather the numbers it required. Then when Almos betrayed it and hid himself for centuries and centuries ..."

"Civilization evolved," Zima said. "Yet the Entity did not, or was unable to, adapt the pathogen to meet the new challenges humanity posed."

"Exactly!" Charlie practically vibrated with excitement. "If the Entity was after numbers, it would have modified the vampires' genetic makeup to counter the new threats humanity was throwing at it so vampirism could spread uninhibited, which strongly suggests it can't. Now, if every vampire had an implant like Anne's, the entire vampire race could be modified to adapt to just about any condition, or meet any threat head-on. Targeted evolution in hours instead of millennia."

"It could eliminate their vulnerabilities," Cappa said, her eyes haunted. "Tweaking Anne's metabolism is just scratching the surface of the implant's capabilities. Sensitivity to sunlight and silver could become a thing of the past."

"Leaving vampires virtually unchallenged as the dominant species on the planet," Zima said.

"I guess it's good that I'm the only one with an implant," Anne said.

Super cyber vampires ... The thought made Anne sick. *Humanity wouldn't stand a chance.*

"An implant may not be required," Zima said. "The foundations for making genetic changes are in the cells themselves. The implant is a convenient interface, but, given sufficient understanding of their function, the cells could be interfaced by other means. Even a non-technical solution, such as biofeedback."

Anne wanted to cover her ears and forget this whole conversation, but she couldn't. She had to see it through. "A-are you saying my cells could be manipulated just by thinking the right thoughts?"

"I suspect it would require more discipline than a human mind can achieve," Zima said. "But it is also likely the Entity is not human, so the possibility exists. More to the point, you are not the only vampire whose cells have been modified by the implant."

"Tim," Anne said, unable to keep the despair from her voice. "And Nick, and Jody, and Conway."

"And every other vampire in their new society, who are all descended from your blood," Zima said. "That includes Orwing's renewed vampire army. And their numbers are multiplying daily."

"My God, if the Entity turns them into super vampires ..." Anne swiped a shaking hand down her face. "In saving me from William, we may have accidentally ensured the Vampocalypse."

Zima brow-knit. "This is mostly supposition, of course, but yes."

Charlie sat heavily on the bed, all traces of excitement gone. "Well ... fuck."

Unfortunately, Anne couldn't have agreed more.

28

DIVIDED WE FALL

T HE REST OF THE POSSE SOON JOINED THEM in Anne and Zima's hotel room. Anne listened in sullen silence while Charlie briefed them on the Entity in her head. Mark, predictably, swore like a sailor, but Dela's smile grew steadily wider. By the end of the tale, she was positively beaming.

Cappa stormed to her feet. "Unbelievable! What is it about dire circumstances that you always find amusing?"

"Are you kidding?" Dela said, losing none of her mirth. "Super vampires! As if Anne wasn't awesome enough already."

"Your comic book privileges are officially revoked, kiddo," Doris said. "Ain't nothing super about what I just heard."

"That's because you're not seeing the bigger picture." Dela brushed past Cappa to address the others. "First off, we've got two of the smartest guys in the world standing right here. It may take a while, but they'll think of some way to turn this into our advantage, or I'll eat one of Cappa's fancy shoes. Second, we've got the Dark Angel — the greatest hacker and warrior in history. By themselves, they're formidable. Put them together, and I pity anyone who gets in their way!"

"That's a naïve and unfair burden to place solely on their shoulders," Cappa said.

"Which brings me to my third point," Dela said, shooting Cappa a withering glance. "We're not the only people on this planet with a stake in keeping it the way it is — i.e., habitable. If we go public with this, we'll have billions of minds working together on a common goal: Survival of the species! Super vampires or no, the Entity doesn't have a prayer with the entire human race working against it. We just need to get the message out there, fast and furious like, and we'll have all the help we could ever want in this battle."

Charlie tapped his fingers together, deep in thought. "Dela's right," he said eventually.

Dela's face split in a gigantic grin.

"With *one* exception." Charlie stood and stretched in his dark blue robe. "The world can fend for itself. I'm done."

He'd said it so matter-of-factly that Anne thought she'd heard him wrong. "You're ... done?"

"Yes, or near enough."

Charlie held a hand out to her, which Anne took. He pulled her to her feet, wrapped an arm around both she and Cappa, and pulled them close.

"I should have died tonight," Charlie said. "But I didn't."

"Maybe you were spared for a reason, Charlie." Dela's smile was gone, her face flaming red.

"And maybe tomorrow I'll die of a stroke." He shook his head. "Anne has the Entity in her head, but she's still herself, and my relationship with Cappa has just begun. I'm going to enjoy what little time I might have left with them, not spend it hunkered in a situation room trying to fix everyone else's problems. You and Mark are engaged, for Pete's sake! Doesn't that mean anything to you?"

Dela shook her fists. "That's not the point! The world needs us!"

"After we disseminate the information we have on vampires, the world can take care of itself for a while." Charlie turned to Anne with a smile. "Has Zima told you where we're going?"

"Not yet. I assumed I was still in need-to-know status."

Which is doubly true now.

Even as they spoke, the Entity stalked on the periphery of Anne's mind, listening. Waiting.

"Let me paint a picture for you, then," Charlie said. "Imagine a twelve-bedroom country mansion on the outskirts of a small town, a hundred miles from the nearest city. We'll chop our own wood in the snowy winter, enjoy air-conditioning in the summer, and swim in the river running through the two hundred acres of forest and farmland we own."

"That sounds amazing," Anne said, resting her head on his shoulder.

"It gets better." He kissed the top of her head. "There's a children's hospital nearby."

Anne perked up so quickly that she accidentally bashed her head into his chin. "Don't tease me. Really?"

Charlie rubbed his jaw. "Really. You said you wanted to help people, to do some good with that venom of yours. I can't think of a better use than curing sick kids, many of whom have little hope for the future."

A children's hospital ...

The thought wasn't just enticing, it was captivating. Enchanting. Enthralling.

"You ... you really think they'd let me work there?"

"A few donations and conversations with the right people, and yes, I guarantee it. Besides, I have some ideas on how to help you blend better with the rest of the population."

"She'll need it," Cappa said. "In a week, the news will be filled with nothing but vampire horror stories."

Mark stood in front of Charlie. Concern etched every inch of his face. "Charlie, are you sure about this? You'd really just walk away and leave the world to its fate?"

"Positive," Charlie said, squeezing Anne and Cappa's shoulders. "We've done our share. Our research on the pathogen alone will put scientists years ahead of the game. Toss a few other gems out there, like our plasma technology, and they should have what they need to carry forward."

Mark's clenched jaw said he wasn't convinced.

"Look, it's not like we haven't done this before," Charlie said. "Remember Prague?"

Mark's gaze became distant. He nodded.

Dela nudged him. "What happened in Prague?"

"The rebels became too dependent on us," Mark said. "We did their thinking for them, which gave them no incentive to think for themselves. Charlie and I ended up fighting their war for them, even though we had no stake in the game. They panicked when we told them we were pulling out, but it forced them to organize themselves and establish their own practices using what we'd taught them. They won in the end." Mark met Charlie's eyes and sighed. "All right. Early retirement it is."

Dela punched his arm. "Mark! Are you *serious?* This isn't some skirmish in eastern Europe: it's the goddamned fate of humanity! Y-you're really going to play little house on the fucking prairie while the planet goes to hell in a blood-soaked hand basket?"

"That depends on how you look at it. Like Charlie said, the information and technology Z-Tech holds — er, held ..." Mark grimaced. "It's substantial. Our micro plasma tech has uses beyond weaponry. Our fusion reactors provide not only clean energy, but a means of establishing bases of operation in remote locations without worry of shipping in fuel, and opens the doors for a range of new inventions previously unattainable due to the weight and size limitations of conventional generators. Nanotech will —"

"Probably stay with us," Charlie said, catching his eye. "But almost everything else is fair game."

Dela shook her head, red hair bouncing on her shoulders. "All right! I get it. You've put the time in already, and the world will scramble to pick up where you left off before it falls into oblivion. It just ... abandoning the fight still feels wrong." She looked at Zima. "Is the Dark Angel on board with this chicken show?"

Zima stood beside Anne, opposite Charlie, and took her free hand. "I wish to be with Anne. Whether sitting in a country house, working in a hospital, or fighting on the battlefront, I shall do it gladly, as long as we are together."

More than anyone else's, Zima's declaration took the fight out of Dela. She rubbed the spot on Mark's arm where she'd punched him, then quietly slipped into his embrace.

"I guess that settles it," Cappa said. "One more task, then we disappear."

"It's still early," Mark said. "Let's get this over with. If we're going to start a new life, I'd like to do it baggage-free."

"Cappa and I will meet you in your room," Charlie said. "Zima, will you join us, too? We have the contacts, Cappa has the research and schematics, but we'll need your help to make sure the information can't be traced back to us. Our exploding factory trick probably won't fool anyone for long, but until they can prove otherwise, we're all officially dead."

The group filed out in subdued silence, but a gentle clearing of Anne's throat called their attention.

"Dela? C-could you … I mean, would you, um … s-stick around for a few minutes?"

"You have not eaten today," Zima said.

Anne shook her head. She felt so awful asking that she wanted to shrink into the carpet, but she'd held out as long as she could, and was starting to feel faint. Experience told her it was better to swallow her pride and ask now than accidentally attack someone she loved in a starvation-induced frenzy.

"Fear not," Cappa said. "There weren't many blood bags left in the fridge, but what we had is packed in a cooler in the van."

"Don't bother." Dela marched into the room with grim determination and rolled up her sleeve. "I could use a pick-me-up. Besides, I should probably get used to the idea of being treated like cattle." She leveled Charlie with a dark stare. "We *all* should."

Not even Cappa called her out on the jibe.

The others vacated, leaving Anne, Dela, and Zima. The moment the door closed, Anne took Dela's arm, spared a grateful glance for the delectable redhead, then sank her teeth into the biggest vein she could find.

Their mutual moans of pleasure were interrupted by a knock. Zima answered, and in walked Charlie. Anne was about to ask what had brought him back so quickly, but then she spotted the bandages across his chest. This was Charlie's cyborg body. Its artificial brain had been killed during the escape, preventing his spirit from inhabiting the body, which meant it was being piloted by …

"Cappa," Anne said, reluctantly parting from her meal. "What's up?"

"Just pinch-hitting for Zima so she can join us in Mark's room." They were definitely Cappa's words, but spoken with Charlie's voice.

Anne fought a shiver at the creepy dichotomy. "It's fine. We'll be done in just a minute, then I'll bring her over and —"

Zima's touch cut her short. "It is best if you remain here, Anne. We shall be openly discussing names, information, technology, and security measures that the Entity may someday use against us."

"Oh, o-of course. I'll be here when you're done, honey."

After Zima left, Cappa's Charlie self took position in the corner and quietly watched. Anne picked Dela's arm up to resume her meal, but set it back down with a frown. Her appetite was gone.

Cappa isn't just here to keep me company, Anne realized with a sinking feeling. *She's my prison guard.*

They had every right to be paranoid, she knew, but it still stung. Anne had worked hard to earn their trust, to make everyone feel comfortable around the super-strong, blood-sucking parasite William had turned her into. It was a cruel irony that killing the monster responsible for her condition had turned Anne into something even worse.

"Keep drinking," Dela said, her words slurred. "The cowardice feels like a knife in my back. Drink me unconscious, Anne. You'll be doing me a favor."

Anne patted her arm, but let it dangle loosely beside Dela's relaxed body. "I know it's upsetting, sitting on the sidelines when you feel you could be doing more. Part of me wants to march out into the sunlight right now and burn myself to a crisp, just in the hopes that it might hurt the goddamned thing in my head."

"Wasn't your fault," Dela said, her expression softening. She laid a heavy hand on Anne's shoulder. "You're a good person who shitty stuff keeps happening to, that's all. You shouldn't have to suffer."

"None of us should. But to your point, I think Charlie, Mark, Cappa, and especially Zima have had a lot of shitty stuff happen to them, too. More than they let on. Maybe more than you and I can understand." Anne took a deep breath, and chose her next words carefully. "They've suffered, Dela. They've made mistakes. They've been betrayed. And they've worked very hard to dig themselves out with their lives intact. They saved Zima, saved me multiple times, and saved everyone at the party last night. They've given more than most people will in ten lifetimes."

Cappa's Charlie self smiled. "It hasn't been all bad, but thanks for the nod."

"Their entire legacy went up in a bright flash tonight," Anne said, turning back to Dela. "While Charlie may not have lost his life, he did lose his life's work." She pointed at the bandages on Charlie's chest. "When Charlie said he was done, I don't think he or the others were being defeatist. Tonight may have been the final straw that broke the back of a strong, but sorely abused camel."

"If you were trying to make me feel guilty, it worked." Dela sagged against her and offered a wrist. "More?"

Anne was going to refuse, but a rumble in her stomach changed her mind. "If you insist."

While Anne was back in happy drinking land, Cappa's Charlie self sat on the bed across from her. A sheepish look crossed her face.

"Anne, you know we love you, and that we wouldn't exclude you from anything unless we had a damn good reason, right?"

Anne nodded, not wanting to relinquish her meal.

"Good, just ... keep that in mind until we get a handle on this master vampire thing, okay? Hopefully this will be the last time we ever have to keep you out of a conversation, Entity or no."

Dela fell to the bed with a lazy smile, eyes half lidded, signaling the end of the meal. Anne grabbed a wet washcloth and cleaned both Dela and herself to reduce the ghoul factor, then sat next to Cappa's Charlie self.

"Thanks," Anne said. "That means a lot."

"Your explanation to Dela did, too. Speaking for myself, you hit the nail on the head."

Anne smiled and leaned in for a kiss, but Charlie's Cappa self raised a hand between them, stopping her short.

"Sorry," Anne said. "I forgot you weren't him for a second."

"It's fine," he — *she* — said with a wink. "But don't take that as permission to try again."

Anne leaned against Charlie's cyborg body and laid her head on its shoulder. "How about this?"

"Very suave," the cyborg said with Cappa's cheerful laugh. "Almos would have been proud."

They sat listening to Dela's happy muttering for a while.

"What's going to happen to Rose?" Anne said eventually. "She doesn't know about Almos yet. He was her lifeline, in a way. I don't know how she's going to take it."

"Badly, if I know myself." The cyborg heaved a sigh. "I'm not looking forward to that conversation when we turn her back on."

"When will that be?"

The cyborg shrugged. "Whether it's a few days, or a few months from now, she's off, so she won't feel the passage of time. I'd rather wait and revive her in a healing environment, like after we've settled in Montana."

"Hopefully she won't be upset by the delay."

"I wouldn't be," Cappa's Charlie self said with a smirk.

Anne snuggled closer and closed her eyes. With rare exceptions, she hadn't been able to sleep since becoming a vampire, but, for a few minutes, she was able to forget the tragedies of the day — and the Entity in her head — and imagine what life in a country mansion would be like with her family.

It was a very pleasant daydream.

29

SURRENDER

CHARLIE SAT ON THE BED in Mark and Dela's hotel room, his fingers steepled in thought. Mark lay on the bed with a faraway look, while Cappa paced in front of the bathroom. A knock on the door stirred Charlie from his concentration.

"It's me," Doris said from outside.

Charlie let her in. "Thanks for coming."

"No problem, sweet cakes." She settled into a chair and threw her legs over an arm. "Though I have no idea how I can contribute to your tech discussion."

"This isn't a tech discussion," Cappa said. "It's an Anne discussion."

"Well that explains it. Who wants to start?"

"We're still waiting for Zima," Cappa said.

As if on cue, another knock rapped the door.

"That's her," Cappa said.

Charlie sighed in relief. They hadn't even started the discussion, but he was already paranoid that his girlfriend — no, the Entity, he reminded himself — might somehow be listening in.

He had, in fact, chosen Mark's room instead of his own because it was on the opposite wing of the hotel, far enough away that even Anne's sensitive ears couldn't hear.

He put his face in his hands. "I hate this."

Cappa rubbed his back. "I know how you feel. We'll fix this, Charlie. It's what we do. We just need a little time to figure things out, that's all."

He nodded gratefully, then looked at Zima. "Do you think Anne bought our story?"

"I did not observe any signs to the contrary," Zima said. "As incredulous as your resignation was, your reasons aligned well enough with her desires that she should have little cause to doubt you. The children's hospital was a compelling addition." She cocked her head. "Your resignation was simply a ruse for the Entity's benefit, correct?"

"Correct." Charlie gave Mark a grim smile. "Thanks for backing me up, buddy."

"It wasn't easy. I should be up for an Oscar after that performance. I thought you were serious when you said you were giving up until you mentioned Prague."

Zima brow-knit. "I do not understand. The circumstances you described with the rebels did not counter Charlie's decision, they supported it."

"Yes," Mark said, grinning, "but I omitted a few key facts. The opposing government knew they would lose because the rebels had us on their side, so they were seeking aid from Russia to offset the balance. If we left the picture, however, Russia couldn't intervene without looking like outright bullies, which would force the United Nations to side with the rebels. So, Charlie and I made a very public exit. We continued to support them in secret, however, with weapons and tactics. And that's why the rebels won."

"Sneaky," Doris said, laughing. "You're right about the Oscar. You sure had me fooled."

"And not just you," Mark said. "I'm surprised Dela didn't call off our wedding right there and then."

"Maybe you should wait to tell her the truth until we get to Montana," Cappa said. "After all that buildup, the makeup sex would be epic."

Charlie raised an eyebrow at her. "Since when did you become such an expert?"

"The moment I got an internet connection after my genitals miraculously stirred to life in China. People post a *lot* about sex, which I had mostly ignored before. I had a lot of catching up to do."

"You ... you read it all?"

"You bet I did," Cappa said with a sly wink. "Eat your Wheaties, dear, because there are many, many things I want to try."

Charlie gulped.

"I look forward to a summary of your findings," Zima said. "My immediate concern, however, is Anne. Her implant appears to be preventing the Entity from controlling her, but the Entity has also demonstrated abilities beyond a normal sire. The implant may only be a temporary deterrent."

"Even so, it sounds like it hears and sees everything Anne does," Mark said. "We need to be very careful about what we say around her from now on."

"I agree," Charlie said. "Even if the Entity is powerless to act now, it might become desperate if it knew we were actively working against it, and find some way to hurt Anne."

And I'll be damned if I let that happen.

Doris, Cappa, and Mark's grim expressions said they were thinking the same.

"Cappa shielded Almos when he was underground," Doris said, "and was able to keep him shielded above-ground. Let's do the same for Anne, then we won't have to worry about it."

Cappa slumped. "I think Almos' brains splattering across the van demonstrated that *chi* shielding is a short-term solution at best."

"All right, so we'll find a cozy basement somewhere and set her up," Doris said. "She ain't gonna like it, but she'll understand."

"That's certainly an option," Charlie said, "but there may be advantages to staying in contact with the Entity."

Mark stared at him, then grinned. "Keep your friends close ..."

"And your Entities closer. If we're careful, we can prevent the Entity from learning anything about our operations."

Cappa brightened. "But Anne can tell us anything she gleans from its thoughts!"

"Like Zima said, it's risky," Mark said. "We don't know what other tricks the Entity has. But if we keep a close eye on Anne and the Entity, we may learn more than it intends, and use the information against it."

Zima brow-knit. "I do not like the risks that plan poses to Anne, but neither do I like the idea of keeping her underground. She was miserable in the reactor room. I do not wish to put her through that again."

"Let's say we run with this idea," Doris said. "You really think Anne's gonna believe we just up and quit for long? She ain't stupid. Sooner or later, she's bound to figure out the truth."

"She doesn't have to believe us," Charlie said. "She just needs to have faith in us. That means doing exactly what she's been doing — which is *not* asking questions, even when she sees something suspicious. It sucks, but it's better than the alternatives. This way, Anne still has a shot at a normal life."

"With supervision," Mark said.

"It will be my pleasure to perform that task," Zima said.

Charlie grinned. "I thought you'd say that. I'll help as well. We all will, I'm sure."

"And if it doesn't work out," Cappa said, "there are always Plans B and C."

"I guess that settles that." Doris leaned back and looked at the ceiling. "The next problem is how the hell we're going to fight a national vampire epidemic from Bum-Fuck, Montana."

"We shall do so indirectly," Zima said. "Tim and Nick have already created the foundations of a resistance. More importantly, they have the infrastructure to support it. They have offered Anne and me high-level positions. I shall dissuade Anne from accepting hers, or indeed contacting them in any way, but I shall accept their offered role of General."

"General? From the middle of nowhere?" Doris frowned. "I know you're talented, sugar, but that sounds like a stretch, even for the incredible Dark Angel."

"It is not. While our location will prevent me from participating in direct combat, a general's greatest contribution is strategy. With proper data feeds, I can greatly assist their efforts by monitoring and coordinating teams."

"You can do that?" Doris said. "I thought you were an up-close-and-personal type of gal."

"I am proficient at both tactical execution and strategy. I have led successful military campaigns on three different continents. In four of those campaigns, my role was purely strategic. I am also adept at parallel processing. I assimilated data faster than an entire team of intelligence specialists, produced concrete strategies from it, and delivered them to the appropriate units in real-time."

Doris snapped her hanging jaw shut. "I, uh, take it things worked out well for your side?"

"Yes. Friendly casualties averaged seventy-four percent lower than comparable campaigns, and we did not lose a single battle."

"I'd call that contributing," Cappa said with a smile.

"All right," Doris said. "What about the rest of us?"

"We'll do what we do best," Charlie said, sharing a grin with Mark. "Research, development, and manufacturing."

"Armies need a steady stream of weapons and equipment," Mark said. "Quality of supplies often determines the victor — at least, that was true when we were the suppliers."

"Ain't y'all forgetting something?" Doris said. "The poor factory is a burning pit of fire two hundred miles away."

Cappa waved it off. "Our manufacturing lines are a snap to set up, and only require simple, raw materials. We brought enough nanites with us to start production immediately, and we can make more later, if we need them.

"As for weapon and equipment designs, they're all in here." Cappa pointed to her own head. "I've even found the perfect place to set up in our new town: an old factory on the outskirts with a big sub-level basement. We can pay cash, and I'd bet dollars to donuts we could have our first shipment ready for Tim and Nick by this time next week."

"A basement ..." Mark scratched his chin. "That's perfect! We could use the main factory floor as a front — something innocuous like chocolate production — which would give us an excuse to receive regular material shipments and establish an outbound supply chain."

Cappa jumped from the bed, bouncing with excitement. "That's right! And I could decorate it this time. I'm thinking white with pastel-colored dots for a pop motif that would ..." She stopped bouncing when she noticed everyone staring. "Sorry. We can decide on the decor later, I guess."

"Setting up a new lab to continue research on the virus will be trickier," Charlie said. "We didn't bring many lab supplies with us. But, with a few calls to the right places, we should be back in business in a couple of weeks."

He looked around the room, and was amazed at the difference he saw. Everyone had arrived despondent or agitated. Now they were practically quivering with excitement about the future. It was an interesting study on the power of hope.

Doris stood and stretched. "Is that it, then? I'm a few hours short on sleep, and I'd love to catch up."

"You go ahead," Charlie said. "I meant it when I promised we were going to share our knowledge with the rest of the world. Mark, Cappa, Zima, and I still have work to do."

"All right. Let me know if y'all need anything, but the best I can probably offer is coffee and donuts."

Charlie and Mark both perked up.

"Coming right up," Doris said with a laugh. She closed the door behind her.

Mark turned to Charlie, his expression grave. "You sure about this, pal? Once we send this information out, there's no taking it back."

"You mean, 'Will our allies abuse our technology again?' Possibly, but the difference this time is that we all have a common enemy. Our tech won't give the vampires many advantages they don't already have, but it'll make all the difference to non-vampires. And if our allies do abuse it ..."

"Then maybe we weren't meant to survive as a species anyway." Mark sighed. "Okay, I'm with you. Let's figure out what we want to share and get it out there. I'd like to catch some sleep myself before we hit the road again tonight."

With the four of them gathered around, discussing weapons, technology, and old military contacts, Charlie was taken back to a few years ago, when only the people present in this room were privy to the groundbreaking technologies Z-Tech held. When vampires were still myths, and the only things trying to kill them were other humans. Life was simpler then. For a moment, Charlie missed those days.

But then he thought about the new people who had entered their lives: Dela, Doris, and, of course, his dear Anne. He also thought of the wonderful transformations he had seen in everyone, especially Cappa and himself, and his wishing for old times vanished.

Vampires were real. The Entity was real. Almos' doomsday prophecy wasn't the fantasy they had all hoped it was. Charlie's hard-earned empire had burned to the ground in a single night. The only things he had to show for his efforts was a cyborg body with a hole where his brain used to be, a few vehicles, and his family.

All of them.

Charlie smiled.

Things could certainly be worse.

30

ROAD TRIP

THE DAY PASSED SLOWLY in Anne's hotel room. As Rose had done while Anne was recovering from her burns, Cappa's Charlie self helped pass the time by reading a book from her extensive electronic library. Dela roused from her venom-stupor around noon and stumbled off in search of lunch. They switched to playing cards, then filled each other in on their time apart: Cappa's adventure in China, Anne's captivity with Calum.

The sun had nearly set when the others finally returned. Anne jumped from the bed and practically pounced on Zima.

"How'd it go? Did you get everything sorted?"

"Yes, it was very productive."

Anne glanced at the other faces around the room. Charlie looked exhausted, which was understandable, given this was his biological body's first day up and around in over five years. Cappa clung to his arm, wearing an eerily similar expression to her Charlie self lying on the bed, both of whom Anne found hard to read. Mark frowned at the floor, but Dela seemed to have snapped out of her funk and had regained some of her usual bounce.

Zima immediately took Anne's hand. "It is eighteen minutes until sundown. If we leave soon, we should arrive at our new home before dawn. Are you ready to depart?"

"Ready as I'll ever be."

Anxious as she was, the picture Charlie had painted of their new life made Anne excited for the future. She finished packing her bags before the last person had left the room, then waited with Zima under the protective shade of the awning, where she stared at the fading sky as if she could make the sun move faster by sheer will.

When the last rays finally disappeared behind the treetops, Anne skipped out to the van, loaded her bags, and climbed into the front passenger seat next to Zima. Charlie and Cappa piled into the back. Stolen hotel sheets now covered the rear bench, masking the remaining stains of Almos that had refused to come out with water alone.

The memory of his murder — there was no other word for the Entity's brutal act — still twisted her stomach. The ancient vampire's wisdom and surety had inspired confidence in everyone around him, a quality that would be in great demand in the dark days to come, she suspected.

"You okay, Anne?" Cappa said, touching her shoulder.

Anne wiped a tear and nodded. "I'll be fine, I just ... miss him. Almos was a good man — and one of the few people who gave me hope when I was chained to the wall in Calum's dungeon."

"His death shall be added to the growing list of crimes the Entity has to answer for," Zima said, looking pointedly at Anne.

"I know, honey, but ..." She glanced at Charlie, who smiled. "Let's worry about fixing us first. What do you say?"

Zima was silent for several seconds before nodding. "As you wish."

The van pulled out of the parking lot, followed closely by Mark, Dela, and Doris in the sedan. Anne watched the hotel behind them grow smaller and smaller until, like the City that had been her home for half of her life, it disappeared from view, leaving a mixture of memories she both cherished and wished she could forget. Anne faced forward again.

Her breath caught.

The brilliant night sky ahead of them was clear and perfect, the vast horizon infinite with possibility. She took Zima's hand, wishing to share the moment. Blue eyes met hers: soft, strong, reassuring.

Breathtaking.

Anne smiled and returned her gaze to the expansive skyline.

She didn't know what the future held, but for the first time in a long while, she couldn't wait to find out.

ABOUT THE AUTHOR

Ryan Southwick decided to dabble at writing late in life, and quickly became obsessed with the craft. He grew up in Pennsylvania and moved to a farming town on California's central coast during elementary school, but it was in junior high school where he had his first taste of storytelling with a small role-playing group and couldn't get enough.

In addition to half a lifetime in the software development industry, making everything from 3-D games to mission-critical business applications to help cure cancer, he was also a Radiation Therapist for many years. His technical experience, medical skills, and lifelong fascination for science fiction became the ingredients for his book series, "The Z-Tech Chronicles", which combines elements of each into a fantastic contemporary tale of super-science, fantasy, and adventure, based in his Bay Area stomping grounds. Ryan's related short story "Once Upon a Nightwalker" was published in the *Corporate Catharsis* anthology, available from Paper Angel Press.

Ryan currently lives in the San Francisco Bay Area with his wife and two children. You can get in touch with him and see more of his work by visiting his website *RyanSouthwickAuthor.com*.

ALSO BY RYAN SOUTHWICK

ANGELS IN THE MIST

THE Z-TECH CHRONICLES BOOK ONE

An ancient, powerful evil is loose in San Francisco. The heart of Silicon Valley must fight back the only way they know how — with compassion, unwavering determination, and, of course, super-technology.

ANGELS LOST

THE Z-TECH CHRONICLES BOOK TWO

A vampire hunter has his sights on Anne Perrin, threatening to unleash the very evil she and her friends are fighting to contain.

ZIMA: ORIGINS

A Z-TECH CHRONICLES STORY

Even artificially intelligent recovering assassins need a home.

ONCE UPON A NIGHTWALKER

A Z-TECH CHRONICLES STORY

Ellen Bloom just wants a normal working relationship with her colleagues at her old job. But, at this point, she'd be happy with a pulse.

Available from Water Dragon Publishing in
hardcover, trade paperback, digital, and audio editions
waterdragonpublishing.com

YOU MIGHT ALSO ENJOY

BUILDING BABY BROTHER

by Steven Radecki

It seemed like a good idea at the time …

GODDESS CHOSEN

BOOK ONE OF THE "GODDESS RISING" TRILOGY

by Jay Hartlove

The man who would beat the devil isn't a hero, but a ruthless madman.

MEMORY AND METAPHOR

by Andrea Monticue

Civilization fell. It rose. At some point, people built starships.

Available from Water Dragon Publishing in
hardcover, trade paperback, digital, and audio editions
waterdragonpublishing.com

Water Dragon Publishing is an imprint of Paper Angel Press
paperangelpress.com